Praise for the novels of J...

'The pages of *Hungarian Dances* just kept on turning! Like all the best novels, it asks unexpected and compelling questions. It's a book for anyone with an interest in how history leaves its mark on people and how they in turn come to live with its scars.'

Martin Davies, author of *The Conjuror's Bird*

'After having read *Rites of Spring*, I am now equally thrilled by *Hungarian Dances*. Jessica Duchen is a very gifted storyteller; her characters are sensitively portrayed. She has observed "Hungarianness" very well indeed. And her understanding of the tragedy and sufferings of the Gypsy people – that is not just history, but very much a problem of our time – gives this book an even more profound meaning.'

András Schiff on *Hungarian Dances*

'The devil in this book is in the detail, the accumulation of every detail that disables middle class life when the unexpected lands, in this case a musically gifted child. You turn the pages with a tremble, in case you crush the fragile family. Unbearably real.'

Yasmin Alibhai-Brown on *Alicia's Gift*

'As in *Rites of Spring*, Duchen demonstrates a gift for vividly sketching, with a few deft lines, the environment in which the characters move as well as their internal emotional landscape, and again her compassion for her characters is persuasive.'

BBC Music Magazine on *Alicia's Gift*

'This is a very well written study of the problem of being and having a child prodigy . . . it's a gripping read and it's very easy to get caught up in the excitement of wanting Alicia to succeed . . . I enjoyed this book a lot'

Muso on *Alicia's Gift*

'An imaginative novel . . . with themes of miscommunication, perfectionism and adolescence.'

Eve on *Rites of Spring*

Captivating, imaginative and fascinating . . . The pace builds powerfully to a dramatic and ultimately very moving conclusion. Completely gripping'

Tasmin Little on *Rites of Spring*

'A haunting, heartbreaking novel.'

Closer on *Rites of Spring*

'Jessica Duchen has crafted a riveting drama set within the arts world . . . For fans of Joanna Trollope and Russian composers alike.'

Classic FM Magazine on *Rites of Spring*

Also by Jessica Duchen

Rites of Spring
Alicia's Gift

Jessica Duchen was born in London and grew up with music and writing as twin passions. *Hungarian Dances* is her third novel. She is also the author of two biographies and several stage works combining music and drama, and as a journalist for the *Independent* she has interviewed most of today's greatest musicians. She lives in London with her violinist husband.

For more information about Jessica Duchen, please visit www.jessicaduchen.co.uk and www.hungariandances.co.uk

Hungarian Dances

Jessica Duchen

HODDER

First published in Great Britain in 2008 by Hodder & Stoughton
An Hachette Livre UK company

First published in paperback in 2008

2

Copyright © Jessica Duchen 2008

The right of Jessica Duchen to be identified as the Author of the Work has been asserted by her in accordance with the Copyright, Designs and Patents Act 1988.

All rights reserved. No part of this publication may be reproduced, stored in a retrieval system, or transmitted, in any form or by any means without the prior written permission of the publisher, nor be otherwise circulated in any form of binding or cover other than that in which it is published and without a similar condition being imposed on the subsequent purchaser.

All characters in this publication are fictitious and any resemblance to real persons, living or dead is purely coincidental.

A CIP catalogue record for this title is available from the British Library

ISBN 978 0 340 93358 9

Typeset in Plantin Light by Palimpsest Book Production Limited, Grangemouth, Stirlingshire

Printed and bound by Clays Ltd, St Ives plc

Hodder & Stoughton policy is to use papers that are natural, renewable and recyclable products and made from wood grown in sustainable forests. The logging and manufacturing processes are expected to conform to the environmental regulations of the country of origin.

Hodder & Stoughton Ltd
338 Euston Road
London NW1 3BH

www.hodder.co.uk

For all the violinists in my life

Author's Note

A great many people have helped to bring this book into being. Immense thanks first to the Author's Foundation for their kind financial support; my agent, Sara Menguc; Carolyn Mays, Kate Howard, Kerry Hood, Marissa Cox and everybody at Hodder & Stoughton; and Éva Norton and the British Hungarian Fellowship, who have been an invaluable source of information and support.

Warmest thanks to the violinist Philippe Graffin for becoming my accidental muse. Without his CD *In the Shade of Forests* presenting 20th-century music influenced by Gypsy idioms and recorded with the pianist Claire Désert on Avie Records, this novel might never have existed. The fictional Marc Duplessis's Suite *Dans l'ombre des forêts* is named after the disc. I am honoured and overjoyed that Philippe and Claire now plan to produce a new recording especially to complement *Hungarian Dances*, featuring some of the violin music mentioned in its pages.

For advice on everything from Hungarian history to Amati violins and the oddities of the British railway system, I would like to thank the Hungarian Cultural Centre in London, John Batten, Sarah Bowles, Simon Broughton, Katalin and Stephen Cass, András Hangveto, Agnes Havás, John Hornsby, Angela Impey, József Koos, Judit Körös, Susan Kramer, Sharon Little, Tasmin Little, Miklós Lojko, Stephen Macklow-Smith, Ben Mandelson, Melanne Mueller, Peter Nall, Jonathan Orr-Ewing, Tony Palmer, Jeremy Preston, Juliet Reingold, Naomi Sadler, Florence Schoemann, Sylvia Szabó, Ariane Todes, Eleanor and Tom Stanier and Katalin Várnagy. Profuse thanks to Lady Ellen Dahrendorf and Lady Valerie Solti for their enthusiasm, sound advice and moral support. And for caffeine, chocolate and endless patience, as well as some useful pointers, Michael, Laura, Hannah, Ben and Luca; and, most of all, Tom for putting up with me.

It would be impossible to list everybody who has been involved with this book – apologies to anyone I've missed – and it's equally difficult to credit everything I've read during my research, but the following books proved essential: *The Voice of Freedom: Remembering the 1956 Revolution* by Katalin Bogyay, *My Happy Days in Hell* by György Faludy, *Revolution in Hungary* by Eric Lessing, *The Sisters d'Aranyi* by Joseph Macleod, *Memoir of Hungary* by Sándor Márai, *And the Violins Stopped Playing* by Alexander Ramati, *Twelve Days: Revolution 1956* by Victor Sebestyen, *Solti on Solti: A Memoir* by Sir Georg Solti, *The Life and Music of Bela Bartók* by Halsey Stevens and Malcolm Gillies, and *Gypsies* by Jan Yoors. These represent the tip of an iceberg.

Just a few of the countless vital websites included: The Patrin Web Journal (http://www.geocities.com/~patrin/history.htm), The Hungarian Quarterly, especially Bálint Sárosi's article 'The Golden Age of Gypsy Bands in Hungary' (http://www.hungarian-quarterly.com/no173/17.htm), the House of Terror Museum, Budapest (http://www.terrorhaza.hu/terror2.html), the Institute for the History of the 1956 Revolution (http://www.rev.hu), the Office of Rail Regulation (http://www.rail-reg.gov.uk) and the stunning performances that can be sampled on the site of the Hungarian Gypsy violinist Roby Lakatos (http://www.robylakatos.com/).

Hungarian is a fearsome language, but here's a basic note about pronunciation. The stress mostly falls on the first syllable of a word. A is similar to O in English unless it bears an acute accent; S is SH; CZ is closest to TCH; GY sounds like DJ. Tamás Veres is pronounced as Tomahsh Vairesh, István Rácz is Ishtvahn Rahtch, György is Djeurdj, Dénes is Dehnesh. The accents that sharpen vowels are vital. If you don't pronounce them in *egészségedre* – 'cheers!' – you'll find you are toasting somebody's solid backside. Still, it usually sounds fine after a few Pálinkas.

Jessica Duchen, London, 2007

I

Air. Movement. Freedom.

Wood, four strings, the scroll. Beyond them, the fireplace and its rose-patterned tiles. When she closes her eyes she glimpses clouds on the horizon, the earth flat and cracked; peaked thatch passing, dust, grass and faraway mirages, the beckoning shadows of the forest, the minstrel. Her bow is his in an unbroken loop through the centuries. Horsehair, gut and metal, vibration. Her fingertips find the pitches of his storytelling; a slide, a flicker of pizzicato, the quietest harmonic she can manage. The minstrel whispers, through Marc Duplessis's music: who are you?

Wheels. Not his, wooden and creaking under a painted wagon. Smoothness. Familiarity. Routine. A twizzle of keys, footsteps in the hall, and Karina is back in her front room, holding her violin; her husband is striding towards her with his arms open, her son is bounding down the stairs and she knows where she is again, even if she isn't quite sure what she's doing there, in her own home.

'Karrie, darling.' Julian's wingspan curls round her. 'How's my little Gypsy? Playing with your toys?'

Karina kisses him and says nothing.

'Karina, are you free this morning? Your grandmother is having a bad day. We need you.'

Karina, clutching the phone, glances at Julian's mahogany clock in the entrance hall. Jamie's at school, and she doesn't begin teaching until four. 'I'll get the next train,' she promises her mother. She brushes her hair and sets off for Lewes station, quick and light on her feet, enjoying the scents of spring leaves and salt blown inland from the sea.

In Twickenham an hour and a half later, Karina finds her grandmother, Mimi, rambling from her armchair in furious Hungarian. Karina's mother, Erzsébet, holds Mimi's hand and tries to soothe her: 'It's all right, Mimi. It's all finished. I promise. Look who's come to visit.' Sometimes only Karina, Mimi's sole grandchild, true-hearted and comforting as a cup of cocoa, can bring Mimi back to herself.

Karina bends to hug her; Mimi's face transforms from scowl to beatific delight. She strokes back Karina's hair with hands distended by arthritis. These fingers used to coax magic out of a violin; the sight of them now causes Karina nearly physical pain. Mimi asks a long question in Hungarian; slipping into her old language on bad days, she forgets that Karina speaks not a word of it and has never set a toe in Hungary. 'Hush, Grandma,' Karina whispers. 'Everything's going to be fine.'

'It is Dénes's fault,' Mimi says.

Erzsébet, exhaling hard, glides away to the kitchenette to make tea. 'Is Dad teaching?' Karina asks her.

'At the Academy,' Erzsébet says. 'It's just as well.' Karina's father, Dénes, is a cello teacher, much in demand. Sometimes, watching Mimi rant, Karina wonders why a woman of ninety-one should turn on her only child like this. The stroke, perhaps; though the doctor insists not. Dementia, Erzsébet suggests, but Karina doesn't believe this either. Perhaps it's sheer frustration that her body will no longer do her bidding.

'Shall I play to you, Grandma?' she says.

Mimi, with her distorted hands, has scarcely been able to play her violin for twenty years. She falls silent, her eyes caressing the instrument while Karina tunes the strings, then begins the Marc Duplessis Suite *Dans l'ombre des forêts*. Duplessis wrote the piece for Mimi in the mid-1930s. Five movements: 'The Minstrel'; 'The Fireside'; 'The Forest'; 'The Storm'; 'The Wedding'. Inspired by Mimi's Gypsy childhood – at least, as Duplessis, an ambitious young composer fresh from the Parisian bourgeoisie, had imagined it. Mimi listens, eyes closed. Tears glint on her lashes.

Until a year ago, Mimi had lived in a West End mansion block with solid walls and high ceilings that she said reminded her of

Budapest. She'd stopped giving concerts when the arthritis grew too bad, but never ceased working, inundated with requests for teaching, competition adjudication, master-classes. Her body aged faster than her mind. A knee; a hip; bladder trouble; then the stroke. Dénes had finally coerced her into moving to a sheltered housing complex with warden, helpline and community lounge, close to the Thames and her family. Her window opens on to the communal garden, and from front door to bathroom the flat has been adapted with specially designed railings and handles. 'Wasn't this a good idea of mine?' she declared, while the family unpacked for her.

'I worry about her losing her independence,' Karina told Julian.

'She's a survivor,' Julian said. 'If you have a hard life early on, you can take pretty much anything later. Not like us spoiled old softies.' Still, every time they meet, Karina senses that a sliver less of her indomitable grandmother exists. It's as if her image is fading away, pixel by pixel.

Mimi is still when the piece draws to its end. Karina glances at the photo on the bookshelf. Mimi in Paris, aged twenty-one; beside her is the composer – her composer – Marc Duplessis. Backstage at the Théâtre du Châtelet, after they'd given the Suite's first performance together, Marc in white tie and tails, Mimi wearing silk. That was 1936. Mimi's black eyes shine out, elongated, opaque. Karina has inherited Erzsébet's elfin face and small, pointed chin. But her eyes are Mimi's and her hair, too, is jet black: straight, simple and very long.

'We must let her have a proper sleep now,' Erzsébet whispers. 'It was good of you to come, Schnooky. Sometimes I despair, I don't know what more to do for her.'

'Sleep.' Mimi's hearing is as fine as a twenty-year-old's. 'I can't sleep. Rest, yes. But I do not need so much sleep, my dears. When I sleep, I dream.'

Karina kisses her goodbye. 'I'm coming to see Lindy on Monday,' she says. 'I'll stop in on the way.'

'Little blonde Lindy Rookfield.' Mimi smiles.

'She's neither blonde nor very little now. She runs a bookshop and dyes her hair.'

'Ach, Karina.' Mimi kisses her. 'You should play that violin, not just teach other people's children. And you should have more children of your own. That's what your grandfather says.'

'He never knew me,' Karina reminds her gently. Tamás Veres had died in the early 1950s. At least, Mimi and Dénes assume so; they never knew what had become of him at the hands of the Hungarian secret police. All Dénes will say on the subject is, 'Rottweilers'.

Guilt needles Karina. She should get to grips with the heritage that drags like a sack of rubble on her family's shoulders; but, growing up in London far from the Iron Curtain and its ghosts, she had never felt that Hungary was part of her, nor she part of it. Besides, she's too busy in the present to focus on the past.

'Karrie, were you in Twickenham today?' Julian asks, pouring himself a drink after the two of them have eaten a late supper.

'Mum said Grandma was poorly, so—'

'I've got a bone to pick.' He surveys her across the room. 'All your mother has to do is pick up the phone, and you go running.'

'My pupils weren't due for hours and Mimi was asking for me.'

'I don't like the way you're always at their beck and call. You've got your own life, but they lean on you all the time. They use you. Why is it your fault if Mimi's having a Hungarian rant?'

'It isn't. I love her, she loves me and I seem to be able to calm her down. What's wrong with that?'

'Nothing, but it happens too often. They take advantage of you.'

'We see plenty of your family, probably more.'

'That's different. They're up the road. And they don't insist on living in our pockets, or vice versa.'

'I'm all they've got.' Karina points out. 'I think you're jealous because we're so close.'

Karina and Julian's domestic spats, though rare, follow a tribal ritual. One hint of disagreement and those old, ingrained dance patterns emerge: the unflinching minuet of Fairfallows Place out of step with the *csárdás*, all lows and highs, of the Veres family's home. Karina has one last refuge.

'I'm going to practise for a bit,' she says.

'All right.' Julian clears away the dinner plates. 'I have to do some reading. Don't wake Jamie.'

'Nothing wakes Jamie.' Karina presses her husband's shoulder; he kisses her hand. It's their habitual signal that the issue is closed – for now.

Karina's violin sits in its case in a corner of the lounge, behind the Victorian chaise longue that had belonged to Julian's great-grandmother. The instrument is old and battered – the scroll must once have come off, as it's clearly been restored and replaced – but she's had it since she was eighteen and she'd feel limbless without it. You grow together with a violin, Mimi had told her. It's part of you.

Free from the pressure of concerts, orchestras and destructive colleagues, Karina can, in theory, practise in peace. Teaching is the most important job a musician can do, Dénes says, but now she does little else, having accidentally become the area's most sought-after violin teacher for small children. She hasn't given a concert since before Jamie was born. Sometimes she imagines her violin pleading for more of her hands-on affection; but it can't. It's just a piece of wood.

Besides, teaching brings different rewards. She loves to mould a small hand around the fingerboard, help a little bow gain its balance and see a child's eyes brighten as the first hesitant sounds stammer out. Nothing makes a noise quite as tooth-shattering as a violin in the hands of a beginner – but the Sussex schoolchildren seem undeterred.

'They make such progress with you,' Karina's neighbour Gilly Pearson remarks when her son Olly's lesson is over and he charges outside to play with Jamie. 'You should teach at the school. They'd give their eye-teeth to have you.' Karina laughs and thanks her, but she prefers to teach privately, so that her pupils needn't be from only one source. Like her father, she believes with a passion that music belongs to everyone and that all children can and should learn. Her best student is a boy from a council estate, whose father is in prison. Karina had helped to find him a violin to borrow and won't take a fee for his lessons.

'You don't need to teach,' Julian protests. As a City lawyer, he earns handsomely.

'It's not about money,' Karina tries to explain.

Her students troop in at weekends, after school and occasionally first thing in the morning. Mondays, though, she keeps clear, mainly at Julian's insistence ('You have to have a day off, darling one'), and now she's glad of it. This is the time when she can visit her parents and grandmother and occasionally slope off for a girly afternoon in London with Lindy, her oldest and dearest friend.

Still, in the end, the violin is her first love. It's always there for her: an unchanging force, perhaps the only constant in her family's history; she relies on its song to replenish her when she feels drained or discouraged. Her music rises through the house, soothing Jamie asleep and dreaming upstairs, calming Julian like a honeyed potion as he tries to concentrate on the *Law Society Journal*, then pours its lonely Hungarian enchantment out into the night and the oblivious hills.

A low whistle near the door. Lindy straightens up: she's been scrabbling behind the counter for some plastic bags. Alban's beaming at her, apparently relishing her back view, long-legged in her denim skirt, bending from the hip. 'Where is camera?' he says.

Lindy laughs. She's used to Alban eyeing her. It's part of his Balkan charm, which doesn't bother her. She's so preoccupied with her current love affair that she feels inoculated against everyone else. She can't explain why she likes to hang out with Alban – but she does, and why not? He'd chatted her up at her till two years ago; he tolerates her sexual unavailability and seems content to be a companion for clubbing and pubbing, and a provider of general words of wisdom to which she doesn't listen. Certain things they don't discuss: she knows too little about where he comes from or how he makes his living, which implies that she knows too much. She suspects that Alban isn't his real name. Still, they're friends: they support one another without taking advantage.

'What you do later?' He leans on the counter, grinning.

'I'm buggering off at lunchtime. Karina's coming up for the afternoon and we're going out. Yes, she is married, and no, you can't come with us.'

'This Karina, you talk about her a lot.'

'She's the closest thing I have to a sister. She's an only child too. They lived across the road from us, so I've known her all my life. She married my cousin, Julian. You know my godson? He's their kid.' Jamie's picture takes pride of place on Lindy's desk: big, dark irises, an overserious expression.

'Special eyes,' Alban remarks, surveying him. 'An old soul.'

'He's only seven and I don't buy reincarnation.' Lindy turns to a woman waiting beside Alban, two paperbacks in hand. 'That's thirteen ninety-eight, please.'

The customer, pocketing change, glares at Alban. Perhaps it's his aftershave, or his chunky leather jacket and fake Rolex. Alban, ignoring her, reaches over the counter and pulls a chocolate biscuit out of a packet by the computer.

'Too much scent, darling.' Lindy pulls a face. 'You don't know the meaning of the word moderation.'

'How is this word? Modern—?'

'Mod. Der. Ray. Tion. Moderation. It's the opposite of excess.'

'No, this word I don't understand. Excess, that I like!' Alban munches. 'Lindy, when you come out with me again?'

'You're coming to see *Distant Beloved*, aren't you?'

'Sure, I bought tickets. Lots of tickets. I bring people.'

'Good, because I'm bloody nervous. I'm hoping to get an agent along, so the fuller the place is, the better.'

'Lindy, where you find time to write plays while you run shop?'

'No idea. I just do. If you've got nothing better to do tomorrow night, let's go for a drink.'

Cold air and exhaust fumes fly in as the paperback customer leaves the door open. Lindy closes it. Heating, or lack of it, is an issue. She's wearing woolly tights; her boots conceal thick socks, and a chunky grey cable-knit jersey is fastened across her waist with a giant safety-pin.

'Alban, off you go,' she says. 'Take another biscuit with you. I've got work to do before Karina gets here.'

'Karina like sister, but not sister.'

'Exactly. Come on, out! See you tomorrow.'

'Lindy, you have no brother. So *I* am brother. Yes?'

'Bye-bye, then, big brother. Love you.'

'Love you too. Till tomorrow.' Alban zips his jacket up to his chin and vanishes, blowing Lindy a kiss through the window. Lindy waves back. An ice-cube seems to have replaced her nose. She must discuss with the owner how best to improve the heating without spending too much. A few more customers wouldn't hurt.

At one forty-five, Karina's slight, dark form blows in with the March wind. Lindy shouts her name and dives across the shop.

'Heavens, it's cold in here.' Karina reaches up to hug her. 'You're frozen!'

'I'm going to do something about it, honest. Let's get going. I booked us into Zucchini's.' Lindy grabs her coat and shouts a goodbye to her deputy.

Camden High Street, south of the lock and the market, is home to a blustery mix of outlets offering bijou gifts, health food, books, recordings and films of all types (legal and otherwise), electrical goods, grungy fashion and second-hand clothes – some for charity, others for retro glamour; an inner-city concatenation where tarmac, lorries, buses, bicycles, roadworks, electric drills and vociferous pedestrians muddle together in too little space.

'Bet you don't miss the chaos,' Lindy remarks while they walk.

'Oh, but I do! I miss – this. There's always something happening. Something to watch, someone interesting to talk to, unusual food, funny noises and smells and sights. And you can lose yourself in London.'

'I can lose myself anywhere,' Lindy quips. 'No sense of direction. Never had one.'

'You know what I mean. You can't be anonymous in Lewes. You can't just disappear.'

When Jamie was born, Karina and Julian had needed more space and Julian, in an executive decision, decreed that they'd move to Lewes, not far from his family at Fairfallows Place. He doesn't mind his lengthy commute – he enjoys driving, with a CD on full blast. 'It's nice for Jamie to grow up in a small town,' he'd pointed out. Karina finds it easier to agree with him than to fight; when his mind's made up, he won't budge. Arguing, he insists, is a waste of time.

Perching on the South Downs, close to Brighton and inviting stretches of coast, Lewes's steep lanes and jigsaw of cottages often attract fugitives from urban sprawl. Still, the town, with its tradition of burning effigies of the Pope on Guy Fawkes night, has been less comfortable for Karina since the bonfire in 2004, when a few locals in a nearby village decided to send up in smoke a wagon painted with images of Gypsies.

She often watches Jamie hurtling ahead on his scooter, staring into shop windows and charging back to plead for a toy or lemon sherbets, with the dark eyes of his Hungarian Roma great-grandmother and the well-modulated English accent of his father, his father's father and many fathers before that; and she wonders how he'll make sense of their different worlds, which will mingle in his blood and affect the way people perceive him all his life. One side, the wandering minstrel; the other, the lord of the manor. On Julian's side, the family baggage flaps about for all to see; but on hers, there exist only shadows and secrets.

At Zucchini's, Pietro, the proprietor, greets Lindy and Karina open-armed and in Italian; he's reserved them a table in the front window. Signed photos of celebrities neither of them have heard of line the wall; from the ceiling dangle bunches of desiccated flowers, strings of garlic and empty wine bottles.

'I was wondering,' says Lindy, while Karina shrugs off her coat, 'have you ever thought of trying to trace your ancestors? Everyone's at it. There's even a celebrity series on telly. Wouldn't it be fascinating?'

'It's too difficult. On my father's side, everything gets lost out on the big flat puszta a generation past my grandmother. Anyway, my parents aren't interested and I can't speak Hungarian.'

'So find someone who does.'

'But it's awkward. The Roma thing. First, it seems they didn't keep records, not reliable ones. And then, people don't like it . . . it's better to keep quiet, for Jamie's sake, if nothing else.'

'But you're only a quarter Roma. It's just Mimi, isn't it?'

'Technically,' says Karina. 'Sometimes I feel that it means more than all the rest put together.'

Lindy winks at Pietro, who brings them a bottle of prosecco straight away. Karina, sitting with her back against the wall, watches Lindy, head to one side.

'What?' Lindy demands.

'I envy you that. Your confidence. I think it comes from the old, grand family, the way you can just *command*.'

'Tripe. Pietro knows I always order prosecco.'

'Yes, but Julian does it too, and, heaven knows, so do his parents.'

'Sod the lot of them.' Lindy lifts her glass. 'Here's to alcohol before six. *Egészségedre!*'

'Cheers,' says Karina.

Lindy isn't sure how she got into her current mess. Tracing the progress is easy enough. You meet people if you run a bookshop well. You order some obscure volumes for a middle-aged musicologist; they look intriguing, so you ask him questions and he offers to buy you a drink and tell you more. Over that drink, you learn all about Beethoven and try to imagine the living hell of a musician who couldn't hear. You realise how excellent the story would be on stage. Your actress friend is overjoyed when you suggest that you could write something for her to perform. Your customer offers to help. Soon, though, it's not Beethoven who's under your skin, but your customer. And how that comes about is anyone's guess.

'But there's real love between us,' Lindy confides in Karina, eating tiramisu. 'I don't know what else to call it. It's just . . . so true.' Charles is twenty years her senior, married, father of three teenagers. It's his second marriage, the first having ended in what he calls 'acrimony and alimony'. Old love turned to stone by lawyers. He doesn't want to go through that again.

It's not all bad. She's lost half a stone since she met him. Besides, the affair makes her write. It polishes her mind, like exfoliation for the brain, and her theatre piece has certainly benefited from her experience of a distant beloved, even if he's only in Primrose Hill.

'It could be the break I need,' she remarks. 'I've been working on outlines for two more plays.'

'Just keep at it. Whatever happens, don't stop writing.'

'Like you and the violin, yeah?'

'Oh, come on.' Karina shrugs. 'You're just getting started. I've finished.'

'Don't be daft. Drink your coffee and let's head out.'

Now that Karina and Lindy live eighty miles apart, they've developed a routine for their afternoons together. Lunch at Zucchini's. The tube to Knightsbridge, where they indulge in a window-shopping spree in

Harvey Nichols, trying on designer gear that they've no intention of buying. Finally, cocktails, the more colourful the better.

Today, though, a notice at Camden Town station tells them that the Northern Line is suspended north of Kennington due to signal failure. 'Fuck,' Lindy says. 'Let's get a bus.'

The rest of Camden Town's would-be passengers, needing to cross London, have the same idea. The girls, screwing up their eyes against the wind, stand at a stop on the one-way system and hang back while what had been a queue implodes into a mush of human forms struggling through the last remaining space in a number twenty-seven.

'Ask Julian why things like this still happen?' Lindy demands. 'I thought it was his job to sort out transport.'

'Why do you think he drives everywhere?' Karina quips. The bus queue watches them laughing, their hilarity brightening the afternoon. 'He's working on PPP stuff at the moment,' she adds. 'It's way over my head. Since Andy Williamson moved to the Department for Transport, Julian's been letting everyone know that they're old mates and suddenly he's got more work than he can handle.'

'Fucking politicians. I hate them all.'

'Andy's all right.'

'Andy's a prat. He's a natural Tory, he only turned Labour to get in power. And that wife of his . . . Is it true it was a shotgun wedding?'

'Yes, but she adores him.'

'God, Karrie, you're so naïve. She's a neurotic twit and Andy deserves everything that's coming his way.'

'Why are you so hard on them? Can't you give them the benefit of the doubt?'

'Which benefit of what doubt?'

Another bus pulls up. Karina and Lindy are half pushed, half pulled with the crowd towards its gaping doors. The interior, body upon body, limbs squashed against the windows, reminds Karina abruptly of a painting of the Day of Judgment.

'Lin, wait – I can't get in there.'

Lindy elbows her way out of the bus's inexorable suck, back to her friend. Karina suffers from claustrophobia. 'Are you OK?'

'I just – never mind. I get panicky in crushes like that.' She takes a breath, watching the doors close.

'Let's go to my place,' Lindy suggests. 'We can do Harvey Nicks next time.'

Lindy calls her flat 'The Rookery'. It's at the top of a white stucco nineteenth-century house off Camden Road; from the first floor, its stairs lead up to a small bedroom and a living room that opens broad and low under the eaves. She's decorated it herself: plain, bright and fresh, with two red sofas posing against white walls beneath the windows. 'Sorry about the mess,' she says, making for the kitchen.

Karina pulls off her boots and settles on her usual sofa. 'My place is a lot worse.'

'Kids.'

'Kid, singular.'

Lindy presses a switch. Karina, eyes half closed, hears the coffee machine, Lindy's one luxury, gurgling into action. 'Do you still not want more kids, Karrie?' Lindy asks, frothing milk under a jet of steam.

'Jules does. I'm not sure.' Karina lies back with her head on the armrest. 'I don't feel ready. It's odd, but for the last seven years I've been . . . Jamie's mum. I'm not sure who I am any more.'

'My trouble's different.' Lindy's back is turned. 'I know who I am, but I don't like it.'

'But you're wonderful! You're strong, you're clever and your writing is fantastic. And I don't know why you dyed your hair black. You looked so great blonde.'

'I got sick of being Miss Mousie. Ugh. I'm just a bony great oaf with flat feet.'

'Rubbish,' Karina says. 'You're straight out of a Pre-Raphaelite painting.'

'I don't like the Pre-Raphaelites.' Lindy brings Karina a mug, then puts on a CD of dusky jazz and flops onto the other sofa. Rain patters against the windows; Karina gazes at the clouds through the glass. The jazz singer describes tears like a river, shed for love.

'I don't want to be in this mess, but I don't want to stop seeing him,' Lindy says.

'If Julian lied to me the way Charles lies to you, I'd leave.'

'Do you think infidelity is always wrong? No matter how strong the love is?'

'Yes, of course. But I blame him, not you. He's the one who made vows. If you make a promise, you should keep it.'

'They've got these wedding photos on the walls. Six of the damn things, blown up huge.'

'You've been to his house?'

'Mostly he comes here. But his wife was away, lecturing in Italy, the kids went with her, and he stayed home . . .'

'But . . . ?'

'Did we do it in his bed? *Their* bed? Yes, we did.'

'Lin! How could you bear it?'

Lindy takes a long swig of coffee. 'Actually, I didn't even stop to think about it. Are you shocked?'

'Yes, but only because I worry about you. What do you see in him?'

'God knows. We laugh together, we have incredible sex. But it's more than that; we're not just in love, we're, I don't know, in harmony. It doesn't make sense, but it's there and I don't want to be without it. But sometimes if I see families go past, dads carrying toddlers on their shoulders . . . I can't even think about that without it hurting. And there's fuck all I can do, because he's got a wife and kids already. And I keep thinking, maybe one day he'll recognise how special things are between us and leave them, but . . .'

'Lin, don't go there. Don't start thinking he'll leave her. He won't.'

'God, Karrie. Sometimes I think I'm going to be stuck here forever. I'll wait for him and it'll never happen, and I'll spend my life wondering how to heat the shop and fighting with my blasted family, and suddenly I'll have my bus pass and I'll have missed everything. Oh, damn it, let's open some wine.'

Much later, Karina walks back to the station, her head spinning. The tube is running again; she changes at Euston. At Victoria, she buys a double espresso to sober herself up during the journey home.

'Mum, you've been to see Auntie Lindy!' Jamie accuses her when she picks him up from the Pearsons'.

'How do you know, sweetie?'

'You always look happy and you always smell like that bar on the high street!'

Lindy, alone, pours the rest of the wine into a large glass and drinks the lot in ten minutes, flicking through the TV channels with tears sliding down her cheeks.

2

One spring day in 1969, Cynthia and Martin Rookfield spotted a removal van outside the house facing theirs in Forest Road, in the Strawberry Hill area of Twickenham. Their new neighbours, two Hungarian musicians named Dénes and Erzsébet Veres, arrived in a spectacular muddle shortly after the van. They'd brought minimal furniture, an ancient baby grand piano, powerful accents and the wrong set of keys. A startled Cynthia hurried out to welcome them, then let them use the phone. Dénes called the estate agents 'Rottweilers', while Erzsébet, her hands clasped, apologised to Cynthia again and again.

The Rookfields' Georgian pile would once have had Forest Road to itself; but between the wars someone had erected opposite it a modest yet profitable row of terraced houses. The Vereses' was the fourth of these. Soon the piano sat in its squat bay window and the dining table was spread with a white cotton cloth embroidered with scarlet wool.

The families' paths crossed infrequently at first. Cynthia was distracted by pregnancy, then Belinda; Martin by work and, covertly, his secretary; and in this street, people liked to say that the neighbours 'kept themselves to themselves'.

Belinda was a few months old when Cynthia, wheeling the pram home, spotted the heavily pregnant Erzsébet struggling up her front path with six bags of shopping. She went over to help, then on impulse invited her back to the Georgian house for tea. Erzsebet's ready smile and lack of pretentiousness seemed refreshing compared to the wives of Martin's business associates and what remained, post-baby, of her own contacts in the fashion world.

Over the first cup of what would become decades full of tea, Erzsébet watched Cynthia, her five-mile legs curled under her on the antique sofa, talking about Dr Spock, pre-labour breathing exercises and how to test the temperature of bottle milk. Erzsébet was grateful; she explained that there was nobody else to advise her, since she had no family. She'd escaped from Hungary as a teenager during the 1956 uprising, by swimming across a river. 'In any case, mostly they were not alive by then,' she added. Her pregnancy was unexpected; she didn't tell Cynthia that she uttered prayers of thanks for her baby every day.

'What about your mother-in-law? She looks quite a type,' Cynthia said.

'She's busy. She travels so much . . .' Erzsébet couldn't imagine asking Mimi, who was recording with Yehudi Menuhin in Switzerland, to discuss childbirth and adjustment to motherhood. Dénes as an infant had been cared for by a Hungarian nanny named Vali, who still sends him a Christmas card from New York every year.

'Anything I can do to help, just say the word,' Cynthia promised. Erzsébet blushed and thanked her. Sometimes she imagined that Twickenham was the dream and the living reality still Budapest in 1956, which reclaimed her and her husband in their sleep almost every night.

Cynthia, fascinated, scrutinised the Veres family: the piano in the front room, the music that seeped towards her from their windows, Erzsébet's slanted, sky-blue eyes, the cello case gliding up the road on Dénes's back like a speedy snail. Their intense privacy was puzzling – Erzsébet's net curtains were the thickest in the street – especially as it didn't reflect their hospitality. When they invited the Rookfields to supper, only weeks before Erzsébet's baby was due, Cynthia went home so stuffed with goulash stew, dumplings and strudel that she imagined she wouldn't have to eat again for a year. 'You see,' said Martin, 'you don't need to be worried about them being poor musicians. They may have nothing, but they eat very well.'

'We must invite them back,' said Cynthia. 'I wonder when – with the Blythes, perhaps?'

'Don't be silly,' Martin snapped. 'You can't invite *them* with the managing director of a merchant bank.'

'Why not? I happen to prefer Erzsébet's company to anyone else's,' Cynthia retorted.

She was the first visitor at the hospital to see mother and daughter. A girl. A friend for Belinda. 'Karina? What a darling name,' Cynthia cried, wishing she'd thought of it first.

Erzsébet, trying not to let Cynthia know how intimidated she still felt by the size and contents of the Georgian house, began to bring the infant Karina over the road to play with Lindy twice a week. And when spelling and pronunciation defeated the Rookfields, Erzsébet and Dénes, who called each other Erzsi and Dini, found themselves gradually transformed into Betsy and Dennis.

Aged six, the little girls loved dressing up. Sneaking into Cynthia's wardrobes, they'd appropriate the rhinestone earrings and party dresses that she'd given them permission to touch. On Cynthia, who'd been a model, the skirts reached mid-thigh, maximum, but on the children they almost swept the floor. Lindy rifled through Erzsébet's wardrobe, but among the subdued tweeds found hope only in an attractive scarf and a full skirt, patterned with yellow and red, that trailed behind her when she tried it on.

'I think those are Hungarian,' Karina remarked – at six, all she knew about 'Hungarian' was that her parents spoke this language when they didn't want her to understand them. She didn't know yet that they'd decided to keep it that way, regarding the usefulness of Hungarian in Britain as second only to Martian.

They walked to and from primary school together, hand in hand, escorted by Cynthia's French au pair; Erzsébet was grateful for this help, which left her free to give piano lessons. When the girls were eleven, Cynthia and Martin enrolled Lindy at a local private school for girls; Karina, distraught at the idea of being left behind, practised her violin so hard that she sailed in on a music scholarship.

Dénes, in the meantime, had been making friends and enemies. Tired of freelance insecurity, he applied for section leader posts in several orchestras until one of them turned him down with an explanation that nearly made him choke. 'You played much the best audition,' the chairman told him, 'but the conductor wants to give the job to an old friend of his from school. Sorry, old man, but there's nothing I can do about it.' Dénes's deluge of invective, spangled with minutely argued meritocratic philosophy and some ferociously onomatopoeic Hungarian swear-words, left the chairman reeling for a week and a half.

'I'm not in Hungary now and if I despise something I can say so!' Dénes stormed at home. 'I will not bow and smile and tug this forelock thing! I tell you, Erzsi, I've had it with these fucking cunts. There's such a notion as human dignity. Orchestras are full of sheep eating shit. I'm never touching one again!' And he never had.

'Let me help,' Mimi suggested, while he sulked. 'I'm earning too much for myself. What do I need with money?'

'Never.' Dénes and Mimi locked wills in the latest round of a long battle in which Erzsébet dared not interfere.

'Please, Dini,' Mimi ordered. 'Why be so proud? It won't always be like this.'

'Because you still blame me, you still think it was my fault,' he growled. And at that, Mimi grabbed her coat from the banister and flounced away home.

'Why is Grandma so angry?' Karina asked, afraid, peering round the kitchen door. 'Why, Daddy?'

'Nothing, little one. Nothing at all.' Dénes ruffled his small daughter's black hair and shook his head.

Fortunately, Dénes was as generous with kind words and good sense as with their opposites. His Hungarian musician friends rallied round, recommending him as a teacher, and soon so many students were seeking him out that he had to set his alarm clock for several hours earlier every day.

On Sunday afternoons, the Vereses' friends would come over to play chamber music after coffee and cake. With the arrival of evening, they moved on to red wine and Erzsébet's stews; a few string quartets or piano quintets later, they'd put down the instruments and analyse the world's evils well into the night, as they once might have in a Budapest café.

Lindy and Karina would creep in to listen to the music, sitting on the floor and feeling the vibrations fizzling through them. Karina's violin teacher, József, Dénes's oldest friend, played first violin; Karina kept very still, scrutinising his every gesture. On one memorable occasion, Mimi turned up, bringing strudel. József took one look at her and fled into the bathroom. After ten minutes, Mimi tapped on the door and talked through it in Hungarian, which, eventually, brought him out; in the bathroom doorway, he hugged her, motionless for minutes.

Karina couldn't work out what had been going on. Was he scared of playing in front of her? Why, then, the embrace? All these silly mysteries, she mused, chewing her pencil over her homework. And her grandmother was always in the middle of them.

Mimi had given Karina a tiny violin when she was three years old. Karina never forgot the frisson as Mimi played to her that day, conjuring the voice of the forests and plains out of her grown-up instrument. Her spell had worked its way under Karina's skin; and it's never left her. Perhaps it had been there already.

They used to make violins out of crates, floorboards and firewood, Mimi told her. Lacking music, the *muzsikás cigány*, the Hungarian Gypsy musicians whom Mimi insisted were the aristocrats of their race, would lose the will to live. In prison, war, times of hardship, they'd make a violin out of any wood they could find. 'It's in your blood,' she'd tell the child Karina, who sat, transfixed, with Lindy big-eyed beside her. 'Don't believe you can get away from it.'

'That's me,' Karina whispered to Lindy on the lounge floor, watching József, Dénes and their quartet. 'That's what I want to do.'

Aged eleven, Lindy came home from school one Friday to find that she'd unceremoniously been assigned the front bedroom on the second floor instead of the back bedroom on the first. She called Karina. Helping her to move her books, toys and collection of foreign costume dolls, Karina pointed out that as she had the front bedroom in the opposite house, they'd be able to wave to each other. Better still, they could send signals.

'All we need is a couple of torches,' she said. 'You switch them on and off, like Morse code. You can do SOS for emergencies. Or we could signal three long flashes for "are you there" and one for "yes" and two for "later" . . .'

'OK,' Lindy mumbled. Her lower lip was wobbling.

'What's the matter? What happened?'

'Dunno. I think my mum and dad don't want to share a room any more.'

'But . . .' Karina sensed something freezing up inside Lindy. 'Did they have a row?'

'Dunno.' Lindy looked down at her feet, biting her lip, keeping back tears.

At home, Karina went straight to her mother, who had just finished giving a lesson, and said, 'Mum, Lindy's really upset, her parents have been fighting.'

Erzsébet gave Karina a long hug. 'They do fight,' she confirmed. 'I'm sorry, it's horrible for Lindy. Hush, Schnooky, try not to let it upset you too. Lindy needs your support, so you must help her be strong.'

Lindy and Karina signalled through the dusk in spring and autumn, and the short winter afternoons. Summer proved frustrating: it was harder to see the flashing torches before dark. Martin complained: why couldn't they just nip over the road? Cynthia insisted that they were doing no harm. But all the parents drew the line at the girls' next idea: rope ladders. 'You can ring the bell like normal people,' Cynthia told them.

'We're not normal people,' declared Lindy, who had learned that her honorary sister was partly Gypsy.

'I have these dreams,' Karina admitted, aged fourteen, walking to school. 'I've always had them, but I never thought much about what they mean.'

'My mum says dreams are all about sex,' Lindy said.

'Well, these aren't.' Karina was wearing one of her serious looks, which sometimes scared Lindy. 'It's difficult to describe.'

'Try. What do you see?' Lindy encouraged.

'It's partly seeing, partly feeling. Rocking, as if I'm moving. There's a long road and a wide horizon. Totally flat. Space, forever, and nothing to stop you moving across it.'

'Are you in a car? Or a plane?'

'It's like something bigger than a car, with wheels but no engine.'

'Horse and cart?'

'Could be.'

Lindy stopped giggling. 'What else do you see?'

'Stars. I look up and the sky is silver with them. I fly into them and then just when it's becoming magical, I wake up, and it's like I drop down into bed. There's an actual jolt. It's as if I'd really been up there. Do you think I'm crazy?'

Lindy's own dreams were more mundane – mainly concerning her cousins' friend Chris, who was in his twenties and extremely charismatic. At Christmas lunch at Fairfallows, he'd been Hilary and Julian's guest, and after they pulled a cracker, he put an arm round her shoulder, hot and sweet, for one point eight seconds. Afterwards she couldn't eat. Asleep, she'd dream that he was kissing her, and no way was she going to tell anybody that. Not even Karina.

Seeing Chris at all was tricky, because, apart from the obligatory Christmas visit, her family hardly ever went to Fairfallows, which was where she'd be most likely to run into him. She'd worked out that her father, Martin, and his elder brother, Arthur, barely spoke to one another. Whether it was jealousy over the estate, unspoken issues about Martin's life and business that went clean over Lindy's head, or some row dating back to childhood fisticuffs, she had no idea.

Martin was the best-looking dad she knew, incrementally handsomer than the overtall and overwide Arthur; she'd thought proudly that he could have stepped straight from the celluloid of a period drama. Her mother's problem was that most other women thought so too, and Martin knew it. Later Lindy wondered why it had taken her so long to recognise his mask for what it was.

Now and then, from her attic room, she heard shouting, her mother's tone shifting up several gears towards hysteria. She tried to block out the noise with Madonna or Alison Moyet records, but even if she couldn't hear the row, she still knew it was happening and it flooded her foundations like a burst water main. For a while, she dreaded that her parents would get divorced, which would mean she'd spend the rest of her teenage years shunting between two homes. It was only after Christmas at Fairfallows, with the remembered sensation of Chris's arm as warm as a fur coat around her, that she began to wonder why her mother hadn't left her father years ago.

Lindy sat on her bed and made a silent vow. From now on, she no longer loved her father, for he appeared to love neither her nor her mother. She felt as if a veil were lifting from her eyes. He talked to her only to hector her about homework and wearing too much make-up. Only to tell her that the boys who asked her out were yobs. Only to decree that she'd never amount to anything. A writer? 'Don't be stupid. You won't even get into university, the way you're going.' She pressed her teeth together until her gums throbbed.

Shaken, miserable, Lindy glanced towards the window and spotted, through the dusk, a light in Karina's room. She took her torch out of her desk and flashed SOS. They were attuned to one another's signals after four years; a soft flicker that half caught the eye during a homework crisis. A halo of net curtain framed the shadow of Karina and the violin cradled under her chin. Lindy opened the window; the skein of music reached her. For the first time it struck her that one day her friend might abandon her, and for this: music, a sphere that spun beyond her grasp. And now as she watched, she saw her father driving away up the road alone, too fast. She threw herself face down on the bed and howled for half an hour.

'Oh, darling,' Cynthia cried, 'it's your hormones.'

A few nights before their wedding, Karina and Julian drove from Fairfallows up to the Seven Sisters and lay on the ground. They gazed at the Milky Way spreading over the sea; jugfuls of starlight seemed to pour down on them, sticky as cream. Nobody was around at that hour: clifftops, waves and stars were all theirs, they had sex on a rug, no holds barred, and Karina told herself that this was what she had been dreaming of in those peculiar night travels. She told herself that as hard as she could.

'I'm so lucky!' Julian, getting his breath, flopped onto his back, laughing. 'I can hardly believe you're really marrying me.'

'If anyone had told me about this ten years ago, I'd never have believed it,' Karina said. 'And you were always there, Lindy had been talking about you forever . . .'

'I worry that you think I bounced you into getting engaged too quickly.'

'You certainly bounced,' she teased him.

'But you could have said no.'

Karina hesitated for a second before agreeing that yes, she could have said no.

'I've never loved anyone the way I love you,' Julian mumbled into her neck.

Karina, melting with a love that sprang somehow from mingled gratitude, hope and continuing incredulity at her good fortune, decided to tell him about her dreams of space and motion, which she'd never confided in anyone except Lindy. 'Sometimes,' she admitted, 'I think I've taken on some of my grandmother's memories, or perhaps something further back, some kind of collective unconscious.'

'But darling one, there's no such thing as collective unconscious,' Julian insisted. 'You shouldn't believe everything your grandmother says.'

'She didn't say anything. She doesn't know, I've never told her.'

'It's more what *she* tells *you*. Those wretched stories about the Gypsy way. For heaven's sake, she left it all behind when she was ten!'

'I've never even been in a wagon, but I can feel the way it moves. I can remember it when I wake up.'

'And I promise the Jag is more comfortable.' Julian kissed her nose. 'Come on, love, let's get going.'

Today, Karina sometimes wonders what happened to her will-power. Wrecked, perhaps, by the Richard incident, when she spent every gram of it breaking off a relationship she didn't wholly want to leave; it has never come back, not with its old strength. Or perhaps it's motherhood, which may have softened her, or may simply have tired her out.

It's a measure of her success that Jamie's happy, popular, and good at everything except maths. She pours all her love around her son, for this treacly affection is his best nourishment. Julian, after a long day at the office, sprawls in his chair and calls her 'Vitamin K', but Karina's Vitamin J is Jamie. Tiptoeing into his room to check on him at night, she watches him asleep, a dark little hump under his duvet; a roaring fire of tenderness consumes her. Will-power, compared to love, doesn't seem so important any more.

The clock ticks towards eleven. *Newsnight* barks out headlines about a Stop The War demonstration, new government regulations about child restraints in cars, and the latest level of terrorist threat. Julian switches off the TV and goes back to an article about rail franchising that he's writing for the *Daily Telegraph*. 'Sorry, love,' he says to Karina. 'It's a bugger, but I've got to get this finished tonight.'

Karina takes the phone to the kitchen extension at the back of the house and calls Lindy. 'Just me checking in,' she says. 'How's *Distant Beloved*? Are you rehearsing yet?'

'So far so good.' Karina can hear Lindy pouring liquid in Camden, probably wine. 'We're wondering how to describe it for the flyers. It's not really a play. It's a *thing* with words and music.'

'How do you mean?'

'Well, Nicki is Beethoven's Distant Beloved, discovering after Beethoven died how he'd felt about her, and Vince plays bits of the piano music. I have this theory about who the Distant Beloved really was.'

'His sister-in-law, I heard?'

'Charles says that's bollocks. My premise is that she's a woman he's seen and watched; but she knows him by sight, nothing more than that. For him, it's only the idea of her that's important. It doesn't matter if she's a complete cow.'

There's a pause. Karina says, 'How's Charles?'

'A pain. A painful kind of pain. He was meant to come round tonight, but he called to say he has a meeting at college, and I don't know whether it's a pile of old porkies. Maybe he wants a nice evening at home with the wife and kids and can't bear to tell me.'

'Is it him you love, or the idea of him?' Karina asks; it seems pertinent.

'Fuck knows,' says Lindy.

'I don't want to say you should break it off. But – you should break it off.'

'I know, but I can't.'

'Yes, you can. I did it once, on your advice. So believe me, I know.'

'Don't use that tone, Karrie. It always makes it sound like you married Jules on the rebound.'

'You know I didn't,' says Karina.

3

Over a late supper, Julian puts down his fork, folds his arms behind his head and says, 'Listen, darling one, I've been thinking about Jamie's school.'

'What?' Karina, who's been reminding herself to ring her parents and invite them to Lindy's play, is off guard.

Julian begins to explain. At thirteen, Jamie should go to the best possible school, ideally Elthingbourne College, where Julian, his brother, father, uncle and grandfather all studied. He'll need to pass an entrance exam; therefore, he needs a prep school that will train him to do so. For instance, St Matthew's, just outside Chichester.

'You want to send Jamie to boarding-school *now*?' The words emerge as though from someone else's mouth. Karina can't believe she has to say them. 'But he's only seven!'

'By the autumn, he'll be eight, which is already on the old side for Year Three. I went away to school at five.'

'But you hated it.'

'At the time. But do you think I'd be where I am now if I hadn't gone to Elthingbourne?'

'I don't understand. What's the point of having a child if you send him away?'

'If he goes to Elthingbourne,' Julian begins, patient, 'he'll be given one very important quality: confidence.'

'But he *is* confident. Can't he be coached for the exams at a normal school?'

'Sweetie, I'd like us to go to an open day at St Matthew's. It's got an excellent reputation for pastoral care. Let's look, and if you don't like it, we'll try somewhere else.'

'I don't want to.'

'Karrie, why won't you discuss this rationally?'

'Because it's not a rational thing to do to a child.' A violin string in Karina's brain is tightening towards snapping point. 'What's wrong with where he is? He loves school, he loves his friends, he's happy. Why uproot him? He'll be lonely, he could be bullied, and he'll be put into the academic sausage machine and when he comes out he'll have been squashed and twisted—'

'Calm down, darling one.'

'Don't talk to me as if *I'm* seven years old! He's my son too – you can't take him away from me!'

'Hush, you'll wake him.' Julian pushes a tissue into her hand. 'You're thinking of yourself, not him. I only want to give him the best chance. It's all very well to imagine that childhood is fun and games, but he's already growing up. And because of our idiotic schooling system, if he's going to have a decent education, we'll have to pay for it. Elthingbourne's the best, but it's very competitive and he's got to be ready.'

'But he won't get into St Matthew's now. You have to put kids' names down for those schools almost before they're born, don't you?'

'Karrie, I did.'

'You did what?'

'I put Jamie's name down for St Matthew's when he was six months old.'

'*What?*'

'Well, you went into Hungarian three-year-old mode at the very mention of boarding-school, so . . .'

'You did that without telling me?'

'I'm telling you now.'

Karina hides her face in her hands and sobs.

'Karrie,' says Julian. She doesn't respond.

On their first date, a decade ago, Julian took Karina out to dinner at Le Caprice in Mayfair. Gazing at the bronze and gold apparition opposite him, he thought irrationally of the scene in *My Fair Lady* (irrational because he doesn't like musicals) in which Audrey Hepburn as Eliza Doolittle is mistaken at a society party for a Hungarian princess.

A week earlier, Lindy had said, 'My friend Karina's in the British Symphony Orchestra. Why don't you come to a concert and meet her?' He'd already met her once, years before, during a rare visit to his aunt, uncle and cousin in Forest Road, when he was a trainee solicitor and she was a skinny fourteen-year-old keener to dash off to youth orchestra than to lounge about in riverside pubs. He'd never given her a second thought. When she glided onto the platform in her concert dress with the rest of the orchestra, he didn't recognise her.

Julian was still smarting, at the time, from being dumped by a blonde Canadian lawyer, whose legs were even longer than Aunt Cynthia's. The legs had walked. He wasn't sure what had happened to Karina; a big love thang, said Lindy. She'd had a boyfriend, something arty – a composer? – but she'd left him. Lindy had been vague, and he could hardly ask Karina outright on their first date.

She seemed made of molasses: her fluid movements, the almost impossible sweetness in her soul, a flavour that was strong, upfront, unique. She was ten years younger than him, yet something in her face – patient, intuitive – made her seem older. She sipped red wine in the candlelight: a vision in sepia superimposed on the black and white sophistication around them; a reel of film spliced from a different movie.

Every man who walked by glanced at her, including the waiters. She was unassuming – her background, Lindy said, was modest, though musical – and her beauty was unconscious, her strange, quiet charisma unthinking. When she laughed, though, she did so explosively, clapping her hands and throwing her head back, a gesture that astonished the besotted Julian. Her face sparkled as if a tub of glitter had tipped over it. Emotions flew across her, volatile as the weather.

He tried to take her left hand, and to his surprise she let him. Her fingertips were slightly calloused: the result of pressing violin strings for hour upon hour. Few women had ever struck him speechless, at least not since he was nineteen. He wondered how he was going to get her into his bed.

His CD collection proved an unexpected asset. In his Bayswater flat, he'd built floor-to-ceiling shelves for it. The leggy Canadian had loathed it, probably out of jealousy; when Karina saw it, though, her face lit up and she begged him to show her how it was organised.

The left-hand side, he explained, was alphabetical by composer. The right-hand side held historical recordings alphabetically by performer. Karina gravitated to the right, hunting for violinists. Heifetz, Kreisler, Menuhin. She pulled out disc after disc, exclaiming in delight at finding so many rarities. Julian hadn't imagined he could meet a girl who'd heard of Efraim Zimbalist, let alone one who knew more about him than he did.

She asked to hear an ancient recording by Jelly d'Arányi: 'She was Hungarian too. The great violin tradition was all Hungarian. József Joachim, Leopold Auer, Jenő Hubay – all the finest teachers in the nineteenth century.' Julian poured some drinks and they listened to an extract from the CD, a whisper of violin crackling out of the past. Karina kept exploring. When she got to R for Rácz she turned round.

'You've got Mimi Rácz in the wrong place,' she declared. 'She's alive.'

'Seriously? I haven't heard of her in decades. The recital with the Duplessis Suite is from the sixties.'

'She'd heard too many musicians giving concerts when their technique wasn't up to it any more and she promised herself she would never do that. So when her arthritis got worse, she decided to stop.'

'You know a lot about her.'

'She's my grandmother.'

Lindy had mentioned a family of musicians, but not their names. Karina held up Mimi's picture on the CD case. Their eyes were identical.

Lost for words, Julian couldn't stay where he was any longer. He crossed the room and took hold of Karina's waist. She frisbeed the CD box towards the sofa and tipped her head back to return his kiss. He faintly remembered, while his innards blistered down to charcoal, that it's the quiet ones you have to watch.

Much later, she lay beside him, stretched out like a dark-furred forest creature, eyes closed: after what had been considerable tumult, she'd disconnected, drifted off to a place where he couldn't follow her. Glowing, elated, he wanted to ask her if she felt good, if she was happy being with him, but he fell asleep too fast.

'He's always collected things,' Lindy told Karina a few days later, sharing a bottle of wine in Camden Town. 'First it was stamps, then CDs. Arthur's the same, with his icons.'

'But thousands of them! It's incredible. He'd put most music libraries to shame.'

'So he said "Come up and see my CD collection," and you were impressed?'

'I haven't been home for four days!' Karina threw her head back and clapped her hands.

'Better than Richard?'

The sunshine fled from Karina's face.

'More suitable, anyway . . . ?' Lindy back-pedalled.

Two weeks later they were engaged.

'Marry me.' Julian pinned Karina to the bed with his full weight.

'Jules, I can't breathe!'

'You have to marry me. Say you'll marry me!'

'But we only just met. Get off, you're squishing me.'

'I know. Marry me, for Christ's sake! Just say yes, and then I'll move.'

'We don't *know* each other.'

'I know you well enough to know that you've got to marry me. Karina, say yes, now, this minute, or I'm going to go clean out of my mind.'

'All right, *yes*. Now let me breathe.'

The next day, Julian sprinted from his office to Hatton Garden and bought the classiest ring he could find – delicacy, not ostentation, for his magical Gypsy violinist. Perhaps she'd thought he was joking, but he wasn't going to waste time telling her otherwise. He hadn't introduced her to his parents, let alone his brother, but he didn't want that to matter. He was thirty-seven years old, madly in love, and he didn't need their approval – even though demanding that a girl he'd only just met should marry at once into the Rookfield family was the single silliest idea he'd ever had.

Erzsébet stared at Karina's diamonds. 'Schnooky, are you sure? This is very quick, no?'

'He's attractive, generous and intelligent, he's crazy about me, he's my best friend's cousin and he loves music. What more could I ask?'

'But do you love him?'

Karina twisted her ring. 'I know it's fast, but I can't *not* love him back. I still can't believe that someone like him could want me so much.'

'Schnooky. You give everything and you give so easily.'

'I can't help it. You're the same. So's Dad. So's Grandma.'

'But these English families sometimes are not. Be careful. You need to learn some of their tricks. Not always showing how you feel. Not giving so much away.'

Karina thought of Julian pressing down on her, crying out that he'd go crazy if she didn't say yes, and burst out laughing.

One thing made her uneasy.

'This is fascinating,' Julian said. The flat rang with the sound of Dinu Lipatti playing a Chopin piano sonata. 'He plays the slow movement in half the time of this Russian bloke I just bought.'

Karina was lying on the sofa, lost in the music. 'Does he?'

Julian switched off the CD mid-phrase and put on his new acquisition. She sat up, disturbed.

'Ugh!' she said after a minute. 'I don't like this one at all.'

'But why should he play it so slowly? What's the marking on the piece?'

'I don't know, but I don't like it. Can we have Dinu back?'

'Let's try Rubinstein. He's meant to be the benchmark.' Julian cut off the unsatisfactory Russian and scanned the shelf for Arthur Rubinstein.

'Better.' Karina tried to listen.

'It would be interesting to hear what Pollini does. I've got him somewhere . . .'

The Rubinstein recording stopped as abruptly as it had started; Julian tossed yet another CD into the slot.

'I still prefer Dinu Lipatti,' said Karina. 'Can't we hear that one right through?'

'Yes, love, in a minute. Look, here's Alfred Cortot, he's interesting . . .'

Karina couldn't get her head around Julian's attitude to music. Either you love music, or you don't. Julian must love it; he spent much of his free time with his discs, listening, comparing and buying more. Yet he put her in mind of a schoolmaster on sports day. To him, musicians were like long-distance runners to be compared, detachedly, for their speed and agility. Sometimes he'd use music to engineer his mood: he'd put on something stirring, Beethoven or Richard Strauss, before a difficult meeting. But Karina would listen only for love – to atmosphere, poetry, personality. None of this appeared to matter to Julian. Surely, some day, she'd discover that it did?

Karina and Julian introduced their families to each other over dinner in the Bayswater flat. All seemed well at first. Dénes, a compact figure in a brown corduroy jacket, shook hands with Arthur, who to Karina seemed twice her father's height, twice his girth and if not twice as eccentric, then easily his match. Dénes's eyes fixed, disbelieving, on the gem-studded Orthodox cross that dangled over Arthur's waistcoat: a souvenir bought during a business trip after the Iron Curtain fell, Arthur explained, chosen for aesthetic reasons, not religious. Erzsébet asked Anne to sign the copy of her latest biography that she'd brought them as a gift. Karina concentrated on the food, flurrying about fluffing couscous, squeezing lemons and unwrapping French cheeses; that way, she didn't have to worry about what would happen if and when the Rookfields wandered on to the piece of Hungarian territory where the land-mines lay.

They'd reached the cheese before Arthur fell foul of the taboo.

'So, Dennis,' he said, 'you both came to this green and pleasant land in 1956?'

Erzsébet replied for him: 'Yes, we were very lucky.'

Dénes stayed silent.

'How fascinating, Betsy,' Anne prompted. 'Was it awfully traumatic?'

'One did what one could.' Erzsébet forced a smile. 'We were both very young. My mother and father were long dead and I escaped with some school friends. We swam across a river in the snow. Dénes and I met here, some years later. I was accompanying auditions, and he came in with his cello. We've been together from that day.'

'And you, Dennis?' Anne pressed. 'Did you have a spectacular escape, too?'

In the ensuing silence, Dénes assessed his daughter's new family, his gaze defensive. Karina held her breath, but her father, to her relief, spoke quietly. 'We don't talk about this,' he said at last. 'It's not important, and who knows, the world may bring us worse things one day. Now, my friends, we've got an engagement to celebrate. Let's have another drink!'

They did. And if, later on, Arthur and Anne discussed in private the suitability as Julian's chosen wife of a musician with traumatised parents, or asked Julian to reconsider, none of the Vereses would ever know, not even Karina.

The wedding took place in Lewes parish church. One bank of pews was packed with the Rookfield family, their long-standing friends and acquaintances and Julian's colleagues. The other side contained Karina's friends from college and orchestra, plus a smattering of Hungarians. And in the porch, Mimi Rácz, born into a family of Romungro musicians on the puszta, looked up into the fair, broad face of Arthur, Lord Rookfield, born in the great house that he now owned, and shook his hand with an intensity that left him briefly speechless.

Mimi's copious anecdotes about Hungary switched off like a terminated water supply as soon as she reached the late 1930s.

'My earliest memories are of my favourite horse,' she told Karina's new husband, in her high-ceilinged apartment overlooking Montagu Square. 'I loved him so! A beauty, brown and shiny like a fresh chestnut. My father sold him. I cried for days.'

'But you were musicians, not horse traders?'

'Yes, *muzsikás cigány*.'

'All of you?'

'Exactly. We were all musicians, my family. A dynasty, like that TV series.' Mimi chuckled, more to herself than at Julian. 'When I was tiny we lived in a beautiful, exceedingly painted wagon while my father and his brothers went from job to job, but later we settled in the very last house in a fearful suburb outside Budapest with our cousins. But musicians among the Roma, the finest *muzsikás cigány*, were like royalty. The others were afraid to speak to us!'

Mimi's recollections of infancy might have been vivid, but her memory of what she'd told them before was non-existent. Julian had heard about the chestnut horse several times. But Mimi skewered him with her eyes, and he shifted in his chair. Few things made Julian uncomfortable, but Mimi, on best form, was one of them. Her accent was as thick as goulash; the stresses fell on the first syllable of the words, the vowels were drawn out, the 'r's rolling, the 'w's emerging as 'v's. If the British voices around her were pastel shades from apple green to strawberry ice, Mimi's was a peppery scarlet. 'What a fine young man, Schnooky,' she told Karina. 'He remembers everything.'

Julian tried to call Karina 'Schnooky' once, but she laughed. It's an imp from an old Hungarian story, she explained. Fine for her parents, but she'd rather he stuck to 'darling'. Anyway, Julian didn't think Karina looked much like a schnook, whatever that may be.

All that remains of the Veres family's own old Hungarian story is confined to Karina and Julian's house in Lewes. At the top is a guest bedroom, and beside it, through a low, lockable door, the unconverted part of the loft, in which they keep their junk and other peoples'. Erzsébet and Dénes, lacking space, have unloaded their keepsakes, and Mimi's, onto them. Ten or fifteen boxes; possibly more. Family relics that nobody dares throw out: Mimi's might include a letter from Marc Duplessis, mementos from important concerts or ancient photographs. But the nature of the boxes and their contents – dusty, chaotic and mainly in Hungarian – has stopped Karina from exploring them as thoroughly as, perhaps, she should. The implications still frighten her away.

'Why haven't you been to Hungary?' Lindy demanded once. 'If I were you, I'd have been on the first plane to Budapest when the Iron Curtain came down.'

'My parents put it behind them. I think it's best to do the same.'

'I don't know what to do with you,' said Lindy.

4

At nightfall, they brought out the violins. Two of them, for father and son; the larger viola; the massive double bass; the tárogató and the cimbalom. With the jangle of the hammers on cimbalom strings and the arabesqueing swoops of the fiddle, Mimi felt the magic begin.

A violin played as István Rácz played his could halt a revolving universe. Like the Pied Piper, István, Mimi's father, could draw everyone to him, regardless of their race, wealth or education. Alone, it wouldn't be the same: the fiddler needs his audience, for the thread between them transforms a string of musical beads into a necklace. The bow gives the fiddle its voice, the fingers of the left hand shape the words of its song. If it says nothing, if it means nothing, then it is nothing. It's not only the notes, but the space, the motion between them, that tunnels into the subconscious and stabs through the heart.

Mimi, under her blanket, was supposed to be asleep. She opened her eyes and breathed the scent of woodsmoke. Her father, grandfather and uncles stood near the fire, playing a *verbunkos*, and Uncle Sándor's cimbalom fizzed into her dreams, with the shadowy whine of the viola, the tárogató rising on currents of air like a strand of silk, the double bass grinding at the bottom, and István's violin leading them all, sliding, soaring and weeping above. That's me, Mimi told herself. That sound will be mine.

It wasn't so easy. 'You're a girl,' her mother, Mária, told her. 'You can sing when you're older, or dance. Playing is for the menfolk.'

'Why?' demanded Mimi, who was three.

'Because that is the way it has always been.'

'But I want to!'

'Mimi, the men go to play in bars and taverns or for parties, and sometimes in restaurants in the big cities. These are not suitable places for a young girl.'

'I want—'

'Stop this, Mimi. Come and play near us, now, while we make dinner.'

That wasn't good enough. Mimi was at the end of the line, with centuries of tradition stacked against her, but just because she didn't understand, that didn't mean they would win. There was only one thing she could do, and she did it. She lay down on the ground, kicked her heels against the earth and screamed and screamed, and the birds flew out of the trees and the horses held up their heads and whinnied with her, for they were her friends. Her mother tried to calm her, but Mimi screamed on. Her father threatened her with a hiding, to no effect. 'Get a grip on your daughter,' he ordered Mária.

Soon Mimi smelled the dinner; her mother was tempting her with a bowl of rabbit stew from the cauldron. Her stomach rumbled. 'No! I won't!'

'Then don't,' István said, glaring at his wife.

Mimi refused breakfast too. She didn't know that she was on hunger strike. 'I won't eat until you let me play the violin.'

Her dreams were always vivid when she didn't eat enough. The second day, she lay in the wagon with its wooden sides spinning around her. She could see her mother, her dark skirts, her long, oiled hair, flying about in strange arcs. 'You must make the child eat, or she will die,' István protested. 'You want to lose yet another child?'

'What can I do? She won't!' Mária stamped her foot, almost in tears. Mimi bit her own lip and tasted blood. She wouldn't give up. Closing her eyes, she saw dragons.

How long it continued, she would never know. But her next memory was clearer: her brother, Péter, kneeling beside her, holding the small violin on which he was learning to play. He took her hand and wrapped it around the fingerboard until she could feel the four strings under her pads. 'I'll teach you, Mimi,' he whispered. 'Now come on, eat something. Just a little piece of bread. It's fresh.'

Mimi half sat up and glared at her father for what felt like a very long time.

'All right.' István Rácz had just met his first ever defeat. 'If that is how it's meant to be, so be it. My daughter will play the violin. It was good for Panna Czinka, maybe it's good for her too.'

The fiddle was never out of her hands. Péter helped her work at it in the mornings; in the evenings, when her mother agreed, Mimi sometimes went with the men to the taverns and sat among them, tiny, wide-eyed and longing to join in, while they performed. It wasn't long before they realised what an asset she was: the *gadje* adored seeing this sweet, serious child with her long plaited hair, and the nights she was there, the money was always better. That was before she had mastered her instrument. When her days and nights were spent drinking up sound, greedy for music, it was only natural that, soon, she'd be part of it.

Before she was ten years old, rumours about little Mimi's performances with István Rácz's Gypsy orchestra were as infectious as the rhythms of their dances. Word reached István, through a haphazard but effective grapevine of other Roma musicians, that the proprietor of Károlyi's in Budapest was making enquiries about the Gypsy child violinist and her family. If they were to go there for a trial run in the restaurant and proved to his liking, he might offer them a permanent position.

The Ráczes made their way across country to Kistarcsa, about sixteen miles north-east of Budapest, where Mária had cousins. The horses plodded along while István and Sándor asked around until one group of young Roma men recognised the names and directed them to an encampment at the suburb's edge that, to Mimi, looked like the end of the world. Sooty factories; tumbledown housing that seemed to be itching to fall into the mud and filth; barely a tree in sight. 'We can stop here, because nobody will move us on,' Mária explained, though Mimi didn't understand. Hungry and fractious after a long day in the wagon, she tagged along when her father and the others – including Péter, who was fifteen and played second violin – set out to perform in the restaurant, up in the hills of old Buda.

They dressed impeccably in their uniforms of dark trousers, white shirts, waistcoats and patent leather shoes, and Mimi wore the long, embroidered red skirt that Mária had made for her, with a waistcoat and red slippers. Climbing into the third-class compartment on the train, with the men carrying their instruments, their embroidered leather waistcoats sticking out a mile among the other passengers, Mimi felt a hundred eyes upon them, but not the usual hostility. Kistarcsa was full of Roma, István told her, and everyone could see they were musicians. Besides, they'd scrubbed down for the occasion. In the social order of the third-class carriage, she divined, they were right at the top.

'Ready, Mimi?' István whispered to her while she dozed against his shoulder.

'Ready.' By now she knew all the most popular tunes – 'Dark Eyes', 'The Lark', the Brahms Hungarian Dances, some tunes by Liszt, Kálmán and Lehár, and many more. 'Hungarian melodies, sometimes classical compositions, not our own music,' István had told her, treating her like a grown-up. 'They're famous and people love them. But we bring our style to them. You see, Mimi, our job is to beat them at their own game!'

Mimi made out later, to her mother, that Károlyi's wasn't so marvellous. She sensed that she ought to prefer the forest to the city, and the wholesome spicy stews of rabbit or chicken, with mushrooms, apples and cherries gathered quietly from the orchards, to Károlyi's fancy sauces. She should favour the simple, low-cut blouses and long skirts that flattered her mother's figure over the silks and velvets that the *gadje* women wore here – they dressed up like that just to *eat*, Péter whispered on the way home, disgust in his voice. But she waited her turn while her family played, watching, absorbing everything – necklaces as long as the Danube, droopy hats that looked like flower buds about to open – and as the waiters bustled past bearing silvery serving dishes, the smell of meat and rich soups made her feel faint, for she was growing fast and it was a very long time since breakfast. Nobody gave them any food.

Our way of life is the best, her mother told her. We're free. We're not trapped by possessions. We work for ourselves, not others, and we pay our debts. We value honour and integrity. Not like them. But by the time Mimi lifted her violin, she was starting to wonder whether perhaps possessions weren't so terrible; that entertaining your family with fine food in a famous restaurant wasn't so dreadful either; and that if she could change places with the young girl at the nearest table, sitting beside a moustachioed father in a smoking-jacket, a mother in a cherry-red hat that sat close against her elegant short hair, and an elder sister wearing a low-waisted white dress with a long string of pearls like moonlight on her skin, who was to say that she wouldn't? She swung her bow into action. The little girl, her own age yet a world away, stared into her face and sat very still.

Mimi slid up the string, held a high harmonic and felt the intake of breath among her audience. She pushed a lethal dose of longing through her tone, and while Sándor rustled tremolando on his cimbalom she improvised, fingers scuttling, bow shivering; and around them the clank of knives and forks on expensive crockery quietened to silence. Her solo was over; it was time for the fast section to close the *verbunkos*. The slow and fast sections, István told her, represent the two sides of the Hungarian character. The dance used to be played as a recruitment trick to stir up young men and make them join the army. The fiddles belted out the tune, one that always induced people to clap in time, and phosphorescence glimmered around them, electricity like the air on the puszta before a storm, so that Mimi, following her father's cues, could imagine sparks shooting out from under the horsehair, and at the end there was such applause that the proprietor, who held the reins of their future, went up to István and almost hugged him. As for Mimi –

'My greatest treasure,' István declared, hand clamped to her shoulder. Mimi didn't like to say 'I told you so,' so she kept quiet, smiling her sweet little smile.

Such was their success at Károlyi's that the Rácz family stayed in Kistarcsa and moved into a cheap room. It must, Mimi thought, be the last house in a hundred miles; beyond it she could see only a stony, devastated road, the crumbling wall of a factory that made bolts, and some open land that even she couldn't really call countryside.

On the first day, she tried to grasp the banister on the stairs and it gave way under her hand; all afternoon she quaked in case somebody blamed her for it. By that evening, though, she'd worked out that no one cared, because the rest of the place was in the same state. There was scant room in the bed for all of them, the hygiene buckets stank, and sometimes *gadje* do-gooders would bang on the door and ask why the children weren't in school. The other Roma families who weren't musicians were afraid to talk to them, and as far as Mimi could tell, her parents didn't want to talk to them either. 'We'll save money and move on soon,' Mária decided. 'We can do better than this. This isn't the way we should live, Mimi. Not musicians.'

Mimi worked. Any minute not spent working was a minute ill used. Péter didn't work as hard as she did. 'It's natural, it's in our family, we don't need to practise,' he told her. But she was sure that wasn't true because she was soon playing much better than he could. He was lazy. He just played the same way over and over again. She wanted to try something different every day, pushing the boundaries – holding a note longer, letting the tremolando blend for another second, extending notes so that the audience had to hold its breath, half begging for release before it arrived in a welter for the whirling finale.

Back very late after the evening's work, Mimi sometimes curled up close to her mother and watched the stars through a cracked window, a longing inside her that she didn't recognise. She missed the forests, the streams, the wide, empty plain, but she didn't want to say so. 'Soon we'll have a better place to live,' Mária told her. 'We'll settle. It's not so unusual any more. Travelling, the old ways, it's not as easy as it used to be when I was a girl. Besides, your father's going to be famous soon.' She stroked Mimi's hair. 'One day we'll all go abroad on tour, and when we come back we'll be rich and everyone will know the name of Rácz. You wait and see.'

St Matthew's is a sensible option. It won't be like Julian's days at prep school. Five is too young; a confident seven is another matter. Walking across herringbone floors, admiring sports trophies and photographs of boys holding footballs and cricket bats, Julian dismisses his memories as irrelevant.

Julian is forty-five; in the four decades since he started prep school, everything has changed. Head teachers are afraid of being sued and will fall over backwards to take good care of the boys.

Caning, slippering, all that is long gone. Now, no doubt, if a child wet his bed, therapists would be queuing up to psychoanalyse him.

He'll never forget the smell in his first dorm. He wasn't the only one – that was the sole comfort against the disgust on the housemaster's face, the shame, the punishments. Probably half the children in that room were bed-wetting.

He remembers watching his parents driving away: the Jag (the Rookfields always have Jags) trundling towards the gate, then pausing while it opened. The gate closed; the car swung out, accelerated, vanished. You don't question things when you're five; you don't know there's an alternative. The emptiness; the misery. That stayed with him. Abandonment. You love someone; they leave you. You trust them; they betray you.

At night, he'd dream he was at home, only to wake up on a narrow mattress surrounded by eleven beds containing other five-year-olds, most of whom he didn't like; usually there'd be someone snivelling in the dark. Then he'd feel his pyjama trousers wet against his skin, and he'd know where the stink was coming from.

At St Matthew's, the boys sleep in private cubicle rooms. They're allowed home every weekend. Nobody censors their letters – a seven-year-old can send text messages on his mobile phone. The showers boast bottles of moisturising body wash and over the dining room door there hangs a huge banner, decorated by the pupils with pictures of farm animals and smiling people of all colours, declaring that at least half the food in each meal has been locally sourced.

Karina walks beside Julian, holding Jamie's hand.

'Look at that, Jimbo!' Julian says, pointing through a window. 'Not many prep schools have sports fields as good as this.'

Jamie stares at the other boys, who might soon be his classmates. 'Are the teachers nice, Mum?' he asks. It's the most sensible question anyone has thought of all day and, of course, the one thing they can't answer.

'We'll find out,' Karina promises him.

'The headmaster was funny,' says Jamie. 'He was so crawly to you, Dad. Was that because he knows Grandad's a lord?'

'He wasn't crawly, just polite,' Julian remarks. 'I'm sure he's met lords and suchlike before.'

'Remember, Jamie, it's important not to talk about that at school.' Karina keeps her voice low. 'It sounds grand, but all it really means is that your grandfather owns a very big house that's difficult to keep up.'

'So everyone who has a big house is a lord?' Jamie asks, disingenuous.

'You know that's not the case, Jamie,' Julian says.

'Will you ever be a lord, Dad?'

'No, love,' Karina cuts in. 'Uncle Hilary inherits the title because he's older than Daddy.'

'Hilary's a girl's name,' Jamie scoffs. ''Sides, it's not fair. Why can't they both be a lord?'

'That's the way it works,' Julian says. 'Always has, always will. The only difference now is that we're no longer part of the running of this country.'

'Why?'

'Because Mr Blair has thrown out most of the hereditary peers from the House of Lords and replaced them with his own best mates. It's like a bully punching you just because they don't like your name.'

'If I was running a country,' Jamie muses, 'I'd get my friends to run it with me too, rather than a load of old people I didn't know who mightn't like me.'

'The important thing, Jimbo, is not to be liked, but to be respected,' Julian lectures.

'There's nothing wrong with being liked, though,' adds Karina, 'as long as you're liked for *who* you are, not *what* you are.'

She thinks of the headmaster's fair, friendly face. He'd been gushing to The Honourable Julian Rookfield – of course he had. He was relatively new to the job and wasn't yet bored by the small boys of the aristocracy, however stupid they were. Jamie, at least, has a good brain. The headmaster likes music, too. 'Mimi Rácz?' he remarked. 'My father was a great fan of hers. The best of classical and Gypsy traditions rolled into one, he used to say. Well, demand for places is extremely high, but James seems a splendid lad. Naturally he's on our waiting-list, and as soon as a place becomes available . . .' Creep, thinks Karina, one arm firmly round her son.

Later, in the car park, they find a family with a boy of Jamie's age admiring the Jag. Jamie smiles at the lad, who grins back. 'Is it yours?' he asks.

'Yup,' Jamie declares, proud.

'Cool!'

'He'll be demanding we get one now,' the father jokes. 'So, what do you make of St Matthew's? Good place, isn't it?'

'I reckon so.' Julian flourishes his car keys. 'We've had our eye on it for years.' The Jag bleeps and flashes its lights.

'Real cool,' breathes Jamie's prospective classmate, goggle-eyed. 'See you here in September, then?'

'Yeah, maybe!' Jamie waves, and climbs in.

At home, when Jamie has gone to bed, the floodgates rupture.

'He's seven years old and you want to send him away!'

'Karina, we've been through this.'

'No, we haven't. We won't have "been through" anything until you listen to me!'

'All you say is "no". I've yet to hear a convincing reason.'

'You're the one who went away to school at five. You told me all about it, don't you remember? We sat on that beach and you spent three hours describing how miserable you were. And now you want to put Jamie through the same thing?'

'I've told you a hundred times, you'll never find a school like that in Britain in 2006.'

'The schools may be different, but kids aren't. Children need their families! He'll be homesick. And the other kids will be homesick too, but they'll pretend they're not, because they won't want the others to know. And they'll spend their whole lives afterwards pretending that they don't feel the things they feel, because they don't know there's another way to be.'

Karina has hit a nerve. 'Supposing we ask Jamie if *he* liked it?' Julian retorts. 'Because I rather think he did.'

Karina's firebrand fizzles out as fast as it flared up. She shakes her head and reaches out to press Julian's shoulder; automatically he turns to kiss her hand. 'Come on, love,' she says. 'We'll feel better for some food. I'll make something.'

Julian fetches a bottle of red wine from the rack under the stairs.

He's never become entirely accustomed to Karina's quick changes of mood. He knows she's as worried as ever, but now she's burned out the fury, at least for a while. That is her 'Hungarian three-year-old mode', as he calls it, though part of him can see the benefits of letting it out, for someone as passionate as she is. If she didn't, she'd burst. It's as if she takes a state of mind out of a carton, drinks it to the last drop, then pulls out another and starts on that instead.

Over breakfast the next morning, there's silence. Karina hasn't slept. Images of Jamie at boarding-school have been pounding round a racetrack in her mind, together with the anxiety about what she'd do without him. A confident mind: what an asset. Certainty, roots, what comfort in a quicksand world. If she had to choose whether her son should be victor or underdog, the lord of the manor or the Gypsy with the violin, would there be any choice? Yet wouldn't something else be lost, like a blossom crushed under concrete?

'Can we ask Olly to come and play?' Jamie asks, oblivious over his cereal.

'Of course, Schnooks,' says Karina. 'It'll have to be this morning, because we're going to Auntie Lindy's play tonight. Your first trip to the theatre!'

'So, what do you think about yesterday? How did you like the school?' Julian says at last. 'Think you'd fancy going there?'

'Sure. I liked it.'

'Why, Schnooky?' Karina asks. 'Why did you like it?'

'That boy in the car park was nice. Maybe I'd have friends.'

Julian emits a noise like a balloon deflating while all its worries evaporate.

'Don't you want to think about it some more?' Karina prompts. 'We could go and see some other schools, maybe ones where you don't have to sleep there all week . . .'

'On the other hand, if you really like this one,' Julian interrupts, 'I could give the headmaster a buzz first thing Monday morning.'

'OK,' says Jamie. 'Cool.'

The British railway system is the oldest on the planet. No wonder Julian drives to work.

Trains, he reflects, are supposed to transport people quickly and safely from one location to another. In an ideal world, more than a century of activity would be unaffected by wear and tear; you'd buy a cheap ticket, step aboard at once, find a seat and arrive on time, without 'signal failure', 'leaves on the line' or 'the wrong kind of snow'. Julian knows too much about the railways.

They'd needed an overhaul when the Tories set about privatisation. Since Thatcher had blasted the unions to hell and gone, surely you could no longer run a transport network, like communist Russia or Hungary, primarily to benefit those who ran it? Still, Julian would never have recommended the funnel-web of complexities springing from the Railways Act of 1993. Back then, he'd been a junior lawyer learning his trade in a glass tower in the City. Trapped in the mountain range of paperwork that supported the breakup of the old, nationalised British Rail, he'd worked hundred-hour weeks, often through the night. Worse, when he'd talked to his friend Andy Williamson, who was a solicitor too but also did time on his local council ('for my sins,' said Andy) in the hope of someday becoming an MP, they'd soon agreed that the new system, the preparation of which was eating away their youth, was relatively unlikely to work in a month of Sundays.

One company owns the tracks. A variety of others run the trains, on short-term franchises. A handful more own the rolling stock and rent it to the train operating companies. You can't have a train company without trains, so the 'rollos' rake it in and have been snaffled up by banks with an eye on easy money. Stations? Run by the train operating companies, which are competitive organisations; when more than one is involved, there'll be dogfights. Every part of this web must be controlled by a legal contract. Who stands to benefit? Why, thinks Julian, it's his son, Jamie. Julian manages the movement of vast sums of money, much of it the taxpayers', and earns some himself. It will pay for Jamie's education at Elthingbourne; and that, in the end, is what matters.

Now that Julian is a partner, half his time is taken up with marketing, tendering for contracts and networking. He steers himself like a ship in full sail through the restaurants, clubs, industry conferences and trade fairs at which the talking gets done. At work, he knows what he's doing.

In his less happy moments at home, before he met Karina, he'd sometimes wondered whether things might have been different if Elthingbourne had offered an A level in Marriage Management. A set of tools for avoiding Ugly Domestic Scenes; how to tell the difference between a woman suffering from PMT and one who means it when she says she's thinking of moving out; how to spot warning signs and defuse a situation before it explodes; how to apologise without losing face. You're supposed to know. You endure years of academic and sporting drill, barely meeting a girl until you're old enough to marry one, and then you're just supposed to *know*.

Women like spontaneity, Julian suspects. But the only spontaneous thing he can remember doing – ever – is falling so violently in love with Karina that he proposed to her within weeks. His family had thought he'd gone mad.

Like a train, a relationship ought to glide smoothly towards a satisfactory outcome. But when Julian sees how many things can potentially go wrong during a single journey, and compares that to the variety of misunderstandings that can block the paths between people as surely as a cracked rail, flooding or frozen points, sometimes he wonders how any couple ever manages to stay together. And, as on the trains, the worst hazard is a SPAD: a Signal Passed At Danger.

Trains in mainland Europe are fitted with a system named Automatic Train Protection that stops them should the driver go through a red light. In the UK, though, 'ATP' is considered too expensive and so far has been installed on only a handful of lines. Julian suspects that if the device had been used sooner and more widely, lives might have been saved. He feels sick remembering this, but all he can do is manage contracts, not persuade decision makers to make different decisions, or make them faster.

Whether he had passed a signal at danger when he ignored Karina's protests about Jamie's schooling, he would never be sure.

5

István Rácz's Gypsy Orchestra had been playing for six months at Károlyi's when somebody noticed Mimi.

He was a doctor, Jewish – István told Mimi that all good doctors were – and much sought after. His son had been killed in the army in 1918, while the Austro-Hungarian Empire met its death alongside him. Music, Dr György Frankl told István in Károlyi's, had greater healing powers than any of his medicines. He bought spritzers for István, Sándor and the other adults in the band, and fruit juice for Péter and Mimi. Then he began to ask István about his daughter. What were his plans for her? Wasn't it unusual for a girl to play the violin? Would she spend the rest of her life in a café orchestra? István shrugged: he supposed she would carry on until she was ready to get married. Mimi, aged ten, calculated that that gave her about four years.

'May I come and see you tomorrow afternoon?' Dr Frankl asked. 'I'd like to talk to you about this a little more. And please make sure Mimi is there.'

Mimi knew what was inside the moment she saw the box. She couldn't read, but she recognised the style of the lettering. Gerbeaud's. A great white palace of a café on a huge, tree-lined square. They'd passed it on their way to work through the centre of Budapest. But they couldn't go inside.

'Why not?' she had demanded, the first time.

'Because we can't,' István had snapped at her.

'But *why*?' Mimi had gazed past the window. Chandeliers garlanded the air inside Gerbeaud's; wooden tables gleamed below. Behind the counter were cakes, row upon row of them. At a table on the terrace, a well-dressed boy her own age was tucking into an artfully striped slice covered in chocolate icing. Watching him, she'd wanted to cry.

And now Dr Frankl, holding a Gerbeaud's box, was standing in their doorway – a figure from another world. Mimi stared, her mouth open. How had he found his way to them? How had he dared? Nobody who wasn't a Gypsy ever came here, other than missionaries and, sometimes, the police. Normally people were too frightened, though she wasn't sure what they were frightened of – boisterous children, smelly buckets and a bit of mud? Soon they'd move, Mária kept saying. If only Károlyi's paid them better. Yet in these times of immense unemployment, they were fortunate to have a job at all.

'István. Mimi.' Dr Frankl, with his blue eyes and his wise, accepting face. Mimi felt the warmth as he smiled at her. Something about his combination of small round glasses, pipe, white beard and waistcoat felt comforting. Perhaps it was the waistcoat.

'Dr Frankl. Please come in,' István mumbled through his moustache. Péter and the cousins stared askance at the visitor until Mária, understanding István with one glance, summoned them all to her side and marched them out into the street, leaving Mimi and István alone with their guest.

Dr Frankl opened the box. A tide of aroma tantalised Mimi: cherry strudel, nut cake, chocolate. Her head spun. They didn't usually eat between breakfast and dinner, and in her stomach a knot of hunger twisted itself tight. 'Mimi, choose whichever cake you want,' said Dr Frankl.

'I had a son,' Dr Frankl told them while they ate. 'A wonderful boy, gifted in medicine and music. Now he's dead; and although I try to make others well, I have little of my own to live for. But the times are changing, István. The era of imperial power is over forever. The Trianon Treaty is a disgrace, but we'll survive it because we have to until it's overturned.'

'Do you think that it will be, doctor?' István asked.

'It must be. How can a country that was so large for eight hundred years squeeze itself into this space? Well, we'll see. At least we've escaped Soviet communism, for the moment. I hope István Bethlen may succeed with his "national unity" plans, but who knows what the future will hold for any of us? You have to take chances while they are there, don't you agree?'

Mimi saw her father sit forward, listening, she thought, with a little more attention, a little more openness.

'I have a proposition for you, István,' said Dr Frankl. 'Send me your daughter. My neighbour is a violin professor at the Ferenc Liszt Academy. Send me your Mimi and I'll take her to play to him. I would wager anything that if he accepts her as his student, he will make her into the finest violinist on the planet.'

'My daughter is a Gypsy,' István reminded him, without meeting his gaze. 'That's the first problem. The next is that she doesn't read music.'

'She's a bright girl. Anyone can see that,' Dr Frankl said. 'She'll learn.'

'I can't let her leave us. She's only ten. My wife won't let her go, our women never hand our children over to strangers. And we have only one other, our son Péter – we lost two infants in the typhus outbreak. It would be difficult for my wife to give her up.'

'Perhaps your wife will be glad that Mimi has the opportunity to better herself. Face the facts, István. I am a Jew; I know about prejudice. I try to be a good doctor; I had a fine training in Berlin, people need me, ask for me and pay me accordingly, and I'm glad of my good fortune. But we should never forget the lessons of history. A majority population can at any time make scapegoats out of those races it perceives as outsiders, especially when a period of instability threatens. It's a natural reaction, however irrational; and politicians have been exploiting it since the beginning of time. And those who suffer the most are always the vulnerable, the helpless. At the moment, Bethlen needs the approval of wealthy Jews, but only six years ago my own cousin was murdered by state-approved thugs for being a middle-class Jew. Our destiny could turn at any moment, on any whim. So what future is there for a Gypsy girl in this city? Your daughter has the chance to escape. With a talent like that, if she's well trained, she could surpass everyone.'

'Who can escape their blood?' István gave a shrug. 'One glance and anybody knows that my family and I are Gypsies. Say what you like, we're stuck.'

'But I choose not to accept this.' Dr Frankl leaned forward and gazed through his spectacles into István's face, in a way that István found unsettling. He rarely engaged with any stranger beyond the call of commerce, but he couldn't deflect the involvement that Dr Frankl was demanding from him.

'I believe,' said Dr Frankl, 'in actively working to *create* a world where everybody, no matter their race, can live together as human beings first and last; where our futures are determined by what we make of ourselves; where everybody, from every background, has the right to fulfil their potential. Christian, Jew, Gypsy, Muslim, Hindu, black, white, brown, yellow, what should it matter? We are *people*. I am a Jew, but I have no religion, István. I am a humanist and I believe in a meritocracy, which can only be created with collective effort. All I ask is that you let Mimi try.'

István was quiet. Mimi, beside him, couldn't talk through her Eszterházy cake – her mouth was full of walnut heaven – but she could read her father's face. She knew him by his expressions as closely as she knew her violin. If she studied with a conservatory professor, if she became the protégée of a wealthy doctor, it wasn't only that she wouldn't go home with the family each night: also, she wouldn't be in the band any more. That was the real problem. They'd grown to depend on her. If the great István Rácz turned pale at the idea of losing her . . .

'Please, what's a merry tock – a what you said?' she asked in a squeak.

'Meritocracy,' Dr Frankl repeated. 'It's a system in which all people stand or fall according to their personal merits, no matter their background. For instance, your merits include your talent for playing your violin, and your willingness to work hard at it.'

Mimi took this in. If Dr Frankl was right, if the professor accepted her as a student, would she find that her chances went far beyond the forest shadows that she'd always thought must mark the limits of her world?

'Perhaps we should let Mimi decide,' Dr Frankl suggested. 'Why not come to my home, Mimi – meet my wife and see if you would enjoy living there with us? You could stay for a few days first, just to try. Then we'll take you to meet the professor and we'll see how it goes.'

Mimi bit her lip. She liked the kindness in his face and she felt sorry for him, losing his son, but what would her mother say? Then a question slipped out of its own accord. 'Will there be cake?'

Dr Frankl's eyes creased up at the edges. 'Yes, Mimi,' he laughed. 'You shall have cake whenever you like.'

Her father stayed silent.

'What will it take to convince you, István?' Dr Frankl asked.

István said nothing.

The doctor nodded. 'We can come to an arrangement.' And Mimi wondered what he was talking about.

The Church Theatre, sandwiched between the houses in a Camden back street, is perfect for a show involving one actress and one pianist: it doesn't cost too much. It's a converted Victorian church; inside, the rows of seating curve around the stage, intimate under the vaulted roof. Nicki, the actress, has coerced the theatre's director into giving them an extra-cheap rate for a solitary Sunday evening. Lindy and Karina have always been astonished by the way that Nicki, with her auburn hair and internal light bulb of performer's charisma, can floor any man with one blow.

When they were students, and for several years afterwards, Karina and Lindy shared a rambling, run-down flat in Willesden Green. Nicki, at university with Lindy, used to come round to eat their Ubiquitous Bean Stew, which they'd adapt with rice on Monday, toast on Tuesday, scrambled eggs on Wednesday and tinned tomato soup on Thursday. On Friday Karina and Lindy often treated themselves to pizza or curry – usually without Nicki. Still, they loved to play at being Bohemians together: writer, musician, actress. They fantasised: Lindy dreamed of writing for the National Theatre, Karina longed to perform a concerto with the London Philharmonic and Nicki intended Hollywood triumph and marriage to a multi-millionaire. Nothing has turned out quite the way they'd imagined.

Unlit while the audience assembles, the stage bears a grand piano, an armchair, a lamp and a table laden with music manuscript paper. Lindy, pale and nervous, hugs Karina. 'It's nearly sold out,' she says.

'Auntie Lindy!' Jamie cries. Lindy sweeps him into her embrace.

Karina tries not to look at her eyes, which sparkle over Jamie, but sometimes turn unintentionally reproachful when there are children around.

'I've never, *ever* been to a theatre before!' Jamie tells his godmother.

'I know, and I've kept the best spot specially for you.' Lindy beckons them to a row near the front.

'Sweetheart, I hope you'll come home with us afterwards,' Cynthia says. 'I'm doing wine and cheese. Everybody's coming.' They're all there: Dénes and Erzsébet, Arthur and Anne. Only Julian's brother Hilary is missing; he's not into theatre.

Lindy steers Karina aside. 'What am I going to do about Charles? He's meant to be here, I left him a ticket. There's no sign of him. I've sent him two texts, but he hasn't replied.'

'There's not much more you can do,' Karina says. Lindy looks as if she hasn't slept for a fortnight. 'Try not to worry, OK? You've got bigger things to think of tonight.'

'Whatever are you two girls whispering about now?' Cynthia crows, too loudly. Lindy's gaze meets her mother's, inscrutable.

Cynthia is the image of Lindy, but tenser, flightier. In the sixties, photographers had adored those legs and her oceanic eyes. She'd modelled tights, short skirts and make-up; her image graced posters around the London Underground. There they caught the roving eye of Martin Rookfield. After he met her, her profession didn't go down too well with his family.

The Vereses, as always, look slightly lost beside the Rookfields, who tower over them. Erzsébet is unobtrusive in tweed, her hair twisted into its usual bun. Dénes is in brown corduroy trousers and a dark purple shirt that suits his swarthy colouring. Karina finds it hard to see her parents and Julian's together without imagining her mother and father as bereft, displaced teenagers, gazing around unfamiliar shores and hoping that someone might be kind to them.

'How about lunch at the house next weekend?' Anne asks Julian. 'I think your father has some ideas he wants to discuss with you.'

'Oh God, Father's had ideas. Duck, everyone!'

Arthur, Anne explains, has decided to apply for a licence to host civil weddings at Fairfallows, his eye on the income. They could hold ceremonies in the entrance hall, receptions in marquees on the lawn with adjacent catering tents, and have Portaloos a safe distance away to minimise disruption. 'Frankly, Jules, I don't like the sound of it,' Anne grumbles. 'How I'm supposed to get my book written with people tramping about . . .'

It's seven thirty. Karina takes the seat between Lindy and Jamie, praying silently that what Lindy has written will be good. The lights dim.

Nicki and Vince stride onto the platform, Vince to the piano, Nicki to the armchair. Vince begins to play the dramatic opening of Beethoven's last sonata. Nicki, wearing a Grecian sea-green robe, rises and walks forward into the spotlight.

A small upheaval disrupts the back of the theatre: a man, a woman and three teenagers are scuffling into some seats. Karina glances round. She recognises Charles from a photo in Lindy's flat. He has brought his whole family. His wife is fair-haired and high-heeled. His two daughters are nymphettes with tight jeans and ironed hair; his son cultivates scruffiness. Just as Karina is willing Lindy not to see them, she turns. Karina feels the shock blow a fuse.

'Ye men who think or say that I am malevolent, stubborn or misanthropic,' says Nicki, reading Beethoven's words as if bewitched by them, 'how greatly you do me wrong . . .'

Lindy's staring at the floor: gone. Her body is in the theatre; her spirit has left.

The play advances. Nicki declaims words from Beethoven's song cycle *An die ferne Geliebte*. 'Will nothing more reach you, then? Is there no messenger of love for me? I shall sing, songs that speak to you of my pain . . .'

Karina, half an eye on Lindy, hopes against hope that seeing *Distant Beloved* performed will counteract the effects of Charles's entourage. If that's love, who needs it? Surely contentment is better – as rare as love, maybe rarer. She's been as desperately in love as Lindy is now, and, in retrospect, she didn't like it. Waking up that first morning with Richard, with the trees glowing, the birds shouting, lights dancing in front of her eyes while she watched him asleep; then his smile as he awoke and reached out for her. Later, back in bed in the early evening with glasses of wine half drunk beside them, they sang together. Simon and Garfunkel, 'The Boxer', in harmony, for the hell of it.

She's content, quietly, with Julian, who can't sing at all.

At the end there's a storm of applause. Karina spots Alban, his outsize watch glimmering as he claps and shouts: 'Author! Author!' Near him, the agent Lindy has invited is making some notes on the programme. Nicki and Vince smile and bow. Vince looks across the rows for Lindy, then holds out a hand as if to invite her to join them. Lindy gets up and walks straight out of the theatre.

Backstage, Karina lets conversation swish past her while she looks for Lindy. Anne holds forth to Vince about her new biography of Ottilie Featherstone, a nineteenth-century novelist with a turbulent private life. Arthur tells Nicki about the theatres he visited in Russia in the nineties: freezing, chaotic, jam-packed and very cheap. Charles comes in and glances about, but only for a minute. His family is waiting in the auditorium. Karina, trailing him, watches him wrap a pashmina around his wife's shoulders before they leave.

She finds Lindy at last: outside, leaning against the wall, smoking. Her face is as blank and shocked as if all her clothes had dropped off.

'I think you should come to Forest Road,' Karina says.

Lindy inhales, then blows smoke towards the sky. 'Actually, I thought I'd go down the pub with Alban and get well plastered. I can't ask him back to the house, can I? My father would have a fit.'

Alban himself bustles up and hoists Lindy off her feet. '*I* think we go get very, very drunk,' he says. 'Lindy, you are star of tonight. When I catch that bastard, I will *do* him.'

'Whatever,' says Lindy. 'I don't care.'

Despite Alban's coaxing, Martin and Cynthia twist Lindy's arm so hard that she ends up in Forest Road after all. They've prepared red and white wine, a tray of biscuits, chunks of Cheddar and Brie, and a bowl of crisps. Erzsébet beckons to Karina and they cross the road to fetch her contribution: a platter of stuffed peppers, another of ham and pickles, and a fresh-baked cherry strudel.

'Whenever anyone comes round, I'm afraid there won't be enough food,' Karina remarks. 'I always make too much.'

'You only need to see Cynthia to know how her mind works, Schnooky. I believe she thinks "Oh no! *People!* How can I stop them from eating my kitchen dry?"'

'Betsy! Karrie!' Cynthia flounces into the hall. 'Oh, darlings, you shouldn't have!'

'We must treat Lindy to good Hungarian food tonight,' Dénes declares – though Lindy herself is nowhere to be seen.

'Oh, Dennis, you are a devil!' Cynthia gives him a kiss, then ushers them towards the biggest, most cat-clawed sofa in the drawing room. 'Come and sit down . . . Tell me, how's your mother? My bridge partner was talking about her only yesterday.'

'She wasn't well enough to come tonight,' Dénes tells her, accepting a glass of wine. 'Tomorrow she will phone and say "So, when can I see Lindy's play?"'

'Is it true,' Cynthia asks, 'that she has a violin that's worth absolutely millions?'

The Vereses look at each other. Julian looks at Karina. Karina looks at Jamie, half asleep in an armchair.

'She had some nice instrument once,' Dénes says. 'But she doesn't have it now. I don't know what happened. And it was never worth millions, no way. Cyncyn, this wine is divine. Like nectar and ambrosia!'

'But the violin must be somewhere,' Cynthia presses.

'There must be documentation about valuable violins,' Anne adds. 'I expect there'd be loads of information on the Internet about what violin was owned by whom.'

'Why you want Internet? What it matters?' Dénes says, with his distinctive half smile, half scowl. 'A good violin is a good violin. If you have it, nice. If not, you have something else.'

'Karina could have used it,' Cynthia points out. 'It can't simply have vanished.'

'But it could.' Erzsébet sighs, glancing at Dénes's face.

'Betsy, are you seriously saying your family has *lost* a *Stradivarius*?' Anne demands. 'And in all this time, we've never known about it?'

'Not a Stradivarius,' Erzsébet says. 'We think it might have been a Nicolò Amati.'

'Amati? How beautiful.' Anne smiles. 'That's "loved ones" in Italian.'

'I thought it was Stradivarius who was the important one,' Arthur grunts through a mouthful of ham.

'The Amatis were the first great Cremonese violin-makers,' Karina tells them. 'There was a dynasty of them in the sixteenth and seventeenth centuries. Antonio Stradivari and Andrea Guarneri were both apprenticed to Nicolò Amati – you could say he taught them everything they knew. Nicolò made the Amati violins that are big-time concert instruments today, and his grandfather was Andrea Amati, who may have made the world's first real violin. So Amatis are older and rarer than Strads.'

'Is it a bit like comparing diamonds to rubies, then?' Anne suggests. 'Diamonds have all the glitz, but sometimes rubies are more beautiful and more characterful too.'

'Well, I've not played one, but I've heard that Amatis aren't quite as powerful as Strads in terms of projection, though certain violinists adore them.'

'And, my God, you have one in the family?'

'Now, *listen.*' Dénes's tone silences the room. 'This story is Chinese whispers, no more, no less. Nobody has seen this violin for fifty years. Nobody knows if it *was* an Amati. My mother doesn't need a posh fiddle now and my daughter doesn't either. So come, my friends, another drink! Enjoy the moment, for the black soup will come later.'

Cynthia beams. 'I love your Hungarian fatalism, Dennis. It's so sexy.'

'Cyncyn, darling, you are as beautiful as a butterfly's wing. If I were a photographer, I would demand you model for me at once, completely nude.' Dénes grabs her hand and kisses it. Karina notices, though, that his eyes are not smiling. She excuses herself and makes for the stairs to look for Lindy.

Lindy's old attic room used to be crammed with Lindyish stuff: posters of favourite actors, pop stars, Snoopy cartoons; jars of flowers, which would stand wilting for days before she could bear to throw them out; notebooks on the desk, where she scribbled ideas for stories; the torch upended close to the window, ready to flash signals to Karina. Now the room is a shell, with only a few ghost objects left languishing inside.

Lindy is sitting on the bare bed, talking on her mobile phone. Karina hears her from the landing. 'What am I going to do? I can't stand it any more.'

'Lin?' Karina whispers.

'Alban, I have to go. Drop into the shop? . . . I'll be there. In body, if nothing else.'

Karina sits down beside her. Lindy leans on her shoulder and Karina soothes her as if she's Jamie.

Since escaping Budapest, Dénes and Erzsébet have been strangers to the stuff that normally accumulates over decades in family homes. They buy only what they need, nothing expensive, fashionable or frivolous; they've redecorated the house only once since they moved in; and their frugal wooden-armed furniture is still as serviceable now as it was in 1970. But when they entertain, Erzsébet spends the whole day cooking and Dénes takes pride in choosing the wine. The most densely occupied area of the Veres house is always the fridge.

The Rookfield home overflows with stuff, mainly inherited, some dating back to the eighteenth century. They own Georgian walnut wood cabinets full of Dresden china knick-knacks, Victorian tablecloths, fuzzy photographs of 1860s Rookfields in top hats and crinolines, Edwardian crockery, crest-embossed family silver, Martin's father's Victoria Cross awarded after the Battle of the Somme, an ancient sampler stitched by Cynthia's grandmother. Cynthia's cat, a fawn-coloured, squash-faced Persian named Pom-Pom, has wrecked the antique sofas; but Cynthia doesn't mind because, she insists, Pom-Pom is a member of the family. Their fridge habitually houses little more than butter, some sliced ham and several bottles of white wine.

'So many *things*,' Erzsébet remarked at home after one dinner at the Rookfields' house when Karina was fifteen. She was slicing three pieces from a home-made poppy-seed cake and pouring three cups of tea. 'You leave it behind when you go.'

'That's why they have it,' Dénes pointed out. 'Because everybody did leave it behind.'

Certainty didn't lie in stuff. Stuff could be lost, burned, stolen, confiscated, blown up. Love, food, drink, music, said Dénes. Those were necessary; nothing more. Sometimes you couldn't be sure of food and drink. That left love and music. If love failed, you must live for music. 'Dad,' said Karina, 'it's 1985. Wake up!'

'So it is, so it is,' her father nodded. 'The twentieth century will soon be over. And good riddance to it.'

It should have been a certainty that Lindy would be happy tonight, having waited for her first play's first performance almost since she had learned how to write her name. Karina kisses everyone goodbye while Julian loads their sleeping son into the car. What's ever certain? Her certainties are her eccentric family, her child who already appears to want to leave her, and the big, fair, bossy man who has become her life's unlikely partner.

Listening to Jamie's sleepy breathing while they drive, she watches a late plane approach low over the motorway near Gatwick Airport. Growing up in a family that lived for music, she'd learned to live for music too. Lindy doesn't have that peculiar spiritual security; emotionally she's hanging on by a fibre. Very soon, Karina decides, she must make sure they have their trip to Harvey Nichols. That would cheer up both of them.

'Darling one,' Julian says, invading her thoughts, 'don't you think it's time we gave Jamie a sibling?' Jamie's breathing in the back is slow and regular; he'll sleep soundly all the way back to Lewes.

'If he's going away to school, what's the point?' Karina retorts, keeping her voice down.

'What's the matter, love? Why are you angry?'

'I'm not. But Jules, I don't feel ready.'

Karina doesn't know how to explain, even to herself, why she doesn't want another child. Everything in her recoils at the idea. Sometimes she's afraid she's expended so much love on Jamie that there'll be none left to give. Other times, she dreads a repeat of the initial shock, the loneliness and exhaustion of those early months. And now, a complication: boarding-school. Anger. Resentment. Sometimes she feels so overwhelmed with fury that she's afraid the neighbours must be able to see it as a scarlet mist around her ears.

'I don't understand,' Julian grumbles.

'I know,' Karina returns. 'That's the trouble.'

How can she have another child with a man who doesn't want

his seven-year-old son to live at home? And if that is the real reason, above any other anxieties, how can she ever tell him?

'The English don't know how to love their children,' Mimi had remarked years ago when Lindy landed on the Vereses' doorstep, a small refugee from the domestic vituperation over the road. 'It's not the Gypsy way.'

'I'm sure Lindy and Karina don't want to hear about the Gypsy way again, Mimi,' Erzsébet soothed.

'The family was the pulsing heart of life,' Mimi reminisced. 'We might have had nothing, but we had love . . .'

'And music.' Erzsébet, with an indulgent sigh, finished Mimi's sentence.

Later, Karina lies awake, haunted. The worst thing is trying to sleep angry. Why does she guard Jamie so fiercely, loathing the idea of him strait-jacketed in school, trapped behind a desk, unable to see his parents for five days every week? Does her passion stem from Mimi's? Or – and this thought is more disturbing – shouldn't it be perfectly natural for any mother to feel this way?

'Karrie?' Julian's hand brushes her back.

'I'm asleep.'

The nightmares come. She's on a train, crossing London. She's on the wrong line. She leaves it, then walks along empty tunnels, devoid of adverts and other travellers. She takes another train in a different direction, but it stops at the next station and goes no further. She takes another, changes again, walks, boards, descends, walks. And she's left her violin behind on one of those terrible trains that carry her everywhere and nowhere. She's had this dream since she was twelve; it recurs as often as its opposite, the moving wagon and the stars.

She opens her eyes. It's dark; too hot; and she can still hear the rumbling of trains passing, one by one. The darkness is the night at home and the noise is Julian, snoring. She feels as if she's suffocating; her world will tip over and she'll be crushed in its rubble. She slides out of bed and goes downstairs for a cup of camomile tea.

6

When Karina answers the phone one bright June morning, she doesn't recognise Lindy's voice. It's choked with tears. 'Are you busy, Karrie? I really need you.'

'What is it? What's happened?'

'I've been dumped. I've been crying all night . . . I just . . . fuck, I'm sorry, I'm in a state. I'm not going to work.'

'I'm on my way,' says Karina.

Lindy's flat bears signs of crisis. Used mugs and a wineglass lie abandoned in the kitchen and a rumpled blanket and hot-water bottle on the sofa, although it's summer. A photo album splays face down on the floor where Lindy must have thrown it. She's in pyjamas, her hair unbrushed, her eyes red and puffy. 'Do you want to come and stay?' Karina suggests, embracing her.

'Thanks, but no thanks. It'd be all over the family in no time and can you imagine what my mum would say? She doesn't know. Nobody knows except you and Alban.'

Karina distrusts Alban, but that doesn't matter. 'Do you want me to call him?'

'No, he's on a job. Besides, he might send his friends to duff Charles up and I don't want him to.'

Karina tries to laugh, but notices in time that Lindy's serious. 'I'll make some coffee,' she says instead, 'and I'll run a bath for you. Have you got any lavender oil?'

'On the shelf.' Lindy blows her nose and slumps on to the sofa while Karina moves from bathroom to kitchen and figures out how to work the coffee machine.

'Have you eaten?'

'No. I feel sick.'

'What happened? Tell me.'

Tears well out of Lindy's eyes. 'I knew he'd been lying. Nothing new there, but it was getting worse. About where he was, what he was doing, using the kids as an excuse not to see me – and I knew something in his attitude wasn't what it had been. Yesterday he called and said, 'Look, there's only one of me, I can't leave my wife and I can't make a go of my marriage if I'm seeing you, so we have to stop.' And I don't know how long he'd been rehearsing that little speech, or even whether it's true. He's told me so many lies that I wonder if he just doesn't love me any more . . .'

'If you know he's lying, don't you think you're better off without him?'

'But it doesn't change how I feel.'

'Your bath's ready. It'll do you good.'

'Come and talk to me in the bathroom?'

Lindy splashes into the tub, which Karina has filled with bubble bath and a drop of soothing lavender. Karina closes the loo lid and sits on it. Lindy tips back, slides under the water and stays there. Bubbles drift across her face and long, pale body.

'Lin?' Karina prompts, anxious.

Lindy lifts her head, mounds of foam like ice floes catching in her hair. 'Don't worry. Even he isn't worth that,' she says.

'We could go out later. We could do Harvey Nicks.'

'I look so crap, I don't want to see myself in a mirror. Let's wait for the sales.'

'Wouldn't it cheer you up?'

'No way. I don't even want to *know* myself right now.'

'Lin, it's not your fault.'

'I don't know. I don't know anything any more. Maybe it is my fault. I put up with all that crap and I don't understand why I did or how I could. Maybe I'm just the proprietor of Belinda Rookfield's Professional Pushovers Limited. Chuck me that towel?'

When Lindy is dry, dressed and calmer, the girls sit on the floor, backs against a sofa, leafing through Lindy's old photo albums. The two of them running together through the Isabella Plantation in Richmond Park, past the pink and purple azaleas; Cynthia dippy in 1970s swirly-patterned dresses and big earrings. Then the eighties: Cynthia bouffed up her hair and wore outsized shoulder-pads, while Karina and Lindy tested their teenage wings beside her, and Erzsébet in tweeds looked exactly as she does now, but with brown hair instead of silver. Back then, Karina was too thin and rarely moved without her violin case, and Lindy was a tad podgy.

'My God, look at those styles! We thought it was so cool,' Lindy smiles.

'No Internet,' says Karina. 'No mobile phones. It was a more innocent time, even if we hated the politics.'

'My dad would have licked Thatcher's boots, given half a chance, assuming the blasted woman ever wore any,' Lindy says with a snort. 'And so would your father-in-law.'

'Look.' Karina turns a page. 'There's Willesden Lane. Do you ever make our bean stew?'

'Make it? I live on the stuff. Charles liked it too. Especially with scrambled eggs.' Lindy pulls another tissue out of a fast-emptying box. 'Sorry. I can't bloody help it. I just – the thing is, I know *why* I fall for men who can't be faithful, but I can't stop myself doing it.'

'Tell me.'

'I've been counselled until I'm blue in the face and they all start by saying 'Tell me about your father'. So I tell them and they nod and try to look clever. So I'm pre-conditioned, right, by his behaviour? I choose men who are like him, even if I don't know they are until later. But knowing that doesn't bloody stop me! That's why you've got nice, reliable Julian who adores you and would never think of looking anywhere else. Because your parents adore each other and that's always been the end of it.'

'Come on,' Karina protests. 'You don't have to be like your parents. My mum lost her mother and father when she was a child, so how would she know?'

'Just at the moment,' Lindy says, without meeting her eye, 'I'd give anything on earth to be in your shoes.'

Karina can hardly tell Lindy in her current state that her own shoes are giving her blisters. 'Hush, Lin. It's not so bad. Really. Everything will look better in a few days.'

'Damn it,' says Lindy. 'Let's open some wine.'

* * *

'Tamás.' Mimi isn't certain whether the voice is inside her head or whether she's spoken aloud. Lately, she's stopped wondering. Does it matter? She doesn't care; why should anyone else? Tamás haunts the flat; he waits until her visitors have left before coming back to explore the hour's discussions, the progress of his son and granddaughter and the great-grandson whom he's never met – well, Jamie has never met him, though Mimi suspects that he's sensed Tamás's presence. Sometimes the boy, who's twice his previous size whenever she sees him, lifts his head, glances about, listens.

Listens? says Tamás. Of course he listens. He's a Rácz. Music in the blood doesn't disappear so fast. One eighth Rácz, Mimi replies. It's not much. Another generation and the great tradition is gone forever. Rubbish, says Tamás. I've been back, I've had a good nose about in all those new cafés and restaurants in Budapest. They're still there, playing for the diners, busking in Vörösmarty Square outside Gerbeaud's, and for the shoppers on Váci Street. Gypsy fiddlers, all over the place, scratching around for a living; it's hard now that everyone uses iPods and digital downloads. Yes, and so what? says Mimi. How do you know they're real *muzsikás cigány*? It's all for tourists now. The Americans, the Japanese. How are they supposed to know whether they're hearing the real thing, or just some conservatory kid dressed up in a waistcoat? Nobody will know the difference.

That phrase, Mimi shouts at her dead husband's ghost, is the curse of the modern age. People don't bother to do things properly, because they think that nobody will know the difference. Therefore, one day there will be no difference. There will be no—

'Grandma?'

Mimi shields her eyes from the afternoon sun. A dark figure with long hair is standing in the doorway, bathed in brightness and holding a bunch of roses. It looks like her mother, in modern dress. Real or not?

'Grandma, it's me, Karina.'

Mimi breaks into a smile and holds out her arms. Karina's lips brush her cheek and her arms encircle Mimi's bony frame. Real.

'I didn't know you would come today. Erzsi and Dini said nothing.'

'They don't know. I came in to see Lindy, so I thought I'd try and see you too.'

'My dear, you look so beautiful. Are you happy?'

'Yes, Grandma, very. Can I make you some tea?'

'Ach, Karina, such a world. Tamás and I were talking. You must never forget, people do know the difference.'

'Yes, of course they do.' Karina, benignly bemused, wanders to the kitchenette where she puts the flowers into a vase.

'A great tradition. Gone.'

'No, it hasn't, Grandma.'

Mimi vaguely gathers that Karina has missed the point. Beautiful girl, Karina, Tamás rumbles from his corner. Just like you. She should have another child, or two.

'Girls don't think that way any more,' Mimi explains.

'What's that, Grandma?'

'You should have more children, my dear.'

'Grandma, please don't start that again,' Karina protests.

'Well, maybe not with that husband.'

She turns, eyes wide. Mimi taps her own wrist lightly – a reproof to herself. Sometimes she doesn't say things she ought to say, because she doesn't realise that she hasn't. Other times, she says things that probably should stay unsaid, but if she doesn't say them, no one else is going to, and sometimes people have to be told.

'You love him?'

'Of course. And I love you too, Grandma, and Jamie, my son, and Mum and Dad.'

Mimi sighs. Will this girl ever understand? 'I loved him,' she says.

'Tamás?'

Tamás's ghost is quiet; he knows what she's talking about. Where I am, he says, it doesn't matter any more. There's enough love, on this side, for everybody.

'Such wonderful music. All gone. Burned away.'

'Grandma, what are you talking about?' Karina takes her hand. Mimi gazes into her face: so young, so very worried. She reaches out and brushes back Karina's hair.

'A long time ago, Schnooky. Your mother calls you Schnooky.'

'Yes, I like it.'

'When you find him, bring him to me,' says Mimi. Tamás and the other one, the one who understands, are telling her to say this.

'Bring who?' says Karina.

Mimi's inner vision clouds for a moment; she says nothing. Why should Karina look all of a sudden as if she's about to cry?

'Grandma, I've always wondered something: why didn't you marry again?' Karina asks her. 'Everyone loved you so much.'

Mimi smiles. 'Maybe that is why,' she says. 'You are good girl, Karina. Come and see me again soon.'

In her room in the Frankls' home, in an enormous dark block in Belváros, the central Fifth District of Budapest, Mimi stood at her tall window, staring down at the street. The window was so thick that through its two layers of glass she could scarcely hear the birds in the trees. The building's front door was so heavy that it was a struggle to move it, and the ceiling in her room was almost high enough for her to pretend it was the sky. It was strange here, lonely and eerily quiet though so close to the Danube and Váci Street; but it was warm. A peculiar contraption stood in the corner, a tall stove covered with green ceramic tiles and fed with coal. The heat wasn't as fierce as the fires she'd once been used to, but it was constant and reliable.

Being alone in the room felt odd, and the first night she couldn't sleep for missing her mother. 'See you very soon,' Mária had whispered when they said goodbye; but her tears told Mimi not to believe it. The Rácz family was not pleased. The grandparents and aunts berated Mária for letting strangers bring up her child; but Mária, though loath to let Mimi go, insisted that exceptional needs called for exceptional strategies, and if Mimi's need wasn't exceptional, then whatever could be? So this was what her mother wanted for her, and she must have good reasons, even if it hurt like being branded with hot irons. Mimi muffled her sobs in the blanket so that the Frankls wouldn't know. She decided to watch out for the good reasons.

On the first day, when Mrs Frankl insisted she take a bath, Mimi disgraced herself by staying in it for an hour. She hadn't wanted to get in at first – the tub was huge and she feared drowning –

but the Frankls seemed to think it was normal (an hour wasn't necessary, but ten minutes were). Mrs Frankl helped her wash her hair with soapy stuff that smelled like flowers and she saw herself in the mirror when it had dried, sleek and shiny. Confusion invaded her. Why were some people convinced that everyday tasks must be accomplished according to one special set of rules while others insisted on the opposite? Mimi knew that if she was going to live with the Frankls, then, as her mother had advised her, she had to learn their methods, fast. One day, she promised herself, she'd impress Papa and Mama and Péter and all the others with the way she'd settled into her new life.

Mrs Frankl brought Mimi a parcel containing schoolgirl clothes – a white shirt with a lace front that buttoned up high, a dark blue skirt and some shiny new shoes. She brushed and braided Mimi's hair, and when she'd finished Mimi looked like a Hungarian child who happened to have dark hair, eyes and skin, maybe a legacy of the Turks, just like Budapest's Turkish baths. At least, she thought so. 'You look beautiful, Mimi,' Mrs Frankl confirmed. 'Now come and sit with me here at the table. Would you like to learn how to write your name?'

'A little Indian,' Professor Gábori joked when György Frankl walked into his apartment in the next block, holding Mimi by the hand.

'A Gypsy, not an Indian, János. This is Mimi Rácz, the astonishing child I told you about.'

'Oh, the Gypsy prodigy. I should warn you, Doctor, impoverished prodigies are two a penny – or rather, children whose parents would like them to be prodigies.' The professor stifled a yawn. 'They think it's a passport to fame and fortune. The reality can be exceedingly different.' He was staring at Mimi with suspicion; but, she sensed, curiosity too. 'I can see she has spirit,' he said to Dr Frankl, as if she wasn't there. 'Those eyes . . . Let's see what she can do. Come, little Gypsy, take out your violin and play to me.'

Mimi wasn't used to performing alone. The atmosphere was wrong. Nobody was drinking, eating or willing her to play a favourite song. Just two elderly gentlemen in a darkish room with a wooden floor and a huge piano, watching her hands like owls appraising mice in the cherry orchards. She must imagine someone to play to, besides them. She began a song by Panna Czinka. Because of Panna Czinka's example as the first woman to lead a famous band back in the eighteenth century, Mimi was allowed to play the violin. She would play for her, the great-grandmother of all Gypsy musicians. She closed her eyes and tried to hear the cimbalom and the bass in her mind while the familiar melody rang out and she improvised its embellishments.

At the end she looked up. Dr Frankl was wiping his eyes with a handkerchief and Professor Gábori, who had been standing, examining her every move, had slumped into a chair.

'Amazing,' he said.

'Is it yes?' Dr Frankl asked.

'It could be,' said the professor. 'It could be. Now, Mimi, you will learn to play some studies . . .'

When Karina tried to improvise, she couldn't. Regimented to books of scales, exercises by Carse and Ševčik and, later, studies by Kreutzer, she could only play when she read notes on a page. József, her father's friend who taught her in north London, fed her Bach, Beethoven and fidelity to the score.

Mimi would listen to her, but wouldn't give her lessons; Karina never quite understood why. Mimi used to hold public master-classes for advanced students and would fill them with tales of how Georg Solti had advised her to phrase a certain passage, how Leonard Bernstein had accompanied her at his home, how Marc Duplessis had consulted her over revisions in the violin writing of *Dans l'ombre des forêts*. 'Storytelling,' said Mimi. 'The Gypsy tradition is handed down by word of mouth. Why use books when you have the human mind?'

That didn't help Karina through music college. Admitted to a concrete bunker of an institution, she found herself fighting with a professor who demanded that she should play Bach without vibrato because it was supposedly 'authentic'. Mimi exploded with rage: 'This sound is ridiculous! How they know? Have they been alive in the eighteenth century?' When Karina answered the professor back, saying that Mimi Rácz's advice was different, he took it personally and advised her to study with Mimi Rácz instead.

The principal threatened to throw her out, until the invocation of Mimi's name as her grandmother – about which she generally kept quiet – induced her teacher to pretend that Karina consulting Mimi had been his idea in the first place. Karina quietly went back to József without telling the college. 'That professor,' Dénes declared, 'is neck in pain!'

Around the year 2000, an influx of Roma refugees, mainly, it was rumoured, from Romania, began to frequent the London Underground. Wearing long, bright skirts and headscarves, carrying babies or toddlers on their hips, the women would wander through congested carriages, showing the passengers written cards that explained their circumstances; they couldn't speak the words they needed, asking for money to feed the children. Commuters recoiled, but the Roma didn't understand the British meaning of being ignored and would stand and plead until a direct reproof sent them away. Behind them, executives, office workers and tourists would clutch at pockets and bags, checking for theft. Tabloid newspapers ranted against them, calling them 'bogus asylum seekers', sniping that they drugged the babies to keep them quiet. Karina fumed over the papers. The equation was simple: olive skin plus headscarf plus fear equalled good sales figures.

Karina, in London for family or Lindy, always gave money to the Roma beggars. She'd look into their faces and see her grandmother. If Mimi hadn't known when to leap from café to conservatory, swinging on a fragile thread from one tradition into another, then Karina too might have been shuffling through a train, trailing children, trying to care for them among a hostile populace that feared anything different from itself.

Riding through a tunnel near Warren Street, she gave a five-pound note to a Roma woman in a purple skirt who was leading by the hand a toddler, around the same size that Jamie was then. The child stared up, silent and great-eyed, finger in mouth; Karina caught her solemn gaze, smiled, waved down at her. The woman thanked her and seemed to offer blessings in her own language before moving on.

A businesswoman nearby glared at Karina over a leather briefcase. 'You shouldn't encourage them,' she scolded. 'They come to this country to scrounge. We let in too many. If people like you didn't give them money, they wouldn't come here.'

'They've got children to feed,' said Karina. 'They're trying to get away from a place that persecutes them. I've got enough money – why shouldn't I help them?'

'This island's so overrun it's going to sink, innit?' remarked a man to her left.

'Islands don't sink,' Karina pointed out.

'Yeah, luv, but the bottom line is, they shouldn't be here, should they?'

Karina shrugged. She'd proved her point by giving away her cash. It was nobody's business but hers. At least today that child would eat.

A couple of years later, there were no more Roma on the Underground. Nobody was sure what had happened to them. Sent back, and good riddance, said Julian. Sent back, Karina protested, to a country where they'd be discriminated against, where their children would be denied education and could never build a better life, just because they're Roma. It was only seven years since a Roma settlement in a part of Austria that was once Hungarian had been attacked with bombs. In a Europe populated by ever more immigrants from troubled countries all over the world, in thrall to terrorism, organised crime and traffickers of drugs and humans, still no people were more loathed than Gypsies, who only asked for money to feed their children—

'Oh, Karrie, get off your high horse,' Julian interrupted. 'We've heard it all before. We know about your grandmother. She bettered herself through her talent.'

'She bettered herself through luck,' Karina insisted. 'She was talented, she worked hard, but it was only luck that someone decided to help her. If he hadn't, she'd still be there now. Do you know, she donates hundreds of pounds every year to an international charity for Roma in Eastern Europe?'

'Karrie, she wouldn't still be there. She'd be dead. She'd have been killed in the Holocaust.'

'She had a chance because she was helped. Jules, sometimes

you forget that people are people, no matter where they come from.'

'And sometimes you forget that not all people are good, honest and trustworthy.'

'I care.'

'Then be careful who you care about.'

7

'The voting was done by pressing buttons,' says Carsten Schmidt. 'Could it be that somebody pressed the wrong button?'

Julian is at his club in St James, having dinner with Andy Williamson from the Department for Transport and a potential client, the director of a German train company named Locomotivation, who has made an unimpressive start by expressing astonishment that London should be staging the 2012 Olympic Games.

'This is crazy,' he goes on. 'Millions of extra visitors, with the roads in such poor condition, the railways so much needing updating?'

'Whoever wins this franchise will have their work cut out,' Julian remarks, glancing down the wine list. 'Still, big challenge, big rewards. How about a Gewürztraminer? A good German wine for good British luck?'

'Something must have been wrong.' Carsten assents to the wine with a perfunctory nod. 'Why would London win this over Paris? There must be an error.'

'Oh, don't you worry,' Andy reassures him. 'We worked hard for this, and the passion with which the team presented the . . .' Andy rattles on – he's taken to government-speak like mallard to duckpond.

Julian doesn't want to alert Carsten, whose business could be worth millions, to the fact that he's likely to press the wrong button himself if he tells a government minister London could only have won the Olympics by accident. He counts to ten, slowly. 'The future of transport is the biggest issue facing this city,' he says. 'I honestly believe that, Carsten. I think we all have a responsibility to make things *work*, the sooner the better.' He samples the wine. It's good, but he'll let Carsten and Andy drink most of it. He wants to keep his wits about him.

Julian can never look across a table at Andy without reliving his first glimpse of him at school. His voice had been breaking in the most embarrassing way, and his acne had to be seen to be believed. Since that day, they've been through everything together: cricket, Cambridge, trial by paperwork; and now their years of plenty, in which they enjoy the fruits of hard graft and try to be good family men. Last summer they'd taken Karina, Sarah and all the children for a day out at Windsor Safari Park in Andy's scarlet people-carrier, and they'd run out of fuel in the middle of the lion paddock. Julian wonders if the story might make Carsten Schmidt laugh, something that's almost as difficult as moving a broken-down car without getting out and pushing. Still, it would rub Andy's nose in the fact that he, a transport minister, hadn't listened when Julian said, 'How's the petrol level?' He keeps quiet.

Lindy is in a Camden pub with Alban, crying. At the next table, a stranger's birthday party is in full swing: streamers, party poppers, songs; it only makes her feel worse. Alban tries to cheer her up. 'You see, there's a future. We look forward, not back. There are good things to come. That is lesson for today.'

'Alban, I know I promised never to ask you exactly what you do,' Lindy says, wiping her eyes, 'but what exactly *do* you do?'

'Lindy, one day I tell you. You won't like me any more.'

'Is it legal?'

'Legal is not issue. We fulfil need. Without us, lots of things that must happen would not happen.'

'I don't get it.'

'Just think: if a system is lousy, unfair, incompetent, what you do? You make another system. Yes? And now, another drink!'

By closing time, they're both extremely merry. Yet the line between laughter and tears is so fine that Lindy abruptly falls on to the wrong side of it all over again.

'Dear, lovely Lindy.' Alban embraces her. 'Is still the married bastard? Come home with me tonight. You shouldn't be alone. Don't worry, I don't touch you. Promise. I put you in spare room. Yuri is away on job, so his room is free. I give you tea and sympathy and when you want, you can sleep. OK?' Lindy is too drunk and miserable to refuse.

At Alban's home above a shop in Wood Green, a short walk from the local main-line station, they drink spirits – Lindy isn't sure what and doesn't care; some virulent Balkan cross, perhaps, between vodka and meths. Eventually she almost loses consciousness at the kitchen table. Alban helps her to the absent Yuri's room and pulls a sheet tenderly over her before creeping out.

'Wake me up in good time,' Lindy mumbles into the pillow as he goes. 'I have to get to work.'

'Don't worry. You sleep now.' Alban turns off the light.

The next morning dawns fine and bright. 'Mum,' Jamie appeals on the way to school, 'please will you get out the paddling pool? *Please?*'

'If I can find Daddy's old bicycle pump to blow it up, then yes, I will.' Karina waves him off at the school gate, then strolls home via the bakery where she buys a croissant to fuel some violin practice.

She's tuning up when the phone rings. 'Karrie?' says Julian's voice.

'Darling? What is it?'

'Don't worry, I'm fine, but I wondered whether you could do something for me.'

'What? What's going on?'

'Put on the TV. I'm afraid there's been a train crash. It's bad.'

Karina fumbles about, shocked, looking for the remote control. Near Wood Green main-line station, a freight locomotive has collided head on with a passenger train in a long urban tunnel on a hill. Half of the double track was out of service for repair. The cause may be a signal passed at danger. Hydraulic fluid had leaked from the derailed carriages and stoked the fire that is now sweeping through the tunnel. Several hundred passengers are believed to be trapped.

'Andy and Sarah would use that line to get to her parents' place,' Julian explains. 'She sometimes goes up there on Thursdays, she only works Monday to Wednesday. I imagine she'd drive, but . . . Andy will be dealing with all hell breaking loose at the department. If he's worried about her, I don't want to make it worse, and now I've got to go into a meeting. Could you find out if she's OK?'

'I will. Call me later?' Karina hangs up.

She finds the Williamsons' home number and dials it. The answering machine comes on at once. She tries Sarah's mobile, only to hear a message declaring the network unavailable. On the TV, a report is in progress at the site of the disaster. Thick smoke pours from the tunnel mouth. Karina stares, feeling a prickling of familiarity. Wood Green? Why does the name alarm her? Some conversation with Lindy, about Alban? Uneasy, she tries Lindy's mobile, only to hear again that the networks are unavailable. All of London is trying to phone its loved ones in the north of the city. At least Lindy walks to work.

She watches the report, hypnotised. The number of dead and injured is still unknown, but the inferno created by the fire in this sloping tunnel, an expert comments, would be horrific: the so-called 'chimney effect' would suck air in from the lower end, intensifying the draught that fanned the flames. With rush-hour overcrowding, if smoke could get in but passengers couldn't get out, people would have been trapped like flies on flypaper.

Karina can feel heat on her skin, tightness in her throat – a hint of the claustrophobia that stopped her from climbing aboard the bus in Camden Town. She watches a spokesman announce the requisitioning of a nearby school's gym as a medical centre for the walking wounded. Ambulances scream by in the background.

At five past eleven the phone rings again. 'Karrie? It's me, Cynthia. Have you spoken to Lindy today? Please say you have. She hasn't arrived at work. She's not at home. I can't reach her by mobile, the networks are buggered. Oh, Karrie, I don't know what to do!'

'She walks to work. She wouldn't have been anywhere near that train.'

'The thing is . . .' Cynthia breaks off, breathing too hard. 'I spoke to Paul at the shop. She hadn't said she wasn't coming in, and she always would normally. And he said she'd gone out with that peculiar friend of hers, the Balkan one, last night, and he thought maybe she'd stayed at his place. In Wood Green.'

'What?' says Karina. 'But Lindy never stays with Alban.' At least, she never used to. With Charles gone, could Lindy be letting Alban console her?

'It's near the tunnel,' Cynthia sobs. 'The main line is faster than the tube from there. I don't know what to do, I don't know how to find her. Oh, Karrie . . .'

This isn't happening. It can't be. Everything will be all right in a few seconds. Lindy might be caught in the backup of other trains on the line – they'd have been told there was a power surge, signalling problems, anything to forestall panic; eventually someone would walk the passengers down the track to safety, and she'd emerge, shaken but unharmed. 'London's full of people trying to get somewhere and finding they can't,' she points out. 'Maybe she's stuck, waiting for a bus. Give it a bit longer.'

'Until when?'

Karina can't answer that. 'Let me know when you hear from her?'

'You too,' Cynthia says. 'Oh, God, my baby, my little girl . . .' The line goes dead.

Karina tries to imagine how she would feel if she didn't know where Jamie was on such a day. In a split second, your child can be transformed into an abstract phenomenon: a person in the wrong place at the wrong time. She wrestles with pain, refusing to panic.

Minutes inch by; segments of hours. Julian calls, but Karina can tell him nothing; no names have been released and among the survivors commenting on the TV there's no sign of either Sarah Williamson or Lindy Rookfield. She dials the bookshop.

'She's not here,' says Lindy's deputy manager, Paul.

'Has she called in?'

'I'm afraid not. But it's too early to get too worried.' It is past one o'clock. The trains had collided before nine a.m.

As soon as she's put the phone down, it rings.

'Karrie,' Cynthia says, 'I hate to ask you this, I know how far away you live. But . . . I know something's happened to her. It must have. She wouldn't vanish like this, she wouldn't not call me.'

'Shall I try to find her?'

'I don't know how . . . but . . . Martin's away at a conference, he won't be back from Stockholm until this evening, and I don't want to move too far from the phone, the mobiles don't work . . .'

'I'll do everything I can,' Karina promises.

An emergency phone number has appeared on the TV screen. She dials it, but it's as oversubscribed as the mobile networks. She turns up the TV. Bodies have been recovered, horrendously burned. There will be more. Both drivers are dead. She finds the north London hospitals' phone numbers on the Internet, but they, too, are jammed. Finally a switchboard operator answers and tells her to try again later. Later, Karina reflects, may be too late. Lindy might be in there, injured, terrified. She swallows incipient tears of fright and calls Gilly Pearson.

'Gilly, it's Karina. I've got to go to London. Someone's missing. Could you take Jamie after school, and either Julian or I will come and get him later?'

'Of course, but for heaven's sake, be careful,' Gilly pleads.

Karina drops the phone, runs out of the house and turns downhill towards the station. Riding into London, she's one of a few isolated, alarmed passengers who sit apart, staring into space, trying not to think about where they might have been had fate, God or chance not determined otherwise. They're calm; they don't talk. The passengers in Wood Green would have started their train journey exactly as they began theirs, in the summer sun. Everything would have been normal, until that moment after which nothing would ever be normal again.

North-east of Muswell Hill, she's astonished, at first, at how usual everything seems in this suburb of mini-roundabouts, terraced houses and council blocks. Traffic grinds past; a church clock strikes the hour. She glances at her map. She took two buses from Victoria – she couldn't face the Underground – but got off too soon, afraid of missing her stop. She's walking too fast, out of breath, her throat grating with thirst, but she doesn't want to pause for water. Her shoes pinch her toes, the arches of her feet ache. Lindy's image hovers, manically expanded, in her mind.

Closer to Wood Green, streets are closed; police in fluorescent yellow jackets stand by the cordons, talking quickly and quietly to anxious locals. Karina stares at an ambulance, its windows blacked out, its siren piercing. Is Lindy inside? Overhead, the sky is wearing a charcoal shroud. The smoke tastes caustic and makes her eyes water.

The school is ahead of her at last; she halts outside, finding herself amid a horde of people with the same mission, in tears or with set, blank faces, everyone asking questions. Some have brought photographs: Karina spots pictures of a woman with spectacles and a denim jacket, a smiling black youth in a suit, a backpacking Australian on a beach, a teenage Asian girl. Somebody clutches her sleeve. 'Have you seen my daughter? This is her photo.'

Paramedics stand by the entrance explaining again and again that they can't let anybody in, that names will be given out as soon as possible and the casualties released when they are able, but the medical effort must take priority. People inadvertently block the doorway; Karina stumbles aside. A group of injured passengers, limping, dazed, their faces stained with soot and blood, are being helped out of an ambulance. It's taken hours to free them from the wreckage. Strange how the more you stare, the harder it becomes to focus; but not one bears any resemblance to Lindy. An official calls out, she can't hear the words, but at once there's a rush of voices, mouths moving, shouting names. Karina says 'Belinda Rookfield,' to no effect. She forces herself to stay calm.

Along a narrow corridor, its walls lined with children's paintings, the official ushers a cluster of the frightened relatives into a classroom where more people – maybe thirty, maybe fifty, she's too frazzled to know – are already waiting. Maps are pinned to the walls and a giant globe lurks in a corner. The pupils have been sent home; they should have been in here, learning geography. Someone is worrying at the catch of a window that won't budge.

'Who are you looking for?' Karina asks a youth beside her, who's clutching a photo.

'My grandmother.' He shows her the picture: a wide smile, a tartan scarf. 'She was going to King's Cross to catch the Edinburgh train. My cousin lives there, she's just had a baby. I was going to fly up this afternoon . . .'

'Why now? Why today? Why here?' a young African woman sobs, her face ravaged. On her hand there gleams a wedding ring that looks new.

Now and then a name is called and someone rushes from the room.

'Is there any news from the hospital?' the young woman asks

the official. He explains as tactfully as he can that the identification of victims isn't proving easy. Many are unconscious; some are burned beyond recognition. Documents that might have helped would have been in handbags and briefcases, destroyed with their owners in the fire. Grey spots leap in front of Karina's eyes. She's drunk nothing since leaving home and her throat is desert dry.

At some point word spreads that some of the seriously injured victims have been identified at the hospital. The official reads out a list. Lindy is not among them. Several people fling themselves through the door.

Karina asks her waiting-room neighbour, searching for his grandmother, if he could possibly listen for Lindy's name while she makes an urgent call. She forces her feet to carry her out into what would normally be a playground. She dials the emergency line again. Now the networks are back in action a recorded message informs her that she must leave her name and number and the name of the person she's looking for, and someone will call her back. She phones Julian instead. 'I should go to the hospital,' she tells him. 'There's no sign of her here.'

'Go home, Karrie,' he begs. 'You can't do everything. If she's badly hurt, they won't let you see her anyway. Cynthia should never have made you go.'

'Any news about Sarah?'

'She's fine, thank God. Karrie, please go home.'

Karina rings off. She hesitates; turns; and walks back into the school. The medical staff are briefly too busy to notice her. She edges across to a side door and into the gym.

The smell of disinfectant penetrates the smoky tinge in the air, mingling with something ironish, sour and animal; on an improvised rack of benches and mats under the wallbars, figures sit or lie, while paramedics clean wounds, bandage limbs, inject painkillers and tranquillisers. Karina takes in plastic dishes, syringes, tubes, piles of swabs, people shivering from shock, swathed in silver heat blankets. Scanning the scene for Lindy, she glances down; close to her a patient lies propped against the wall, asleep or resting, blood seeping through a bandage from a head wound.

'Madam, I'm so sorry.' A paramedic approaches, her eyes red and sympathetic. 'I have to ask you to wait outside. We can't have people wandering in and I'm afraid if you do, everyone else will too. I'm very sorry.'

'Of course,' Karina says in a whisper. 'I'll go.' She hadn't realised how bad 'walking wounded' could be. If this can mean bleeding head wounds, broken bones or embedded glass, what injuries have befallen those who've been taken to hospital? She's certain now that Lindy isn't here. That means one of four things: she was never in the train; she's in hospital, severely injured; she's waiting for rescue inside a crashed carriage; or she is no longer alive.

Tracing the wall with one hand, Karina finds her way into the open air. Blood has always upset her, but now she feels so sick that the ground lurches under her feet. She makes it round a corner into a side street, where she doubles over and vomits. Getting her breath, ashamed of her own feebleness, she steels herself, then begins to wander back towards the main road.

It is past nine o'clock when Karina, defeated, wrung out, opens the front door. Jamie is asleep. Julian sits her on the sofa and pours her a brandy. 'Have you eaten?' he asks.

Karina shakes her head. 'Did Cynthia phone? Paul? Anyone?'

'Cynthia says they've heard nothing. They've left ten messages on that helpline, but nobody's rung back. I'm sure they're flooded with calls, it may take a while.' The news has confirmed that this is the worst calamity on the main-line railways since the Hatfield crash in 2000, and a fearful adjunct to the London Underground's terrorist bombs of 2005. 'It's awful, Karrie,' Julian says, holding her hand, 'but you've done all you can. More than that, from the look of you.' His pale eyes are furious.

'I haven't done enough. I could have tried the hospital, I only went to the school. And we're just assuming she was at Alban's place last night – she could have been anywhere, she could have slept late and not bothered to tell anyone she wasn't going to work . . .'

'I'll make you some supper.'

'I couldn't eat a thing.'

The TV news is piecing together the background to the accident. No foul play is suspected; this, the reporter opines, may be a case of incompetence at every level. A case in which it is difficult to assign responsibility, because numerous different companies are involved and each can no doubt find a way to blame the others.

Why should a driver pass a signal at danger? Exhaustion? Distraction? Would it have helped if the train had carried the ATP system? Is this the government's fault for valuing life in terms of pounds spent, then failing to provide safe transport for its citizens? Or the privatised train companies, doing likewise? Forty-six people have died, a hundred and twenty more are injured; nobody dares to admit fault. Perhaps the drivers will end up taking the blame, because they aren't alive to pass it elsewhere.

'What a mess,' Julian growls. 'What a beastly, idiotic, bloody mess.'

Karina hides her face on his shoulder and lets herself cry at last.

8

Karina wakes with a splitting headache after Julian's gone to work. Her son needs breakfast and yesterday's abandoned pupils must be rescheduled. How can the sun rise and routine carry on if Lindy is dead? Normality feels corrupt. Wandering back from Jamie's school, she pictures the empty Rookery, the bookshop, their table at Zucchini's. In the hall, she picks up the phone.

No news. Erzsébet is with the distraught Cynthia. Paul, in the shop, has heard nothing. Karina asks him for Alban's number, but nobody had ever had that, or even the man's surname, except Lindy.

She looks up Charles on his college's website and phones his office. Having loathed him, in principle, for two years, she controls her voice. 'You don't know me, but my name's Karina and I'm a friend of Lindy Rookfield's.'

'I do know you, very well,' comes the reply. Charles's voice is a civilised baritone, less snooty than she'd expected and much more worried. There's a long pause; he must be alarmed by her call. What is this? Blackmail, pregnancy, suicide threats?

'I was wondering whether you might have seen her.' She puts him in the picture, choosing her words as carefully as she can.

'Christ, no. Oh my God.' He sounds as frightened as she is; it's obvious that Lindy matters to him, greatly so. 'Please, Karina,' he says, 'call me the minute you hear anything at all? Please?'

'I will – and would you call me, if she contacts you first?'

'Of course . . . though I think she won't. Please, Karina, promise you'll call me?'

She promises, humbled, her opinion of him changing shape.

The day passes; she goes through its motions. Nobody rings

from the helpline. Martin and Dénes, who's furious that yesterday's burden fell on Karina, take over the search, trawling the hospital, the school and even the station. Karina curls up on the sofa, eyes hurting, body aching.

She forces herself to eat toast. She pulls out weeds in the garden. She tries to convince herself that there's still time and hope. Later, she fetches Jamie, who hasn't been told; she wants to say nothing until they know for certain what's happened to his godmother. Her first pupil arrives; she guides her through exercises, Grade III pieces, scales and a little sight-reading. It feels pointless.

By bedtime, she has spent hours on the phone. Cynthia, Erzsébet says, is under sedation. Martin and Dénes have found no trace of Lindy. Identifying the dead, the TV confirms, is difficult because the fire was so intense: in some cases, it's impossible to tell whether a victim was a man or a woman. 'If nobody's found her by Monday,' Julian reflects, 'then we probably have to assume the worst.'

Saturday. Karina watches the gyrating hands of the kitchen clock. At lunchtime Jamie wants ice-cream. She lets him have seconds, then thirds. Later, he's sick. Julian scolds her for spoiling him. Karina bursts into tears.

Arthur and Anne invite them to Fairfallows for Sunday lunch, but it's the last straw. Karina refuses to get out of bed. Julian agrees to go without her, taking Jamie. 'Sweetheart, you have to be strong,' he insists, bringing a cup of tea to the bedroom for her. 'Everything may still be all right. Lindy wouldn't want you to give up like this.'

'I haven't,' Karina protests in the dark; she's kept the curtains closed. 'But I can't face your parents and Hilary. Sunday lunch, *today*? Why do we have to pretend that nothing's happened?'

Monday. Sunlight glows into the house. The clock ticks. Karina slumps at the kitchen table. The silence is preternatural. If Lindy were alive and in hospital, surely someone would know by now? Lindy's image in her mind has reversed like a photographic negative. Where she'd occupied white space, there's a black void.

She drifts, dazed, to the nearest newsagent. The papers are full of pictures and lists. Those confirmed dead; those miraculously saved. The narrow escapes of some who would normally have taken that train, but hadn't. Lindy's photo, with wide-set, light eyes and high cheekbones, stares out at her.

Jamie is by the school gate when she arrives to collect him. He's leaning against the fence, staring fixedly at the ground.

'What's up? Out with it, lovey,' she says.

He shuffles along, eyes lowered. 'They're saying Auntie Lindy's dead,' he mutters. 'Sebastian said he saw her picture in the paper. But it's not true, I know it's not true.'

Bloody hell, thinks Karina. Beastly children. She reaches for his hand. 'Schnooky, the truth is that nobody's heard from Auntie Lindy since the train crash, but that doesn't mean she's dead. What the newspaper's saying is that nobody actually knows where she is. That's why they ran her picture, in case someone's seen her.'

Jamie looks up into her face, his eyes full of tears. How dare those stupid children talk to him like that? How dare Lindy put him through this by getting herself burned to a frazzle? She takes him in her arms and as he howls into her sternum she blames the government and the train companies and Julian, besides all the Rookfields and Charles and Alban, for bringing him a pain that no seven-year-old should have to feel.

Jamie's school term is drawing to a close. The three of them are supposed to be going on holiday to Portugal. Julian says it will do them good; Karina begs him to cancel it. She doesn't want to go away, in case – though in case of what, she isn't sure.

Two charred, unidentified bodies remain. Martin and Cynthia steel themselves to visit the morgue.

Julian takes Martin's call afterwards. Martin, he tells Karina, wasn't sure, but Cynthia is convinced that one body is, or was, Lindy's – the decision spurred by the presence of a filling in one back molar. She hadn't looked at the face, Martin said; he had, then advised her not to; but they had talked to the pathologist who had examined what remained of the teeth. The other body remains unclaimed; perhaps a homeless person, the police suggest, someone who had nobody to miss them. The horror is, perhaps, better than the uncertainty. 'I'm sorry, darling,' Julian says to Karina, his face turned away to hide his emotion.

Karina goes upstairs to put Jamie to bed. She feels as leaden as if she'd drunk hemlock. In the soft evening light, Jamie is standing at his window, mumbling something rhythmical under his breath. He's repeating a chant, over and over again. Karina hears the words: 'Lindy Rookfield, you will come back, you will, you will, you will. Lindy Rookfield, you will come back, you will, you will, you will . . .'

'Hush now, Schnooky. Bed.' She kisses him and closes the blind.

After the quiet, private cremation, the Vereses go back to Forest Road with the Rookfields. While the others drink tea and whisky, Cynthia, her butterfly-wing iridescence tarnished through neglect, leads Karina up to Lindy's old bedroom. The space gapes, its energy inverted like a black hole.

'I've got a few of her things,' Cynthia says. 'We went to her flat and brought back the valuables. I didn't like to think of the place sitting there empty. Please, Karrie, take something as a memento.'

Cynthia has arrayed Lindy's knick-knacks on the desk, its wooden surface lightly etched with the word 'Chris' enclosed in a heart. From here Lindy used to flash the torch at Karina's window. SOS. Karina strokes Lindy's moonstone necklace; the charm bracelet, a thirteenth-birthday present; a watch from the Chelsea Craft Fair that she and Lindy had chosen together. It's silver, which had suited Lindy. She'd liked light, frosty blues, wintry greys and white. Karina, with her darker skin, prefers chocolate browns, bronzes and red; gold suits her better than silver. She caresses the watch with a fingertip; she knows she'd never wear it. 'What's going to happen to The Rookery?' she asks.

'We've started to clear it. Once everything is sorted out we'll put it on the market. She hadn't made a will, you know. The stupid girl! How could she not have made a will?'

'Hush, Cynthia. It's OK. Can I help with anything?'

'Darling, you're too good. I'm sorry if I lose it sometimes, Karrie. I do try – but it's so difficult. Every morning I wake up and there's one blessed moment when I've forgotten. Then I remember; and it's like going through the first shock all over again.'

'I know.' Karina squeezes her hand. She feels exactly the same. 'How's Martin coping?'

'You know him, he shows nothing. He doesn't talk to me. He's busy calling all the other survivors and victims' families and he wants to form an organisation to sue people. That's all that really interests him. Not me. I never did.'

'You'd think this would bring you closer,' Karina suggests.

'Some chance. He's doing the paperwork, the flat, all the practical things. He's good at *doing*. What he's not good at is feeling or talking.'

'Most men aren't.'

'Oh, Karrie, look at all these things. There must be something that you want?'

Karina pulls out a drawer in the desk. Inside lies the torch: a clunky old object with a red plastic switch. Her hand closes round it. 'Could I have this, please?'

Karina and Gilly Pearson spend an afternoon walking on a wide-skied section of the South Downs Way with Jamie, Olly and the Pearsons' chocolate Labrador. Chalky pebbles leave dust on their shoes; the sea sparkles in the distance beyond the ripening wheat fields, cobalt against the reddish gold. The view from the Downs brings Karina nourishment. Something is inherently heartbreaking in the caressing curves of the hills, the clumps of trees in the valleys and the way the land comes to an end with such grace at the sea – sorrowful despite its beauty; perhaps because of it.

The boys shout and run, the dog prancing beside them, and Karina, watching them, finds she's in tears again. Gilly pats her arm, but doesn't know what to say. Nobody knows what to say when they hear that your best friend has been killed.

Later, after sending Jamie off with the Pearsons, she reads Lindy's old emails for comfort, although it's also a torture. It's all that's left.

> Hi K,
>
> Sorry I was in such a bloody mess the other day. It was sweet of you to come over. You were right, we should have had a Harvey Nicks trip. Best thing I can do is doll myself up and find another bloke prontissimo. My God, it's all so stupid. Can you believe the idiotic things that come between people? Makes me sick. Reminds me of Jules's legal bullshit – no relation to reality, but everyone has

to stick to the system. What about feeling, what about love?

There'll be none left anywhere soon. It won't be allowed.

I'll shut up now. If you see Charles, tell him from me: BASZD MEG.

Lxx

How extraordinary that Lindy's last online words had been 'Fuck off' in Hungarian.

The phone rings. 'Is that Mrs Rookfield?' The voice is female, unfamiliar.

Karina's heart bungees into her throat. The helpline? The hospital?

'This is Mary Woodrow, I'm the admissions' secretary at St Matthew's School. We met briefly when you and your husband and Jamie came in for the open day. Mrs Rookfield, I had a chat with your husband the other day and he told me how keen Jamie is to come to St Matthew's, which is lovely news for us. I promised I'd see what I could do, and it so happens that a child has just dropped out. We're now in a position to offer Jamie a place in September.'

'What, you mean next term?' Karina's mind roots frantically for any conversation with Julian about St Matthew's. She's effectively wiped out any experiences of the last weeks unconnected with Lindy's death. 'I need to talk to him,' she says. 'Can we get back to you?'

Karina and Lindy's school was a twenty-minute stroll from home, mostly along the river. Yet on their first day she'd felt stranded, muddling through a hymn in assembly with hundreds of girls who, it seemed, all knew the words, maybe even believed in them.

She'd never been to a Church of England service. One Christmas, they'd gone to the Hungarian church in Hammersmith, but her parents weren't interested in attending regularly. Music was their religion; art and culture make us human, they'd tell her, though Erzsébet used to joke privately that Dénes's god was his mother. Among rows of pasty-faced schoolmates piping out the tune off key, Karina thought with longing of her grandmother's expressive face, her warmth, her energy, her *giving*ness. Soul, Mimi had told her, is everything to a musician.

'Karina Veers.' The form teacher was taking the register.

'*Vairesh*,' Karina corrected her. The other girls tittered. Lindy silenced them with her best withering look.

Other people felt comfortable in clumps. They went to the same churches. They ate bland food with names like corned beef and Spam. They played team games that they knew from mothers, older sisters or even grandmothers. Karina had never heard of hockey. 'I'll show you, Karrie,' Lindy said, encouraging her.

The bullies targeted Karina at lunchtime. She was always eating, they declared, because she was always Hungary. She couldn't take a mouthful without them trying to force her to put down her fork, lunch uneaten. She can still feel her own hand moving the cutlery across the plate, wondering whether she could endure the consequences were she to lift it and eat – her hair yanked, her fingers bent back, her arms rubbed with 'Chinese burns'.

Her father eulogised the London that had taken him and his mother to its heart when they had arrived as refugees: cosmopolitan, welcoming, paradise for a good musician. School was another matter. Karina didn't even fit in with the minorities: Asian, Jewish, Afro-Caribbean. She was the only Hungarian, she felt, in a hundred miles, even though she'd been born in a hospital ten minutes from the Thames. She began to avoid the dining hall, taking her violin to the music wing and finding a room where she could escape into practising.

When Erzsébet noticed that Karina was losing weight, the truth emerged. The headmistress, after the shock of facing two fierce, furious Hungarian parents, quickly took action. Karina's lunchtimes were reinstated with a supervising teacher on stand-by. The next time anyone tried to taunt her, Karina had the courage to throw some of her father's Hungarian swear words at them, then fix them with a look that she pretended was the evil eye, learned from her Gypsy grandmother. That caused almost as much trouble as the Hungry Hungarian had in the first place.

Karina couldn't articulate her sense of being at sea among so much self-confidence; or why life was so different at home – quieter, simpler, but much warmer; or how crushed she felt, knowing that because she had a funny name, black hair and parents with odd accents, the others would never let her fit in even if she wanted to.

'You fit in with me,' Lindy announced, 'and I've got the oldest English family in the school. My uncle's a lord. So *neuur* to them!'

She imagines Jamie in school. Perhaps he has the best of both his parents: her treacly warmth, combined with Julian's old-established self-assurance. But he's so small. He sees St Matthew's as Hogwarts and himself as Harry Potter; and he only thinks he wants to go there because his dad has talked it up to him. Isn't that, in itself, wrong? As wrong as pretending that when someone you love dies, life can continue as if nothing has happened?

Karina wants desperately to do the right thing. She seems to have spent much of her life trying to do the right thing.

'Of course it's the right thing,' Julian insists. 'You may have issues about fitting in, but Jamie doesn't, and if I've got anything to do with it, he never will.'

Faced with a watershed, Karina would once have called Lindy. She thinks of Lindy's last visit to Lewes: her energy shining blue and silver through the sunny entrance hall, Jamie hurtling in to embrace her, the presents Lindy placed in his arms. She knows Lindy's face so well: the tiny mole above her left eyelid, the fine golden down on her upper lip, the flecks of grey scattered through her pale, bright irises. In a year's time, two years, five, ten, will she remember the details of Lindy's face? Will Jamie?

Karina goes up to him. He's lying in bed, awake, his lips moving.

'Hey, Jimbo.'

'. . . will come back. You will, you will, you will,' mutters Jamie.

'Hush, now.' Karina sits on the bed and strokes his hair. 'It's very late, darling. Try and sleep.'

'She will come back. She will. She will.'

Karina kisses his cheek and slinks out. Downstairs, her eyes meet Julian's, reproachful. 'He's doing it again,' she says.

'Karrie, can't you see? Once he's busy getting used to school and making new friends, he won't have time to fret.'

'It could be too much change, too fast. This upset at home; then being sent away.'

'Darling, if we turn it down, there may not be a place for the next academic year. It's been a bad time, but we have to move on. This is about Jamie's future.'

Karina's sanity seems fastened on with a loose pin. One false move and it'll fall off. 'I'm not sure I can handle it,' she manages to say.

'Of course you can. You'll have more time to yourself. You'll be able to do all kinds of things – practising, chamber music, whatever you like. And he'll be home most weekends.'

'Time to myself?' repeats Karina. Take Jamie away, and Lindy, and she's not sure what her 'self' will be.

9

On the day of her debut recital, going home after the rehearsal, Mimi looked backwards. Taxi-cabs clanked along the road; the villas and embassies along Andrássy lay still under the heat and overhead the leaves quivered in the sun. Far away beyond the city boundaries was Kistarcsa. Mimi hadn't seen her family for nearly four years.

Dr Frankl read her mind. 'Homesick, Mimi?'

'No,' Mimi said, violin case clasped to her chest.

'But?'

'I miss them, sometimes.'

'I have an idea. Would you like to bring your father to the concert? We've got plenty of time, so we could go and fetch him. If he's not playing tonight himself, of course.'

Dr Frankl leaned forward and spoke to the driver, who looked startled – outraged, Mimi thought – until the doctor offered him rather a lot of money.

Perhaps it was her imagination, but Budapest didn't seem so glamorous any more. One day the doctor had come home depressed and anxious; Mimi saw him musing over a newspaper. Something had happened in America, a place named New York, Mrs Frankl said, something to do with a stock market crash, which was going to cause problems for the whole world. 'Budapest will be all right in the end,' she remarked. 'We're good at bouncing back, heaven alone knows why.'

Mimi, practising alone in her room, wondered what a stock market was. She remembered, from when she was tiny, the market place in Temesvár, now called Timisoara because somebody had decreed that it was in Romania, not Hungary after all; István and the band had had a job in an open-air café for the summer, and they'd been gearing up for the St Stephen's Day celebrations on the twentieth of August. Mária had walked her round the market, teaching her the names of fruit and vegetables, which lay sweltering in the heat. She could still picture the jumbled wooden crates of lettuces, peppers, melons and apricots; the peasants unloading them from their carts, looking like walking walnuts. She imagined all those crates stacked up high, swaying then toppling, scattering their gaudy contents around the gutters. New York, Dr Frankl had told her, was a huge city full of enormous new skyscrapers. If crates fell down there, well, that did sound bad.

A few years earlier, Budapest's terraces, cafés and shining shopfronts had sung a more hopeful song to her. The city tonight felt tired, oddly shattered. The wind across the river made her anxious. As the cab jolted further and further from the city centre, Mimi began to wonder whether this was such a good idea.

The roads deteriorated and the motion of the cab tossed Mimi and her violin from side to side. Several times the driver tried to make them get out and walk; he didn't want to be there. He was afraid. Outside, the smell was rancid – drains, or lack of them. Many of the buildings, factories and housing alike, seemed near-derelict; doors and windows were patched or in pieces in front of shadowy gateways; children played feral, unsupervised games across the lot. Odd to think that she and her brother and cousins used to play like that.

They pulled up beside an arched entrance missing half its door. 'It's here,' Dr Frankl told her. 'Shall I come with you?'

'No, thank you.'

Mimi stepped down, trying, in her smart shoes, to avoid the smelly refuse at the roadside. She wanted to get back in the cab and go home to the Frankls' apartment as quickly as possible. Instead, she lifted her head and walked on. The children in the courtyard paused in their game, watching her mount the staircase on the right and peer through the door. This couldn't be the place, could it?

'Do you know István Rácz? The violin player, the *primás*?' she asked a child who looked no more than six years old. The boy, as dark as she was herself, gawped at the mismatch of Mimi's face and clothes; then he pointed out of the courtyard and across the street, where a doorway and dark window concealed a bar.

The place was dimly lit and stank of coffee and spirits. She hesitated just inside. A group of men, all Roma, were in heated discussion around the tables, drinking strong coffee.

'Papa,' said Mimi.

Her father, sitting slightly away from the others at the back of the room, stared back as if he'd never seen her before. 'Mimi . . . Is that our Mimi?'

'Papa, I'm giving a concert tonight. Would you like to come?' said Mimi in a small voice. 'Dr Frankl's outside. There's a cab . . .'

'Little Mimi!' István leaped up, his face transformed in a split second from darkness to light. He grabbed Mimi round the waist and lifted her into the air. 'Look at you! What a little woman!' The reek of his unwashed suit, a smell that used to signify home and familiarity, struck Mimi for the first time as revolting. A retch caught in her throat, the shock of it as upsetting as the sensation itself.

He put her down and tipped her face towards him, a finger under her chin. 'It wasn't the same after you left.'

Now she knew how things were today with the Rácz family. 'Where's Mama?' she asked.

István didn't reply. 'So,' he said instead, 'you're giving a concert. A proper concert in a proper hall. Have you learned to read notes on the page?'

'Ages ago, Papa.'

'So, you play classical music. Rich people come to listen to you and sit in rows and applaud?'

'Yes, Papa.'

István shook his head. She saw an odd flicker of sadness cross his face, unexpressed. 'My daughter, my Mimi, a star for bourgeois Budapest,' he muttered, as much to himself as to her. 'Who'd have thought it? Have you forgotten everything of our music?'

'No, but Professor Gábori wants me to learn some concertos.'

'Don't forget it. Don't forget everything I taught you. Don't forget that they've never produced a player to touch János Bihari.'

'Professor Gábori says there's never been a great soloist who was a Gypsy,' Mimi said. 'He thinks we've got something missing in our brains. He said we can be good players, but not great artists. And anyway, we don't know how good Bihari really was because we never heard him and nobody made gramophone records then.'

István's face clouded over as abruptly as it had brightened a few minutes earlier. 'So what are *you* doing with this horse-shit professor who doesn't believe we're great artists? What's he training *you* to be?'

Mimi, chin lifted, took a step back. She had come in with a purpose and she was going to see it through, come what may. 'I shall be the first,' she said. 'Papa, please will you come and hear me play tonight?'

'Little one. Come here.' István sat down and patted the bench beside him. Mimi, trying to smell the coffee and nothing else, perched on the edge. She imagined the concert hall of the Ferenc Liszt Academy, the audience assembling, her classmates and Professor Gábori – and her father walking in. He'd been her inspiration. A great violinist, in his own way. She mustn't forget. She must never forget. But . . .

'If I come with you now,' István began, 'the whole of Budapest will know that Mimi Rácz's father is a loud, smelly Gypsy, all washed up without his little star. Is that what you want?'

'I want you to be proud of me, Papa,' said Mimi.

'Proud? Of course I'm proud!' He thumped the table with a fist; the other men turned to see what was happening. 'Look, my friends! My daughter the classical virtuoso!' István shouted, punching the air above him with both fists. A cheer went up, so loud that Mimi's ears buzzed with it.

'I have to go,' she said. 'I have to get ready to play. *Please* come, Papa?'

'Go, Mimi Rácz. Go,' said István. 'Spread your wings and fly. And don't come back. I never want to see you again.'

'Papa—?'

'Don't come back. You heard. Go on, get out!'

'But Papa!'

'I'm not your father any more. I sold you to your fine daughter-less doctor. Get back to him before I throw you out.' István's hands curled into fists; Mimi, swarming with fear and confusion, stumbled to her feet and began to back away. 'You want to be around a father who sold you? *Out!*'

Her fingers were shivering like the surface of the Danube. If they didn't stop, how would she hold her violin?

'Goodbye, Papa,' she said; it came out a terrified rasp. In his eyes she caught a last glimpse of the pride and defiance of all the generations that had once been her family, before he turned his back.

In the cab, Dr Frankl let her cry while the cobbles beneath shook the misery down into her soul. 'Don't you see what he's trying to tell you, Mimi?' he said. 'Don't you see what he wants you to do?'

'I think my mother's dead,' said Mimi.

Four hours later she was standing on the Liszt Academy's wooden stage, playing Beethoven's 'Spring' Sonata with the most sympathetic pianist the Academy could find her – one who didn't mind accompanying a Gypsy if she played well. Mimi's hair was wound into a chignon; her dress was simple, but made of silk; and as she leaned into the melodies, pouring her spirit out like treacle, the audience was silent and attentive. Nobody would ever know what had happened that day. Professor Gábori, arms folded, exchanged a look with Dr Frankl and nodded.

Sunday at Fairfallows. Karina is there, going through the motions. She takes her usual seat in the blue drawing room, on the sofa beneath the largest of the icons, which Arthur had brought back from Moscow in 1992. The image of Jesus, against a dull glimmer of wood and gold, has mournful eyes; Karina always feels that they're following her around the room. She sits with her back to it.

'How's the book going?' she asks Anne.

'It's rather fascinating, darling. Ottilie Featherstone had quite an open marriage, unusual for Surrey in the 1860s even for a romantic novelist, so I'm trying to find out whether her son could actually have been the child of . . .'

Across the room, Hilary is talking to Arthur, pacing back and forth on the threadbare carpet that used to be Persian. Hilary's shock of hair is white, above watery eyes and strong eyebrows; he's wearing a striped shirt and his habitual red corduroy trousers. He's two years older than Julian, but looks over fifty.

Arthur is having second thoughts about renting out Fairfallows's front hall and garden for weddings. 'You know what will happen when it rains,' he's saying. 'They'll be tramping back and forth from the marquee to the Portaloos and they'll wreck the lawn.

Never be the same again. It's bad enough having the great unwashed plodding through the place as it is.' Fairfallows opens to the public as a private museum on Saturday and Wednesday afternoons and a former stable block well away from the house has been transformed into a tearoom.

'Money,' Hilary reminds him. 'Lovely money for lovely heating. Do we need it? Yes, we do.'

'It's going to cost more than it earns at first,' Julian points out. 'The house will have to meet safety standards. I'll arrange to get the wiring checked.'

Jamie tugs Karina's arm. 'Mummy, can we play hide-and-seek?' he begs.

Fairfallows contains more secret nooks and crannies than even Jamie has yet discovered. The oldest part of the house dates back to the seventeenth century: its rooms are set with generous windows, inglenook fireplaces and giant beams. At the centre lies a courtyard resembling a cloister, which boasts a fine collection of old roses. In the modern section – 'modern' in Rookfield terms meaning eighteenth-century – are the marble-floored entrance hall and the blue drawing room. Arthur's icon collection douses the entire place with an incongruous whiff of exoticism.

Jamie could hide in any of the upstairs bedrooms, in a wardrobe, the wicker laundry basket, or the airing cupboard off the flagstoned kitchen. It will take Karina a good while to find him, which suits her well.

'Cam belt went on the Jag last week,' Hilary tells Julian, walking up and down, twisting his fingers together at interesting angles. 'I was on my way to the golf club when I hear *phutt-per-clonk* and bingo, that's that. Highly discombobulating. I waited three hours for the breakdown brigade. Could have fixed it myself if I'd had the tools handy. Had to push the car to the side, there was a steep camber so it was a matter of not shoving the vehicle right over . . .'

Karina, counting to a hundred while Jamie runs off to hide, watches Julian's expression while his brother talks. She's always impressed by his patience with Hilary, who couldn't have fixed a cam belt himself and couldn't push over a car if he tried to. Hilary lives in an apartment on the top floor of Fairfallows. His six-year spell in a tranquil lakeside hospital at Keswick is rarely mentioned.

Anne, Karina reflects, is seventy-five and has had to watch her elder son reach his late forties without being able to sustain a long-term job or relationship. He'll never become independent. It's not his fault; it's a chemical imbalance. Technically there's nothing to stop any company employing him, but Hilary has always insisted on honesty about his condition. He's not a killer, a psychopath or an embezzler. He's a well-educated man who happens to have a chemical imbalance, which most of the time is medically corrected. Unfortunately, employers haven't seen it that way and won't take the risk.

The Rookfields' estate, which includes extensive land and some cottages, is managed by an agent. Arthur had preferred to run a business consultancy, specialising in strategy and planning, which boosted the family wealth for many years; but extending the business to post-perestroika Russia hadn't proved an especially helpful strategic plan for his own finances; and the upkeep of the house and the estate, as well as Hilary's time in hospital, leached away the Rookfields' resources.

Temporary measures are fine – temporarily. They've sold off some land, auctioned some of the most valuable furniture, cut back the team of gardeners, and regretfully let the cook go. Yet the only obvious long-term solutions – turning Fairfallows over to a heritage organisation, or selling the Gainsborough – still seem out of the question, however much the air of shabbiness encroaches. 'Whole way of life's disappearing,' Arthur expostulated when he lost his seat in the 1999 House of Lords reforms.

Karina silently hands Arthur an accolade for the fact that he never complains about Hilary. She's painfully aware, though, that after Hilary inherits Fairfallows, the person next in line to it is Julian; and ultimately Jamie. A decade ago they'd still hoped Hilary might marry and have children; but that has seemed less likely by the year.

'Bloody hooligans on the field,' Arthur grumbles. 'The council says we can't get rid of them. Blasted scroungers.'

Karina pauses in the doorway. 'Travellers?' she asks.

'Gypsies, or so they say. Sorry, Karina, nothing to do with your musical ones, these are different. They have hundreds of children, live on benefits, never do an honest day's work, trespass on your land making a muck of it, then call it their traditional way of life.'

'Aren't you being a little harsh?' Karina tries not to snap. 'Why do people still think it's all right to hate Gypsies for the sake of it?'

'Oh, Karina, darling, what ruffled feathers. You know it's nothing to do with your lovely granny,' says Hilary. 'Why don't I make you another G and T?' Hilary mixes uncommonly fine gin and tonics. He isn't allowed to drink them himself.

'Thanks, but I promised I'd play with Jamie before we eat.' Karina flees.

Upstairs, between checking cupboards for her son, she gazes out at the grounds from Julian's old bedroom window. Great trees bend under the weight of their own branches and summer clouds scud across the sky. She imagines Julian, as a child, waking up to this view every morning. She can't see any caravans.

There's a tiny cough under the bed. Karina lifts the valance; Jamie's eyes sparkle at her out of the murk. 'Gotcha!' she cries. He crawls out, laughing, and she brushes the dust off his trousers. The Rookfields' latest area of cost-saving is the cleaning bill.

'Mum, why doesn't anybody talk about Auntie Lindy?' Jamie demands, on the way downstairs.

'Sometimes people find it difficult to talk about things like that.'

'But it's like they're pretending she wasn't ever there.'

'I know, love.'

Karina sits beside Jamie at lunch in the panelled dining room. The Gainsborough hangs on the largest wall, well away from the sunlight: a portrait of the Lord and Lady Rookfield who had built the entrance wing. Albert, the third Lord Rookfield – an Enlightenment hero and patron of the arts, according to Julian – poses in a blue frock-coat and his wife, Frances, in grey satin with a white wig; three dogs sit to attention, a gun lies on a table and the parkland beyond is painted with the detail and delicacy of antique lace.

Karina cuts up Jamie's meat for him and stays out of the conversation. Anne chats about how appalling bookstore discounts are for biographers' incomes. Arthur declares that they'll have to make Fairfallows souvenir merchandise to pay the government's stealth taxes. Hilary, shifting constantly in his chair, rambles on about his car. Jamie, blithe and hungry, is only interested in food. Karina can hardly believe how much he eats; where does he put it all? She wants to raise an issue that Cynthia has recently mentioned: a memorial service for Lindy. But finding the right moment to interrupt the inanities of Fairfallows chit-chat is next to impossible. After almost ten years, Julian's family still feels as alien to her as if they'd come from a different galaxy.

When Julian brought her to Fairfallows for the first time, announcing his *fait accompli* – 'This is my fiancée' – Karina hovered in the doorway, diamonds glinting on her hand, sensing the Rookfields sizing her up: young, exotic, slender in flattering black trousers and scarlet blouse. She couldn't have felt more foreign if she'd been born in a wagon herself. How was it possible, she reflected, sipping sherry and trying to make small-talk about roses, cricket, agricultural fêtes and Orthodox icons, none of which she understood, that she was marrying into this? On the way home, she imagined what they'd be saying about her behind her back.

'I don't care,' Julian said, pressing his foot on the accelerator. 'You're marrying me, not them. Anyway, they adored you.'

'I don't want them to think I'm a gold-digger.'

'Don't be silly, darling. First, they know about you from Forest Road. Secondly, there's not much gold left to dig.'

In the end, it was Mimi who cheered when she heard that her granddaughter's future father-in-law was a lord. For all her platitudes about meritocracy, Karina teased her grandmother, Mimi was enchanted by what she still saw as social betterment.

Once the shock wore off and the wedding plans were underway, Karina started to enjoy Anne's company, her devotion to her work and her sense of style. She tried to copy the way Anne draped her scarves and chose discreet yet perfect earrings, necklaces and handbags. Arthur was more difficult – not that Karina could blame him for his grouching. 'He wasn't like this when I was a kid,' Julian told her. She'd explore the family photos from holidays in the South of France, the cricket matches Julian organised for his schoolfriends in the Fairfallows meadow, family trips to test matches at Lord's with laden hampers. She began to read up on rose varieties.

Fairfallows had housed the same family for more than three hundred years; now she, too, would belong to that solidity.

'I'm a creative person,' Richard declared, over a bottle of organic wine and a macrobiotic supper of beans, mushrooms, rice and broccoli. 'Placid surface, volcano beneath.' Karina still wonders, sometimes, what would have happened if she'd married him instead.

Julian treats sex like an all-you-can-eat buffet: hearty and satisfying, requiring a good sleep afterwards. But for Richard, that wasn't enough; he wanted to possess her and become her, and the edge between tenderness and violence sometimes wasn't blurred, but obliterated. Karina often ended up with cystitis, but such intensity seemed worth the risk. She met Richard during her last year at college, and barely scraped through her final recital exam because she hadn't had enough sleep for three months.

When they weren't wearing each other out in bed, they'd cry over the same old movies; they'd read the same books, then spend hours talking about them; they'd make macrobiotic food in homage to Richard's composition hero, John Cage, who'd sworn by the diet, especially the mushrooms. Richard was fascinated by her background, had identified with it. He too was an outsider, he declared. He and his mother had lived in a caravan when he was a toddler – through hardship, not tradition – and he'd worked his way into music college by talent alone, though his face, he insisted, would never fit. Each seeking somewhere to belong, Karina and Richard tried to belong to each other.

'You can't live like this,' Lindy protested to the exhausted Karina in their Willesden Green kitchen. 'You're burning out. There'll be nothing left of you. How will you keep up with the pace in the orchestra if you're keeling over?'

'I love him.'

'But you're being devoured, not nourished. Look at you! You do everything for him. You copy out his music, you type his grant applications, you're virtually being his secretary. You give and give, but don't you need something back from him now and then? What does he offer you? He'll never give you a home, he doesn't even want you to move in with him after three years, and I bet he still says he can't afford to move out. You can't pay his way, not on your salary, while he just sits writing weird noises that nobody wants to hear.'

'I can't live without him.'

'You know I'm fond of him. He's an amazing bloke in many ways. But he's a taker. You'd be stuck with him, working your socks off to support him and your kids and probably his mother too. And what are you going to do when the sex goes off?'

'It won't.'

'It will. It always does.' Lindy's longest relationship to date had lasted eight months.

Karina had crossed London to his flat in Lewisham the next night; they'd cooked a mushroomy dinner, then went to bed. Two days later she had raging cystitis. She took antibiotics for the infection, plus paracetamol for the fever and pain, and swallowed gallons of cranberry juice. Performing a very long symphony by Mahler at the Royal Festival Hall while her bladder twinged and cramped, she was horrified to catch herself wondering whether things between her and Richard were quite as marvellous as she'd thought. Lindy had jarred her certainties enough to make her wobble and keep wobbling.

She hadn't known what it meant to miss someone until she broke off with him. Crying her eyes out, she'd buried the telephone under an iron casserole and three cushions to stop herself calling him. Lindy, taking the blame, cooked bean stew for her and let her mourn. What if she hadn't mustered every ounce of her will-power to leave him? Wouldn't she be happy, instead of devastated? First, she'd wondered this once an hour. Then once a week; slowly, less.

With Julian, sex is as comfortable as morning coffee. She hasn't had cystitis for years; free from the pain, anxiety and exhaustion brought on by recurrent bladder infections, she long ago decided that since she'd experienced unimagined heights of passion with a lover once, perhaps she doesn't have to again. At least Jamie proves that she must have made the right choice.

Karina opens her eyes early, in the too-bright summer morning. Music is blaring through the house, a full orchestra going hell for leather in the living room.

'Jules? What are you doing?'

Downstairs, she finds him in his armchair, opposite and precisely midway between the two Bang & Olufsen loudspeakers, eyes closed, head raised, hands folded. Karina puts a hand over one ear.

'Why are you playing *Ein Heldenleben* at this time of morning?'

'Lunch with Carsten Schmidt,' Julian says, without moving. 'Strauss helps to get me going. Trying to feel I can be a hero too.'

'It's very loud.'

'So it should be.'

'It's six o'clock in the morning.'

'Well, I have to leave at half past. Come on, darling one, why don't you pop on a pot of coffee? I promise you,' he adds, while Karina turns away, recalcitrant, 'if you had to have lunch with Carsten Schmidt, you'd do exactly the same.'

10

Julian is accustomed to stress, but not this kind. He doesn't generally lose clients. Carsten Schmidt is sipping red wine at the club, his face like granite. They've been discussing the Wood Green collision.

'We will have to reassess our costs,' Carsten says. 'I'm not sure we should go ahead unless we can ensure greater protection for our customers, our employees and our business.' The government's reluctance to help fund safety systems on the trains has become a major sticking point.

Julian tries to be diplomatic: naturally Locomotivation will only bid for the franchise if there's profit in it. He's restated the obvious advantages: international expansion, raising the company profile, the prestige of running one of the lines that will carry crowds hundreds of thousands strong to the Olympic Games in 2012. He's also noted that Germany is not immune to train crashes.

'What about security?' Carsten demands. 'The Olympics are a prime target for terrorism. This I don't like. You have to admit it, my friend, this country's strong ability is not in organisation.'

'Everything will be extremely well planned,' Julian says in his most soothing tone. He wishes he liked Carsten. He tries not to give way to ancient British prejudices about Germans – putting out the towels, and so on. 'Carsten, my own cousin died at Wood Green – I of all people know how vital it is to prioritise safety. I swear I'll do all I can to support you.' Under the table, he presses his own left toe with his right heel, trying to keep irritation at bay. A stress band is tightening above his ears. If he doesn't convince Carsten, if he's responsible for losing Locomotivation's business . . . well, it won't affect his position, it won't do any damage, but it won't look good and it won't help him make this year's target.

Of course, there's no danger he won't make it. But if there's something Julian hates, it's wasting time.

Now that it's September, Jamie must be made ready for St Matthew's. Karina takes him to Brighton to buy his uniform, sports boots and new pyjamas; she spends a numb afternoon stitching name labels into socks and pants. She notes the cost of forthcoming school trips to London, Cornwall (the Eden Project) and Snowdonia (an activity weekend including, to her horror, white-water rafting). Presumably such excursions have to be good for the boys, and safe – haven't they? Everything progresses smoothly until the last moment.

When it's time to go, though, Jamie decides that maybe boarding-school wasn't one of his better ideas after all. He grows quieter and quieter while they drive to Chichester, then falls silent walking up the stone stairs into the hallway. Karina and Julian shake hands with welcoming teachers and try to forge links with some other newcomers. In Jamie's cubicle room, Karina, a lump in her throat the size of a cricket ball, arranges his clothes and books, puts his favourite toy dog on the pillow and makes sure that the right blockages are set up on his mobile phone. But when they walk him towards the dining room for tea with the other boys, Jamie's face begins to crumple. He throws himself at her and locks on to her waist, howling like a two-year-old.

'Hush, darling.' She clutches him, trying to remember how his hug feels, to sustain her during the week ahead. She hadn't realised how strong his grip could be.

'Come on, Jimbo,' Julian says. 'You're a big boy now.'

'*Mummy!*'

Karina wants to howl with him. She prises his left arm away; then his right. 'It's only a few days until the weekend, Schnooky,' she whispers. 'Before you know it, you'll be home again, and by then you'll be able to tell me about all your new friends.'

'Don't go, Mum.' He looks so small and pale, bereft in the middle of the entrance hall, that Karina cracks.

'I can't do this,' she whispers to Julian. 'I'm bringing him home.'

'Don't be silly. He'll be used to it in half an hour.'

'Can you look at him like this, and leave him?'

'I can, and so can you. Don't throw away this chance, Karrie. Don't let him throw it away.'

'Jules, you're heartless.'

'Karrie, you're brainless.'

The Year Three tutor breaks the deadlock for them, glancing from tearful child to resentful mother and impatient father. She puts a hand gently on Jamie's shoulder.

'Come along, Jamie,' she says. 'We're all going to have tea with scones now. Come and meet your new housemates. Mr Rookfield, Mrs Rookfield, please don't worry. Leaving the lads is always hard the first time, I know, but we'll take good care of him.'

Karina can't speak. Julian shakes the tutor's hand, puts an arm round Karina and says, 'See you Friday night, Jimbo.'

'See you.' Jamie's eyes turn to the floor as the tutor leads him off. Karina, following Julian, doesn't dare look back while her son pads away round the corner.

After a dismal five days, the weekend feels like an oasis. Karina picks up Jamie on Friday night; the three of them spend quality time on Saturday afternoon and Sunday, with a windy walk on the Downs and tea with the Pearsons. Jamie chatters and laughs, full of stories of the other boys and the teachers, just as she'd told him he would be. She feels idiotically disappointed.

'Don't you want him to settle in?' Julian demands.

'Of course I do, but I also want him to be home.'

Reality kicks in with the second week. This is how it will be from now on, probably for the next ten years. Alone, when she isn't teaching, Karina wanders through Lewes for the sake of it. She breathes sharpening autumn air from the sea, explores hilly back-streets, decides to train herself to walk quickly for exercise, but also to notice the plants changing colour in the cottage gardens and the way each house is different from the last. She wonders whether to advertise for more pupils, now that she has too much time.

'I'll recommend you to the head of the junior Academy,' Dénes suggests on the phone. 'They should be so lucky to have you.'

'Dad, it's difficult – the junior Academy's on Saturdays and I need to be home for Jamie.'

'We'll meet next Monday to discuss the memorial service with

Cynthia, and we can talk about this then,' Dénes suggests. 'I don't like it that you have first to send away your son, then your life is ruled by a schedule that does your teaching no good. Your work is important too, no?'

'What choice do I have?' says Karina. Her father grunts an annoyed goodnight.

On Monday afternoon, Karina arrives to find Cynthia pacing about in the Rookfields' kitchen, planning Lindy's memorial service. Her weight is melting in her grief. As etiolated as a light-starved seedling, she explains in a great rush that she wants to book St Mary's Church, send out invitations, have Karina and Erzsébet play.

Karina, too, is thinner. There's a gnawing emptiness inside her, a plughole of lassitude that swallows her energy. Would a memorial service make any difference? Lindy would still be gone. 'Perhaps rather than calling it a memorial service,' she suggests, 'you could call it something like Service for Lindy. Make it a celebration of her life. I'd love to play, if you want me to.'

'If I can convince Martin to celebrate his daughter's life,' says Cynthia, acid, 'that would be very nice.' Pom-Pom, the squash-faced cat, loops the loop round Cynthia's legs. She picks it up and hides her face in its long beige fur.

Dénes and Erzsébet appear on the doorstep a minute later. After an hour and a half thrashing out the service's content with Cynthia, who needs their company more than their advice, they take Karina home with them for an early dinner. Finally she leaves at eight o'clock, tired out. She takes a train to Clapham Junction, then makes her way through the underpass to platform 13 for the Lewes train.

The platform is thronging. The electronic information sign, announcing the next train in a sputter of yellow lights, says DELAYED. Karina, her feet feeling heavy on the asphalt, passes groups of anxious travellers who are trying to get to Gatwick Airport. An announcement blares out: 'Due to signalling problems, we regret that trains to Eastbourne and Southampton are experiencing severe delays and Brighton trains are currently suspended north of Haywards Heath. We are sorry for any inconvenience this may cause to your journey.'

After ten minutes of stasis, Karina asks a stationmaster what's happening.

'Wish we knew, love.'

Since the accident, any delay on the trains upsets Karina too much. Those words could mask anything: a security scare, a fire, an explosion. Stalled trains on the line, ostensibly harmless, could indicate that further away, people are losing their lives. Maybe this isn't rational, but Karina's stomach lurches. At least Jamie isn't waiting for her. She phones Julian, hoping that he could come to meet her somewhere else in Sussex, where the trains are working.

'Oh, Karrie.' He sounds as exhausted as she feels. 'I've just got in. Darling one, I've had a shit day. Lousy meeting, bloody Carsten. Normally I'd come out, but . . . Just hang on a little longer, all right? They must get things moving soon.'

Since Jamie went away, Karina has felt reluctant to spend extra time in Julian's company. If he'd helped her, just this once, that would have helped them both. She tells herself it's bad luck, nothing more. 'I'll keep you posted,' she says, and rings off.

At nine fifteen, the headlights of a train gleam in the distance. Frustration hums through the station. The Gatwick passengers are white with fury: they may miss their flights. Karina hurries to the end of the platform as the train pulls up, hoping to find a carriage less crammed than the others. The doors open; there's scant room even to climb aboard, but while she's picking her way through the crush, a woman jumps up from a seat nearby and rushes out, having fallen asleep during the extended trundle from Victoria. Her seat is the last available. Nobody else takes it, so Karina flops down, grateful. She closes her eyes to keep her claustrophobia at bay.

'Signal failure, hey?' the man opposite her remarks. He has an interesting accent, familiar, although she can't place it. 'Not leaves on the line this time?'

'Something like that,' Karina mumbles. She wonders where he comes from – his voice is pleasant, oddly warm – but she's too tired to bother asking.

There's a warning squeal, the doors thump shut and the train begins to move. Sleep swims through Karina while she inches towards home.

Just before Haywards Heath, there's a screech of brakes and a jolt. The train stops. Groans go up around her. She drifts awake.

'Over two hours from Victoria,' someone grumbles. Anxiety shreds the back of her mind. An announcement from the guard crackles out: 'Ladies and gentlemen, we're sorry for this delay, which is due to signalling problems. We hope to be on our way again as soon as possible. Please listen for further announcements.'

The carriage settles into disgruntled acceptance. Things are quieter now. The Gatwick passengers have gone; few boarded in their place. A whiff of burgers and chips rises from the waste-bins. The man with the interesting voice, who has dark hair, a long face and a green scarf, is trying to peer at his neighbour's newspaper without being noticed. Why do people so dislike other people reading over their shoulder? What does it matter? Karina is about to close her eyes again, when she hears something that shakes her alert. Of all things, a violin.

She turns, then blinks. A swarthy-faced man in a dark T-shirt and jeans is walking through the carriage, playing Monti's *Csárdás*. Behind him walks a small boy, bright eyed, dusky skinned, not much bigger than Jamie, carrying a beret upturned to receive coins. Middle Eastern? Indian? Roma? As Karina watches, the violinist tosses out from the instrument a stream of shimmering, decorative phrases that make her gulp with amazement. She has to be dreaming. Gypsy violinists don't go busking on trains in Sussex.

The fiddler and his child reach the space by the doors; the father tunes a string, then begins a new number. The child wanders from bank to bank of seats, holding out the hat: 'For the music.' Passengers staple their gazes to their books and newspapers; they only want quiet at the end of a long day.

Karina, listening, feels her throat constrict. This man is playing out the sorrows of centuries: piercing truth in the middle of a train trapped at a red signal. She opens her handbag. When the child trots over, she holds out a two-pound coin. At the same moment, a hand holding a similar coin extends, mirrorlike, opposite her. The child looks from one to the other, flashes a delighted grin and rattles the coins triumphantly together.

Karina glances up into the face of the man with the interesting voice. He's watching her as if he knows her.

'That really got to you, didn't it?' he says. Can she detect in his eyes, which are dark and rather beautiful, a trace of the tears she's been holding back? A question mark flickers in her mind.

'It did,' she admits. 'You too?'

'Wow.' The stranger gives a sigh. 'He can really play the fiddle, hey?'

'Your accent's familiar,' Karina says. 'Where are you from?'

'I was going to ask you the same thing.' He leans his head to one side and smiles at her. He's wearing a brown jacket, a deep green sweater and, beneath, a bright linen shirt. His shoulders are very broad and his hands look twice the size of Karina's.

'I don't have an accent, do I?' she asks.

'Well, do I? I shouldn't. Tell me yours and I'll tell you mine.'

'Twickenham.'

'Go on! Something exotic. East European?'

'All right, Professor Higgins.' Teasing this sudden friend who feels the busking fiddler's music as deeply as she does, Karina's wide awake. 'I was born in Twickenham, but my parents are Hungarian.'

'So you know a Gypsy violinist when you hear one.'

Karina hesitates. To explain to a total stranger on a stalled train . . . 'Your turn,' she suggests.

'South Africa. Saarth Iffrica.' He gives a wide, soft smile, poking fun at his own accent. Karina watches his features: long, pointed nose, high cheekbones with a certain refinement to their tilt, and a gaze so direct that it's nearly uncomfortable. 'I'm originally from Cape Town,' he says. 'I've lived here all my life, but I picked up a bit of the voice from my parents, though I shouldn't have any left. Only someone with a very good ear can spot it.'

'It's nice. Musical.'

'And *you* have a way of *puuut*ting *the* stress on *the* first *syl*lable *of ev*ery word.'

'That's good,' Karina laughs. 'Very good. You must be an actor.'

'No way. I'm a musician.' He points up at the luggage rack.

Karina looks: above them sits a violin case. She'd been too tired to notice it earlier. Her breath becomes confused for a moment, between in and out. 'But I'm a violinist too,' she says.

'You're kidding!' The smile widens, and now Karina spots the violinists' giveaway, which his scarf had hidden: a red weal on the neck between chin and left ear. 'So, where do you play?' he asks.

'Nowhere, really, not any more. But I used to be with the British Symphony Orchestra.'

'Wow! And you left?'

'Yes. I hated it,' Karina confides. Funny. It had taken her months to confess to Julian how much she loathed the orchestra.

'Don't I know the feeling,' says the violinist. 'I don't do orchestras any more either. I'm in a string quartet. The St Francis Quartet.'

Karina recognises the name. 'I've heard you on the radio, then. You're doing well, aren't you?'

'Theoretically. It's hard to make a living, but it's fun. I freelance too, when I can – concertos, recitals sometimes. I've got a New York debut recital next spring – that's pretty terrifying, though it's a great opportunity. Do you ever play quartets?'

'Mostly I teach – mainly little ones, at home.'

'So, where do you live?'

Karina tells him and when he nods – he knows Lewes – she finds herself describing the street and the house.

He lives in Brighton. He wouldn't normally be on the Lewes train, but the Brighton line is screwed today, like everything else; he'll change at Haywards Heath. 'I've been up for a rehearsal,' he explains. 'And to collect something. We just made our first CD.' He jumps up – he's easily as tall as Julian, and moves with a fluid, appealing grace; unzipping the pocket of his violin case, he retrieves a CD box. Karina takes it: Schubert, played by the St Francis Quartet. Harry Macintosh, second violin; Yevgeny Koslovsky, viola; Malcolm Griffiths, cello. And first violin: Rohan Masterson.

'That's you?'

'Guilty,' says Rohan, smiling.

'It sounds Indian.'

'It's from Sanskrit. My parents had funny taste in names.'

'Sanskrit?' Hadn't Mimi once told her that Romany was derived from Sanskrit? Is this any moment to start explaining what little she knows of this history? She glances at the backs of the fiddler and his son, who are making their way through the connecting door to the next carriage.

'I often hear that Hungarian musicians don't really like Gypsy playing,' Rohan remarks, following her gaze, perhaps puzzled by her reaction.

'I'm kind of both.' She'd normally hesitate over admitting this. 'Do you know Mimi Rácz?'

'Of course! She's one of my heroines.' Rohan's expression fills with light.

Karina takes this in, then says, 'She's my grandmother.'

The information seems to hit a nerve beyond the norm. 'I don't believe it,' Rohan says eventually, shaking his head. 'But this is incredible. The thing is, Marc Duplessis—'

An announcement interrupts: 'Ladies and gentlemen, we apologise for the delay, but we now have the signal to proceed. We will shortly be arriving at Haywards Heath. Please remember to take all your belongings with you when you leave the train.'

'Shit,' Rohan says.

He and Karina gaze at one another, each wondering where they go from here. The train shivers into motion. Rohan glances at Karina's left hand, where diamonds and gold catch the light.

'So, what's your name? Are you a Rácz as well?' he asks.

'Veres. Karina Veres.'

'Pleased to meet you.' He squeezes her hand. She has a fleeting impression of heat, strength, enthusiasm – before she realises what she's said.

'My married name's Rookfield,' she adds, guilt-stricken.

'Is your husband a musician too?' His expression doesn't change.

'No, he's a lawyer. A proper job!'

'What kind of law? My sister, Liora, is a solicitor.'

'He's with a city firm. His speciality is the railway business.'

The train begins to move in earnest while Karina and Rohan crease up laughing together at this unintended irony. Once they've started, they find they can't stop. Karina claps her hands and throws back her hair. Other passengers glance at them, amused.

'Oh, God!' Rohan wipes his eyes. 'That was priceless. Karina, listen, I've got to get off this train in a moment. Please, please, *please* give me your number? There's something I want to tell you about Marc Duplessis. It's important, but it would take too long right now.'

Karina opens her bag, looking for a pen. Then she freezes.

'It's OK,' Rohan prompts. 'I know you're married. I'm not going to pester you, I promise.'

Karina says nothing. Her mind is pounding out warnings, louder than an orchestra at full throttle. But it's a straight choice between seeing a kindred soul again, or not.

'Please, Karina,' Rohan presses. 'Like I said, it's important, you *will* think so too, and I can't squeeze it into two minutes.'

Karina thinks of Jamie's face when she dropped him at school on Sunday night, and of Julian, pale eyes betraying impatience: don't waste time. She thinks of Lindy. And whether it's Rohan's words that sway her, or the fracas over Jamie, or Lindy's lost life, or simply the fact that if Julian had come to meet her she'd have been home hours ago, she isn't certain. The lights of Haywards Heath station pull into view, a sickly off-white in the dark. She can give him her number; or not. If she doesn't, he'll go and she'll never see him again, and she couldn't bear that.

'Hey,' says Rohan. 'Take my number. Call me now and then I'll have yours.' Karina finds she's pulling out her phone and pressing in the number he recites. His handset tinkles out a phrase of Mozart. 'Great. That's it, then. Karina, wonderful to meet you. See you soon, I hope.'

Rohan swings his violin case and a small rucksack down from the rack and makes for the doors. As they open, he glances back and smiles at her. She lifts a hand. A second later, Rohan Masterson and his violin have disappeared into the night.

Karina shuts her eyes and, bailing out her inundated mind, waits for the train to take her home.

11

Mimi is having a good day, playing her old recordings and dreaming about the past. Karina, spending a late October Monday afternoon with her, basks in the brief resurrection of the tigerish energy she once knew so well.

'Listen to this one, Schnooky.' Mimi prises a CD out of a case. 'Marc Duplessis.'

Karina listens.

'The first movement represents the wandering minstrel, the Gypsy fiddler,' Mimi tells her. Karina knows, but nods. The violin speaks: skittering, swooping, enticing with the hint of exotic places in off-centre intonation. 'Telling strange tales, fascinating the child who listens and watches. That's the child – that swoop up. A question mark.'

'What was he like, Duplessis?'

Mimi sits back in her armchair. The room resonates with the sound of her violin, captured forty years earlier. 'Time goes fast, Schnooky. Isn't it funny? I can remember forty years ago, but I cannot remember yesterday. Marc. Ach, Marc Duplessis.' Mimi shakes her head; then, to Karina's astonishment, she winks.

'Was he in love with you?'

'Such a long time ago . . . Now, my dear. Tell me your news.'

'Not much. I haven't seen Jamie for over a week. The school took them on an activity weekend in Wales. But, Grandma – about Duplessis—?' Tantalised, she wants to ask a thousand questions, but Mimi won't have it.

'How do you feel? In *you*?'

'I feel . . . lost. Perhaps it's Jamie going away to school, or Lindy, or both. Does that make sense?'

'Why do you need it to make sense, Karina? Things don't.'

That doesn't help as much as her grandmother probably intends it to. 'I feel as if I were on that train with Lindy. I feel as if I've been blown up too. I don't know where I belong any more.'

'Shh. Listen.' Mimi's recorded violin whispers the forest scene from the Suite. To Duplessis, she'd once told Karina, the forest represented the central force of childhood, where the mystery lay: the symbol of everything tempting and forbidden. Karina remembers the skipping song Lindy used to tease her with when they were small. '*My mother said I never should, Play with the Gypsies in the wood.*'

'One doesn't need to belong somewhere,' Mimi says. 'We belonged with our own kind, but nowhere in terms of place. In the old days.'

'The old country,' Karina smiles.

'Not ours, though. The Roma are a people without a homeland. Why you think people make us scapegoats all these centuries? That's why. Music is my homeland and my language, and when you're a musician, you belong with other musicians. The place doesn't matter. You speak through music, and they will understand. I tried so hard to forget my childhood, my dear, but you cannot forget, you cannot betray your roots. I learned this in such a hard way. Ach – listen to this – this was my favourite part . . .'

Where can you belong, when your ancestors belonged nowhere? Nowhere too? Or everywhere? Karina goes home by train, musing. Everything runs smoothly. No buskers appear. Opposite her, a bored girl ruffles a magazine with claw-nailed fingers. Weeks have passed since Karina met Rohan Masterson; for all his eagerness, he hasn't called. She hasn't listened to his CD. It lies under a heap of letters and magazines on the ex-Fairfallows bureau she uses for her paperwork, the only proof that she didn't dream that strange journey.

As she unlocks the door, her mobile rings. 'Darling, there's a smash on the M23. I'll be late,' Julian says.

'OK,' says Karina. 'See you later.'

She will have, potentially, two hours to herself; it's Monday. No pupils; no Jamie to feed, play with, read to and put to bed. Nothing worth watching on TV. Perhaps she should start taking pupils on Mondays after all. She retrieves Rohan's CD from the bureau and slots it into the machine.

Schubert: the soft opening of the A minor quartet. The second violin purls an accompanying figure, the cello shudders beneath. The melody drifts over the top, a sigh from Rohan's violin. Sweetness; fine, intense, edgy sound; delicate variations in the vibrato drawing out the nuances; occasional slides between notes, which show that Rohan is a romantic. He plays almost the way he talks. The weeks roll back; she seems to be with him again, at ease and alarmed all at once. She drinks the music like a tonic. When the disc finishes, she restarts it.

She looks him up on the Internet: ROHAN MASTERSON VIOLIN. The St Francis Quartet's website shows four men in their thirties and forties. The cellist, Malcolm, sports a fountain of prematurely silver hair. A bespectacled, gingerish younger man – Harry – is holding another violin; the violist, Yevgeny, is on the right in a leather jacket, looking as if he personally is hiring out the entire group. Rohan stands to the left, wearing an open-necked shirt patterned in earth colours; his head leans to one side, his dark, sugar-laden eyes are just as she remembers them. She reads.

> **ROHAN MASTERSON (first violin)** Rohan was born in Cape Town in 1968 and moved with his family to Britain in 1970. He studied at the Yehudi Menuhin School, then at the Royal Academy of Music in London and with Ernő Nagy in Canada. Prizes at the 1989 Leopold Auer Competition in Philadelphia and the 1990 Ravel-Morhange Competition in Lyon helped to launch him into the international arena. Rohan often appears as soloist in concertos and recitals across Europe and he enjoys teaching and leading youth projects for budding musicians. He also composes, counting a string quartet and several pieces for violin and piano among his works.

Ernő Nagy was Hungarian, Karina remembers, with a disproportionate thrill. And Rohan composes? For a moment, she's disturbed by the thought of Richard, the other composer in her life. She resumes her search.

> **REVIEW – St Francis Quartet, Wigmore Hall, October 2005**
> Taking its name from the most gentle of saints, the St Francis String Quartet is a dynamic group in which tension is as productive as passion: four strong personalities each with a

> contribution to make, adding up to a thoroughly satisfying whole. The penetrating, eloquent timbre of Rohan Masterson's violin spearheaded an evening of edge-of-the-seat musicianship . . .

Karina finds photos, a concert schedule, more reviews. She stumbles on an interview in an American magazine that tells her even less about him than she'd learned during their conversation on the train.

The phone rings. 'Sweetie, I'm just leaving the M23,' says Julian. 'I'll see you in about twenty minutes.'

Karina closes down the computer, switches off the CD and takes out her violin. She should have used this time to practise for Lindy's memorial service, not to snoop into the life of a complete stranger who's vanished every bit as fast as he appeared.

'Karrie? Hello? Anybody home?' Julian stares across the dinner table at the silent Karina. 'If you won't talk to me,' he says, 'how can I help you?'

And if you won't let me grow, her mind replies, if you won't grow with me, I'll have to grow without you. But how can I leave you behind if I love you? The phrases don't make sense even to her, so she says nothing.

'Darling,' says Julian, 'what, other than losing Lindy and getting used to Jamie being at school, is making you so unhappy? What do you want?'

'Isn't that enough?'

'Do you want to go back to the orchestra? Do you want to move back to London? What's got into you? I don't understand.'

The rain beats down on St Mary's Church while Karina, Julian and Jamie, huddled together under two umbrellas, join a throng of people trailing up the path to the Service for Belinda. Inside, the resident grand piano stands near the altar, almost in lieu of a coffin.

Martin, inscrutable behind his glasses, shakes their hands formally; Cynthia, whose grey and black dress appears stitched from a hundred silk handkerchiefs, hovers fluttery and tremulous beside him. Friend after friend greets them. Karina embraces her parents and takes her violin case into the vestry.

Warming up, she watches the assembling guests from a safe distance. There's Alban in a black suit; the horse-chestnut gleam of Nicki's hair; Charles, aquiline-nosed and wearing a trench coat, keeping to the shadows at the back; and a confluence of Rookfield relations, none of them close to Lindy, each horsier than the last. Karina retrieves a pack of beta blockers from her purse and bites off half a pill, hoping it will work fast.

She carries out her violin and joins her family in a pew near the front. Beeswax, flowers and damp mingle their scents around her; raindrops patter overhead in muted counterpoint to the organ music. Bitterness lingers in her mouth, not only from the medicine. Gradually, she senses her heartbeat calming and the tremble in her hands with it.

The vicar intones words and prayers; everyone sings a hymn. A reading and a speech go by, then a psalm – the shadow of the valley of death; next, Karina and Erzsébet walk up to the piano. This music had no significance for Lindy. Beethoven would have been better; Lindy deserved nothing less furious than the 'Kreutzer' Sonata – but tranquil Mozart could create a time for reflection, geared to the living, not the dead. Karina's violin sings out; while she plays, occasional snuffles sound in the congregation, people rustling for hankies, a child asking a question. Going back to her seat afterwards, she looks at her watch. Another twenty minutes and this ordeal will be over.

By the time the last hymn finishes and the vicar announces that tea will be served in York House, Karina has begun to wonder how to keep her self-control. Beta blockers stop physical symptoms, but not mental ones. Rage isn't what you should feel at your friend's memorial service, but she can't help it. As if anything in this frightful afternoon could so much as begin to do justice to Lindy's memory. She wants to grab Lindy's shoulders and shake her: how could you put us through this? She itches to shop Alban to the police. What does he do? People-trafficking? Drugs? Both? He was the last person to see Lindy alive. Why didn't he stop her getting on that train? As for Charles, she'd string him up by the ankles and whip him black and blue. Yet tea, which she can't avoid, will be full of polite condolences, delivered in the same tone as remarks about the miserable weather.

'Mummy?' Jamie cuddles up, looking sorry for himself. Karina puts an arm round him and forces herself to smother her anger, as she always does.

When the door opens, November chill swamps the church. People Karina doesn't want to see keep wanting to see her.

'Karrie, darling!' Nicki sails up and hugs her. 'Karrie, you played *so* beautifully. You should do more playing, it's such a shame to let it go. Listen, we absolutely must get together and have a little catch-up.'

'That would be nice,' Karina lies.

'We're doing a memorial performance of *Distant Beloved*,' Nicki adds. 'It would be so lovely if you'd come.'

'I'll try.' Karina forces a smile. 'Please excuse me, I have to say hello to someone.'

Alban kisses her hand. 'Of all memorials,' he says, 'music is the most beautiful. This expresses everything we cannot express any other way.'

'Alban, tell me what happened that last night?' Karina demands.

He stares intently into her eyes and begins to talk. Karina wonders how much to believe. Lindy was drunk and extremely upset, he explains; he hadn't wanted to leave her on her own. She'd come back with him, crashed out in the spare room, and, as he'd promised, he woke her in the morning for work. She'd had a massive hangover, but set off for the train at a run saying, 'See you later.' He never saw her again.

The academic in the grey trenchcoat waits until Karina passes him to say, 'Karina? Thank you for your playing. I'm Charles.'

She's not certain how to greet him. She holds out a hand.

'It's wonderful to meet you at last,' Charles says, taking it, 'though I wish it could have been in other circumstances.'

'Likewise.' Karina looks up at him. His eyes contain myriad sorrows.

'I don't know what to say,' he adds.

Nor does Karina. She manages, 'Thanks for coming today.' Julian has led Jamie over to his grandparents; they're out of earshot.

Charles lowers his voice. 'I did love her, you know. She was the most extraordinary woman I'd ever met. I had the greatest respect for her, and the greatest love. Karina, I know you must hate me. I can only imagine what she must have said to you about me. Please try to understand. I'd have done anything for her. It's just that . . .'

Anything except leave your wife, Karina thinks. Anything except tell the truth. Yet she remembers Lindy saying, 'There's real love between us . . .'

'Christ,' says Charles. 'It's too late to put it right now. I miss her so much.'

Karina wonders why grief changes your attitudes to people. She has nothing to say to Nicki, who had once been her friend; and now, instead of whipping Charles, she wants to hug him. 'Are you coming to tea?' she asks politely.

'I'd better not, but thank you for asking. And Karina – please stay in touch if you can? Here's my card.'

'Charles, take care.' Putting the card in her pocket, Karina watches Lindy's lover dissolve into the dusk. His words echo inside her. Perhaps Lindy was right. Perhaps they really did love one another and it's only now that he recognises how much. But how to admit you love someone when all sense militates against it?

She slings her violin case over her shoulder and calls to Jamie. It's time she forgot about Rohan. He's lingered in her mind for a month. What of that undisclosed 'important thing'? A ploy to get her number? From today, she decides, bundling Jamie into his rain jacket, she'll never think of Rohan again.

Tea means wine and fish-paste sandwiches in a reception room overlooking the river. Nicki and Alban have both vanished. Julian is soon trapped by some buck-toothed Rookfield acolytes who are grumbling about the fox-hunting ban. Dénes and Erzsébet talk to Arthur and Anne. Dénes turns on the charm and begins his best impersonations of famous conductors and politicians in an effort to liven things up. 'Well, my name is . . .Tony Blair, and I must . . . say that . . . Gordon and I are the . . . best of friends . . .' he squeaks, morphing his tones into the most parliamentarian he can manage. But after a few minutes, Cynthia crumples and runs out, with Anne hurrying after her.

'I hate fish paste,' Jamie whines; he's tired, overwrought and upset at how he's had to spend his Saturday. Karina swallows a second glass of claret too fast, then realises that she can't walk in a straight line. 'Let's go,' Julian mutters.

In the car, Jamie begins to chant under his breath: 'Lindy Rookfield, you will come back, you will, you will, you will.'

'Jamie,' Julian says, 'this has got to stop. I know you miss her. We all miss her. But you can't keep doing this. It's been five months now. It's an important lesson: we have to carry on.'

Jamie begins to wail instead. Karina doesn't know what to say, so she stays silent, hunting in her bag for a tissue for him.

Her mobile phone is beeping. The screen declares: *New message from ROHAN*. Had someone told him that she'd decided, this very afternoon, never to think of him again?

'Back. Lunch? R.'

12

According to Magda Frankl, the French language was the most elegant, precise and poetic in the world. Mimi struggled to learn it, but communicating with Marc didn't require much talking. Marc with his big, kind eyes and soft voice, forward and shy all at the same time: her swain. The Amati violin in her arms, her perfect voice. She shouldn't accept it, but how to refuse? What possessed a Frenchman to write a suite about a Hungarian Gypsy child? 'You possessed me,' said Marc. It was a year since she had met him and Tamás Veres within four days of each other.

Tamás said that he wanted to marry her. Marc just sat opposite her and gazed. Tamás was Hungarian; he spoke her language, he understood her situation and looked for ways to circumvent the barriers between them. Marc saw no barriers; he only heard the music inside her. He looked, listened, then went away to write. Meeting him again to play his composition, Mimi had no idea what to expect.

Perhaps every life holds one immortal night that unfolds in slow motion, the culmination of all that's gone before and the seed of everything that will follow. 'The Wedding', the last movement, whirls to a false end, then quietens into an unexpected coda: the piece's kernel is not in the force of their love, but in its softness. That night, while the Châtelet held its breath, Mimi knew that Marc had understood that hidden tenderness inside her before she understood it herself. He'd even spotted her ideal violin – the Amati was strong but intimate, a mirror for her inner self, concealed from everybody yet apparently not from him. How can any person know another so well, simply by intuition? She stood centre stage, holding Marc's hand; together they raised their arms to the crowd. Flowers, bouquet after bouquet; stray petals of yellow and white caught in her red silk dress. The audience was on its feet, roaring approval.

They walked out of the light, Marc's hand around hers. In the shadows, his arm circled her waist. She looked up. One kiss. She'd kissed Tamás Veres in Budapest. They'd been meeting in secret because his family hated Gypsies, and they'd kissed. Before she left for her tour, he'd said that she must consider herself engaged; he didn't care what his family thought. Still, nothing was settled. One kiss couldn't hurt. She tried it, and it didn't.

The dinner at the hotel, chandeliers, champagne, oysters – then some comment from a newspaper man at the far end of the table, something about Jews and Gypsies and gutters, and Marc leapt up, held out a hand to Mimi and led her out. She hadn't heard the remark properly, but it made her cry in any case, wrecking her perfect evening, and Marc wouldn't leave her to weep alone.

It was all slow motion, though in memory it was too fast, playing and replaying, twizzling through fast-forwards and rewinds; Mimi can still feel the way his body pleaded with hers, and as he unpeeled her dress she said, 'I'm supposed to be engaged,' and Marc just said, 'Hush,' and then they hadn't spoken for over an hour. One kiss couldn't hurt.

'Then what happened?' Rohan leans forward, chin on hand, elbows propped on the wooden table. Over their heads fly angels and stars. Brighton's favourite health food restaurant, piping out Christmas carols, is decked with tinsel and shining seasonal cut-outs. Karina, too warm in her bronze cashmere pullover, is outlining why she left her orchestra. Neither of them has made much headway with their lunch.

'My bow started to shake,' she says; she knows Rohan empathises. 'Once someone in your section starts telling you that your playing doesn't blend in, it's impossible not to feel you're being watched. They kept saying I was too loud . . .'

'Too much Hungarian vigour?'

'Probably.' Karina smiles.

'Did József talk about controlling the bow as if it's a pencil?'

'All the time! And the sound comes from the weight, the way you manipulate gravity.' They've already worked out that József and Ernő Nagy had been classmates under the same professor in Budapest.

'But seriously,' Rohan presses, 'that was enough to make you leave?'

'When you can hardly keep your bow on the string in long, quiet notes because you're terrified that you'll stick out and then lose your job, and you're on the platform of the Royal Festival Hall, it doesn't feel great.'

'That's awful. We have fisticuffs in the quartet, but when it comes to playing, we pull together.'

'So did we. But it just wrecked me. My father has two ways of describing people he doesn't like – either they're "fucking cunts" or they're "Rottweilers". In this case it was both. Anyway, I started taking beta blockers, but eventually I'd taken so many that they stopped being effective, I had to up the dose, and my GP said that if I carried on I could end up with serious digestion problems. Sorry, I don't want to put you off your lunch!'

'Go on. I want to know.'

'And Richard – my boyfriend at the time – kept saying I should leave, but I didn't want to freelance and he was a composer, he wasn't earning much, just going from grant to grant and doing a bit of teaching . . .'

'Was that why you broke up?'

'Not really.' Karina stalls, remembering that Rohan composes too. 'There were all kinds of problems.'

'I can imagine. My girlfriend ran away with the dog trainer.'

Rohan had lived with a flautist for four years in south London. She'd wanted children, but he'd hoped for more stability first, preferably enough solo work to support a family. Lonely at home while he travelled, she'd adopted a boisterous golden retriever puppy. 'I was away all the time,' Rohan explains, 'so she took the pooch to dog-training school. Then she seemed to get obsessed with it. Only it wasn't the dog she was obsessed with, but the trainer. I came back from Norway and found she'd moved out and taken Goldie with her.' He grins. 'I really missed Goldie!'

They laugh together, Karina clapping her hands and flinging back her hair. Rohan watches her, head on one side.

'So that was when?' she asks, calming down.

'Two years ago. What about you and the composer?'

'It didn't seem to be going anywhere, and eventually I left him. Then Lindy introduced me to her cousin Julian. Before I knew what had happened we'd got married and Jamie arrived . . .' She hesitates. How much to tell him? 'I didn't know what had hit me. At the antenatal group the other mothers were all older than me, and they seemed so confident. I'd left the orchestra because Julian saw how I was living, said I was crazy and made me get out. But one minute I was playing at the Royal Festival Hall twice a week and going on tour to Paris and Berlin and the Salzburg Festival, and next thing I know, I'm miles from my parents and my friends with this – little creature. Who needs me. And I adore him, I'd lay down my life for him . . .'

He taps the back of her wrist with a fingertip. 'Are you happy? Or content?'

'How do you mean?'

'I'm happy, but not content. I get the impression that maybe you're content, but not happy.'

'I don't know.' There's a pause.

'There's something aristocratic in Julian's family?' Rohan prods. Karina puts down her fork and describes Fairfallows.

'. . . and then in 1999 with the House of Lords reforms, Arthur lost his seat,' she adds.

'Did he leave it in Edinburgh?' Rohan laughs, delighted. Why doesn't Julian laugh like this? Then he says, 'Tell me about your grandmother. She must have been amazing.'

'She still is, in her own way. Her focus comes and goes. She had a stroke a little while ago. Some days she's fine. Others . . . But yes, she's wonderful. She's a big personality – old style, the way people often were in that generation, especially in music. I've learned so much from her – just by her being there.'

'Karina, I don't want to impose, especially if she's not well,' Rohan begins, 'but, you know, I'd love to meet her. There's such a lot I'd like to ask her.'

'What kind of things? I can't promise she'd tell you much.'

'About her background. About why she stopped playing. But especially about Marc Duplessis.'

'Do you play the Suite?'

'It's one of my favourite pieces. Don't tell me – yours too?'

Karina smiles. She and Rohan, meeting for only the second time, can communicate with their eyes alone.

'You remember there was something I wanted to tell you about Duplessis?' Rohan moistens his lips. 'The thing is, it's actually thanks to him that I'm where I am today.'

'*What?* Tell me more.'

'How long have you got?' Rohan beams straight into her gaze. Karina stares back, floored.

'After the war, Marc Duplessis emigrated to South Africa,' Rohan begins. 'He wanted to make a fresh start, and a year before apartheid came in he arrived by boat and settled in Cape Town. There weren't too many composers in Cape Town, certainly not real European ones with French accents, and the university snapped him up and gave him a lectureship. My father was studying medicine there at the time and he adored music. He got to know Duplessis through playing in the student orchestra. Duplessis married one of his students, a girl called Shirley Cohn, who, obviously, was a lot younger than him, and she was friendly with my dad, so they all started to see a lot of each other. Then when my dad married my mum, Shirley tipped them off that there was a small house for sale near theirs in Stellenbosch, so they ended up becoming neighbours. And when Duplessis died, my parents were round with Shirley the whole time, helping her get through it, sort his papers and so on.'

'So you didn't know him?'

'No, he died in the early sixties. I met Shirley once or twice when she came to Britain, but she didn't travel much – she hated flying – and my parents settled here when I was two. They were communists, you see, they got hounded out – and they wouldn't or couldn't go back until after 1991. But when I started the violin, and it seemed like I might be OK at it, they were incredibly supportive, mainly because Duplessis had made them so idealistic about music. When I got into the Menuhin School, my mother wasn't too happy, but Dad said that Duplessis would have been all for it. So I went, and now I almost feel I owe my violin-playing to Duplessis – and also any composing I do, not that my stuff's much use. But I play his Suite in his memory whenever I have a recital, as long as the promoters let me.'

'Heavens. That's beautiful.'

'He died rather young,' Rohan adds. 'My father told me that he was kind of depressed. It seems something had happened that affected his state of mind. At first Dad thought maybe it was apartheid – that Duplessis had recognised what was going on, and after his experiences in Europe it was the last straw. But later he said that he was certain it was more personal.'

'I don't really know anything about him,' Karina admits.

'Another thing he told me is that there was a legend that Duplessis had written a concerto for Mimi Rácz, but she never performed it. Before he died, Duplessis burned a lot of manuscripts, and Dad thought the concerto, if there was one, probably went too. Has your grandmother ever—?'

Karina's head begins to spin. She trawls her mind for any trace of this, but finds none. 'A concerto? By him? No, she's never said anything about it.'

'Karina, are you OK?'

'A little fazed.' Karina takes out a tissue.

'Ya. Me too.' Rohan pats her wrist. 'Sorry. I didn't mean to upset you.'

'I'm just very – touched, I guess. That there's this connection, or whatever it is. That there's my grandmother, who's been maybe the most important person in music for me, and Duplessis, who's the same for you – and he wrote for her . . .'

'Whatever it is,' Rohan echoes, nodding, turning away. 'Wait here, I'll get us some coffee.'

While he goes to the counter, her eyes trace his outline. His profile, alert and long-nosed, seems peculiarly out of place in Brighton. She imagines him as a creature from an African landscape – an antelope stag, perhaps, with gangly legs and huge dark eyes, head lifted, listening and watching, ready to think on his feet.

'Cake?' he calls. She holds up a thumb. He chooses her favourite, carrot cake, and places two spoons beside one piece, which is what she'd have asked him to do.

'You're a mind-reader,' she says.

'Now, listen.' Rohan puts a coffee cup in front of her and pours in the milk. 'Could I come with you to see Mimi? I'll treat you to lunch or dinner and a few drinks. And maybe, also, you'd play to me?'

'Of course you must come and see Mimi. And *you* should play to me.'

'I'll send you the list of our quartet concerts.'

'Concertos? Recitals? And what about your own pieces?'

'There aren't many concertos and recitals at the moment, and those there are, I'm not sure I'd like you to be there. Especially not for my pieces. I'd be too nervous.'

'But I'd love to hear them,' she protests. 'Look, let's do a deal. Play me all your music, and on that condition I'll take you to see Mimi.'

'OK. Done.' Rohan clinks his coffee cup against hers. Then he says, 'Mimi had a very good violin, didn't she?'

'My father always says "she had something nice once". I don't think it made it out of Hungary with her.'

'What happened? Why did she leave it behind?'

'I don't know.' Karina is embarrassed to admit that she's entirely ignorant of how her father and grandmother left Budapest during the Revolution in 1956. Through Mimi's musical contacts, they'd come to Britain and embraced a new life. Nobody's told her anything more.

'Was there a grandfather?' Rohan prompts.

'Yes. Tamás. He was an academic. He disappeared in Hungary. My grandmother never knew what became of him.'

'Murdered by the ÁVH?'

'The what?'

'The state security police. I heard about these things from Mr Nagy in Canada.'

'You know more than I do, then. My parents never talk about it.'

'That's odd.' Rohan stirs his coffee. Karina curls both hands around her cup and lets the heat sear her palms. 'Most Hungarians I know,' Rohan adds, 'never *stop* talking. And building on it, making everything incredibly colourful.'

'Maybe they're trying to protect me.'

'Could be. My parents are similar. They never told me much about what really made them leave South Africa. Your family left their country to get away from communism. Mine were communists who left to get away from fascism. My mother's a teacher and she used to hold classes in Soweto for township women who were so downtrodden they couldn't see how the system was wrecking their lives. She's back there a lot now. Dad died years ago, but when he first qualified as a doctor he used to work in mission hospitals, just trying to improve things for so many people who were poor, uneducated and unhealthy because the state wanted them to stay that way.'

'I'm sorry about your father,' Karina says. 'What happened to him?'

'I was only twenty, I was away studying in Canada and it turned out he had cancer, but he didn't want to worry me and never told me. So they called me too late and I rushed back, but by the time I got there, he'd gone. I was kind of in shock.'

Karina wants to take his hand. She links her fingers around her cup to stop herself.

'It focused me, later,' Rohan goes on. 'It made me more curious. There were so many things I'd never asked about his background and his family, and now it's too late. Look, don't you want to know where you come from? Don't you want to know who you really are?'

'Yes,' Karina says. 'There's nothing I'd like better.'

'Take me to see Mimi, then. And we'll do some investigating. We'll be musical sleuths together. If anyone knows the truth about the concerto, it's her; and maybe we'll find the violin. What do you say?'

'Only if you let me hear your music!' Karina laughs. 'Promise?'

'I promise.' He breaks into a helpless grin, watching her. 'I've never seen anybody laugh the way you do. You're incredible. You give so much.'

Rohan and Karina wander through the pedestrian lanes and up the hill towards the station. She glimpses their reflection in a shop window. Rohan towers over her; when he bends to talk, something in his face seems protective and gentle. Now that they're out in the sea air, she feels less sure of herself beside him. He's a footloose bachelor – the absconding dog owner has had no permanent successor – and a far better violinist than she could ever be. What would he see in her, a lapsed musician, a married mother? Other than that she's Mimi Rácz's granddaughter?

At the station entrance, she smiles, hiding her anxiety. 'So when do you want to come and see Mimi?'

'Call me. Let me know when's good.'

'You're the one who travels. I'm always here.'

Rohan touches her shoulder. 'Karina, listen. Don't vanish. Whatever happens, please don't vanish.' He stoops and kisses her on both cheeks.

'I have to run,' she says.

Karina bends to avoid hitting her head on the cross-beams. She props Lindy's torch on top of a precarious tower of boxes; in its dim light, she surveys the remnants of her family's past. The attic smells of ageing paper and dust. Erzsébet and Dénes's piles of stuff are stacked to the right; to the left are Mimi's, older, more daunting, more tempting. Where to begin? Karina hoists Mimi's dustiest box into her arms and manoeuvres it out through the spare bedroom and down the stairs.

'Ah.' Julian glances up from the contract he's checking. 'You're doing a clear-out.'

'Not exactly.'

'Oh. Couldn't you do a clear-out at the same time as whatever you *are* doing?'

'Not really.'

'So what's this in aid of?'

'I'm looking for something.'

'What?'

'I don't know.'

Julian gives a sigh and turns back to his work.

In the kitchen extension, Karina puts down the box and lifts out a pile of smaller containers, biscuit tins and shoeboxes. She dampens a cloth and wipes away a layer of fuzzy filth. Then she lifts the lid of a tin that in 1950s lettering declares its contents to be English leaf tea.

The Hungarian language soon feels like the least of her worries. The handwriting splayed in front of her would have been equally unintelligible in a passage of Jane Austen. Karina squints at a date at the top of the letter. 1935? Mimi would have been twenty. This writing seems unformed enough to be a child's; but the pressure is too strong, the aspect too peculiar. Erratic, uncontrolled, scribbled across cheap paper, and splodged with brown stains that could once have been coffee. Several similar letters lie below, the dates later, the handwriting the same. She lifts a page and tries to think herself into Mimi's skin, reading these letters when they were new. She'd obviously treasured them enough to bring them out of Budapest; Dénes has often remarked that they arrived in Britain with nothing.

Underneath the letters, she finds concert programmes. Liszt Ferenc Academy, 1929: Rácz Mimi, violin; Székely Géza, piano. Mimi would have been fourteen, playing the 'Spring' Sonata. A larger, grander pamphlet heralds the Tchaikovsky Violin Concerto, with the Academy's orchestra, 1932. The programmes are sepia, scrunched at the edges. The typefaces and borders morph from art deco to modernist. Famous names; foreign countries. 1935, Vienna; Wilhelm Furtwängler. Mimi had played with that greatest of conductors when she was only twenty. 1936, Paris. Marc Duplessis: Suite *Dans l'ombre des forêts, création mondiale.* Mimi Rácz, violin; Marc Duplessis, piano.

Julian peers over her shoulder.

'How did she get these out of Budapest?' Karina says.

'Well, she evidently did. Isn't that all that matters?'

Karina wants to say that it isn't the half of it.

'Darling, your grandmother was a famous musician. It's fun to overdramatise this business of leaving Hungary, but I bet she simply walked across the border with a few suitcases, a violin and a visa.'

'If only I'd learned Hungarian.'

'You don't need to waste your time tackling an impossible language that you'll never use. Just ask your parents. How about some tea, love? I have to do some more work before bed – we've got a meeting with the great Carsten Schmidt and the Office of Rail Regulation first thing.'

Julian's family has spoken the same language for hundreds of years. There's no reason he should grasp the frustration of not understanding your own grandmother.

Why hadn't her parents encouraged her to learn Hungarian? Those weird, extended phrases, the vowels astringent, the first syllable stressed, the rest stretched out like a string of red peppers

– the ambient sound is familiar when she encounters it, but leaves her adrift.

She calls her parents.

'You're not going to ask your grandmother about Hungary, are you?' Dénes growls.

'Do you think she won't talk?'

'It's not that she won't, Schnooky. She can't. And she shouldn't. It was then a big trauma, you know? Don't put her through this strain.'

'Dad, what *happened*? I wish you'd tell me. Why all the secrecy?'

'The past is the past. Life can be hard, so when times are good, we must make the most of them, no?'

'Yes, but—'

'I tell you, Karina, we have had a marvellous life. This country has made possible for us so many things that would never have been so in Hungary. Career, travel, Chinese food, Californian wine. Why do you want to drag out these old stories?'

'I just want to know what happened.'

'You never wanted to know before.'

'But I do now. It's different . . .' She hesitates. She hasn't told him about Rohan.

'Why it's different? Why suddenly after thirty-five years? You want to "find your roots"? You've done very nicely without them, my child. You want to learn Hungarian? Did you know there are over forty cases to understand in this crazy language? No, I didn't think you did. Now, get some rest and let the men in your life rest too, yes?'

'Sorry, Dad. I didn't realise it was so late.'

'I would give you your mother, but she has gone to bed already. We'll call you tomorrow, Schnooky. Go to sleep. The past is the past.'

Karina hasn't even had a chance to mention the letters.

13

Rohan doesn't use email. He prefers texts. Short ones. 'Mon OK', Karina reads. 'Clpm Jct #5, 1 p.m. R.'

Karina spins Rohan's image around in her mind. Why him, why now, why, of all places, Clapham Junction? If the trains had worked properly that day, would she ever have met him? Perhaps he's a figment of her imagination, created when she needed him: a friend now that her closest friend is dead; a sympathetic ear when her husband is least sympathetic; an inadvertent connection with a past she doesn't understand; a distraction from missing Jamie.

Jamie's first term is almost over. Boarding-school, peculiarly, causes more disruption to daily life than normal school. He's too little to take a train alone, so she fetches him on Fridays; she's moved her Friday pupils, so other days are commensurately busier, though she finds she's guarding her free Mondays more zealously than she might have three months ago. Julian does the return run most Sundays, though not all. 'If he's too little to take a train,' Karina says, 'then he's too little to be away from home.' Julian, tired after difficult negotiations as Locomotivation's franchise bid judders forward, tells her not to fuss: Jamie is fine.

'What's the best thing about school?' Karina asks Jamie, as jauntily as she can, on the way back for the last week of term, a Sunday when Julian has to work.

'Midnight feasts with Calum and Laurence,' he says, with a grin.

'I'm sure you're not meant to have midnight feasts.' She tries not to smile.

'It's cool. We hoard up cake and biscuits for a bit, then we pretend to go to sleep and at midnight we go into someone's room and eat everything!'

'But where do you hoard stuff from?' Karina remembers the dining room banner and the school's obsession with healthy food, locally sourced.

'They give us all this *salad*,' Jamie grumbles, without answering. 'And things like broccoli. It's revolting. We only have chips once a week, and they never do pizza.'

'Salad and vegetables are good for you.'

'It's *horrid*.'

'But what do I give you at home? We eat lots of vegetables too.'

'They taste better when you do them. At school it's all soggy. Yuck.'

'But where do you get the cake and biscuits?'

'Oh . . .' Jamie licks his lips, a guilty flicker crossing his face as if he's just remembered that maybe he shouldn't tell his mother such things. 'First it was Calum's mum, she always sends him back with some, but Laurence has this big brother, Piers, who's at Elthingbourne, and Piers told Laurence that he'd bought a pack of biscuits that were all broken, and Piers and his friend wrote to the company to complain, and then the factory posted them a whole load of new packs free. So what we did was, we wrote to—'

'Oh, you didn't!'

'Well, Calum did. We wrote to this place that does these really wicked chocolate brownies and said they were stale.'

'And?'

'They sent us five packs. They were really yummy. You won't tell the teachers, will you, Mum?'

'What if you get caught?' Perhaps Jamie sees her as a rebellious child like himself, not an adult who ought to be in league with authority.

'But *you* won't tell, will you?' he begs, as crestfallen as a cartoon puppy with droopy ears.

'No,' Karina promises, 'but I want you to not do it again.'

'But Mum, please, *please* don't tell, because we'll get detention. We'd be shut in this room and have to write lines. It's horrible. There's this teacher who's really mean. He always does the detentions, and he supervises prep too, and—'

Karina's humour leaves her abruptly. 'Why? What happens?'

'It's just like, well, like when the maths is difficult, some of the others, like, cry, and when he knows who the ones are who get upset, he picks on them.'

'How does he pick on them?'

'He's mean. He calls them names.'

'I'm afraid teachers sometimes can be mean, love. He hasn't been calling you names, has he?'

'He called me a "Gypsy joker".'

'Good God.' Karina's foot nearly slips off the accelerator.

'Dad said it'll be better at Elthingbourne because once you're old enough to go to proper school the masters aren't so much bigger than you any more.'

'You told Daddy about this? When?'

'Yesterday, when you were teaching.'

Why hadn't Julian mentioned it? 'I'll talk to him,' she says, her mind thumping with anger.

At school, she settles Jamie back in his room. 'See you Friday, Schnooky, and then it's Christmas!' Jamie trots away to find Calum and Laurence – Calum is the lad they met in the car park at the open day. Walking alone down the corridors, she casts around, watching the boys, trying to gauge the atmosphere. Locally sourced food is all very well, but . . .

She remembers what Julian told her about his own prep school and wonders whether she will sleep a wink until Jamie is home again.

'That was forty years ago,' Julian says, later. 'Everything's different now.'

'But Jamie says there's a teacher picking on them and calling them names. Can you believe it? Calling Jamie a "Gypsy joker"? Does that sound normal to you? Supposing this man's not only a racist—?'

'Darling one, it's *school*. It's part of the rough-and-tumble. Can you imagine the scandal if there were a paedophile at St Matthew's? There are countless checks to prevent that kind of thing. Everyone's so paranoid that you can't take a photo of your own kid playing with his friends in case their parents think it's something nefarious. We'll write to the headmaster about the name-calling, but you mustn't start panicking like that for no reason. It's ridiculous.'

'But at your school—'

'Some weird things went on, but it didn't affect me.'

'And Hilary? I suppose it didn't affect *him*?'

'Look, Hils has his problems, but there's no evidence that being touched up at school had the first thing to do with it. It's a chemical imbalance. Honest to goodness, Karrie, there's nothing like that going on at St Matthew's. Come on, darling one, let's get an early night.'

Half an hour later, Julian is proving to Karina that nothing he experienced as a schoolboy has remotely affected his sexuality.

'I love you,' he mumbles into her neck.

'I love you too,' she mumbles back, her arms encircling his body – warm, comfortable, comforting. Her mind is somewhere else, but fortunately he doesn't notice.

There's the now familiar lanky figure with his slight stoop and wide shoulder line, his brown-sugar eyes smiling at her. She wants to run the length of the platform to reach him faster. She stops herself. She's taking a fellow musician to meet her grandmother; nothing's wrong with that.

Rohan gives her a peck on the cheek. 'Karina, this is fantastic – I'm so thrilled. How are you? How's Jamie?'

Now that he's arrived, she feels confident, as reckless as a girl half her age. The anticipation was altogether different. 'We're fine, thanks. I hope you didn't forget our deal. Did you bring your music?'

'Here.' Rohan gives her a CD box with a white handwritten insert. 'Take it, quick, and don't let me think about it again.'

Karina pounces on the box. ROHAN MASTERSON: String Quartet, says the insert. Then the violin pieces: *Adagio and Rondo*; *Vocalise*; *African Skies*; *Brighton Beauty*; *All At Sea*; *Fiddle Fingers*. 'They're just useful encores, that kind of thing,' he mumbles into his scarf. 'I'm hoping they might get published. Someone from Boosey's is looking at them.'

'I can't wait to hear them.'

'So, how's Mimi?' Rohan, bashful about his compositions, is looking so hard for a way to change the subject that she lets him.

'Look, she mightn't be all there,' she says. 'She has good days, and less good days.'

'I'm crossing everything I can cross for a good day.'

They wander up the platform, waiting for the Twickenham train. As it approaches, Rohan puts a hand on Karina's back, guiding her further from the edge. She doesn't look at him.

'What do you want to ask Mimi?' she says.

'I'll show you.' Rohan takes out a much-folded sheet of A4 bearing a list of questions scribbled in pencil, full of loops and underlinings.

'Don't hope for too much,' Karina warns him.

'I think they've taken my spoons,' says Mimi.

The couple sitting well away from one another on her sofa stare at her, bemused, with two pairs of matching dark eyes.

'I had silver spoons that were given to us as a wedding present,' she tells them. 'I've had them for sixty-nine years and they took them.'

'Who took them, Grandma?' Karina asks.

'The cleaner. This girl who comes in the mornings. She thinks I don't notice. Karina, will you write to them for me and complain? Your father won't. He doesn't believe me. Eiyiyi, my own son.'

The tall young man gazes at Mimi with such fire and respect that if she were sixty years younger she'd blush. 'I've loved your recordings since I was a boy,' he says. She can hear a faint trace of an accent – very faint, but her ears never deceive her. Good, he's an immigrant, like Dini. What is it? South Africa?

'Grandma,' Karina says, 'Rohan has something to tell you.'

Mimi turns her piercing gaze towards him. He looks back, without blinking. A connection bounces to life: South Africa? What's going on?

'Madame Rácz,' he says, 'you knew Marc Duplessis.'

'Of course.' Mimi's words sound terser than she intends.

He reaches forward and takes both her hands in his own, engulfing her swollen knuckles. 'My father knew him very well in Cape Town.'

An arrow catches in her throat. 'There's a name I haven't

spoken in some time, except for teaching the Suite,' she says through the pain.

'He was a kind of mentor to my dad. It's because of him that they let me become a musician.'

She listens, bemused, while he talks. The house with the swimming pool and the proteas – so it was all true; he was married, he had two children and they still exist six thousand miles away. His son, Michael, runs a Stellenbosch winery; his daughter, named Annette, is a human rights lawyer. And he died, too early, from cancer. Nobody has talked to her about Marc Duplessis, except about the Suite, for thirty years or more. The last person who tried to ask her questions was that French journalist, writing his biography, and after taking one look at his tape recorder she'd clammed up and told him nothing.

'Let me make us some tea,' Rohan offers. His ears have flushed red – he's a tad overcome. He jumps up and goes to the kitchenette.

'Rohan's a fantastic violinist,' Karina tells Mimi. 'He leads a string quartet and he's got a New York recital next year. He composes too.'

'I dabble,' Rohan mumbles, giving the teapot a good scrub. 'I wish you hadn't stopped playing so soon, Madame Rácz. I'd have loved to hear you.'

'Once one can't play so well any more, what's the point? It's embarrassing,' Mimi says. This information is harmless. Perhaps he'll find it useful sometime. Will he tell her anything more? Or will it be questions, questions, questions, for the rest of the day?

'What was your violin?' Rohan asks.

Questions. Mimi sighs. 'I had a very nice violin,' she says. 'A Guadagnini, bought for me by my sponsor, through Goldsmith's. But when I stopped, we sold it. A fine violin must be played. It mustn't just sit.' She closes her eyes. Under the circumstances, she doesn't want to make too much sense.

'But before that.' Rohan pours tea. 'What violin did you use for the Duplessis premiere?'

'Ah. That. Yes. A nice violin. Gone. Two spoons of sugar, please, my dear. I don't diet.'

He brings her a mug, stirring in the sugar. She sips: the flavour is perfect. A meticulous fellow, just like Marc.

'I heard once that you had a wonderful violin,' he says. 'But that perhaps it never made it out of Budapest?'

Mimi shrugs. 'It is so long ago, my dear. I don't remember.'

Karina catches Rohan's eye; he goes quiet. These two, Mimi sees, can communicate without words. With the other one, the tall, fair one who looks like a rugby player, Karina can't communicate at all, no matter how many words they use.

Rohan takes her hand again; it's many years since a strange man held her hand and she smiles. 'Also, there's a rumour that Duplessis was going to write you a concerto, but it was never played,' says Rohan in a rush, apparently encouraged by the smile. 'So I just wondered . . . whether it was true?'

'Why you young people need to look back so much? You should look forward. You two. It is more important.'

'We're interested,' Rohan says simply. 'We'd like to know more about it.'

The years crowd in on Mimi. Images dance through her memory, changing places, switching partners, carving out an unconscious pattern on time's floorboards. Where to begin? Nothing begins; nothing ends, not even in death. So much explanation defeats her. So much pain. Why do the youngsters need that in their comfortable, modern lives?

'Our destinies,' she begins, 'carried us in opposite directions. So much I didn't understand when I knew him. What a wonderful man he was, and I never truly appreciated it, my dear. I tried, you know, to forge myself. To make my own life, not bound by any tradition. I had my Gypsy family tradition, then the Frankls tell me no, that's not going to be my tradition any more, then the other students at the Academy tease me and pull my hair because I'm a Gypsy. And Dr Frankl tells me, music is a meritocracy. That was his favourite word. In Hungarian, of course. That is the only honest way to run a world, he said. My mistake was believing other people would think the same way. My dear, we learn hard lessons.'

She can't remember why she started on this; it's not what he was asking. He wanted to know about Marc, not Dr Frankl's meritocracy, but now her mind is trapped in the years before she knew Marc and she can't find the gate through to the right part of her life.

She turns to Karina. 'And, darlink, those days it wasn't like now. Today you young people don't know about love.' She waves her free hand. 'You like someone, you jump into bed, vip vip, finished. You don't understand real love. There are as many kinds of love as there are people loving one another.'

Karina and Rohan avoid each other's gaze in a silence that Mimi senses is more awkward than it should have been. Karina, no doubt, is preparing to change the subject.

'Grandma, I wanted to ask you something else, too,' she begins. 'I was in our attic and I found some old letters that belonged to you. I was wondering who they were from. This is one.' She takes an ancient sheet of paper out of her bag.

Mimi hasn't seen her brother's writing for more than sixty years. Saliva evaporates from her mouth.

'My dear, so long ago, how I am supposed to remember?'

'Oh, Grandma. Please.'

Mimi shakes her head. She's losing language all of a sudden. Somewhere between English and Hungarian there's a no man's land where words need to be winnowed out faster than she can manage. 'I don't know,' she says eventually. 'You want to ask questions. Ask something else.'

'Well, then, what about 1936?' Rohan ventures. 'Paris, the Duplessis premiere. What happened?'

Mimi puts down the letter. Time to shut the memory shop. She finds her voice. 'What *happened*? We went to the Châtelet, we played the piece, people clapped. What else should happen?' She shuts her eyes. She can still feel flowers bouncing off her dress, the waterfall of applause, the stage lights in her eyes, adrenaline shaking her like an apple on the tree, tasting his tongue, tonight one kiss can't hurt. She can't remember what she did yesterday, but sometimes she thinks she's been living that night for seventy years.

Rohan picks up all the mugs and, with a glance, beckons Karina into the kitchenette while he refills them. Mimi can hear them whispering. Can't talk? Won't talk? Maybe there's no difference. It's such an effort to sift through all those memories, all those words. The letter – her brother's – there are more where that came from . . .

No. Not now.

'I am very tired,' she declares. 'Please excuse me, my dears, I must lie down.'

Karina and Rohan, moved but frustrated, transfer to a café on the high street. Karina imagines they could be sitting in any café in any era and any country; two violinists on a journey, drinking coffee.

'Violinists were always wanderers,' Rohan remarks, as if reading her mind. 'You can go anywhere, with nothing else, and earn your crust by playing.'

'That's what Mimi's family used to do.'

'What happened to them?'

'Her father led a Gypsy band in a restaurant in Budapest, but more than that – well, maybe she doesn't know. Dr Frankl, who she kept talking about, adopted her and sent her to the Liszt Academy and as far as I can tell, she never looked back.'

'And your grandfather?'

'He was a linguist and philosopher and he translated Balzac into Hungarian. He sounds like a kind of enlightened freethinker. One of the few people, I suppose, who was open-minded enough to marry a Gypsy. She still talks to him as if he's really there.'

'You should go to Hungary. You could jump on a cheap flight.'

'It's not so easy, because of my parents. I don't want to upset them.'

'Come on, Karina, it's your past as well as theirs. I've got an idea.'

'Your quartet's going?' Karina knows, from the website, that it is.

'In April. Why don't you come with us?'

'How can I?'

'Let me work on it.'

She watches him. He's miles away, eyes lowered, dreaming. Men aren't often dreamers, Karina reckons, but this one is. A careful, precise, sparkly, sweet dreamer who – to judge from the recordings – turns into a demon when he picks up his violin. She wonders what he's dreaming of.

Fancy meeting *him* on a train. The last seat opens up for you, and he's opposite. Is there some crazy cosmic design to this? Or is it chaos – quantum mechanics determining the future by accident? Chance operations. Karina sips her coffee and begins to tell Rohan about Richard.

Her composer ex-boyfriend had had a fascination for music made through 'chance operations': sounds selected not by the composer's will, but by the throw of a die or the I Ching. Random events, he used to say, were closer to life's processes than one person's decision that a particular note followed by another should constitute music. John Cage had pioneered composition by chance operations in the US; Richard wanted to carry similar ideas into the new century, morphing them electronically. Unfortunately for him, not many people fancied listening to music created in this way; but the theories were powerful enough to coax money out of funding bodies, and the sounds had enough otherworldly appeal to fascinate Karina.

Rohan gives a wry laugh. 'I'm afraid I commit the cardinal sin of writing tunes. No wonder nobody will play my pieces!'

'I'm sure they're wonderful,' Karina protests.

'But you bought into all that? Really? Did you wear black and eat macrobiotic food? Sorry, I shouldn't laugh, I'm sure it's a very good thing, if only I understood it, but . . .'

'We did eat macrobiotic a lot,' Karina admits. 'Aduki beans, brown rice, lots of mushrooms. I was thinner then! But you're right, it was never really for me, although for years I wondered what would have happened if I hadn't forced myself to leave him.'

Rohan nods. 'I've felt that way a few times.'

Karina scoops up chocolate-speckled cappuccino froth in her spoon. Her mind's eye seems to glimpse snow sprinkled with blood.

'What are you thinking about?' Rohan asks.

'Lots of things.' Her imagination is full of questions, too many to consider systematically. Was this why Mimi couldn't talk about the past? Was there simply too much of it left inside her? 'Chance operations, I suppose. Whether the things that happen to us are preordained in some way, or just plain chaos.'

'Either way, the trick is to make something good out of them,' Rohan suggests. 'Here's another idea. Why don't you come to Brighton and bring your violin? I'll give you lunch and we could play some music. How about Bartók duos?'

Karina twinges with longing. She hasn't played Bartók duos for years.

'After Christmas,' she says. 'Once Jamie's back at school.'

As the words come out, she hates herself. It means that not only has she accepted Jamie's exile to boarding-school, but she's planning to take appalling advantage of it.

14

'I tell you, they're fucking cunts,' says Dénes. Cynthia and Martin, eating Hungarian fish soup, Erzsébet's Christmas Eve speciality, have been outlining in alcohol-fuelled detail the problems that currently surround the Rookfield family.

Christmas Eve is the main Hungarian celebration of the season and the Vereses have tried, as usual, to provide a suitable occasion, with a lavish meal, good red wine and plenty of presents for Jamie. Lindy's absence, though, is a great rend in the ozone. Julian tries to keep the peace between his uncle and aunt; Karina, dusky in a red silk blouse and black trousers, quietly helps her mother. While Jamie was awake, everyone manufactured jollity; at nine o'clock Karina put him to bed in her old room, then went back down to discover what was really going on in Forest Road.

'We're being asked for money,' Martin explains. 'People write to us saying, 'I saw you on TV talking about the tragic death of your daughter. Please consider donating to x, y or z to help prevent other loving families from suffering too . . .'

'There must be types,' Cynthia says, 'who deliberately target people like us. I mean, I'd be happy to give money to a bona fide charity. But how do we know it's genuine?'

'Scams, left, right and centre. You'd think people would write and offer condolences. Instead, they try to fleece you while you're down.' Martin shakes his head. 'Fortunately they don't appear to understand my legal background. They usually back off when I tell them what I've done and why I can see through them.'

'Like I tell you, they're fucking Rottweilers,' says Dénes.

'You should send Dad in to sort them out,' Karina says, trying to smile. 'He'd scare them off!'

'My students call me Dracula,' Dénes growls. The bushy

eyebrows – a legacy, perhaps, of the vanished István Rácz – have turned white, but remain as imposing as ever.

'Dennis, darling, you couldn't hurt a fly.' Cynthia fumbles for a tissue.

'Cyncyn, darlink, just you try me!'

'It is a shame,' Erzsébet says, 'that people will stoop to such things. There is so little dignity left. Money is before all else. It shouldn't be like this.'

Cynthia blows her nose. Martin looks the other way.

Karina, who normally adores her mother's fish soup, finds that her appetite is failing. The soup is made with freshwater fish, tomatoes and plenty of paprika; she's eaten it every Christmas Eve for as long as she can remember. This is the first time she hasn't asked for seconds.

'We should have had more children.' Cynthia weeps into her handkerchief. 'How can children die? It should have been me, not her. I would give anything to have been on that train in her place.'

'Cynthia, please,' Martin protests. 'Not now.'

'Why was she the only one? It wasn't my fault! Don't you remember?'

'Cynthia, don't *start*. You've had too much to drink . . .'

'I told you,' Cynthia accuses Martin, 'but would you listen? Never! You never cared about her and me, you were always off diddling your little yo-yos, and don't think Lindy didn't know – she wasn't blind, she wasn't stupid, not like I was. And now it's too late . . .'

Erzsébet puts a soothing arm around Cynthia's shoulder and leads her away to the sofa.

Aged four, Erzsébet hid with her family in a Budapest cellar beneath the falling bombs, while the only thing more dreaded than a German was a Russian. Ever since, she has carried with her slivers of darkness, heat bearing down, the choking grey dust thrown out by a city breaking apart; these are her first memories, impressions stronger than the faces or embraces of her parents. Before she was eight, her mother and father had both succumbed to ailments that might have been curable had they not been so weakened by wartime hunger and infections. She went to live with her piano teacher, who taught her scales, studies and the skill of living in the present. Years later, a matter-of-fact English doctor informed Erzsébet that childhood trauma might have affected her hormones and therefore her fertility. To have one child had seemed a miracle.

Her experience is a world away from Cynthia's. One morning, when Lindy and Karina were eleven, Cynthia saw something on Twickenham High Street that made her order Lindy to move to the upstairs room. She appropriated Lindy's old bedroom, installing a bolt. Erzsébet couldn't have another baby; Cynthia wouldn't, because her husband was too busy with his latest mistress.

'Leave him,' Erzsébet had urged her.

'I can't. Think of the family. Think of the disgrace. We have to stay together, for Lindy's sake.'

'You can leave if you want to,' Erzsébet encouraged. 'It's your decision.' But Cynthia wouldn't hear of it. All you can do while your friends are making mistakes, Erzsébet thought, is listen and be ready with the tissues. Of her own experience, she never said a word.

'Betsy,' Cynthia weeps now, 'you're too good. You're such a good person.'

'We're going home,' Martin snaps. 'You're drunk.'

'I'm not drunk! I just want to tell the *bloody truth* for once in my life!'

'Darling one, we should hit the road,' Julian mutters to Karina. 'We're due at Fairfallows reasonably early tomorrow.'

He goes upstairs and carries down the sleeping Jamie. Karina embraces her parents. Cynthia, steered out by Martin, hugs her too; she can feel Cynthia's ribcage shaking. She can barely bring herself to say, 'Merry Christmas.'

'I don't know what to do to help them,' Karina tells Julian, in the car. 'I knew there were problems, but . . .'

'There's also such a thing as decent reticence. I'm deeply embarrassed that my aunt should ruin your parents' Christmas Eve. Thank God she isn't coming to Fairfallows tomorrow.'

'I'm sure Mum and Dad understand. Mum's really Cynthia's best friend. If anybody's been holding life together in Forest Road, it's her.'

There's a long silence, but for Jamie's sleepy breathing and the roar of a passing motorbike.

'What happened?' Karina asks. 'Do you know? Because I don't.'

'It's not too pretty. Martin never could resist a secretary in a short skirt. Cynthia was out shopping in Twickenham and he drove past her in broad daylight with a nubile blonde next to him in the family car.'

'Did Lindy know?'

'Of course she bloody knew. This idea that you have to stay together for the sake of the children . . . you can end up with children who hate their parents for it.'

'But Lindy didn't hate hers.'

'Oh, didn't she? Maybe she didn't tell you everything the way you think she did, Karrie. Because she knew about her father, and I can tell you she loathed him for sleeping around and rowing with Cynthia, and she also loathed her mother for putting up with it. Sometimes in the summer holidays, when you girls were teenagers and Hils and Chris and I were in our twenties, she'd come down to Fairfallows and we'd sit in the meadow and smoke, and take everyone in the family to pieces. You should have heard her, Karrie. Vitriol isn't the word.'

Karina pictures Lindy sitting on the Rookery floor by the red sofa, her computer on the coffee table, a bottle of wine beside it. By the time she was forty, Lindy had declared, she wanted to be settled with a partner and have two children. She'd have left the bookshop in order to write. Her plays would be West End hits. Quotes would hang above theatre doorways: 'Wonderful!' 'Enthralling!' 'Lindy Rookfield, the new voice of British drama!' Then she'd asked Karina where she'd be. 'Probably right where I am now,' Karina had said, 'but older.'

Karina is resigned to Fairfallows Christmas lunch tomorrow. She'll get through as usual, by going through the motions. Is that any way to live? Doing the right thing, but deliberately switching off your real self?

When Jamie is in bed and asleep, she fetches his Christmas stocking from her cupboard and fastens it to his mantelpiece. He gets Veres presents on Christmas Eve, Rookfield presents on Christmas Day and parent presents in between. She kisses his forehead, tiptoes back to the bedroom and slides down beside the snoring Julian. There she lies awake, waiting for dawn. Rohan's music, full of harmonies that make her catch her breath, plays and replays in her inner ear, as if his CD had downloaded itself directly into her brain.

Karina had bought gladioli on Christmas Eve, ready to take to Fairfallows. She leaves them soaking in Anne's kitchen sink while she adds a heap of presents to the pile under the tree in the blue drawing room.

'The least they can do is leave one in peace for Christmas.' Hilary is pacing up and down, drinking orange juice.

'It takes such a long time to get anything *done*,' Anne says. 'There'll always be some reason why nobody can help. And then they lose your letters.'

'What's going on?' Julian asks.

'Damnable travellers,' Arthur expostulates. 'They're putting couples off wanting to get married here. We've only a fraction of the bookings I wanted for next summer.'

'But you can't see them from the house,' Karina protests. 'I've never seen them yet.'

'You should go and look, Karrie,' Hilary suggests. 'A pretty sight, I don't think.'

Anne turns up the Bach Christmas Oratorio. 'Did you have a lovely Hungarian Christmas Eve yesterday?' she asks. 'How's Cynthia? Is she bearing up all right? I was so sorry they decided against joining us today.'

'The loss has hit her very hard,' Julian says.

'Mum, can we play hide-and-seek?' whispers Jamie.

'Not right now, Schnooky. We only just got here.'

'Julian, come with me, please? I want you to look at something,' says Arthur. They disappear to the study. Karina, arm round the wriggling Jamie, sits with her back to the mournful-eyed icon and asks Anne about her book. Hilary butts in and tells them lots of things they didn't want to know about his car. 'And those blasted people see me driving past and they throw things,' he adds. 'I mean, this is my home! They're trespassing, and they throw things.'

'Don't you think there should be some kind of amnesty for

Christmas?' suggests Karina, who used to be able to cope with Hilary's obsessions, but now can't.

'Tell *them* that.' He folds his arms. 'In my humble opinion, it's time for "*Arrivederci* Roma"!' He tries to whistle a tune and laugh at the same time.

Karina remembers Mimi's words about learning the hard way not to deny your roots. She spent most of the night tussling with her sense of dissatisfaction, and her guilt over feeling it. Now she's tired of everybody else's. There's no point asking Arthur or Hilary, however politely, to be positive; Hilary's condition affects everyone at Fairfallows. At least he took a computer course while in Keswick, and now helps Arthur with the Fairfallows wedding business paperwork, which they are trying to administrate themselves, rather than handing it over to the estate manager along with a hefty fee.

There's an exclamation and the sound of heavy footsteps. Julian makes for the drinks cabinet and refills his sherry glass so fast that it nearly overflows.

'Later,' he mouths at Karina.

When Anne ushers them into the dining room, Julian hangs behind and Karina goes over to him. 'What's happened?'

'Total mess. Figures that mean nothing. He's made it up. He just pretends he's helping. It's a disaster, and what's more, it's an illegal disaster. You're legally obliged to keep accurate business records, you know. There's a pile of receipts and another of bills and everything's there – it will be possible to correct it – but the bookkeeping isn't just a shambles, it's a fictional shambles.'

'Jules, darling! It's your turn to carve the goose!' Anne sings.

Erzsébet is holding Mimi's hand. With Karina spirited away by her husband's family, Erzsébet and Dénes have come to take Mimi to Forest Road. She was poorly the day before and declined to join them for Christmas Eve. Erzsébet had hoped to find her in better spirits, but Mimi is rambling in Hungarian. 'No! . . . I don't know him . . .'

Erzsébet is more accustomed to speaking English than Hungarian after fifty years in London; but it always comes back, each word bearing a thousand needles. Thirst. Cannon fire. Numbing, habitual fear. Odd to be without it. The cellar is still inside her, somewhere. Is that why her daughter is claustrophobic?

'Who don't you know, Mimi?'

'Leave me alone.'

'Miss Rácz, there's someone who wants to see you.' The doorkeeper glared at Mimi and her violin.

'Who is it?'

He gave her the name.

'I don't know him.'

He told her who the youth had said he was.

'I tell you, I don't know him!' she exploded. 'Send him away. I have to practise.'

'Looks like a Gypsy and smells like one.' The doorkeeper gave a snort. Mimi glowered back: yes, she thought, I'm a Gypsy, but I can play the violin and there's nothing you can do to stop me. Meritocracy.

She complained to her manager, Herbert Wilhelm from Berlin, who'd come to Budapest for the concert, that the petty officials backstage were calling her names, tarring her with the same brush as the beggars and the layabouts.

Wilhelm shrugged. 'My dear, I'm sorry, but it's only to be expected.'

'I shall never go back to that life.' Mimi drummed her fingers hard on the dressing-room table. Please tell me I'll never have to go back, she wanted to add; but she mustn't show Wilhelm her weakness.

'Mimi, if you ever go back, I shall eat every hat in Berlin,' Wilhelm assured her. 'Now, I suggest that afterwards we go for dinner at the Café Károlyi. Apparently there's a Gypsy orchestra there which—'

'No,' Mimi snapped. 'I hate it. I hate Károlyi. Anywhere but Károlyi.'

A tap on the door. 'Miss Rácz, ten minutes, please.'

She picked up her violin. 'I must practise.'

Wilhelm, faced with a twenty-year-old girl whose will-power could burn down the whole city, bowed his head in contented agreement and left to find his seat beside the proud Frankls.

Another triumph. Curtain call after curtain call; bouquets knee high. Later, out in the windy night, people crowding her for autographs by the stage door. Among them, a man perhaps ten or fifteen years older than her, with a fascinating face: alert, pointed features, a smallish chin, and round spectacles over sweet eyes, the sweetest and greenest she had ever seen. She hadn't known eyes could be as green as that. She smiled straight at him. 'Thank you for coming. Are you a musician?'

'If only I were,' he said, pressing a card into her hand. Dr Veres Tamás; a smart Pest address, near the university. What a gaze he had: studious, full of spirit. 'An academic doctor, not medical. If you have backache, I'm afraid I can't cure it.'

'What about heartache?' said Mimi.

Tamás, smiling with those eyes, extended a programme and a pen towards her. Mimi scribbled 'With my best wishes, Rácz M', then on impulse added her phone number at the Frankls'. She wanted to tell him to call her, but Wilhelm took her arm and steered her away towards the cab and thence dinner (Gundel, not Károlyi). Tomorrow, the train to Paris. Tamás could call her – but not for three months.

Why couldn't he be stronger? He could have spoken out: 'Have dinner with me, not them, Mimi. I want to know you better.' But he hadn't. Perhaps he'd forget her. For the first time, the idea crossed Mimi's mind that having left one world behind her, she might leave another. Inconceivable – wasn't it?

One more face, at the back of the crowd. Shouldered aside by the concert-goers. Women skirting the crowd to avoid him. She looked away. Wilhelm, beside her, cradled her violin case and radiated pride over his young Gypsy fiddler, the first classical star to emerge from such a background.

'Mimi!'

Heads turned.

'Mimi! Don't you know me?'

'Who is this fellow?' Herbert Wilhelm breathed.

'I've no idea.' Mimi kept her eyes on the cab door. Focus. Get there, fast.

'Mimi! Why won't you talk to me?'

A nearby couple muttered about the police. Was this desperado set upon killing the soloist?

'Come, Mimi,' Wilhelm whispered. 'Let's go.'

Wilhelm, at least, only wanted her for her music. Her playing was so inflammatory, so extreme, that he didn't have to discuss her background to sell her which, with racist nationalism increasing at a fearsome rate, was fortunate. Mimi Rácz and her violin would chew up Europe overnight, given the chance.

'Legend says that Gypsies can't celebrate without fire,' he said to her over dinner, while she wolfed down well-earned goulash soup, 'but your fire is inside you. Make sure you never lose it.'

'Perhaps it will be stoked in Paris!' Mimi laughed, raising her glass. Twelve people around their table were toasting her in champagne and soon Mimi began to forget about the green eyes of Dr Tamás Veres.

Seventy-two hours later she was clinking another glass in another café, in Paris, with Marc Duplessis, a young composer she hadn't heard of three days earlier, gazing for the first time at his necklaces of notes on the staves: his new piece, inspired by her playing. The ink was so fresh that she could almost smell it. 'I can see several passages where you could perhaps rethink some of the figurations,' she said. 'We could work on it together. Maybe next year.'

'I don't know him,' mutters Mimi, seventy-one years later.

'Oh, Mimi,' Erzsébet whispers. 'What are you talking about?'

Mimi's troubled breathing begins to settle. Erzsébet strokes her hair, as she used to stroke Karina's when she was a child falling asleep. Soon she'll take her husband's mother home with her, away from those unfathomable dreams.

It's one complaint too far. 'Damned EU,' Hilary says. 'Meddling bastards. Managed just fine without them. Can't even send back the damned immigrants because of these bloody bureaucrats . . . Whole thing ought to be dismantled, pronto.'

Karina swallows the largest mouthful of coffee she can take without choking, then gets up. 'Excuse me,' she says, and beckons to Jamie.

In the kitchen, she scoops up the flowers that Anne hasn't yet arranged, then grabs her son's hand.

'Where are we going, Mum?' Jamie asks, excited, as she leads him across the entrance hall and out into the pewter afternoon.

'We're taking some people a Christmas present.'

At the long drive, she turns away from the public tearoom in the stables, and marches, with Jamie trying to keep up, along a neglected pathway lined with the bare torsos of elder and hawthorn trees. She gasps in the dank air as if it's the only oxygen available at Fairfallows.

A whitish blur through the branches shapes into a clump of caravans, arrayed on a field of what's now mud. There must be at least ten, maybe twelve. Washing is strewn over lines suspended between them. Peculiar whiffs reach Karina and Jamie – there's not much here by way of drainage or sewers, except some makeshift portable loos that the council's environmental health department has hastily erected; but there's also an aroma of cooking meat. The windows of the nearest caravan have steamed up. Karina can hear the patter of Christmas TV, a soap opera's seasonal special. People still like to spend Christmas watching fictional people spending Christmas together. Outside, some small boys are playing football.

'Now, listen, Schnooky,' says Karina. 'I don't know them, so this is an experiment, OK? Hold my hand.' Jamie does so, tightly, glancing several times over his shoulder at the football game. The traveller children stare back, curious.

Karina strides up to the caravan door and taps. A second later she's face to face with a plump woman who looks ten years older than herself, but, she guesses, probably isn't. Her face is red, prematurely lined; half annoyed, Karina thinks, but also half afraid. Three more children peer round her at assorted heights.

'Yes, and what can we do for you?' she demands.

'Happy Christmas,' Karina says. 'We brought you some flowers.' She pushes the gladioli towards the startled woman's large, chapped hands.

'And who'd you be? We're not going nowhere today, it's Christmas.'

'It's OK. I'm not here to tell you to go.'

'That makes a flippin' change. Dave, turn that down, can't hear myself think!'

'Fine move, sending the lady of the house down to chase us off at Christmas,' grumbles the man in the background.

'She says she's not. Oh, hello, love.' She's spotted Jamie, who's peering at her from behind Karina in an inadvertent mirror image of her own children.

'I'm Karina and this is Jamie,' Karina says. She glimpses used plates, a small battery-operated TV, empty beer cans on the floor and more people than she'd imagined could get into a caravan. Condensation seeps along the inside of the windows; gazes fix on her. Hostile, she's sure, but that's natural. She stands her ground. The woman, after a minute's uncertainty, reels off a list of names – her three children, her sister, sister's husband and their two children, plus an uncle and aunt. They've been eating turkey burgers fried over a gas ring attached to a cylinder in the middle of the caravan. 'He's Dave,' she says, pointing to her husband, 'and I'm Caitlin.'

'We just came down to say merry Christmas and make sure you're OK,' Karina ventures. 'Won't you take the flowers? They're for you.'

Caitlin stares at them, nonplussed. 'That's kind of you, love. Not that we've got any place to put them, but it's very kind.' She gestures towards Fairfallows. 'You got anything to do with them?'

'My husband's their younger son.'

Dave, a hefty man in his forties with reddish stubble on his cheeks, lumbers up to the door and assesses her with a sharp once-over. 'Is he, now?' he remarks. 'You tell them from me, then, this is traditional Romnichal land. Our people were here centuries back. Now they can't get rid of us fast enough. Used to be that councils had to provide land for our caravans, but about twelve years ago there was a government act what changed it. There's no obligation now and it bloody shows. Now we're supposed to apply to buy land, and ask those stuck-up councillors nicely for planning permission, but nobody never gets it. So them social workers were here last week, wanting to take the kids. We sent 'em packing. How'd you like it if they tried to take *him* from you,' he adds, pointing at Jamie, 'just seeing as they don't fancy living like you live? Whole way of life's disappearing.'

Jamie shuffles closer to Karina. 'This government is always talking about how good diversity is,' Karina remarks, feeling anxious and stilted, putting an arm round her son.

'Any diversity except us, see? Anything but Gypsies. Terrorists, drug dealers, people traffickers, no problem, here you are, come to Britain, happy to have yer. But Romany folk? Dear oh dear. They go on about strong families and that, but let me tell you, families don't get stronger than ours. We're all family here.' He points around the field. 'We look after each other. That's real family values. But we don't count, do we, seeing as we're Romany?'

'They thought you were Irish,' Karina tells him.

'Doesn't make no difference anyway,' Caitlin says with a snort. 'We get the same crap. How come you care, love?'

'It's a long story, but I do,' Karina tells her.

What had she wanted? Some sense of kinship with the travellers? Some assurance that they have shared roots in the wandering tribes that arrived in Europe from the Punjab in the fourteenth century? The possibility that she belongs with them, not the Rookfields? It strikes her that the travellers' family is not so different from the Rookfields after all. The trappings – surroundings, food, accents, attitudes – can't or won't mix. But both families believe in their own history; both have their problems and their pride; and both are trying to enjoy Christmas Day as best they can.

'Look, love, I'd ask you in, but there in't much room, really,' Caitlin says. 'Though you're welcome enough to stop for a cuppa.'

'Thanks, but we should get back. You take care now.'

'You as well. Merry Christmas.'

'Merry Christmas,' Karina says; Jamie pipes an echo beside her. The children glance from the muddy field at his warm, padded jacket and Timberland boots. He gazes back with equal longing at their football. Up at the house, he'll be expected to watch a DVD of *Bedknobs and Broomsticks* for the sixth time.

'I think it'd be *brilliant* to live in a caravan,' he says as they walk.

'A lot of things look brilliant unless you're doing them because you have no choice.'

'But they want to, don't they?'

Karina isn't sure exactly how much of the travellers' life is choice and how much is vicious circle. 'Possibly,' she says.

After the caravan, Fairfallows feels absurdly vast and colder than ever. Inside, they stamp their feet to warm up – the chill is the damp, insidious kind that eats into the bone – then venture to the kitchen, where Anne is making tea.

'Karrie, darling,' she says, 'wherever have you been? Hilary thought you'd taken the flowers down to the travellers.'

'We did. It's Christmas.'

'But Karina – heavens! You're a brave girl.'

'Not at all. I just gave them the flowers and we had a chat.'

'And Jamie – oh dear . . . please take those muddy boots off, darling. Why don't you go upstairs and watch *Bedknobs and Broomsticks* in the den?'

Given a choice, Jamie would have preferred to be playing football in the mud with the caravan children. When he's plodded obediently away, Karina tells Anne, 'I thought it might be good for him to see how they live.'

'Well, it's not a bad idea. I'm glad you made contact and Christmas is a good time to do it.'

'You don't mind?' Karina is mortified to realise that she'd been hoping her in-laws would be furious.

'People are people,' Anne remarks. 'We're all different, but we're all the same. That's one reason I love biography – because you can see that across time, people don't essentially change very much. I don't mind the travellers, as it happens, but Hilary's obsessed with getting rid of them. And I think they sense he's an easy target. How about a piece of Christmas cake?'

'"She's gone with the raggle-taggle Gypsies-oh!"' Hilary sings in the distance.

'I can't believe you did that,' Julian says, at home.

Karina, changing out of her Christmas Day clothes, doesn't reply.

'And taking Jamie with you!'

'I didn't want him to think that Fairfallows is all there is.'

'You're not related to them, you know. Roma my foot. Those travellers are originally Irish.'

'That's not the point,' says Karina, although to some extent it is.

'You were lucky to escape with your life. They could have taken their pick of robbery, rape or murder.'

'Christ, Jules, they're not dangerous. They're ordinary people, they just live in caravans. Caitlin even offered me a cup of tea. They were fine.'

'They weren't fine when father called the authorities about the children last week. Some of the blokes set on them with knives.'

'Wouldn't you set on someone with a knife if he tried to take Jamie away?'

'Look, we have to get them off the meadow,' Julian insists, ignoring her comment, 'and we shouldn't have to make the police do it. Don't you see? We don't *want* to criminalise them, but they're forcing us into it. You don't understand, darling one. It's a financial disaster for Fairfallows, and you taking them flowers and saying "Merry Christmas" isn't going to help.'

'Oh, Jules, stop it. I don't feel like being lectured now.'

'I'm sure you don't. But what am I meant to tell Father? That my wife has more time for trespassing layabouts than for our own family?'

'Why not?' Karina snaps. 'They're more interesting.'

Julian's expression slides a notch beyond irritation to incomprehension.

'Karina, are you insane?'

'Maybe.'

Rohan is away, but Karina goes to Brighton in any case while Jamie is rekindling his friendship with Olly Pearson, and Julian, confined to his study, tries to unravel the cat's cradle that Hilary has made of the Fairfallows accounts. She tells him she's going to the sales, but instead she walks along the stony beach, letting the wind bite into her. She talks inwardly to Lindy. She can still hear her voice. What alarms her is the thought that one day she may forget it.

'It's not you, it's them,' Lindy seems to tell her. 'Arthur's one of the biggest stiff old traditionalists you'll ever meet. As for poor bloody Hilary . . .'

'But Julian isn't like them,' Karina answers. 'There's more to him.'

'Give him half a chance. Look at him again in twenty-five years' time.'

'Lin, what's it like? On the other side?'

'I'm still here.'

Karina gazes out at the sea, which is as grey as molten mercury. 'If I'd met Rohan earlier . . .'

'You didn't. You've just got a thing about struggling composers whose names begin with R. Don't start saying "if only". There's no point.'

'You can talk.' Karina imagines teasing her friend.

'I know. But you've got to make the best of what you've got, Karrie. Because it's over too soon.'

'Does that mean that if you're miserable, you shouldn't try to change things?'

'No. But be careful what you change. You might replace one set of problems with another.'

'Like—?'

'I'm not even going to begin on that.' Karina imagines Lindy, nose in the air, shaking her head, turning to walk away.

'Lin, don't go. I miss you.'

'Yeah. I miss you too. But I'm here. We can talk whenever. And remember: it's not who he is that counts. It's what he means to you . . .'

'I think who he *is* does matter, quite a lot . . .' says Karina, aloud.

Her friend's shade dissolves like salt into the waves. Tears burn in Karina's eyes. She walks back towards the sea-front road and buys coffee in a plastic cup to rekindle her connection with reality.

15

Time begins to dance, stamping its feet to Bartók's rhythms. A few points anchor Karina: her violin, her ears, the music on the stand and the other violin; the two sounds are alike but separate, blending, jousting, playing games.

'It's the first beat, isn't it?' says Rohan, fingertips skittering, bow as sure as a laser. 'Always that Hungarian first beat. Like a Scotch snap.'

'Yes,' says Karina, without stopping. She hasn't played with another musician, except her parents, in years. They stand side by side, breathing together naturally. If only the orchestra had felt like this.

At the end, Rohan says 'Great! Next one,' and flips over the page.

Rohan lives in the tidiest one-bed flat Karina has ever seen. She'd passed it, without knowing, when she walked by the sea a week earlier; it's in a side-street, at the top of a house in a Regency terrace. Brighton, he told her, isn't cheap, but it's slightly cheaper than London: a better home for what money you can make as a freelance fiddler. The staircase from the ground floor sweeps up in a graceful curve, and the tall windows of Rohan's front room offer a sea view, if you lean as far out as possible and crick your neck to the right. On the sills stand terracotta troughs of yellow and white winter pansies. In the kitchen, overlooking the downstairs flat's back garden, Rohan made her a lunch of lentil soup, baguettes and three different cheeses with tomatoes and grapes. Then they took out their violins and began.

It's only when Karina's shoulders start to ache that she realises they've been playing for an hour and a half, and she suggests a break.

Rohan puts down his violin and stretches his arms, catlike. 'Can I try your fiddle?' he asks. Karina hands it to him and he plays some figurations. The instrument seems to like him as much as he likes it. 'Nice,' he says. 'Very nice. It's really responsive, much more than mine. Pretty carving, too. What is it?'

'It's nothing special. My dad got it for me through some deal with a colleague at the Academy. I think it's Polish. Julian calls it "The Matchbox".'

'It's a very good instrument, though. Mine's OK, but I'd give my eye-teeth for a really fantastic violin. This one was apparently wrongly identified. The guy who sold it to me said it was Italian, eighteenth century, but last year I took it to Jonny Goldsmith and he said it's not Italian and it's not worth anything like what I paid for it. It's crazy.'

'I've never taken this one to Goldsmith's. I just go to a local guy if anything needs fixing.' Karina tries Rohan's violin. The fingerboard is warm from his grip. 'It sounds like you,' she says. 'I feel like I'm playing your voice.'

'Karrie, you're amazing,' Rohan says, watching. 'You have to start playing again, properly.'

'Maybe, if I had something to work for.' She rubs her sore left shoulder with her right hand. Rohan shifts, then stops – as if he'd have liked to help her, but doesn't dare.

'Let's find something,' he says. 'How about Mozart string quintets?'

'Quintets? Not with your group? I can't play the viola.'

'Harry can. He's clever, is Harry, and he's always saying he ought to play viola more often. We'll shunt him onto first viola, which will put Genya's nose beautifully out of joint, and you can play second violin. It'll be nice to have a girl in the group.' Rohan's eyes tease her. 'Might be good for the energy, it needs a kick in the pants. Heck, I'll shut up, I don't want to put you off!'

'I'm not sure I'm *on*. Isn't it a bit weird to book an extra violinist instead of a violist? And at this kind of notice?'

'I'll talk them into it, it won't be a problem. And there's still time to change the programme for Budapest. We were going to do Mozart, so we'll do the G minor and C major quintets, and we're already set up for a trial run in Beaconsfield. It's not remotely scary. What do you say?'

Karina founders. 'I don't want to say no. But I'm not sure I ought to say yes.'

'That's yes, then. What you *want* has a lot to do with it. Coffee?' Rohan dives into the kitchen. Karina leans against the door-frame.

'Ro, I'm not sure.'

'What's stopping you?'

'Everything. Giving concerts, because I haven't for years. Whether I'm up to it. And what the others will say. You've been playing together for ages, you're making CDs, and I'm just a nobody.'

'You'd still be playing in the best orchestra in the country if your husband hadn't decided for you that you should leave and have a baby. You're fantastic and after the first few times, you'll be back in the swing of it, no problem. As for the others, they'll adore you. Let me talk to them.'

'But do you really want me to play with your quartet? I mean – I'm not expecting it, I'm not asking you for anything like this – you mustn't feel that just because—'

'Just because what, Karina?' Rohan turns, coffee pot in hand. Then he puts it down. The thread of energy between them is so powerful that he simply walks along it to her and draws her forehead against his shoulder, one large hand scrunching her hair. Karina feels his jersey on her cheek, his pulse thudding beneath. Her hand grasps the wool of its own accord.

'I can't do this,' she says.

She keeps her head down so that he can't kiss her, but he doesn't try to. Instead, he says, 'I can't either.'

She looks up.

'You matter too much,' he says. 'I've had lots of affairs, but I can't have them if they matter the way you do.'

'I'd better go.'

'No, wait. Come here.'

Rohan takes her arm and pulls out a chair for her at the table. Karina sits on it and puts her hands over her face. She feels seasick.

'Either this is too dangerous and we say goodbye now,' Rohan says, 'or we accept that this is too special to throw away and we have to channel it differently.'

'How?'

'There's all that history pulling us together – we can't just ditch it. I know you're married, I wish you weren't, but you are and I respect that. So let's do something worthwhile instead. Like playing Mozart, or finding your grandmother's violin, or both. Unless you really want to say goodbye, which is your prerogative.'

Karina imagines crying all the way home, then having to explain her gutted condition to Julian in a heap of lies. She says nothing.

'Mozart quintets,' Rohan presses. 'What do you think?'

'Are you sure?'

'You bet. So we're on.' Rohan takes her hand, squeezes, then lets go. A tacit understanding: they won't touch each other again.

Julian's face bears a familiar, purposeful look. 'The G minor Quintet,' he muses, running a finger along his Mozart chamber music CD shelf. A minute later he's placed a stack of discs in front of Karina. 'Which shall we try first?'

Telling Julian about the Budapest concert has had an instantaneous result, which, with hindsight, she could have predicted. She picks up the top disc. 'Tokyo Quartet and friend?'

They listen. Julian notes the timings written beside each movement on the CD booklet, the degree of the players' vibrato, the balance that the recording engineer has organised. After three minutes, he stops the music and puts on another disc. Karina closes her eyes. 'Beautiful.'

'Old-fashioned,' comments Julian. 'Too much vibrato.'

'I think it's wonderful. I love the first violinist's tone.'

'Let's try this one.' He pulls out a disc bearing the logo of a specialist early music label.

After a few seconds, Karina winces. 'It's thin. It's horrible, cold, soulless. They're so busy trying to be correct that they've forgotten about the feeling.'

'Still, this is what people expect today.'

'I don't care. If there's no heart, there's nothing worth hearing.'

Some while later, they settle on an account by a group of young international soloists recorded live at a German festival, which they both enjoy, if for different reasons: Julian likes the brisk tempi, Karina the beautiful tone.

'So, little Gypsy, which is most like Rohan?' asks Julian.

Karina points at the second CD.

'All that schmaltz?'

'It's not schmaltz, it's heart. Rohan plays like a violinist from fifty years ago. He plays like my grandmother – at least, he wants to.'

'He wants to play like your grandmother and he wants to take you to Budapest.' Julian raises his eyebrows. 'What else does he want, Karrie?'

A Nicolò Amati violin, last seen in Budapest in 1956. 'Not impossible, though unlikely,' Jonny Goldsmith remarks, scratching his ear. 'Let's see . . .'

Karina and Rohan stand behind him, staring at the computer screen in the office of his Soho showroom, where the shelving buckles under the box files. The Goldsmith family's stringed instrument dealing and repair business dates back to the mid-nineteenth century; almost every fine violin, viola and cello to pass through London has been here, and the Goldsmiths keep meticulous records. Karina and Rohan have been hoping to discover, somewhere in this dizzying archive, the truth behind the rumours about Mimi's Amati.

'She says that her Guadagnini was bought for her through your father,' Karina tells Jonny.

'Right, but not by trading in an Amati. There's no trace in the records of Mimi Rácz bringing one in, either for sale or repair. And if it's true, if she really did have the Amati that belonged to Francesco Avignola, I can't think why she'd have switched it for that Guadagnini.'

'Avignola?' Rohan asks, amazed. 'Are you sure?'

Jonny goes to a set of shelves by the window and pulls down a fat volume.

'This is my fine fiddles bible,' he tells them. 'This book has the history, as far as it's been traced, of the top five hundred violins, those whose whereabouts are known and those that are currently lost, made by Stradivari, Guarneri, Amati and a handful of others. Let's look up Rácz in the index . . . Here we go. A Nicolò Amati, made in Cremona in 1671, no less. So first it's played in Italy, whereabouts uncertain, then finds its way to France, where it promptly vanishes for the duration of the Revolution. Next, it pops up in Paris, 1831. Played once by Paganini.'

'Jesus,' mutters Rohan.

'Things start getting really interesting, and better documented, in 1865 in Baden-Baden, where the young virtuoso Francesco Avignola, visiting with his "patroness" and attending an operetta at Pauline Viardot's private theatre, hears on the grapevine that there's an important instrument in town. By then Avignola was being called the next Paganini, and his willing lady-friend, an outcast Habsburg with a penchant for young Latin lovers, buys the fiddle for him. Instruments didn't cost anything like today's prices then, but they weren't cheap. So Avignola takes the violin to Venice, Vienna, Berlin, Bucharest and back to Paris, but there, one day, he drinks too much absinthe, doesn't obey the Green Cross code and ends up flat as a crêpe under a hansom cab on the Boulevard Montparnasse. His heartbroken princess gets the violin back and won't let it out of her sight, so it sits in her Venetian palazzo and nobody plays it until 1910. That year, she knows she's dying, and she holds one last party while she still can. The Princesse de Polignac brings all her arty friends, including a young fiddler from Paris; in a final gesture of generosity, the patroness bestows her beloved's Amati on this French fellow. He guards it with his life until the 1930s when he falls on hard times and puts it up for sale in Paris. At which point, it's bought by – get this – an anonymous French buyer, who gives it to Mimi Rácz.'

'Not Marc Duplessis?' says Karina.

Jonny shrugs. He reaches up for another book, entitled *Great Violinists of the Past and Present*. 'There's a nice little biog of her in here.'

'There is?' says Karina, who's never seen this book before.

'Here you are. Karina Rookfield, This Is Your Grandmother. My God, she was gorgeous. Look at those eyes.' Jonny shows them the photo of Mimi, taken in New York in 1940, beside her biographic details. Rohan waits, on tenterhooks. 'So . . .' Jonny licks a finger and turns the page, reading. 'It says here that Mimi Rácz gave the world premiere of the Suite *Dans l'ombre des forêts* on Avignola's Amati in 1936. After that, it's another saga. She goes back to Budapest in a piece of stonking bad timing, marries

Tamás Veres and has her son – your dad. Just as the Second World War's getting underway, someone invites her to America for six weeks; she goes, but doesn't come back for nearly seven years because while she's gone, Europe starts tearing itself apart – for her, worst of all, in 1944 the Germans surge into Hungary from one side and the Russians from the other. But then, after it's all over, she's homesick, yes, *homesick*, and heads back over the pond. More marvellous Rácz timing. She thinks she can keep up her international career, but the communist regime has other ideas. Finally, 1956. Revolution. Bang bang. Russians. She gets out, with her son – your dad – but, apparently, not with the Amati. Since then, zilch.'

'Heck,' Rohan says, 'so she left it behind.'

Karina stares at the fire escape in the Soho backyard. 'You mean, all this information has been sitting in a *book*, and I never knew?'

'Your father never told you?' Jonny asks.

'He keeps saying the past is the past, and we have to look forwards, not backwards. And my grandmother's never told me anything either. She's very stubborn.'

'Yet Duplessis may have bought the violin for her. Unbelievable.' Rohan presses Karina's shoulder.

'We don't know that.' She shuffles away. 'It only says "French". That doesn't mean a thing.'

'The question is, how accurate is this book?' Jonny says. 'It was published twenty years ago – there's bound to be new info since then. The Internet's a seething great sewer full of it, but you can't be sure what's reliable.'

How come her grandmother had had a violin that had touched some of the greatest figures in the history of music, yet she has never said a word about it? If that violin had been in the Rookfield family, they'd have talked of nothing else. But her father? All he says is 'Rottweilers'.

Later that evening, Karina phones Jamie at school. While he moans about the difficult fractions he's trying to learn, she's still trying to marry past to present. 'Night night, Mum,' says the reluctant Jamie as eight thirty approaches.

She lights the log fire and stares into the flames. Lewes maintains a quiet, hilly existence around her; it will liven up with Glyndebourne's opera festival-goers in summer, but spends the winter in firelit semi-hibernation. Her life, too, is quiet and routine: teaching, housekeeping, mothering. At least, it was before all this began. She's an ordinary woman with an ordinary family and a settled life – but is there any facet of her family's history that doesn't touch her? Is that why her parents kept back so much, because they knew that otherwise it would transform her as inexorably as fire transfigures wood?

She watches a log shunt, luminous and sizzling, down the pyramid of sticks and twisted newspaper in the grate. Wood has to grow, burn, or transmogrify. As a tree, it provides oxygen, shelter or food. Set alight, it gives warmth. Fashioned into furniture, it can support anything from a backside to a heap of books. Carved into a violin, it makes music. Cut down and discarded, though, it rots away.

Karina phones her parents. 'Dad? I need to ask you about Grandma's violin,' she ventures, fidgeting. She's not normally so nervous talking to her father.

'Who's been telling you fairy tales now?' Dénes sounds exasperated.

'I went to see Jonny Goldsmith. There's a book of five hundred . . .'

'Oh, bloody hell.' Dénes groans. 'Eiyiyi. Karina, you don't know the damage that book has done. Since it was published, since the information got onto the *Internet*' – Dénes loathes the Internet above all other modern inventions – 'this happens a hundred times. People call me up: "Oh, Mr Veres, how wonderful to talk to you, the great cello teacher, the son of Mimi Rácz, and by the way what happened to the Amati?" Karina, I tell you, be careful. Everyone wants that fucking violin. Anybody who comes to you saying they want you or me or my poor old mother is *bloody lying*. They want that fiddle, because now it would be worth a lot of money. Either they want to sell it "on your behalf", in other words rip you off, or they want to play the thing themselves, for nothing.'

'I see.' Karina feels unaccountably cold.

'Fucking cunts. Tell them *baszd meg*! Now, how's that boy of yours getting on at his posh school?'

When Karina puts the phone down, she's more confused than ever.

Her mobile is beeping. She reads a text: '4tet happy with 5tet. 1st rehearsal Feb 28, OK? R.'

Julian, home from work half an hour later, finds her huddled in her armchair by the fire, shivering. 'Darling, you're ill. Have you got a fever?'

'No, no, I'm fine.'

'Oh, darling one, what's eating you? And what are we eating?'

Karina hasn't made supper. She's not hungry.

'What's going on? Shall I call the doctor?' He rubs her chilly hands.

'No, love, I'm fine.'

'Why don't we go for a pizza? Would that cheer you up?'

She pulls herself out of her chair. Reality check needed.

Eating salad, Karina watches Julian cut his pizza into symmetrical slices. Everything in his dinner is tidy and ordered. She had pizza earlier, for lunch with Rohan in Soho. He plunged straight into the centre where the juiciest vegetables and the gooeyest melted cheese lurked; he left the hard, dry edges. Is he cultivating their relationship in the hope of getting hold of her grandmother's violin? All that empathy – but is he using her? And now she has to play Mozart quintets with him in, of all places, Budapest.

'What *is* the matter?' Julian demands. 'Are you getting your period?'

'I miss Lindy,' says Karina; it's true.

'I know. So do we all. But why don't you go and see your other friends? Nicki left you a message the other day, didn't she? Why don't you go out with her sometime?'

'I don't want to. She reminds me too much of the old times. And I don't want to sit there listening to her grumbling about how she can't find a man and she's got no work. She could find both very easily if she wanted to, but she's always thought the world owed her a living.'

'Well, what *would* help?' Julian looks exasperated.

Karina wonders why men always have to do things, rather than simply live them, and furthermore expect that instant superficial action will change the fundamentals at their roots. 'Maybe I should look for some bereavement counselling,' she says.

'You don't need counselling,' Julian protests. 'You've got me.'

Over Sunday lunch in Forest Road, while Jamie tucks into Erzsébet's goulash stew with the gusto of a boy adjusting to the rigours of cross-country running, Karina explains her forthcoming trip to Hungary. 'I've been thinking about taking Jamie with me,' she adds.

'Budapest?' Jamie pauses, fork in mouth. 'When's that, Mum?'

'During your Easter holiday.'

'What's Jamie going to do in Budapest while you give your concert?' Julian demands.

'It's not much fun for a child,' Erzsébet remarks gently. 'I mean, you could take him to Margaret Island, which is a lovely outdoor thing to do, but . . .'

Karina hadn't considered enough the time pressures of going abroad as a performer rather than as a holidaying parent. 'He could listen,' she suggests. 'Couldn't you, Schnooks? And we can go and find the places where my grandmother lived, and where your grandfather was born. You can learn something about what it means to be Hungarian.'

'I'm not Hungarian.' Jamie munches. 'I'm English, I mean, British.'

'You're second-generation British, on my side,' Karina tells him. 'Do you know what that means?'

'You were the first generation of your family to be born in this country,' Jamie rattles off. St Matthew's has been drilling its boys in the phraseology of immigration. 'And I'm the second. But Dad's completely British, so I'm not second anything.'

'You are, a little bit. Wouldn't you like to see where Grandma and Grandad come from?'

'They're here now, aren't they? Grandma, can I have some more goulash, please?'

Dénes catches Karina's eye over the bread basket. 'You were the same,' he tells her. 'You didn't want to know, when you were younger. First you were busy with school, friends, boyfriends, college, orchestra. Then you got married. Then you had Jamie. When were you going to think about Hungary? And, like I tell you, why should you? Besides, it was another world then. We didn't believe the Iron Curtain would ever come down and I don't believe it's possible to live in another country unless you assimilate.'

'I do want to go there now. Very much. I hope you don't mind,' Karina ventures.

'Mind? I should mind? It's your life – if you want to waste your time on old stories . . .'

'Dad, I want to see it. And I think you're maybe more Hungarian here than you ever would have been there,' Karina points out.

'You can take Dénes out of Hungary, but you can't take Hungary out of Dénes,' Julian adds.

'You're right, I am still in another world.' Dénes, whose posture has the poise of a lead cellist in full flight, gestures broadly. 'And sometimes I despair of this one. I see people in the supermarket, like fat slugs with their children just like them – I don't care if people are fat, but they shouldn't set this example to their children! They fill their bodies with junk food and their minds with junk TV. But these people are *free*! They don't have the ÁVH, they're not going to be arrested and tortured or sent to Siberia, they don't have Russian tanks rolling through the streets, they have every luxury money can buy. And what do they do with freedom? They put it down the sewers! They have freedom to learn, think, explore, create, but they don't do none of it. My God, what an opportunity is life! And to be an artist, to create, to raise us up – this is the way to be fully human. Jamie, you listen to your old grandfather. You have one life: this life. Don't be like animals. Use it well.'

'Why'd we have Russian tanks rolling through the streets, Grandad?' Jamie asks.

'More stew, Julian?' Erzsébet coaxes. 'Look at all this food. You must help me.' She loads three extra spoonfuls onto his plate.

'You don't need to take Jamie to Hungary,' Julian tells Karina, tucking in. 'He's already there . . . Seriously, though, I'll take the Friday off – I haven't had a day off in months – and I'll make sure I'm home all weekend. We'll run you to the airport and pick you up again on the Sunday. How does that sound?'

'Karina, it's good you suddenly start playing professional chamber music. Why you do it now?' Dénes demands, snapping out of rant mode.

Karina seems to see her parents through a soft gauze. 'You can take the girl out of music, but you can't take the music out of the girl,' she suggests.

'It'll do you good,' Erzsébet declares. 'You need something more than motherhood and teaching in your life, Karina.'

Jamie looks up and asks, 'Why?'

16

Rohan laughs when Karina tells him how outraged Jamie was that she might consider playing the violin as fulfilling as motherhood. Curled in her armchair on a cold afternoon, talking on the phone, Karina pictures him in his flat: the curving banister, the bright window-boxes. He's been on tour for a week with the quartet.

'I hate him being away,' she says. 'I really do.'

'But I'd have thought – forgive me, Karrie, I don't know anything about bringing up kids, though I'd like to – but shouldn't the school be a joint decision between you and Julian?'

'You'd think so, wouldn't you?' Karina's mind takes an ill-advised turning: Rohan wants kids?

'Families are never easy, I guess,' he remarks.

'What was your family like when you were growing up?'

'Loud! We used to row very noisily, then kiss and make up and forget it. I wouldn't have liked to live next door to us, because apart from the shouting, there was me playing the fiddle and then Liora got into punk, bought a guitar and dyed her hair pink. That set off a few ructions in Kingsbury! At least they were free of me during term-time.'

Karina laughs, trying to imagine Rohan as a teenager. 'Were you a rebel too?'

'God, no. I wish I had been. I just practised. I was horribly studious and shy.'

'You? Shy?'

'The kids at my primary school used to tease me about my accent. I didn't know I had one, but they used to tell me to say "four" because apparently it came out sounding like "fooor". I'd just picked it up from my parents.'

Karina tells him about her experiences in the school dining room.

'Jeez,' says Rohan. 'It's hard to believe how cruel kids can be.'

'But we still have them.'

'Or would like to.'

'Ro, I've got a pupil turning up any minute, I have to go.'

'Karrie, can we have lunch on Monday? There's so much I want to tell you. One o'clock, Lane's?'

'Wonderful. I'll be there.'

Karina's first pupil is due in five minutes. She plays a few exercises to warm up, and removes the Mozart quintets from her music stand. She's already worked so hard that she can play her part almost from memory. Through the window she glimpses the little girl and her mother walking towards the house. At least while she's teaching, she can't think about anything else.

'Look at this.' Rohan lifts a paper bag out of his backpack and hands it to Karina across the wooden table at Lane's. It contains an old book, its cover slightly stained, its pages yellowing. *Marc Duplessis: His Life and Works* by Pierre Vincente. 'It's been out of print for decades and I reckoned you mightn't have it,' says Rohan. 'I got it second-hand on the Internet. There's a fantastic picture of Mimi.' He opens it and points.

There is her grandmother, sitting in a Paris café, smiling up at the tall, heavy-set Duplessis, with his big feet and hands and floppy hair. Karina has never seen this photo before. She's never heard of the book. Not from her father, not from Mimi, not even when she was learning the Suite at college.

'Pierre Vincente? Who's he?'

'He was a critic in Paris, a close friend of Duplessis. It's a very human book, which is probably why it went out of print. Apparently the musicologists don't like anything that suggests that music is actually created by a human being. Have a look at it while I get the lunch.'

'Ro, for heaven's sake let me buy lunch, just this once?'

'Nope, you stay there and read. Lasagne?' It's their routine now, whenever Rohan has a free Monday. They eat lasagne and salad, and drink fresh orange juice; later they have coffee and share a piece of cake, which they always start by insisting they won't eat this time.

Karina sits back and reads.

It was at Paris's Gare de l'Est that Duplessis met for the first time, by accident, the woman who was to become his muse: the Hungarian virtuoso Mimi Rácz. He was at the station seeing off his brother, who was travelling to Switzerland, when he spotted Rácz with her suitcases and violin, leaving the train on which she had just arrived from Budapest; she was to play the Brahms Violin Concerto in Paris in several days' time. Duplessis had heard Rácz play when the young violinist, then only nineteen but already world famous, gave her debut recital in the French capital the previous year. He had been intensely moved by the vitality of her playing and the magical variety of her expressive tone. When he heard the rumour that she was descended, some way back, from a long line of Hungarian Gypsy musicians, that only served to stimulate his interest further.

'Some way back?' says Karina, incredulous.

Duplessis navigated the crowded platform against the flow of arriving travellers, and with his usual gentle manner was about to introduce himself to Rácz as a composer and admirer. Rácz, however, mistook him for the cab-driver whom the orchestra's management had sent to meet her, and duly handed him her suitcases. Struck by her beauty, Duplessis was only too happy to oblige. She was lively and talkative, speaking error-ridden but enthusiastic French, and by the time Duplessis had walked with her to the taxi rank, he had heard many anecdotes about her journey from Budapest.

It was only when they joined the queue that Mimi Rácz realised Duplessis was no driver, but an opportunistic musician. Turning on every shred of his considerable charm, Duplessis acknowledged the accidental deception and persuaded her to agree to have dinner with him. He had already written a piece of music with her in mind.

'It's crazy – I don't know the first thing about Duplessis,' Karina remarks, pulling herself back to Brighton. Rohan has placed a plate of lasagne in front of her almost without her noticing.

'She didn't talk about him?'

'Not much. She was too busy talking about Tamás, my grandfather. She was so in love with him. Sometimes I think she believes he's still there, after fifty years.'

'God,' says Rohan. 'That's real love.'

'I'll read this. Thanks so much.' Karina closes the book and smiles across at him.

'So, rehearsal next week,' he says. 'How do you feel?'

'Nervous about meeting the others.'

'They can't wait to meet you!' Rohan laughs. 'Poor guys, they won't know what's hit them. When Malcolm gave our Budapest agent a Hungarian name as our extra player, apparently he was rather happy. You want to be Veres for this, don't you? Not Rookfield?'

'Oh – yes, that's fine.' Karina has never stopped thinking of herself as a Veres, though it's easier to live as a Rookfield in Sussex.

'Are you sure?' Rohan spots her hesitation. 'I thought it'd be nice, recapturing your musical identity in your name. There's a lot tied up in that name. People there might remember your father.'

'I doubt it. He was only eighteen when he left.'

Rohan and Karina tuck into their food. Energy twangs between them like a plucked string.

'I've found some interesting stuff on the Internet too,' Rohan says after a few minutes, rummaging again in his backpack. He hands Karina a clump of printouts, the top page bearing a photograph of a violin. There follows a list of the exhibits at a museum of musical instruments in Budapest. She reads: *VIOLIN – late 17th century. Bearing Nicolò Amati label, not thought genuine. Acquired 1958.*

'What makes you think this is Mimi's?' Questions career through her. Supposing it is the right violin? Would her father and grandmother try to get it back? Why was it there in the first place? Why is it 'not thought genuine'? How can they believe what Mimi says, when her mind is so often in orbit somewhere between Twickenham, Budapest and outer space? Could it be true that Rohan only wants to see her because of Mimi's lost Amati?

She opens the Duplessis biography at random. Words catch her eye:

'. . . *in 1938, when her son, Dénes, had just been born.*'

'What is it?' asks Rohan.

'There's something here about my father.'

Mimi Rácz and the baby Dénes arrived in Paris with an entourage of nurse, agent and secretary. Again, Duplessis met her at the Gare de l'Est. In roughly two and a half years following the premiere of Dans l'ombre des forêts, *Rácz's career, boosted by healthy sales of her gramophone records, had blossomed into full-scale stardom. Now she was on her way to Cherbourg, to catch the* Ile de France *to New York. Her husband, Tamás Veres, had remained in Budapest; whether because of his commitments at the university, the pressure of deadlines for his next translation (Balzac's* Cousin Bette*) or some difference of opinion between himself and his wife, we shall never be certain.*

'I love the way they used to call a quarrel a "difference of opinion",' Karina remarks.

'Go on,' says Rohan.

Mimi left the baby with the nurse while she went to dinner with Duplessis, who gave her the revised version of Dans l'ombre des forêts, *parts of which he'd reworked in the light of her observations. Mimi read through the manuscript at their restaurant table. Then, Duplessis related, she suggested: 'Marc, my dear, why not write a concerto for me? Give me a Gypsy violin concerto, with full orchestra and cimbalom, and we'll be immortal together.'*

Marc explained as best he could that to write such a concerto in a climate of depression, poverty and rising nationalism was futile and potentially dangerous. 'Who's going to play it?' he asked.

'Come with me to America,' Mimi said at once. 'We will find our audience there.'

Marc told her that this was impossible. He had his teaching post at the Conservatoire; she was a married woman with a child. But she insisted. If he were to go with her to the States, she could present him to every orchestra with which she was performing and together they could put forward their plans for a concerto that, in the New World beyond strife-torn Europe, could be welcomed with open arms. It would be six weeks well spent. Rácz was persuasive; and Marc Duplessis – despite, he said, his better judgment – set sail with her on the Ile de France *in July 1939.*

* * *

Karina reads on the train back to Lewes; she reads for hours before Julian comes home; she reads after their late supper while Julian, exhausted by last-minute ructions with Carsten Schmidt, valiantly tries to stay awake over the *Law Society Journal*. How is it possible that for several years Mimi had been the most important person in Marc Duplessis's life, and she'd never known?

'I haven't met your new quartet,' Julian remarks, yawning.

'Neither have I.'

'But this fellow, Rowan or whatever his name is. You seem friendly with him.'

'He's fascinated by Mimi. He's convinced her Amati must exist, if we can only find it. And his father knew Duplessis.'

'Isn't he just using Mimi and that blasted fiddle as a way to chat you up?' Julian suggests. 'If a bloke wants to have an affair with a married woman, he has to persuade her. And being interested in her famous grandmother and her missing violin would be quite a good way to do it.'

Karina puts down the book. First her father thinks Rohan is using her to get to Mimi's violin. Now Julian thinks Rohan is using Mimi's violin to get to her. Either is moderately plausible. 'Rohan's a good friend,' she says.

'Invite him to dinner, then. Let's have a name-day bash for you on the twenty-fourth of March.'

'It could wait for my birthday,' Karina stalls – that's not until June.

'Why? You always liked the name-day thing. It's a cute idea, a day to celebrate a name, and it's only a month off. We could invite Andy and Sarah, we owe them one, and we can ask Ro-thing and anyone else you like.'

'If you want to,' Karina says, 'then we will.'

'So, little Gypsy, what are you learning from your new book?'

'A lot. Did you know that my grandmother was in America for the whole of the war? And so was my dad. And Duplessis.'

'Where was Tamás?'

'Budapest. He was too old to be drafted. He was hiding in the university cellars while the Russians fought the Germans.'

'So did she take the Amati with her, or was it hiding too?'

'That's the first problem: the book doesn't say. The other problem is that everyone thinks about the violin. Not the people.'

'You mean . . . Duplessis went with her and Tamás didn't?'

There's a long silence.

'My grandfather's always been such a hero,' says Karina. 'I'm sure there was nothing more to it.'

Because Mimi talks about him all the time – sometimes talks *to* him – Karina's image of Tamás is one step short of apostolic. Tamás was the perfect man, Mimi would insist. Handsome, intelligent, loving, honest, idealistic, a good father, a strong human being. Where did Duplessis come into this? Without saying so outright, Pierre Vincente makes it perfectly clear that Duplessis was manically, insanely and helplessly in love with Mimi Rácz.

Her grandmother had said, 'It's a long time ago.' Karina had taken that to mean: 'I can't remember.' Perhaps it actually meant, 'Don't disturb such memories now . . .'?

Karina goes to her music cupboard, takes out the Suite and runs her fingertips across the notes, as if they're written in Braille. She needs to feel it, in muscle, nerves and skin. If Marc Duplessis were her real grandfather . . .

'Let's turn in.' Julian yawns. 'I'm dog-tired. You wouldn't believe the stuff Schmidt finds to chuck at me.'

'At the moment, I'd believe anything.' The weary Karina knows that she won't sleep. 'I just want to phone my parents.'

'*Ha*llo, Schnooky, I can hear you're full of questions,' Dénes says, when Karina gets through. 'What happened?'

'Dad, is it true that you went to America with your mother when you were a few months old? Just at the beginning of the war?'

'Well, just at the beginning of the war, I was recently born. So if my mother went on tour to America, I expect I went with her. You'll forgive me if my memory doesn't extend quite so far.'

'And is it true that Marc Duplessis went too, while your father stayed in Budapest?'

'My father had students, he had his translations. It's not unusual.'

'It's just that – I've got a book about Duplessis, and Grandma once said . . .' Karina stops. Her father's silence is louder than any she's heard to date.

'Schnooky, don't put two and two together and make ten,' he

says finally. 'It's not so simple. That's all I can say. And now I am going to bed. With your mother. Goodnight, Karina.'

'Mum,' says Jamie's forlorn voice, 'can I come home early this week? Like Thursday? Please, Mum?'

'Darling, what is it?' Karina is standing in Lewes High Street with two bags of groceries at her feet.

'I can't do the maths prep. I don't understand it.'

'Can you get someone to explain it? One of the others?'

'Not really. Because Mr Whitehouse would be livid, and . . .'

'Is Mr Whitehouse the one who called you names?'

There's a silence. Karina can hear Jamie's breathing.

'Well, if I get detention, I won't be the only one.' Jamie sighs. An eight-year-old trying to make the best of a bad job.

'We wrote to the headmaster about him, darling.'

'I know, and Mr Whitehouse won't let me forget it. He doesn't call me names now, but what he does instead is he picks on Calum and Laurence and makes sure one of us always has detention when there's something nice we'd all be doing together. It's horrible.'

'You sound tired.'

'Yeah. We had – well, you know. We went to sleep quite soon after, but I had a tummy-ache and I kept waking up.'

'Oh, Schnooky, this has got to stop! I want you to *not* sit up all night eating cakes, please. And listen, with the maths, do the best you can, all right? Nobody can do better than that. It'll be the holidays again soon and we'll ask Calum and Laurence to come and stay one weekend.'

'OK, Mum.' Stiff upper lip, aged eight.

At least at a day-school, he could get away from mean teachers every afternoon; besides, if your son is asleep in your own home, you'll know that he isn't guzzling excess sugar in the small hours, then feeling too tired to understand maths the next day. She doesn't know whether to laugh or cry. Should she just drive there and bring him back? It's tempting. There's a problem, though: tomorrow she has her first rehearsal with Rohan's quartet in London.

After agonising through her teaching, she waits for Julian, but he's preparing for a European rail industry conference and calls at seven thirty to say he's still at the office, working on his speech.

'Darling, Jamie has to learn to deal with this,' he says when she reports the evening's chat. 'You can't turn him back into a baby at the first little hitch.'

Torn in more directions than she'd thought possible, Karina puts on Rohan's CD, then lies on the floor near the fire, reading about Duplessis, losing herself in visions of the past.

17

In Harry Macintosh's pine-floored living room in Camden Town, three strange pairs of eyes scrutinise Karina over five musical instruments.

Harry is to her left, playing the viola instead of his usual violin. Over a welcoming coffee he'd quizzed her with the alacrity of a *Newsnight* presenter. Who were her teachers? How long had she been in the orchestra? Did she know his friend, its principal cellist? Karina swallowed her coffee and tried to smile.

Malcolm, the white-haired cellist, had unnerved her even more. 'Rohan is very persuasive,' he'd said, his tone cutting. 'You know, of course, that the St Francis is *my* quartet. I'm the founder and I do the management. You have any trouble from them, Karina, you come straight to me, all right?' Karina tried to smile again.

'One thing very important here: food.' The violist, Yevgeny, whom the others call Genya, made her smile at once. 'We play. Then we eat! Karina, please, have biscuit. Lyuba, my wife, makes biscuits for rehearsal.' He handed round a Tupperware box of chocolate chip cookies that didn't so much melt in the mouth as collapse into liquid bliss.

'Lyuba's cooking will be the death of us all,' remarked Harry, munching his third. 'If Rohan's music doesn't do the job first. Has he forced you to listen to his home-cooked CD yet, Karina?'

Rohan caught Karina's eye and winked. She winked back. Harry noticed. It hadn't taken Karina long to work out that Harry noticed everything. His gaze flickered towards her gold rings.

'Come on, you chaps,' said Rohan. 'Let's get stuck in.'

Now, in her place in the open circle of the quintet, Karina concentrates. She attunes her ear to Harry as the player with whom she has most often to blend.

'What you've got to do is play up a bit, Karina,' Harry tells her after they've run through the first movement. 'Try to match Ro as well as me.'

'You're doing great, Karrie,' Rohan adds. 'Your sound is lovely.'

Malcolm's face betrays discontent. 'I think the tempo is a little slow,' he says.

Rohan sets Harry's metronome to the mark at the top of the first page. It clicks out a pulse at exactly the speed they've been playing.

'The period-instrument ensembles have upped Mozart tempi, generally,' Malcolm points out. 'People expect something a little brisker now.'

'You want to use a different edition?' Rohan asks. His part is covered in the most detailed pencilling of fingering, phrasing and dynamics that Karina has ever seen.

'No, I'm just saying we should try it a notch faster.'

'I'll try anything once.' Rohan turns back to the beginning. They start again; Karina, keeping up at the new pace, sweats and tries not to worry.

The prickly atmosphere smoothes out; the five of them are so focused on their task that soon there's no room for sniping. Disagreements evolve and dissolve. Malcolm wants to change a basic concept while the others disagree; Harry and Malcolm declare Genya too loud; Malcolm and Rohan gang up to joke about viola players. The two violins, though, exist as one. Playing together, Karina feels overwhelmed by the sense, usually kept at the back of her mind, that she's known Rohan forever.

'Nice one, Karina,' Harry says when they break for lunch. 'You'll have me out of a job.'

'Of course I won't!' The new kid on the block. Was this how Jamie felt at school?

Rohan touches her arm. 'Are we near where Lindy lived?'

'Not far.'

'I'm sorry it had to be here.'

'It's fine. It'll do me good to see that Camden still exists.'

'Let's go out for a bit and you can show me things. Hey, chaps. Back here, two thirty.'

* * *

It's a long time since Karina last walked down Camden High Street. Tourists head for the market, in winter-reduced numbers; litter and cigarette stubs blow against the kerb; traffic crawls through the one-way system. Across the road is the stop where she and Lindy didn't board the overcrowded bus for what would have been their last trip to Harvey Nichols.

'It's as if every paving-stone is a picture of Lindy,' Karina admits.

'Are you OK? Would you prefer to go somewhere else?'

'No, I had to come back sometime. Do you want to see her shop?'

They stop at a Greek bakery where Karina and Lindy had often feasted on olive bread or almond croissants. Eating on the move, they walk towards the railway bridge and round the corner towards the bookshop; en route is Zucchini's.

'We used to eat here a lot,' Karina says. 'I should pop in and see Pietro.'

'Let's all come here for dinner later, if you'd like to?' Rohan suggests. 'It might help exorcise it.'

Karina pushes the door open. The restaurant is busy; Pietro, a stately figure in his black and white apron, is serving a platter of antipasti. He glances up, does a double take and, leaving the antipasti on its table, comes towards Karina with open arms. 'Miss Lindy Rookfield of the bookshop, I am so sad, I miss her!'

'So do I, Pietro.' Karina hugs him.

'This poor lady. Just innocent, you know? Doing her job. And somebody don't care about safety. Mrs Karina, you are coming back to us?'

'Dinner tonight, with some friends, if you've got room for five of us? Pietro, this is Rohan. We play music together.'

'You make beautiful music! So I reserve the best table.'

'See you later.' Karina smiles.

The bookshop is as chilly as ever. At first Karina, hesitating by the door, thinks that nothing has changed, but soon she senses that the shop has mislaid its purpose. Where Lindy's handwritten notices used to perch on the tables, quirky captions recommending unusual novels, now there are mass-produced signs reading SPECIAL OFFER: 3 FOR 2. On the shelf where Lindy had instigated a section named IF YOU LIKED THIS, TRY THIS, Paul has placed TOP SELLERS. Paul, at the counter, stares at Karina as if seeing Lindy's ghost. She shakes his hand and introduces Rohan.

'We're making more of an effort to compete with the high street heavyweights,' Paul tells them.

The shop hasn't been dusted for a while. Lindy used to do everything herself. 'How's business?' Karina asks.

'As good as can be expected. The owner's talking about either revamping the place or selling up.'

'It would have broken Lindy's heart if the shop went under.' Karina doesn't add that it would have been equally upsetting for her to lose the personal touches, the maverick enthusiasm that had attracted her loyal customers.

'You won't believe it, but we had some train crash tourism last summer. People coming in to gawp because they'd read about Lindy in the papers.'

Karina looks at what was once Lindy's desk. The photo of Jamie has gone.

'Come on, Karrie. We should get back.' Rohan notices her distress and guides her to the door.

'I don't want to cry before this afternoon.'

'It's OK. They know about Lindy. They'll be tactful, I promise, even Malcolm.'

'Ro, you think of everything.'

'Just wanting to make things go smoothly for you.' Rohan puts an arm round her waist.

'My husband wants to invite you to dinner at our house,' Karina says.

'Your husband?' Rohan echoes, moving away. 'When?'

'March the twenty-fourth. It's my name day. It's an old Hungarian custom – every name has a special day that's assigned to it for a celebration. Julian's curious about you, so he suggested we have a dinner party.'

'If I'm not playing somewhere, I'd love to. Will you make Hungarian food?'

'Maybe. I hadn't thought about it. Jules is asking a friend from the Department for Transport. It wouldn't be quite what he's used to. It's heavy – lots of lard!'

'All the better!'

Karina gives up her gloom and laughs with him; when Harry opens the door, they still have the giggles.

'What's got into you two?' Harry asks.

'Long story,' Rohan says. 'We found this fantastic restaurant that Karina used to go to with her friend Lindy.' He lowers his voice – Karina wonders why. 'We booked a table for dinner, if you'd like to come.'

'Sounds nice. Alison's working late. Good that someone around here earns some money, but still. Genya? Dinner?'

Karina notices that her three colleagues don't issue an invitation to Malcolm.

Later, she sees why. They cluster into the restaurant at six thirty, tired, hungry and happy after a good day's work. Pietro greets them with prosecco, which he declares is on the house in honour of Lindy; then he insists on choosing antipasti for them. The musicians clink glasses. 'To our new violinist!' says Harry, surveying Karina.

'Thanks for letting me in.' Karina beams. 'I've loved today.'

'You fit like a glove,' Rohan assures her.

'Karina, you are wonderful violinist. You must play more. To you!' Genya holds up his glass.

'And you can stand our cellist?' Harry asks.

'He's an excellent player.' Karina tries to be tactful, but the others keel over laughing.

Malcolm, they tell her, is a control freak, a horsewhipper, a bullshitter who's upset everyone in the music business. They need the quartet, and enjoy it despite him; but they can't sack him because technically the St Francis Quartet is his operation. The name, they explain, comes from the fact that he'd originally brought them together for a week of concerts he'd organised in Assisi; the ensemble worked so well that afterwards he suggested they should continue.

'That was five years ago,' Harry says. 'People seem to like us and we've got a recording contract, which is pretty rare these days. But still . . .'

'He thinks, is his group, so he should control music,' Genya points out, saturating ciabatta in olive oil. 'But we don't always like. For example, I like quartet that Rohan wrote, but every time I say we must play it, Malcolm finds reason to do something else.'

'We should stop grumbling or Karina will get out while the going's good,' Rohan says.

Relaxed by the prosecco, enjoying the long-missed familiarity of Zucchini's, the brush of Rohan's sleeve against hers and the contented ache in her arms after a whole day playing her violin, Karina begins to tell them about Jamie, the orchestra, the lost Amati, Mimi, Duplessis. They listen, entranced, and Rohan lifts a long arm and quietly orders more wine. And if Harry and Genya want to question Rohan as to whether there's anything between him and her, they don't do so. She can't remember when she last talked so much. She imagines Lindy watching, approving: this is where you're meant to be.

'Mummy?' says Jamie.

It's half past nine; Karina's on her way home. The train is late. Her violin case is in the luggage rack, where Rohan's had been when they first met. Her mind is full of music, but through it, Jamie's voice on the phone sounds like a distant alarm.

'What is it, Schnooky? How did you get on with the maths?'

'It's horrible.' The train's rattle is so loud that Karina can't tell whether or not her son is crying.

'What happened?'

'It's the way he talks to us when we're trying to concentrate. He makes out like we're all total idiots. He's really, like, what's the word – Calum told me – sacrastic?'

'It's *sarcastic*, darling.'

'He just does it cos he likes it. Cos he can. And Mum, please don't write to the headmaster again because it only makes it worse!'

Karina closes her eyes. What price her beautiful day now? 'He doesn't touch anyone, does he?' she ventures.

'No, but I really, really hate him.'

Amid the national terror of paedophilia, Karina reflects, there's not been much recognition that teachers still exist who enjoy inflicting purely psychological pain on their small charges. 'Listen, love, it'll be Friday soon,' she encourages. 'What do you want to do on Saturday? We'll do something nice, whatever you like.'

'Dunno. Watch a DVD, maybe. Just be *at home*.'

On Saturday at teatime, Julian retreats to his study to work, leaving Karina and Jamie sitting together on the living room floor near the fire, absorbed in a black and white wartime adventure movie.

Julian's eyes feel shrunken with tiredness. Certain clients expect him to produce perfect paperwork as if by magic; he hasn't had a day off for weeks, and with his new BlackBerry, which had seemed like a good idea at the time, being uncontactable is a bygone luxury. When Karina came back from her rehearsal, he'd barely glanced up from the desk. She and her new friends had evidently been out for a merry meal. But she'd chosen that moment to invade his study and say, 'Jules, we have to bring Jamie home. That Mr Whitehouse is a madman.'

'Don't be silly,' he said, clauses and subclauses bouncing in front of his eyes.

'But we complained to the headmaster, and now Jamie says it's made things worse. That's not good enough.'

'Karrie, we'll talk about this in the morning.'

Today, though, devouring a Bath bun while he watches the film, Jamie hasn't said a word about Mr Whitehouse.

'Children move on quickly,' Julian tells Karina when he breaks for a caffeine injection.

'Not always,' she retorts.

The guilt appalls Karina. What's worse? The recognition that she'd been in London enjoying chamber music and Italian food while Jamie struggled through a nightmare without her, miles away? Or the anxiety that she should have fought harder in the first place? She should have stood up better to Julian and his family. None of this should have happened. Jamie shouldn't be at boarding-school and she should never have met Rohan.

She slinks up to the bedroom with her mobile phone. 'Ro? It's me. Listen, I can't do the Mozart. You'll have to find someone else.'

* * *

'What's up, darling one?' Julian asks later, while she's cooking dinner.

'I'm not going to Budapest. I can't go away and leave Jamie during the holidays. It's not fair on him. We'll have his friends to stay that weekend . . .'

'Oh, for God's sake! How exactly is that going to help? Wearing hair shirts? Beating yourself up? Do you think Jamie's going to have a better time at school just because you give up your little treat? He's going to stay at that school, face it and deal with it. It's neither here nor there whether you go to Hungary for a couple of days.'

Karina turns her back on him.

There is no doubt, wrote Pierre Vincente, *that Mimi Rácz was the most galvanising inspirational force that Duplessis had yet encountered. The son of well-to-do bourgeoisie, his father a banker who heartily disapproved of young Marc's musical aspirations, he had never been permitted to experience the more bohemian side of musical life in Paris. Hearing the mesmerising young violinist brought about an earthquake in the soul of this impressionable and over-sheltered youth, the effects of which would never leave him.*

How much music he wrote for her is unknown, for much was consigned, tragically, to the bonfire in which the composer later ensured the posthumous obscurity of his past. Whether he was in love with her, or simply the idea of her, is debatable; their sojourn in the US was, he remarked, by turns a fairy tale and a horror story. True to his usual form, he would not elaborate.

Alone in the kitchen extension while Jamie sleeps and Julian works, Karina examines the photos of Duplessis. Big, stooping, rough around the edges – he reminds her of Gérard Depardieu on a bad day. There's certainly no resemblance to her father, whose compact, chunky build takes after Mimi and, apparently, Mimi's father, István. Still . . .

In the morning she phones her parents and reiterates her curiosity once too often.

'Listen, Schnooky.' Dénes sounds exasperated. 'You know your grandmother has many stories about the Romany way of life. Now, for a girl brought up in that tradition, fidelity was a big deal. You hear about "Bohemian lifestyle", but that's horse-shit. If your grandmother hadn't been adopted by Dr Frankl, she'd have been married while she was still really a child, to someone her father had chosen for her who would definitely, absolutely be Roma. And it would be expected that she was a virgin on her wedding day and would remain faithful afterwards. Fidelity and the family were the core of their lives. They guarded their women like there was no tomorrow.'

'But she left when she was ten.'

'Yes, but such things are hard to forget. Your heritage stays with you, even if you don't know it. Do you realise what a big deal it was for a Roma girl to marry the son of a Hungarian landowner? It was crazy. It was unheard-of. It was the most stupid risk. His family would have disinherited him, if there'd been anyone left alive to do it. As for her family, they might have killed them both. Karina, Tamás Veres was my father and you are wasting your time if you think otherwise. Don't.'

While Karina is talking to her father, the doorbell rings. A delivery: white and yellow flowers, tied with a gold ribbon.

'Dad, I have to go,' she says.

DEAREST KARINA,
WE NEED YOU.
PLEASE COME BACK.
Rohan, Harry, Genya & Malcolm

'You never could resist being needed,' Julian remarks later, spotting the vase on the table and the card lying nearby. 'Anyway, it's not very professional to go to one rehearsal, then change your mind. You agreed to go, so you have a responsibility. Call him and say you're coming back.'

'Jules—'

'And don't forget your name-day party. Make sure he's there.'

Karina, wondering whether her husband knows what he's doing, phones the overjoyed Rohan.

'What can I bring to dinner?' he asks.

Karina thinks for a minute, then says: 'Cherries.'

18

On 24 March, Julian goes to the office, although it's Saturday. Karina marshals Jamie, who's jubilant with freedom, into her Golf and off to the biggest supermarket in Lewes. Jamie halves the length of her shopping slogs: he knows exactly where everything is and enjoys darting between the aisles to retrieve whatever she asks for. The trolley fills with the most Hungarian ingredients she can muster: cabbage, mince, rice, mushrooms, onions, apples, peppers, sour cream, paprika and the inevitable lard. Karina can imagine her mother's voice bewailing the impossibility of finding real Hungarian red peppers in Britain.

'Please can I stay up, Mum?' Jamie begs. 'Please?'

'It'll be long past your bedtime, Schnooks.'

'Oh, *Mum* . . .'

'They won't arrive until eight, and you need to eat before then.'

'But I could stay up and say hello, couldn't I?'

A text arrives at that moment from Julian: '2 BOTTLES OF NUITS ST GEORGES ON DRESSER, PLSE OPEN 6PM TO BREATHE X.'

Posh wine, one of Julian's favourites. Perhaps leg of lamb, chicken casserole or roast beef would accompany it better. But it's her name day and if Hungarian stuffed cabbage doesn't match his Burgundy, she can't help that.

At six, when Karina has been cooking for an hour, the doorbell rings. Rohan is outside, his green scarf wrapped round his neck against the wind, a bulging plastic bag in one hand and a bouquet of flowers – yellow and white, somehow familiar – in the other.

'Happy name day,' he says, kissing her three times while she tries to get used to the incongruous sight of him in her home. 'I brought you these, because the others probably died ages ago.'

'Thanks, Ro. They're beautiful.'

'What a lovely house.' He lingers in the hall, taking in the bright landing, the tall window at the side of the stairs, the sleek wooden floors. 'I've been trying to imagine what your home would be like, but it's more *you* than I expected.'

A motion by the kitchen door makes him glance round. 'Hi,' he says. 'You must be Jamie. I'm Rohan.'

'Hi, Rohan.' Jamie walks forward and extends a hand, which Rohan shakes. Karina watches their eyes meet. Jamie, with his round, brown irises, looks more like Rohan than like Julian. How crazy.

'Your mum talks a lot about you,' Rohan tells Jamie. 'I want to hear about your fantastic school while we cook.'

'While *we* cook?' Karina echoes.

'I'm your slave for the evening. And here are your cherries.' Rohan plumps down the carrier bag on the kitchen worktop.

'You managed to get fresh cherries?' Karina had expected morellos out of a jar, which she'd normally use for this recipe.

'You bet. I scoured Brighton until I found them. I hope there's enough. Now, what can I do?' He rolls up his shirtsleeves and stands to attention.

'You can pit the cherries.' She takes an apron from the hook behind the door and ceremoniously places its strap round his neck. 'First, let me pour you a drink and show you the CD collection.'

Rohan walks into the living room, where Julian's CD shelves line the largest wall. 'Unbelievable! How's it arranged?' he asks.

'I'll show you,' Jamie volunteers; he adores the concept of his father's record collection, even if not always its contents. Rohan, exploring, follows his instructions.

'Oh my God,' he says. 'You've got Zimbalist playing the Brahms Concerto.'

Brahms, against its aged, crackling background, is soon singing out through the house. Karina installs Rohan with the cherries at the extension table; Jamie, who should be eating his own supper, bounces over and chatters about school as if he's known Rohan all his life. Placing the stuffed cabbage leaves on a bed of sauerkraut to bake, she keeps her back to them. She doesn't want to catch Rohan's eye; she knows what she'll see there and the only way not to see it is not to look. At six thirty, she remembers Julian's instruction to open the wine at six.

'What are you going to do with the cherries?' Rohan's fingers are stained carmine with juice.

'Soup. Cold soup.'

She tips them into a saucepan, squeezes over a little lemon, spoons in some sugar, adds a cinnamon stick and some cloves, pours over the water. Rohan watches, intrigued. 'This is traditional?'

'It's my mum's recipe, but she says every family has its own version. It's called *meggyleves*.' She mixes a spoon of flour with sour cream, then, when the cherries have turned mushy, she takes them off the heat and stirs everything together with a little white wine. A heady, velvety scent rises from the pink mixture. 'There we are – it's thickening – so now, we put it into a big bowl, let it cool, then stick it in the fridge. I should have done it yesterday. Ro, could you be an angel and set the table? Everything's in the dresser. There's five of us.'

'You didn't invite an extra girl for me?' Rohan quips.

Karina hadn't even thought of that. Idiotically, she's been thinking of herself as Rohan's girl.

An engine sounds in the drive. 'Dad's home!' Jamie trots to the door.

Julian comes in and hoists Jamie into the air. Rohan leans against the kitchen door-frame; he's still wearing Karina's apron.

'You must be Rowan.' Julian holds Jamie with one arm and extends the other hand towards the guest. His eyes fix on the apron.

'My hands are a bit sticky,' Rohan apologises. 'I'm Karina's slave.'

'I see. Well, it's good to meet you at last. I hope my little Gypsy has poured you a drink, besides working you so hard?'

'*You* don't usually help,' Karina points out. She looks at Julian's eyes. Something's wrong, badly wrong. 'What—?'

'Come upstairs a minute.'

In his study, Julian empties his briefcase. 'What's going on?' Karina asks.

'Have you spoken to Cynthia or Martin?'

'No. What is it?'

'My mother called. Apparently Cynthia went off the rails the other day and screamed blue murder at Martin about how she's wasted her life with him. And now she's upped and left.'

Karina reels. 'It's because of Lindy,' she says. 'It must be.'

The doorbell rings. 'Damn,' says Julian. 'They have to be early, today of all days. We'll talk later.'

Andy and Sarah, fair and polished, are at the door, the model of a respectable government minister and his devoted wife. Karina imagines how they must view this chaotic scene: Julian thundering about upstairs, Jamie splashing in the bath, herself with dishevelled hair and a distracted expression, and a strange violinist in a Tate Gallery apron, his hands bloodied with cherry juice.

'Happy name day, Karina.' Sarah stoops to give her the requisite pecks.

'Darling, what a nice idea, I wish we had name days. We brought you a little something.' Andy hands Karina a long, narrow box containing a pricey champagne bottle. Beside Sarah, elegant in a chiffony dress that shows off her slenderness, Karina, in dark trousers, bronze-brown jersey and a silk scarf, feels self-conscious and underdressed.

'This is my colleague, Rohan Masterson. We're doing a concert together in Hungary next month,' she explains. 'Rohan, meet Andy and Sarah – Andy's the junior transport minister I mentioned, and Sarah's a legal eagle like Jules.'

Rohan lifts his stained palms into the air. 'I'd shake hands, but . . .'

Sarah looks up at him and giggles. 'What's going on?'

'Since the name day's a Hungarian custom, I'm doing Hungarian food,' Karina says. 'Come on in, Jules will give you a drink.' Julian, breezing down the stairs pretending that all is well, greets his friends and takes a bottle of champagne from the fridge into the living room.

Rohan slinks into the kitchen after Karina. 'I'm a bit out of my depth here,' he tells her. 'Did you say he's a transport minister?'

'Don't worry, Andy's a terrible talker. You'll be lucky to get a word in edgeways.' Karina hears the cork popping in the next room.

When she's checked the cabbage leaves and popped some ice-cubes into the cooling soup, she rejoins her guests, only to find that the normally loquacious Andy is finding it hard to turn the conversation towards himself, because Rohan has been quizzing Julian about the CD collection. Julian's showing off his computerised cataloguing system and bewailing the trend towards digital downloads on which sound quality is often inferior. Andy and Sarah look on, impressed if baffled.

'Some famous conductor once said that the English don't particularly like music, but they love the noise it makes,' Andy remarks. 'That's us!'

'I do enjoy the opera,' Sarah says. 'Especially Covent Garden. We sometimes have company seats.'

'Ooh,' says Rohan, 'you've got Toscha Seidel playing Korngold!' Andy and Sarah's eyes widen further while he explains that Seidel is the violinist who plays on the soundtrack of *Intermezzo*. 'I can't watch it without crying,' he admits. 'That bit when Leslie Howard goes home and his little girl is knocked down running across the road to him . . .' Rohan places the CD tenderly in the player and a second later the room is filled with a hot, extreme violin sound that grabs Karina in the gut, much as Rohan's can. Andy and Julian exchange glances; she knows they wouldn't be seen dead crying over soppy movies from the 1930s, or, indeed, anything else.

'For my sins, I've been investigating the effectiveness of classical music in keeping yobs away from stations,' Andy puffs. 'Apparently it works a treat.'

Jamie, in his dressing-gown fresh from his bath, appears big-eyed in the doorway and squeaks that he's just come down to say goodnight. Andy and Sarah greet him with overdone smiles. Their children, Marsha and Cosmo, are banished during dinner parties and tonight have been left at home in Pimlico in the capable care of a Bulgarian babysitter.

'Night night, Jimbo,' Julian says.

'Night night, sleep tight, don't let the bedbugs bite,' Rohan adds. Jamie gives him a bear-hug.

Karina goes upstairs to tuck Jamie in. Turning off the light, she hears a whisper behind her. She knows the rhythm too well. 'Lindy Rookfield, you will come back, you will, you will, you will . . .'

* * *

Downstairs, Julian and Andy are regaling Sarah and Rohan with school memories. 'Do you remember "crocket"?' Julian says.

'Cricket with crockery,' Andy tells the others. 'That was some day! Are you a cricketer, Rowan?'

'I love watching it,' Rohan bluffs.

'Well, I'd just come into the common room with my bat, fresh from the field, and I suppose one can go a little trigger-happy,' Julian begins. 'Andy was in there and had a tin of biscuits open, so he chucked this plate towards me. Andy's like that, very fastidi4ous – you have to use a plate for your biscuits. But I just saw this circle frisbeeing through the air and it was . . . irresistible . . .'

'Next thing we knew,' Andy adds, 'we'd got through all the common room plates, there was broken china absolutely bloody everywhere and these poor fags were caught in the middle the whole time, ducking behind the sofa!'

'Fags?' says Rohan.

'First-years who "fag" for the big boys. You order them about and they have to do your bidding.'

Karina imagines Jamie, a few years older, entering his first term at Elthingbourne. She feels Rohan's eyes on her, understanding.

'So you chaps have known each other all this time?' he asks Julian.

'Since the first day at Elthingbourne. Now Andy's my greatest asset. You see, Rowan, a lot of my work is about who you know. It's pressured: we have targets, sometimes jolly demanding ones, and one has to attract new business. If a company's in the transport industry, it helps if their lawyers have good contacts in government.'

Sarah turns to Rohan: 'And you and Karina have known each other for years, too, haven't you?'

'Actually, no. We only met about six months ago.'

'Really? You seem as if you go back forever.'

'It's funny, but I almost feel that we do.' Rohan explains the Duplessis connection. Sarah's eyes widen. Karina slopes away to attend to dinner. Ladling her pink starter into soup bowls, she finds that her mouth is dry, and not only because of the champagne. She's not the only woman who finds Rohan attractive, and she'll have to get used to that.

Over the cold cherry soup, which the guests greet with a variety of responses ('How fascinating . . .' – Sarah; 'Interesting, very interesting . . .' – Andy, who leaves most of his; 'Amazing . . .' – Rohan, who wants a second helping), Sarah prods him for the full story of how he and Karina met.

'I guess we have to thank Julian and Andy for *not* having sorted out the railways yet,' says Rohan. Karina wonders how he manages to seem striking and modest, shy and at ease at the same time.

'Gypsies busking,' she adds. 'It was unbelievable.'

'But where did they come from?' Sarah wants to know. 'Would it be Romania? I thought most of the Romanian Gypsies were sent back.'

'Maybe some slipped through the net,' says Andy. 'Though I say it myself, our immigration system's a total shambles. The Tories left us this mess, of course, but it's a deep-seated thing. Endemic lack of communication. The departments don't talk to each other. The more ways we have of contacting people, the worse it gets. We have phones, faxes, mobiles, emails, instant messaging, BlackBerries, you name it, and nobody communicates.'

'Signal failure,' Rohan remarks. 'It's everywhere. Messages don't get through. Systems don't work. People can't connect with each other. And as for the Roma – I mean, look, chaps, I was born in South Africa, my parents had to get out because of their politics and I was lucky enough to grow up here. The system that chased them out was a fascist government based on the stupidest thing on earth. Don't you think racism is just the worst form of *stupidity*? What could be more idiotic than one set of people judging another set as inferior just because of the colour of their skin?'

'It's more than that with the Gypsies,' Julian points out. 'It's about a way of life.'

'But it's the same principle. Anyone who looks or lives differently from the masses. Religious Muslims, Orthodox Jews – someone's a little different, and at once people have the same reaction. Different equals inferior, bad or dangerous. That was one reason my parents became communists. They thought it would equalise everyone, they hoped it would be the opposite of apartheid.'

Andy and Julian look horrified. 'Are you a communist too, Rohan?' asks the mesmerised Sarah.

'No, but I believe that however different we are from each other on the outside, we *are* all the same. We have the same needs. Our bodies work in the same way. We have the same human rights, or we should have.'

'So what do you think about the matter of our strength being in our diversity?' Sarah's eyelashes are working overtime. Even Andy is gazing at Rohan as if somewhat dazzled.

'Oh, I believe it is,' Rohan says, 'but more specifically, it's in our unity within that diversity. Don't you think so?'

Andy sits up, eager. 'Well, one issue facing us in government right now is that it's essential to find a balance between respecting civil liberties and protecting the—'

'Blimey,' Julian cuts in, glaring at Rohan, 'why don't we redraft the European Constitution while we're about it? Come on, people, lighten up!'

Rohan watches Karina carry the baking tray to the table and place it ceremoniously on a trivet. 'Karrie, that smells amazing!'

'Stuffed cabbage. Another of my mum's recipes.'

'I understand that Karina thought of doing Romany food tonight, but ruled out wild rabbit and baked hedgehog,' Julian says.

'So do you really have Roma blood, Karina?' Sarah asks. 'I had no idea. I thought it was just a rumour.'

'Not something to shout about at the club,' Andy remarks, still looking none too pleased to have had his political contribution pushed aside. 'Karrie, are you going to tell our fortunes?'

Karina, serving spoon in hand, glances from one to the other. She wonders why, after thirty-six years, she still never knows what to say when faced with comments like this, even when they come from supposed friends guilty only of thoughtlessness.

Rohan stands up. 'You all have to listen to this,' he says and disappears into the living room. A minute later, the sound of Mimi Rácz's violin fills the house, playing Ravel's *Tzigane*. 'This is Karina's Gypsy grandmother in her heyday,' Rohan announces. 'I'd have thought *this* was something to shout about.'

Karina's eyes, watching him, brim with tears. Mimi's violin weaves its spell, silencing the room.

'The tragedy of a whole people,' says Rohan quietly at the end. 'You can hear it in every note she plays.'

'It was hardly a tragedy for her,' Julian points out. 'She got famous, moved here, did very nicely, and she's alive and well and living in Twickenham.'

Rohan glances at Karina; she can sense him thinking, 'But at what cost?'

'Do you speak Romany, Karina?' Sarah asks her.

'Not a word. Nor does my grandmother – she says the Romungro were very assimilated, they spoke Hungarian and only a smattering of Romany. Anyway, she was adopted when she was ten.'

'Well, do you speak Hungarian?'

'Unfortunately, no. My parents wanted me to grow up only speaking English.'

'We'll start learning in Hungary,' Rohan suggests.

Julian harrumphs. 'My father-in-law insists it's a complete waste of time.'

Karina changes the subject by offering more food.

'It's delicious, but it's quite robust, isn't it?' The willowy Sarah has made slow headway with her stuffed cabbage. Karina doesn't mention that the dish is cooked with lard and wouldn't taste the same without it. She suspects that Sarah's refused carbohydrates ever since the Atkins Diet became fashionable, but probably binges on chocolate when nobody's looking. There's stewed spiced fruit for dessert, but everyone declares that they are, at least for now, a little too full.

At that moment, the doorbell peals – and continues to peal, insistent. Julian leaps up; the others exchange glances. There's a commotion in the hall: Cynthia, drenched and almost incoherent with emotion, has blown in from the wet spring night.

'Darling,' she weeps as Karina runs to her, 'I didn't know where to go. Bloody Martin and the whole lot of bleeding, stuck-up—'

'Cynthia, calm down,' Julian orders.

'Come and take off your wet things.' Karina hugs her.

'Can I stay with you? Please, Karrie? I just don't know where else to go. I couldn't go to your parents, Martin would have come and found me at once . . .'

Julian is stony-faced. 'Karina will show you up to the spare room.'

'We've got a few friends over.' Karina takes Lindy's mother's arm. 'Do you want to join us? I made all this stuffed cabbage, it's good comfort food.'

'No, no, heavens, I'm sorry, I've barged in at the wrong moment. I couldn't eat a thing, I'll just disappear. Oh, my God.' She begins to sniff, gulping back tears. 'I've wasted my life. I've spent my whole fucking life with the wrong man. And now Lindy's dead and it's too late. *Too late.* I'm sixty-bloody-five. Can you imagine, Karrie? To know your life's gone and you've spent it in the wrong place? And it'll never come back!'

'Hush, Cynthia, Jamie's asleep.' Karina leads her upstairs, past Jamie's door, towards the narrow loft staircase and the spare room at the top. There, she gives Cynthia a tissue, a towel and a brush; she left home in such a hurry that she's brought only a basic change of clothes.

'Make sure you do something with your life, Karrie.' Cynthia stands at the window, her back to Karina. 'Don't throw it away. Don't waste your talent. Not like me. I was doing fine, thanks. The photographers were clamouring for me. I modelled for Lord Snowdon, for Christ's sake. And then I had to get pregnant, and after that nobody fancied taking my picture again. As for the damned Rookfields, they said they wouldn't have "let" me carry on modelling. Not *nice*, is it, for the daughter-in-law of Lord Rookfield of Fairfallows to appear on twenty-foot billboards? How *dare* they talk about "letting" me? Oh, Karrie, your life is *yours*. Don't let them wreck it.'

'Tell me what happened. Why now, why today?'

'You won't believe it.' Cynthia sits down on the bed and pulls off her wet shoes. 'It's because it's your name day.'

'But—?'

'Because Lindy didn't have one. We should have had a celebration for her last birthday, but we put it off because Martin said he was too busy. She had a party of her own, without us, and we said, "Oh, next time". But there never was a next time. And what was he busy with? This bit of fluff he's been dandling. And it's not like I didn't know, it's not like there haven't been others. I've always turned a blind eye – it's not as if he was threatening to leave, I knew it was just sex, it was horrible but it didn't *matter*. But now I can't take it any more. Because if Martin hadn't pushed

Lindy away, if he hadn't been so cold with her, so judgmental . . . And I've been kidding myself, because the sex does matter. It always did, I just didn't want to believe it. Today, your mother mentioned that it was your name day and something just – went.'

Karina shakes her head, speechless.

'He never gave Lindy a shred of encouragement,' Cynthia goes on. 'She could have been a wonderful writer, Karrie. She could have had a play commissioned. And to him, what was she? An encumbrance. He was stuck with me because of her, and he didn't care, he pushed us aside all the time . . .'

'Cynthia, hush. It's OK.' Karina embraces her, her own heart splintering.

'Are you sure you don't mind me being here? You're so kind. You really are.' Cynthia blows her nose. 'It was *ghastly*. I've stood it for nearly forty years. I can't talk to him, he won't talk to me, and if I try he just tells me to shut up. Without Lindy, there's no point any more. And I've left my poor cat . . .'

'Cynthia, try and relax. Why don't you have a hot bath and I'll make you some tea? We'll talk properly in the morning.'

Downstairs, Julian is fuming over his aunt's unscheduled arrival. The Williamsons consult one another, then take their leave in a flurry of kisses and platitudinous farewells.

Amid the mayhem, Rohan has vanished. Karina finds him in the living room, browsing the CDs.

'Is she OK?' he asks.

'Kind of. Ro, I'm so sorry, tonight wasn't meant to turn out like this.'

'It's supposed to be your day.'

'But I wanted you to have a good time . . .'

'Nobody could have seen this coming. Not even a clairvoyant.' Rohan puts an arm around her. Karina leans her head on his shoulder for a second. 'Let's hear something beautiful,' he suggests. Reaching T for Tchaikovsky, he pulls down a disc of music from *The Nutcracker*. Soon it's radiating through the room, full of snow, sweets and transformations.

'This piece means childhood to me,' Rohan remarks. 'Christmas with my sister and my parents.'

'Me too. It's Christmas with Lindy. We went to this ballet so many times.'

'Karina, why don't you see about having *Distant Beloved* recorded? It sounds as if it could work beautifully, with an actress and the piano music, and it would be a good memorial for Lindy.'

Karina reflects. 'It's a nice idea. It would probably be up to Cynthia to agree. I'll mention it to her in the morning, if she's compos mentis enough.'

'Imagine losing your daughter and then deciding you're in the wrong marriage.'

'It's a longer story than I'd realised. It's not easy being married to the Rookfield family.'

'Harder than being married to anyone else?' Rohan raises an eyebrow.

'Maybe, because you don't just marry one person. You take on your partner's whole family and all their baggage. And it's accumulated over decades, sometimes centuries, especially in families like Julian's and mine.'

'You find it hard, don't you?'

'I'm sure Jules does too. God knows my family's got baggage, it's just that normally they don't talk about it.'

'Karrie?' Julian is glowering in the doorway, mug in hand. 'Since you seem to be busy, I'll take Cynthia her tea. And I'll try not to murder her.'

Tchaikovsky's snowflakes flicker through an off-centre waltz. Karina feels as if she's eight years old again, sitting in the theatre with Lindy and an escorting parent, entranced by the weaving patterns of dancers. Once, they'd come out afterwards to find the snow was real, a frosting that left London sparkling and ghostly under the street-lights. Another transformation; a new world. And the little girls they were then had bounded through it, kicking, crunching and laughing, the white path unmarked ahead of them.

Later, Karina lies in bed, remembering, music still ringing through her mind. Who would have thought, that day, that in twenty-eight years' time one of them would be dead, one set of parents would have crashed headlong, Jamie would exist and Karina would be trying to keep everybody on an even keel while half deranged with longing for a sweet-eyed man who wasn't her husband?

'Karrie?' Julian mumbles. 'Can't you sleep? What's the matter?'

'Nothing.'

'You and Rohan . . .'

'*What?*'

'You're quite a double act. You're like a pair of kids. Having a little play together, cooking things up.' He turns on to his back, yawning. 'You musicians never really grow up. Your orchestra used to behave like a bunch of schoolchildren.'

Presumably to Julian, with his responsible job controlling the movement from place to place of ridiculously large sums of money, choosing to spend one's life playing the violin could seem a tad childish. 'He's a wandering minstrel, of sorts,' Karina remarks. 'But so am I.'

'I'm not worried about the two of you.'

'Why not?' she teases.

'That's exactly why not. You behave like little kids. And little kids, thank God, don't bonk. Goodnight, darling one.'

19

The quintet sits in its crescent in the centre of a cool, dark church in Buckinghamshire. The audience is dotted among the pews. Beside her, performing the Mozart G minor Quintet, Rohan's violin invades Karina. Whatever Julian thinks, he hasn't reckoned on the elixir of that tone pouring into her right ear.

She and the violists spin the hypnotic accompaniment to the last movement's introduction; Malcolm's pizzicato punctuates it and Rohan's song soars above, a lamentation. Karina, trying to concentrate, is lost in the sound; his unique violin voice burrows into her bloodstream, tempting her spirit out of her body. When the music bounds back to earth, she's left half of herself behind.

At the end a cheer goes up. In the vestry, which doubles as their dressing-room, the St Francis Quartet is pleased, too.

'Beautiful.' Genya kisses his fingertips to Karina.

'That took off,' Rohan agrees. 'All we have to do is the same again next week in Budapest. Karrie, how do you feel?'

'Good.' Karina fusses over her violin case, keeping her back turned so that he won't see how overcome she is.

'I just thought that maybe the beginning of the G minor . . .' Malcolm begins.

The others shout him down. 'Stop grumbling, Malc,' Harry snaps. 'It was fine.'

'Rohan was too loud.'

'Listen, guys,' Rohan intervenes, 'this was Karina's first proper concert in eight years and we should be celebrating that, not fighting.'

'Let's go eat!' Genya puts his arm round Lyuba, who has bustled in to find him. 'I have booked restaurant.'

'Karina?' Rohan's dark irises turn towards her.

She glances back over her shoulder. 'Can I join you in a few minutes?'

'I'll wait for you.'

'*I'll wait for you forever,*' Harry sings.

'Don't worry, you go ahead.' Karina picks up her violin case and paces out into the church.

The first people she sees are her parents; they hug and praise her, but decline her invitation to join the group for dinner. 'Go with your friends, no?' Erzsébet encourages. 'Where is your family?'

'Julian had to work late, Jamie's with the Pearsons and Cynthia's probably in our bathroom. Mum, I'll phone you tomorrow.'

'Karrie? You go when to Budapest?' Dénes asks, as if in afterthought.

'Next week.'

'You must please give my regards to one place. Andrássy Street number sixty. It's an address. A museum. I write it down for you before you go. I will give you a list. Don't forget.'

'All right.' Karina hopes he'll elaborate; but her father, pulling on his gloves, is saying no more.

A grey-haired man in a trench coat stands in the lamplight, gazing up at the vaulted wooden roof. Why does she always see Charles hovering at the back of churches? Her anger towards him has vanished; he's contrite, and a living link to Lindy. Besides, with his contacts, he's the perfect person to talk to about Rohan's suggestion for a *Distant Beloved* CD. She'd emailed him about this and mentioned the quintet's concert, but hadn't expected him to come all the way to Beaconsfield. She gives him a kiss. 'Charles. Great you could make it.'

He offers to buy her a drink, but Karina explains she's due at dinner. They sit in a pew together. Grief is eating away at him; the hollowness in his face wasn't there before. Unlike her, he has to hide his loss from his family.

'It's not been easy,' he admits. 'I'm thinking of taking early retirement. Academia's going downhill so fast that there's no point staying longer than I have to. Anyway, I've got some news. My producer friend is rather enthusiastic about *Distant Beloved*. He thinks it could work, especially if there's a charitable element in Lindy's memory. They could give a donation per copy to a fund for the families of victims. I've written a proposal so that he can pitch it to the boss. Here.' Charles gives her a printout. 'I thought you might like to see it.'

'Thanks, that's fantastic. I'm glad. And I know she would be too.' Karina puts the paper away in her violin case.

'Karina, this is nowhere near as much as I'd like to do – but nothing ever could be. Are you happy for me to take it forward?'

'More than happy. Thanks for coming all this way, Charles.'

'Not at all. Thank you for the music. It was wonderful – very comforting. There's nothing on earth as cathartic as music. Lindy would have been glad you're back on stage. She always used to say you should never have quit. Look, I'm going out for a drink with Nicki next Saturday – we have to discuss some adjustments to the script for the recording. Would you like to join us?'

'Thanks,' Karina says, 'but I can't. I'll be in Budapest.'

She wanders out of the church alone, thinking about Martin and Cynthia. Martin had come down to Lewes the day before. Karina and Julian took themselves and Jamie out for a pizza; but by the time they returned, he'd gone and Cynthia had retreated to the bath. When she hadn't emerged after an hour, Julian panicked and forced the door. Karina discovered her befuddled in the cooling water, dosed up on a sleeping-pill. She helped her out and tucked her into bed like a child, all the while remembering Lindy thirty years ago, swinging between her parents' hands in the park.

In a nearby Italian restaurant, the others are picking the performance to pieces. They stop when Karina walks in.

'She won't think he's too loud,' Malcolm remarks, sour, once they've called the waiter to take her order. 'Rohan can do no wrong.'

'You want to bet?' Rohan exclaims. 'Karrie, was I too loud?'

'No,' says Karina. That sets them off again. While they battle, she pulls out Charles's paper and glances through the proposal.

Rohan peers over her shoulder. 'What's this for?' he asks.

Karina lowers her voice and explains.

'I didn't know Lindy, but I feel as if I did,' Rohan says. 'I want to be part of this, Karrie.'

'You are already. It was all your idea, remember?'

'Is Lindy's mother still at your place?'

'We're keeping her either until she goes home or until Friday when Jules has decided to send her to her sister in Harpenden. Whichever is the sooner, as a contract would say.'

'Why did she go to you first, not her sister?'

'I think, because of Lindy. Because I was close to her; perhaps I remind her of Lindy's childhood. I can't bear to think what she's been through. She needs more help than I can give her. And all Julian can say is that he'd like to murder her.'

Rohan squeezes her hand under the table. She lets him; she craves the comfort more than she feels the guilt.

'Nonsense,' Julian says, around one a.m. 'It's nothing to do with Lindy. Cynthia knows you're a pushover.'

'How can you say that?' Karina is trying, hopelessly, to sleep. The fingers of her left hand are smarting from her violin strings, her triceps muscle has started an involuntary twitch and her mind is saturated with Mozart.

'But the imposition!'

'She's in pieces. So would you be, if it was Jamie.'

'That's bloody sick, Karina.'

'You're heartless. You don't care about anybody except precious Andy who brings in the work.'

'I care about us and our privacy and I don't believe in washing dirty linen in public.'

'Well, we're taking her to Marion's on Friday. Or you are. I have to catch a plane.'

'I'm taking you to the airport.'

'You can't do both, and I don't imagine you want her here a minute longer than necessary.'

'We'll take her first, then you. Heathrow's on the way back. I've got time off specially, Karrie, at a really bad moment, so I may as well use it.'

'You want me to sit in the car to Hertfordshire and back on the day I've got to go to Hungary to give a concert?'

'Oh, aren't we precious and sensitive?'

'For Christ's sake, Jules, I'll drive myself and use the long-term car park. Or I'll get a train.'

'No, I'm driving you. I promised. Sleep tight, little Gypsy.'

Mozart sears Karina's mind like a grill. She lies awake while Julian begins to snore.

The *Ile de France* slid westwards through calm waters, the air so pure that Mimi imagined it tasted of the pearls forming inside the oysters on the ocean bed. She stood by the rail, the stars outsized above her; she could see the swirls in the galaxy. She breathed, soaked up the starlight, heard in her mind the shiver of the cimbalom Marc had intimated he wanted to put into his concerto.

'You blot out the moon,' he told her. 'You've colonised my creativity. Everything is for you now.'

Mimi crossed the deck and went downstairs, along the corridor to her room. A few minutes later, he knocked.

'Marc? Darlink, I am asleep.'

'It's only five past eleven,' he called through the locked door.

'I am *so* tired. I see you in morning. Dini is asleep, I must sleep too.'

'Mimi!'

The baby was with Vali, the nurse, in second class; Mimi had no idea whether he was asleep. Her hands lifted, hankering to open the door and let Marc into her room, her bed and her slumber; but guilt pounded on her with the chug of the ship's engine.

Marc had told her that whenever he thought of Tamás Veres, whom he'd never met, left behind in Hungary, where he'd never been, he could strangle whatever was nearest out of misery. Balzac in Hungarian? What gave him the right, this academic, bespectacled, green-eyed monster, to possess a creature as unpossessable as Mimi Rácz? Since the premiere, and the night that followed it, he was nothing without her. A day away from her was a day when he wasn't alive. During those first two years when she went back to Budapest, married the other man and had a baby, he'd gone to sleep every night hoping to die before morning. Mimi, listening, wished that he would keep some of this to himself.

'Mimi!' The tapping on the door went on. She didn't reply.

She knew he thought her a master of control. She let him in, sometimes, when she couldn't resist, when she was too lonely and wanted him too much; other times, beset by guilt, she'd lock him out. In Hungary she loved Tamás, yet when she was with Marc, she loved him just as much. To form your own moral universe when life has forced you to walk a tightrope between different worlds causes pain to you, and consequently to others; Marc was unfortunate enough to be among those others.

At one a.m., Mimi woke, aware of noises outside her room. She opened the door a slit. The *Ile de France*'s first mate was bending over a figure on the floor: a tall, flabby yet robust body, big hands, big feet, hair flopping over his closed eyes. Marc Duplessis, his fountain-pen protruding from his pocket, was fast asleep in the corridor. The first mate was rocking his elbow.

'Monsieur Duplessis,' he was saying, 'please come with me, I'll take you back to your room. Good evening, Miss Rácz.'

Marc, rousing himself like a mountain turning inside out, struggled in stages to his feet. His eyes, the colour of the sea, met Mimi's in a gaze that combined reproach, incomprehension, adoration and much, much more.

'Goodnight, Marc,' she said; the words barely came out. The first mate stood aside, looking the other way. What would the ship's gossips say tomorrow?

Back in bed, alone, she hid her face in the pillow and scrunched her hands into fists of frustration. She loved Tamás, but she also loved Marc. Why was this supposed to be impossible? It was possible; it was true. Why did each of them have to think he owned her? Love had to be a good thing; why shouldn't it flow?

She rose and opened the door. The corridor was deserted.

20

Karina is ready to leave, violin case on her back, when Julian clears his throat and says, 'Oh, Karrie, I promised Hils we'd drop him at the garage to collect his car. I didn't want to, but he rang up and kind of begged.'

Karina's plane leaves at four. She needs to be at Heathrow by two thirty. Cynthia has to be ferried to Hertfordshire, on the other side of London.

'I want to come too,' Jamie whines. He's being dispatched to the Pearsons' for the rest of the day: less easy than it used to be. Since Jamie left for St Matthew's, Olly has a new set of friends and isn't interested in posh prep school toffs.

'There isn't room, mate,' Julian says, artificially jolly. 'We've got Great-Auntie Cynthia and her suitcase, Mummy and her suitcase and violin and Uncle Hilary too . . .'

Even as he speaks, the bell rings. Outside is Hilary in his red trousers, pacing about and smiling too broadly, fidgeting with the keys in his pocket.

Cynthia, pausing on the stairs, sees him and freezes.

'Hello, Auntie Cyn. Heading for Herts?' Hilary says. 'Got Pom-Pom with you?'

Pom-Pom the cat is Cynthia's Achilles heel. By the time Julian has loaded the cases into the boot, Cynthia is sobbing into a handkerchief. Hilary, oblivious, has forgotten his taunt and is explaining how he discovered an expert garage tucked away in a country lane behind the M25. Gilly and Olly Pearson are waving up at the house. Karina hugs Jamie and, her heart twisting, watches him wander down to join them.

There's heavy traffic around Gatwick; it takes twenty minutes longer than usual to reach the junction with the M25. There, Hilary, finger tracing the route on the map, tells Julian to turn right. They circle four roundabouts. Hilary can't find the road. 'I think it's this one,' he says. Julian swings left onto a dual carriageway. 'Here on the right.'

'There's nowhere to turn,' Julian points out.

'There should be a gap.'

The barrier is unbroken. 'This is wrong,' says Julian.

'It can't be. Just here. Any moment now . . .'

After five minutes they reach another roundabout. Julian goes round it twice while Hilary squints at the map and mutters, 'I don't understand.'

Julian doubles back along the original road. Karina shuts her eyes.

'Normally when I come here, there's a gap,' Hilary says.

'You always approach from the west?'

'Of course. How very discombobulating.'

After ten more minutes it becomes clear that Hilary usually approaches from the east. Neither Julian nor Karina can work out how or why.

'I feel sick,' Cynthia says. 'Jules, please stop the car.'

'I can't, there's no hard shoulder.'

A speed camera looms out of the central reservation and blasts silver light at them. 'Fuck!' Julian shouts.

'There it is. That little road on the right.' Hilary points. 'Turn here.' Julian can't; there's no slip-road.

'Jules, I'm going to throw up,' Cynthia says, chest heaving.

Julian circles another roundabout and doubles back again. This time he's on the right side of the road and turns down the lane, where some desultory trees soon give way to a run-down collection of lock-ups and corrugated iron sheds. Nearby stands a muddy car, around twenty years old, with a dent in its door. 'Thar she blows!' Hilary cries. 'That's my beauty.'

Julian slams on the brakes. The Jag squeals to a halt. Cynthia tumbles out towards the trees.

'Dearie me. Car sickness,' Hilary remarks.

'Hils, we're late. We have to go,' Julian says. 'Drive carefully, all right?'

'Thanks, little bro, ride appreciated. See you.' Hilary paces off towards his car.

'Vintage Jag indeed,' Julian mumbles. 'Fit for scrap.'

Karina climbs out. 'Cynthia?' she says. 'How are you feeling?' Cynthia is drifting back towards her, pallid. In the dappled shade, she looks more like Lindy than ever.

'Thanks, darling,' she says. 'I'll be fine. I will. I'm sorry. I'm so sorry.'

'Do you still feel sick?'

'It's going. It is.' Cynthia gives a wan smile; Karina holds the back door open for her.

Julian executes the fastest three-point turn Karina has ever experienced. Her violin case, on the back window-ledge, slides about. Lindy would have laughed over all this, she reminds herself.

Cynthia slumps across the back seat and falls asleep. Karina and Julian drive in silence for an hour until they reach Harpenden and have to wake their passenger to ask how to find the house. Fortunately, it's easier than finding Hilary's garage. In the red-brick cul-de-sac, Marion flutters around her sister while a large brown dog slobbers enthusiastically over them all. It's past one thirty. 'You must come in and have a cup of tea!' Marion cries.

Finally they escape Harpenden and Julian dodges the speed cameras back to the M25. Karina's phone rings. 'Where are you?' Rohan asks.

'Nearly there. Turning on to the M4.'

'Are you OK?'

Julian overtakes a Mini; a lorry, looming behind where there'd been none before, gives a vicious hoot. At last they pull up outside Heathrow's Terminal 1. Karina unloads her violin, which has weathered the ride better than she has.

'Darling one, take care. I'll expect you to speak fluent Magyar on your return.' Julian embraces her.

'Give Jamie a hug. See you Sunday, darling.'

She stands on the pavement among the cascade of arriving passengers, watching him drive away. Then she walks inside. Amid the throng, there's no sign of the quartet; she's about to wander alone to the check-in desk, assuming they've gone through security already, when a warm arm encircles her. She turns and hugs Rohan as if he's about to save her life.

* * *

On the plane, Karina, the smallest of the quintet, is sandwiched in between Harry by the window and the long-limbed Rohan on the aisle. Behind them, Genya and Malcolm have both demanded aisle seats and sit across from one another, without talking. Genya brings out a Tupperware box of Lyuba's cookies. Malcolm vanishes behind the *Telegraph*. Harry, beside Karina, dons some outsized headphones and switches on his iPod. She and Rohan are free to talk.

'He's nuts,' Karina says. 'He's my brother-in-law, but he's completely bonkers! They're driving me to distraction, but I'm stuck with them, I don't know what to do.'

'Stay strong,' Rohan says. 'Don't let them squish you.'

'I don't want to grumble, Ro, I know how lucky I am. But this trip is the biggest thing that's happened to me in years, I'm so nervous about going to Hungary and playing with the quartet, and none of it means a thing to them. Maybe it shouldn't, I don't know, but I can't help feeling that if I do something different, I don't count. It's like being married to a family of juggernauts. I should be used to it by now, but it's bothering me more, not less.'

'Of course, because now you're doing something meaningful of your own when you haven't for years. That's one reason I wanted to bring you. You've got so much to give, Karrie, and you've been squashed. I don't know if this makes sense, but I want—' He glances at the stewardess, who's miming safety instructions with a yellow oxygen mask. Sunlight slants into the plane, illuminating the side of his face. 'I want to bring you back to yourself,' he says. 'I don't know where you left yourself behind, but if I've found you, then you can too.'

The plane taxis and takes off. Malcolm, who hates flying, closes his eyes. Genya has struck up a conversation with the lorry-driver beside him about Malcolm's cello case, which occupies a seat of its own. 'He must always buy ticket for it,' he explains, 'but when I ask if I may look after its meal, which is part of ticket, they never give me!'

'Fuck that, mate,' says the lorry-driver, who's on a jaunt with an entourage of tattooed friends. 'Save yourself for the lager. Dirt cheap in Budapest.'

'Let's have a drink,' Rohan says to Karina. 'You deserve one.'

* * *

The buzz in Budapest airport dazzles Karina with a sound she knows well: those chains of astringent Hungarian syllables. She half expects her parents to appear. In her pocket is the list of addresses that Dénes has given her. After some confusion and disagreement, Harry works out that the best way into the city, and the cheapest for five people and five instruments, is a minibus.

Karina gazes out of its window, her heart thudding, part of her wondering whether she should have stayed at home. She hadn't expected so much grey. The city was heavily shelled during the Revolution, as well as bombed in the war, and the Soviet-style concrete that went up over the craters hasn't worn well.

Imagining. Fifty years ago; and sixty. What does her father remember? Her mother? And Mimi? She takes in wide streets, lined with trees. Big, solid apartment blocks are plastered dark red, brown and what was once terracotta under the grime; some bear wrought iron balconies that remind her incongruously of Paris. A warmth in the air suggests that spring has arrived here faster than in Sussex.

'It's Vienna plus communism,' Harry remarks.

'Or not,' Rohan mutters to Karina, pointing at pock-marks high on an apartment block, where shells must have struck.

Now the Danube is before them, meandering through the town, green and grey in its wide bed. On its far side, the castle and the Fisherman's Bastion stand on the hilltop, as if hoisted aloft by the parkland below. The minibus passes the Erzsébet Bridge. 'That's my mother's name,' Karina remarks.

'Who is this Erzsébet Bridge?' Harry jokes. 'A close relation of Albert Hall?'

'And Victoria Line,' Rohan quips back. 'Here we are, chaps.' The minibus pulls up outside a concrete tower sandwiched between two elegant old blocks on a busy street.

Posters in the lobby announce the Budapest Spring Festival, with the Hungarian musicians' names written, to British eyes, back to front: Schiff András, Kocsis Zoltán. Foreign musicians, though, are in Western format: Alfred Brendel, the St Francis Quartet. But – Veres Karina? They've decided that she really is Hungarian.

The hotel receptionist speaks perfect English, rattling out an Americanised welcome.

'It's wonderful to be here,' Rohan tells her. 'Our guest violinist, Karina, is Hungarian.'

'Not quite – my parents were born here,' Karina explains.

The receptionist grasps her hand, uttering words she can't understand. '*Isten hozta itthon!*'

'I'm sorry, what's that in English?'

'This means welcome home,' the receptionist beams. 'Have a nice day.'

The quartet's local agent has faxed over their schedule. On Saturday they'll have a morning rehearsal in the hall of the Ferenc Liszt Conservatory, a quiet afternoon, then the concert at seven thirty. The next day, they'll fly home at ten a.m. There isn't much time for sightseeing.

The sky is dark over the Danube and Genya's tired eyes have begun to brighten at the prospect of dinner. Rohan shifts his weight from foot to foot and Karina asks him silently, with a glance, what the matter is. 'I need to do some practising,' he tells her. 'Would you mind terribly if I didn't come out with you right now? There's a bit in the C major that's bugging me, I've got to refinger it.'

Karina is surprised, but knows better than to put a musician off his practising. Probably she should do likewise; but now that she's here, she's longing to see her ancestral city. Malcolm is having dinner with the Hungarian agent – he insists, to the others' annoyance, that they don't need to join in. While Rohan disappears upstairs and Malcolm departs in a taxi, Karina finds herself standing outside the hotel with Harry, Genya and her father's list of addresses.

'Karina, where we go to eat?' Genya says. 'Maybe near river, or up hill, near castle?'

'Let's walk and see what happens,' Karina suggests.

They set off along Váci utca, the central pedestrian shopping street; Karina spots fresh-scrubbed facades plastered with designer logos, the companies ravenous for Eastern Europe. Eventually they turn towards the river; ahead, the Danube glistens under reflected lights, and the castle stands floodlit on its hill on the opposite bank. Some way along, there rises the florid pale stone of the Parliament building, which is being cleaned. Karina glances at her list. 'One place my dad told me to look for was close to there.'

Harry, who likes navigating, consults the map he picked up in the hotel and finds their way to the far side of the Parliament and the first address on Dénes's list. It's a postwar concrete monolith, housing, they deduce, public swimming baths. The apartment block that had been the family home of Karina's great-grandparents is gone for good.

'This cannot be place?' says Genya.

'I think you'll find something happened to it,' Harry remarks.

'A direct hit,' Karina says. She pictures the scene: rubble, chaos, looting. With cars and buses streaming by, horns at the ready, and the leaves fresh on the trees overhead, it's hard to imagine that anything could ever have been different. Yet, she thinks, it's not so long ago; it could have been us.

Three men of two generations sit on a low concrete wall between buildings, in heated discussion over plastic cups. Near them, an elderly woman in a headscarf and long, bright skirt holds two small girls by the hand, while their mother, her cheekbones protruding and her hands bony, stands among the parked cars at a pay-and-display meter, pushing the coin return button again and again. A Roma family. Karina watches passers-by avoiding them.

She takes some forints out of her purse and walks up to the young mother at the parking meter. 'Please,' she says, pushing the money towards her. The woman takes a step back, gazes at her in amazement, then accepts it with a mumble of '*Köszönöm*'. Karina goes back to Genya and Harry, ignoring their raised eyebrows.

Genya peers at Harry's map. 'Maybe by river are places to eat,' he says. 'Let's walk over bridge. Karina, what we eat in Hungary?'

Karina glances round at the mix of buildings, soot-laden, crumbling plaster revealing the bricks beneath; among them stand art deco gems, prioritised for clean-up. Friezes of carved figures crawl, petrified, along shrugged arches and curvaceous corners; glimmers of stained glass and mosaics flash like hallucinations high above the street. Communist-era monstrosities are notes from the wrong chord, but the total meshes together into a visual melody of its own, with a pulse gentle and enduring, yet infused with something that makes Karina shudder. Is it the ghosts of those who didn't escape; or the lingering imprint of years of occupation and fear?

She's read somewhere that stones hold energy. Memory? Collective unconscious? Imagination?

But if she's honest with herself, she's not looking along this Budapest street for signals of her family's past. She's looking for Rohan and he's not there.

They take the next bridge towards Buda. Halfway across, Karina pauses and rests on the railing, gazing towards the shadowy expanse of trees on Margaret Island, and beyond, to the gold-illumined castle and the hill of lights and weaving streets beneath.

'Fuck,' Harry says. 'It's *beautiful.*'

'Is odd place,' Genya comments.

'It's more beautiful than Vienna,' says Karina.

'The heart's been knocked out of it,' Harry opines. 'All those invasions and revolutions. You can see it must have been a great city, but it's been buffeted back into the history books.'

'My father sometimes says that no good Hungarian musicians have had international careers if they stayed in Hungary,' Karina tells him. 'The biggest names are all people who left. It's too out of the way.'

'But it's bang in the middle of Europe. Doesn't make sense, really. Bloody Nazis. Bloody – sorry, Genya – Russians.'

'I am not Russian, I am Ukrainian Jewish.' Genya smiles. 'Let's walk. We need food.'

They take a wooden funicular railway up the hill to the old town. Beside the castle courtyard, they meander along a cobbled street where low-set terraces are painted sultry shades of ochre, terracotta and deep pink. Antique shops, craft markets and restaurants cluster together, attracting tourists. It's warm enough, just, to sit outside. Beside a restaurant in a building declaring itself six hundred years old, a sliver of music catches their attention: two violinists and a double bassist are playing to the diners at the outdoor tables.

'Tourist trap,' Harry comments. 'We should go somewhere less obvious.'

'You *know* somewhere less obvious, Harry?' Genya says.

'How hungry are you?' Harry, turning his nose up at the translated menu though he wouldn't know what any dish was without it, wants to keep exploring.

'How hungry?' Genya echoes. 'Very hungry! Is long time since lunch.'

'What about Lyuba's biscuits? You ate the lot!'

'*Karina* must eat.'

If this is how decisions are made in the St Francis Quartet, no wonder there's strife. 'Why don't we stick with this tonight?' Karina suggests, arbitrating in the absence of the usual peacemaker, Rohan. 'Then after the concert tomorrow, perhaps your agent can suggest something more radical.'

The solo violinist looks forty, but she suspects he's younger, aged by his developing girth, his close-cropped hair, his formal outfit of black trousers and waistcoat, white shirt and tie. The second violinist accompanies, alongside the bass; he must be twenty years older, commensurately plumper. Both faces are wide of cheekbone, the dark eyes heavy lidded, set into deep olive skin; they're evidently father and son. The sweetness of the leader's tone speaks to Karina: intimate, coaxing, swooping, a little like Stéphane Grappelli.

'Two a forint here, Gypsy fiddlers,' Harry remarks. 'I heard somewhere that they go to train at a special school where they learn the restaurant repertoire, and that real folk fiddlers use a totally different technique. I once saw some Hungarian folk fiddlers at a gig in London – they keep the bow arm elbow really close to the body. Let's grab that table under the pergola.'

Karina lets them hurry towards the sheltered terrace at the side of the restaurant; she lingers, watching the musicians. She doesn't care where they trained or what technique they use: she loves the warmth in the sound. The solo violinist reminds her intensely of the fiddler on the train.

The pergola surrounds its tables with a trellis, supporting a vine full of green shoots. Genya and Harry are arguing over the menu when Karina joins them. She can imagine her mother's voice saying the names of almost every dish, though the restaurant also offers burgers for the less adventurous. They order a bottle of Bikavér, Bull's Blood wine; goulash stew for Karina, stuffed cabbage for Genya, and Harry chooses Vienna schnitzel.

Karina gazes at a nearby church spire, the cobbled street, the lights of Pest in the distance below. 'I can't believe I'm really here,' she says.

Harry sips his Bikavér. 'When did your parents leave? During the war?'

'No, in 1956.'

'The Revolution.' Genya nods.

'And your parents left Kiev?' Karina asks him.

'They went to Israel, I came to London. Karina, listen: I had nothing. I had viola; I had Soviet prize for playing my viola; I had one suitcase. Now I have house, I have my Lyuba as my wife, we have lodgers, our kids are British and I can play chamber music in Budapest! Is wonderful life, I am so happy.'

At the front, the band has begun a *csárdás*. Karina listens; it's familiar. Isn't this something that her grandmother used to play her, when she was a child?

'Do you know what this piece is called?' she asks the waiter. He shakes his head, but promises to send the band over to them.

If only Rohan had been there to hear this playing. 'Does Rohan always stay in and practise?' she asks Harry.

'Rohan is one hell of a practiser.' Harry swirls his wine in its glass. 'It's good escapism, though. If he's practising, he can't fight with Malcolm. His strategy is that whatever's going on around him, well, he's just going to play his violin. It's the answer to all his problems.'

'You hoped he would join us?' Genya says to Karina, pointedly.

'It would have been nice to do something all together.'

'Your husband, what is he like?'

'Julian's a good bloke. Very dependable. Responsible. Though he's insisted on sending our son to boarding-school, and I'm not too pleased.'

Genya draws in his breath. 'Boarding-school, I don't like,' he says. 'I would never send my son away. A child needs his family. Your son is how old?'

'He's eight.'

'But this is still baby! How is possible you send him away from you?'

'In Julian's family, the boys have always gone to boarding-school. It doesn't matter how miserable any of them have been there, they still send their kids.'

'The English are bloody stubborn sometimes,' Harry says.

'You are English,' Genya protests.

'Scottish. We're even more stubborn than the English. I can tell you, though, if Alison and I ever have kids, I don't know how we're going to educate them. She earns well, but I don't, and with our mortgage we wouldn't be able to afford a private school. I don't know what the fuck's going on in Britain. Everything's polarised according to whether you've got money or not, and if you're a musician, you haven't. It's funny how the minute we get to France or Germany or Scandinavia, things feel normal. Alison says Britain's become unreasonable.'

Karina glances along the street. Compared to what Budapest has been through, the problems at home seem a tad silly. She's beginning to understand her father's frustration over the squandering of Western freedom. But she doesn't want to argue with her new colleagues, and Rohan isn't there to back her up.

'If you're wondering about Ro,' Harry says, 'he'll be ordering room service and refingering every bar of both quintets. Then he'll emerge around midnight, realise how late it is and ask if anyone wants to go for a drink, and just as you're about to turn in, he'll say, "Oh Karina, you know such-and-such a passage? I think we should change the bowings." And then you must make sure you don't lie awake all night worrying about it.'

Karina tries the stew, a comforting mound of meat, peppers, garlic and onions, sprinkled with tiny pieces of pasta which the English menu calls 'nipped paste'. It tastes of home. She's ten years old again, at the table in Twickenham with Lindy. She wants to cry.

A movement by the door, a glimmer of white shirt, and the lead violinist is beside them, fiddle in hand. He gives them a brief, formal bow; Karina notices that his smile doesn't entirely engage with them. 'Good evening, you have question?' he says.

'I just wondered,' she says, 'what that last tune was? It sounds so familiar.'

'That? It is song by Panna Czinka. Panna Czinka was great *Cigány* lady player. *Cigány* musicians are great tradition. This band is my family. My father, my cousin. Our grandfather very famous.' He points at a photo on the wall inside. 'We play this café long time.'

Karina goes inside to explore. The restaurant walls are dotted with historic photos. Late nineteenth century; early twentieth; pre-war; then, tucked away out of clear view, postwar. Once, this restaurant had been elegant. Each table had a little more space; the musicians much more. They'd performed on a dais, away from the bar area. One photo shows a bushy-eyebrowed violinist, a cimbalom player with a huge moustache, another violin being played by a teenage boy.

'I'm a violinist,' Karina tells the fiddler. 'Can I try your violin?'

He holds out the instrument with a nod; Karina takes it and plays some twiddles. Under its fingerboard are stowed banknotes with which the customers have been tipping him.

'The band in that photo – that's not your family?' she asks. He shakes his head. 'So, even if we don't know who they are, what would have happened to them?'

He looks blank. The waiter comes over to translate, and then the violinist understands. He shrugs; then pulls a finger across his throat. 'Hitler.'

Shaken, Karina thanks him. He gives her handbag a brief, barbed glance; she takes a note from her purse and tucks it with the others below the fingerboard. Then she watches him turn away to serenade the next table. This was how her great-grandfather would have earned his living, while he could.

Back at the table, Genya has already finished his food and mopped up the sauce with bread; now he's picking hopefully at the edge of her stew. She gives him half of it. She doesn't want her stomach to feel as laden as her mind.

After eleven, they wander down the steep hill to the Chain Bridge and across the river towards their hotel in Pest. The night is chilly; Karina shivers.

'You are cold,' says Genya. 'Take my coat, Karina.'

'No, thanks, I'm fine. I'm not cold. Just haunted. I keep seeing my parents. I keep thinking of my grandmother. She never seemed to know what happened to her family and the violinist in the restaurant said . . .'

'Did he know them?'

'I was looking at a photo of a Gypsy band, but when I asked what would have become of them, he just said "Hitler". It feels much more real, now that we're here . . .'

'Oh, Hitler hated the Gypsies as much as the Jews,' Harry remarks. 'Everyone knows *that*. He killed something like half a million of them, nobody's certain of the exact number. They were the second most murdered race after the Jews. They occupied a whole section of Auschwitz.'

'Stalin was biggest murderer,' Genya points out. 'Sixty million people die under Stalin. But, Karina, *we* are here. We are proof. We live.'

'Karina, here's what you should see.' Harry, map-reading, points at a symbol on the page. 'The House of Terror Museum. It says here that the building was the headquarters of the secret police. It's at 60 Andrássy.'

This address is on her piece of paper, in her father's handwriting. It's the building to which he had asked her to 'give his regards'. 'I'm supposed to go there,' she says.

'What else on list?' asks Genya.

'There's a musical instrument museum I want to see. There's a violin which – well, we think it might have been my grandmother's. Rohan said he had a hunch.'

'Is good violin?'

'A Nicolò Amati.'

'Bloody hell,' Harry says, 'no wonder Ro has a hunch. He'd kill for an Italian job.'

'Would he?' Karina asks.

'Well, he's making a sound like a fucking angel on a piece of firewood. So, the theory goes, just imagine what he could do with a really good fiddle.'

In the hotel lobby, while they're waiting for the lift at ten to midnight, her mobile rings. 'Karrie?' says Rohan's voice. 'I'm sorry it's so late, I didn't realise. You're not asleep, are you? Do you want to come out for a drink?'

Harry looks at Karina's expression and smirks.

'It's very late,' she stalls.

'Well, hang on downstairs for just a mo and I'll come and say goodnight.'

Harry and Genya roll their eyes heavenwards, kiss Karina three times each and get into the lift. Karina fidgets with her phone.

Her head is aching with exhaustion, but when the lift doors slide back to reveal Rohan walking towards her, she takes one look at him and knows she's going for that drink.

'Jeez, I'm sorry,' he says. 'I'm *so* sorry. You came all this way and I have to practise. But I just wouldn't be able to walk into that hall tomorrow without—'

'Don't worry. I know the feeling.'

'I saw a bar round the corner. We could go there?'

They stroll out into the night's blue and brown shadows. The bar is several blocks away and down a flight of stone stairs: it's a cellar, the ceilings arched, the walls painted with murals of grapevines and cornfields. Cigarette smoke traps light in opaque spirals. Rohan orders a beer; Karina asks for apricot Pálinka, her father's favourite Hungarian fruit brandy.

'Karrie,' Rohan says, 'you know that bit of the C major where we're in unison?' He sings it; she nods. 'I think I've found a better bowing.' He demonstrates. The drinks arrive and Karina tries not to down hers in one.

He talks her through the new bowings, which extend considerably further than this one passage. Eventually she asks to borrow the part so she can copy them in overnight. Since she's practised the original patterns obsessively for a month, changing them on the day of the concert won't be easy.

'I'm sorry,' Rohan says again. 'I'm afraid I often do this – changing things just before the show. Harry will tell you all about it.'

'He did.'

'And I'm sorry I didn't come to dinner, but . . . look, tomorrow afternoon, let's go for a walk or something?'

'Do you want to come to the House of Terror Museum?'

'What's that? Dracula?'

'It's the secret police's former headquarters. My father told me to go there.'

'Why?'

'I'm not sure.'

'Do you find there's something menacing about this place? Or am I imagining it? This cellar, for instance. I keep thinking: what happened here sixty years ago? And fifty? How many people hid in here? What became of them all?'

'I thought I was feeling that way just because of my family. There's a special soul here, and it's the same as the soul in my parents' house. It's gentle and positive and sad, all at the same time.'

'It's like me and South Africa.' Rohan swigs his beer. 'It's got everything to do with me, yet nothing. Sometimes I love it; a lot of the time I hate it. I'm proud that my parents left when they did. It hurts to go there, but I hardly know why.'

Veins protrude on the back of Rohan's left hand; his fingertips are calloused, like her own. It would be so easy to reach out and touch him that the idea becomes upsetting.

'What's that like?' he asks, looking at her Pálinka.

'Try it.'

Rohan takes her glass, then turns it so that the stain of her lipstick is towards his mouth. He lifts it and sips. 'Gorgeous.'

'We should go,' Karina says. 'I have to write in your bowings.'

At the hotel, they hesitate fractionally in the lobby. 'I'll come and get the music,' Karina suggests while they wait for the lift.

Rohan's room is on the sixth floor. He dashes inside, without inviting her. In the doorway, he hands her two slender folios. It would be so simple to step through that door and close it behind her, and he wants her to.

'See you in the morning,' says Rohan.

'Goodnight,' says Karina.

21

Marc and Mimi, walking through Manhattan with Vali the nanny pushing Dénes in his buggy, pretended to be an American family. It was easy to pretend in New York. To some degree, Mimi suspected, everybody was pretending. She and Marc were both convinced that the conflagration in Europe must end in disaster if America didn't intervene – yet apart from the influx of Jewish refugees on the Lower East Side, little around them suggested much awareness of the world's precarious state. One thing was certain: going home wasn't an option.

Marc had rented a studio close to the music college on the Upper West Side where he taught, but it was mainly for show; he spent most of his time at Mimi's place in the Dakota Building. When he wasn't there, trying to compose, he was at the college, giving lessons in orchestration, harmony and counterpoint. Mimi got up early each morning to do her administration, write to Tamás and practise; Vali fed Dénes and took him out to Central Park. Marc listened to the radio and obsessively read every word of the *New York Times*, which Mimi Hungarianised into the 'Tim-esh'.

Saul, the New York impresario who was effectively her employer, advisor and lifeline, had arranged her apartment rental, on the ninth floor of the outsized block by the park: an enormous living room drenched in light, a big bedroom for Mimi, a small one for Dénes and a glorified cubicle for Vali. Everything was black and cream, even the coffee cups. And Mimi, as usual, did things her own way. 'Still,' Marc reflected, teasing her, 'you wouldn't be human if all this didn't go straight to your head.'

'All this': concerts, money, fame. Sometimes she had to pinch herself to make certain she wouldn't wake up back in Kistarcsa. Plucked from a Gypsy family simply because she could play the violin, catapulted halfway round the globe into the hands of New York's most powerful event-maker to grace packed concert halls and the most glamorous parties she'd ever seen – and she'd seen plenty: Mimi was living in a fairy tale. Invitations arrived to meet patrons of the arts in their luxurious homes. Admirers gave her diamonds, Renoir-owning heiresses clucked over little Dénes. Nobody minded that she was a Gypsy; perhaps nobody knew. She looked exotic and spoke with a heavy, middle-European accent; that was enough to enchant them.

Here, too, she could mingle with the finest of her peers as she rarely could in Hungary. Once a sepulchral-looking Russian glided up to her outside her dressing-room, escorted by Saul. 'This is Sergei Rachmaninov,' Saul declared. Mimi flushed from her nose to her fingertips as the composer stooped, lifted her hand and kissed it. Another night, another concert, and a moustachioed gentleman with greying hair and the most enchanting, melting eyes she had ever seen on a man knocked on her door and addressed her in soft Viennese German. Her German wasn't good, but she didn't need it to recognise Fritz Kreisler, whom she regarded as the greatest of all violinists. Kreisler in turn presented her to a beady-eyed piano virtuoso from Russia who was taking the world by storm: Vladimir Horowitz. Both of them had settled in New York. Mimi, laughing, glittering, yet feeling overwhelmed in this company, found the presence of mind to note that these great musicians were fleeing Europe not by fortuitous accident, like her and Marc, but by design and in fear for their lives.

The doorbell in the Dakota rang one warm spring evening just after six. Vali was giving Dénes his supper. Marc, since returning from teaching mid-afternoon, had been alternating between drafting the second movement of the concerto, reading the Tim-esh and listening to the radio. Mimi had sifted through her post and read the latest missives from Tamás and the Frankls three times through. Now she was lying on the settee, enjoying a Martini that she considered well-earned thanks to a vile rehearsal that morning. Vali answered the door and Mimi heard her give a stifled cry of astonishment: the unexpected visitor was speaking Hungarian. Vali hurried back to the living room and carried a card on the salver over to Mimi, who stared at it, disbelieving, briefly paralysed.

'Are you all right?' Marc exclaimed as she scrambled to her feet. She rushed to tidy her hair and then in a flood of Hungarian greeted the stranger in the doorway as if he were her father, even though he didn't look quite as she had imagined him. He was a diminutive, haunted-looking man, modestly dressed, his skin a sickly, yellowish hue, his black eyes vast and filled with inexpressible terror. The fear of death; she saw it at once.

'My friend, Marc Duplessis,' Mimi presented him. 'Marc, look who is here!'

She saw recognition, tinged with dismay, cross Marc's face, for their guest was Béla Bartók. And those fathomless eyes were straying, instinctively, towards the notes that Marc had set crawling over his manuscript paper. With one swift motion of the newspaper, he hid his composition. Bartók held out his hand and Marc shook it, speechless, the great composer's fingers swamped by his fleshy palms.

'Professor Bartók, you must stay to dinner,' Mimi cried. 'Vali, darling, what do we have in the house to eat?'

'You are *here*? In America?' Marc stammered. 'I had no idea.'

'It is a tour,' Bartók explained, 'but I don't know if will always be tour. Perhaps I will stay. Have you been to Hungary, Monsieur Duplessis?'

Marc shook his head.

'Then stay away,' Bartók said. 'I am in despair for my country. I am attacked for my work and each day the crookedness brings less stability – how it's possible for the government to align us with this foul thing in Germany, I don't understand. What's left may be our country, but not, perhaps, our home . . .'

Mimi wondered how to explain Marc's presence. Their situation wasn't exactly conventional: a composer semi-living with a violinist who was married to someone else yet showed no inclination either to go home or to file for divorce. Mimi had cultivated a mask for Marc as family friend, a protective, watchful eye and honorary uncle to Dénes; sometimes she even thought people believed it. She decided it was easiest not to explain at all.

If Bartók was perturbed, he didn't show it. Throughout dinner, he took care to steer the conversation in Marc's direction, and to speak French or English so that Marc could join in. He asked

Marc what he was writing, what style he preferred, what his opinions were of their various colleagues. Marc gazed at Bartók as if he were God – which, Mimi had to admit, he more or less was. She thought of Bartók's concertos, the operas, masterful mixes of visionary poetry, folk idioms and modernistic writing. Marc idolised Bartók and often complained that he could never dream of matching the Hungarian giant's music. Many were the times that Mimi had told him he didn't need to; he should just be himself.

The conversation soon turned to Marc's view that music in France was going to pot. Ravel was dead, Poulenc was too clever by half, and Messiaen, the great young hope, was too religious and had an odd enthusiasm for transcribing the songs of birds rather than those of people. Marc alone seemed intrigued by the possibilities of folk influence in the manner of Bartók. Not that he regarded French folk-song as particularly fertile ground, Canteloube having cornered the market with the *Chants d'Auvergne*, the musical equivalent, to Marc, of *crème pâtissière*. He wanted, he told Bartók, to follow him and Kodály into the puszta to hear folk-song born of the union of nature and humanity.

'And we would welcome you,' Bartók told him. 'My ideal is the brotherhood of all peoples. I won't close my music to any influence, as long as it is a force for good.'

'So, just because I'm French, why shouldn't I draw on sounds from Hungary, Romania or anywhere else?' Marc agreed. 'But I'm out of tune with my time, my country and, to be honest, most other things too.'

'I am certain you are not,' Bartók reassured him. Mimi watched Marc glow.

When they'd put away two bottles of wine and Vali's Hungarian home-cooking, Mimi grabbed her violin and began to play Bartók the Gypsy tunes she remembered from her childhood. She wanted to preserve every second of this evening: the May night deepening beyond the windows; the yellowy-pink gleam of Bartók's bald pate and the fine silver hairs around it; the folds of Marc's white shirt, shifting as he watched her, and the silkiness of the Amati's wooden chin-rest against her cheek.

One glance at Marc's face, though, told her that he wanted to stand up and scream. If Bartók fell for her – he was known to have a weakness for young female violinists – then he'd write for her. And if he did, maybe a concerto – oh, if only – then Marc would take umbrage; he'd demand to know why she would even consider playing his work instead, just because he was her lover. Why settle for second rate, he'd say, when you can have the greatest genius alive? It would be in vain that she would assure him his work wasn't second rate. Marc was too sensitive, too touchy, too self-absorbed for his own good. If she told him this, though, he'd only retort that she was, too.

When Mimi stopped playing, Bartók went to the piano and beckoned her over, asking her to show him some of her favourite tricks in intonation and colour. Talking, demonstrating, she was vaguely aware that Vali had tiptoed in, touched Marc's sleeve, whispered in his ear. He followed her out in the direction of the kitchen and its radio.

Mimi found the music for Bartók's *Romanian Dances*; the composer placed the piano part in front of him. 'Shall we?' he asked. Mimi stood next to him and led the way. By the time Marc wandered in, his feet as unsure as a sleepwalker's, they were halfway through the third dance and she was certainly not stopping now, with Bartók accompanying her in his own music. At the end, she put the Amati down on the piano and glared at Marc. 'And what's wrong with *you*?'

'Germany and Italy have invaded France,' Marc said. 'The report says Paris is threatened.'

Mimi, struck dumb, reached for a chair. She could hear Vali sobbing in the kitchen. Vali, poor girl, was fond of Marc.

'It can't be true,' Marc added. 'They're making it up. Or else I'm dreaming. Or it's all a dreadful mistake, perhaps the news report is garbled – a misread signal. Or . . .'

'I'm so sorry, Monsieur Duplessis,' Bartók said quietly. 'Where is your family?'

Later, when Bartók had left and Dénes was asleep and Vali too, Marc slid into Mimi's bed. She held him and let him shudder with tears. After a while they made quiet, desperate love, which Marc sometimes told her was worse than not making love at all, because he never knew when he'd be allowed back for more.

'It'll be over soon,' Mimi whispered, around two a.m. 'It can't carry on. Someone will assassinate Hitler and then it'll be finished.'

'What about Tamás?' Marc said.

'Why do you ask about Tamás? Hungary isn't involved in this, whatever Professor Bartók says.'

'Because, Mimi, he's still your husband. Because you write to him every day, and he writes back. Because he expects you to go back to him eventually, and because you want to. Because you still love him.'

'Maybe I do,' Mimi said. She knew this wasn't what Marc had hoped for.

'And me? Don't you love me, even a little?' His eyes, blue as Lake Balaton, were reproachful, yet she'd never glimpsed any tenderness on earth that could match theirs.

'Yes, my dear. I love you with all my heart.'

'But then . . .'

'I love Tamás, who is my husband. I love you, who are my soul mate. It's not the same. There is room in my heart for both.'

'Do you honestly believe that, Mimi?'

Marc waited, but Mimi, her cheek against his chest, was falling asleep.

'Can't we do something, Daddy?' It's nearly lunchtime and Jamie is standing by the stairs, looking up at Julian with big, beseeching eyes.

'All right, mate.' Julian tries to be jovial. He's up to his eyeballs in paperwork, worried sick about the franchise decision, which is only weeks away, and still fuming over the behaviour of certain members of his extended family. He's glad for Karina that she has a couple of days' break. 'What do you want to do, Jimbo?' he asks, fidgeting with his BlackBerry in case Carsten has sent yet another email besides his earlier ten, although it's Saturday.

'Can we go to Brighton?' Jamie begs. 'Just go round the shops and see the sea?'

'Why don't we go to the Pavilion? We're always saying we must take you to the Pavilion.'

'That's the big place with the domes?' Jamie looks doubtful; presumably he'd prefer the largest local toy-shop to anything that could be misconstrued as educational.

Julian switches off the BlackBerry. He decides to have a house-husband afternoon. He'll take his son to Brighton, show him the Pavilion and explain the Regency. Later, he'll begin to attack the invasive mess at home. There's too much Veres junk in the loft. Karina seems reluctant even to reduce it, let alone get rid of it. Perhaps he could whittle it down to subsections marked 'Keep' and 'Chuck'.

Karina phones from Budapest while they're putting on their coats. He'd forgotten how she used to sound on tour with the orchestra: wrung out like a damp tea towel.

'Is your room noisy?' he asks. 'Couldn't you sleep?'

'The room's fine. But I was up half the night writing in the new bowings and double-checking that I'd done it right, and then I was worried I wouldn't get to grips with them fast enough, and our rehearsal started early.'

'How's your home town? Is it pretty?'

'It's not my home town, but it's amazing.'

'Here's Jamie,' Julian says, and hands over the phone.

Karina is standing outside the museum with Rohan, who's pacing up and down, hands in his pockets. She melts at her son's voice. 'Schnooky, I miss you!'

'Dad's taking me to Brighton and we're going to see the Pavilion, but he said we could go to a toy-shop too.'

'That's nice, sweetheart. I'm coming home tomorrow.'

'What's the food like in Hungary?'

'Like Grandma's.'

'Mum, will you phone later?'

'Of course, darling. Have a lovely time in Brighton.'

Karina rings off. She's so tired that the museum's entrance seems to be shivering. They've come straight from the rehearsal to view the violin that Rohan spotted on the website. Rohan doesn't want only to see it; he wants to try to play it, which means they need to chat up a curator. 'Let's see if we can bluff our way through,' he says, making for the doors.

It takes a little doing; there's a language problem, and a remainder or two, Rohan later suggests, of communist-style recalcitrance when the officials question their lack of advance planning. Eventually the security guard obliges with a phone call; a few minutes later, a brisk woman in a suit appears and asks whether she can help them.

The violin is suspended in a glass case alongside five other instruments. Stripes glow in the wood. The instrument is strung, ready to play, so that it looks like a violin, not a relic. Rohan gazes at it and voices his request.

'Take it out?' The curator is horrified. 'No, sir. I'm sorry. We never take it out.'

'Is there some way that we can find out how it came to the museum?'

She shrugs. 'You make an appointment, we can find in archive. Today, this minute, we are busy, we need time to find it for you. Archivist is not here tomorrow. Monday museum is closed.'

'I'm the leader of a string quartet, playing in the Spring Festival,' Rohan tries, 'and if this is the Amati that we think it is . . .'

'It has Amati label, but not thought genuine.' The curator points, speaking the words on the description beside the violin.

Why would a museum hold an instrument if it wasn't valuable? Any old violin in a glass case isn't an object of pilgrimage. When the curator is looking the other way, Karina whips out her mobile phone and takes a photograph of it.

'So you make appointment and you come back,' says the curator, 'or you write your question and we will reply to you.'

Karina, out of view, pushes buttons on the phone and sends the picture to her father, with a note: 'Please show Grandma. Hers??'

While they're outside the museum, discussing their next move, Dénes's answer arrives. 'ROTTWEILERS.'

'Clarify?' Karina asks.

'NOT HERS,' texts Dénes.

'Wherever it comes from, someone should be playing it,' Rohan says. 'It shouldn't just sit there.'

'Were you hoping you might be able to use it, on loan?' Karina ventures.

'I can dream, can't I?' Rohan turns his back on the museum and begins to walk. Karina hurries after him.

'Don't be too upset,' she appeals. Her father had never given any indication that hope was justified; quite the opposite. And although she knows Dénes doesn't tell her everything, he's never misled her.

'It's so stupid,' Rohan says, while they march towards the Danube. 'There are all these marvellous violins, sitting in glass cases in museums or in bank vaults, nobody's playing them, so many of us need them – and nobody can touch them because of how much they cost. It's such a bloody waste.'

She's never seen him so annoyed, not even with Malcolm. 'You want one pretty badly, don't you?'

'So would you if you were me. Oh, Karrie, you're right, I'm making too much of it. But it reminds me of – it makes me think of – oh, shit, let's grab something to eat and find your other museum.'

They lunch on the move, on *lángos*, which Erzsébet used to make before Dénes was warned to watch his cholesterol: deep-fried bread dough, plastered with garlic and cheese. On Andrássy, Budapest's answer to the Champs Elysées, the Opera House looms, grey and arched, amid some intensive building work; across the street a layer of scaffolding thrums with restoration activities. Cranes rear up in the distance. Karina and Rohan cross a road decked with a web of trolley bus wires, and pass teeming shops and a large Burger King. The air is gentle, faintly fetid around the drains. On a bench under the ash trees, a dark-skinned man is asleep, wrapped in an anorak, a cigarette still glowing between his lips. A couple in an open-topped Saab speed round a corner, ignoring the red light. A Trabant, forty-five years old, is parked close by.

'Here it is,' Rohan says.

They come to a stop outside the museum and gaze up. No. 60 Andrássy is a corner block, battleship grey. First the ultra-right Arrow Cross Party rented space in it in 1937; three years later, they made it their headquarters and when they came to power in 1944 the basement was transformed into a prison. Later, when the Communist Party took control after the postwar coalition government, the State Security Police moved in and morphed into first the ÁVO, then the ÁVH. Now an iron canopy, bearing the museum's name hewn out in huge letters, stretches up one side and across the top of the block. 'Ready?' Rohan asks.

They walk through the marbled entrance hall, buy two tickets, then turn to find themselves gazing into a covered courtyard. In its centre stands a tank. Behind it, a wall, five storeys high, of photographs. Innumerable faces in silver and black and white, all of them, and thousands more like them, lost in the wreckage of Hungary's twentieth century.

After hauling the boxes out of the loft, Julian arranges them in a semicircle on the spare room floor. Jamie, replete with fish and chips, is glued to the television downstairs. So much stuff. So much *crap*. Julian can imagine Karina's likely response when she gets back, but he has designs on converting the loft, which would make a far better study than his cubbyhole off the landing. Currently it's a waste of space.

What's in here, for God's sake? Karina had started, but had so little help from her parents in understanding what she'd found that she'd virtually given up; now she's preoccupied with playing her violin. Julian decides to be Machiavellian. What she hasn't seen, she won't miss.

He wipes down the top of a box and lifts out a large tin that had once held leaf tea, its lid decorated with 1950s-style writing. Inside there's a sheaf of papers. Letters. What peculiar handwriting. Childish – or is it? The black ink is stark, a little wild; the words are overwhelmed with underlinings and exclamation marks. He deciphers a date: 1944.

Julian regularly encounters human misery in the course of his work, but all the same he feels a chill. The Nazis occupied Hungary in 1944. Mimi? Tamás? Surely not with writing like that?

It's a long way to Twickenham from Lewes – he can't just pop round to the in-laws with the letters; besides, there's no reason Erzsébet and Dénes should be any less recalcitrant with him than with Karina. Julian, though, is good at solving problems. The country is full of Eastern Europeans. London's building, cleaning and service industries have been revolutionised by young Poles, much to the Williamsons' joy ('so cheap and *so* efficient,' Sarah enthuses). He's been to at least three restaurants recently in which the waiters have hailed from Kosovo, Croatia and Slovakia. He's even seen posters here and there advertising a meeting of a Lewes

Hungarian Society. Therefore there must be Hungarians in Lewes. All he needs to do is find them.

'Jimbo,' he calls to his son, bounding downstairs, 'let's go for a stroll.'

'I'm watching this.' Jamie doesn't turn round from the TV.

'I need to find someone who can read Hungarian. You can help me.'

'Don't want to.'

'What's got into you today, Jimbo? Out of bed the wrong side?'

'Why did Mum have to go to Hungary at a *weekend*?' Jamie grumbles.

'Ask her that when she gets back tomorrow. Come along, chop-chop.' He claps his hands and holds out Jamie's coat.

Making brisk progress through the town, Julian and Jamie pop into the pizzeria (waitresses from the Czech Republic and Holland); the bakery (Scottish, Irish and Surrey); and a newsagent (Pakistani). They try a corner shop (Indian) and the best local hotel ('Eight nationalities, but no Hungarians,' the receptionist says, apologising).

'Your turn, Jamie,' Julian says, outside on the High Street. 'You choose where we try next.'

Jamie watches a white minibus approaching, the name GLYNDEBOURNE embossed in green capitals on its side. 'What about them?' he says. 'They do opera. They might be foreign.'

'Jimbo, you're a genius.' Countless nationalities of singers and musicians pass through the portals of the countryside opera house every year – it's worth a go. As if in response, the minibus, which ferries Glyndebourne staff to and from Lewes and the station, halts at a stop a few metres away. They approach as the vehicle disgorges several members of the *Così fan tutte* cast from the Touring Opera's spring season. The remaining passengers gaze with curiosity at the large, inquisitive man and his serious-eyed child.

'Excuse me,' Julian begins in his best Elthingbourne voice, 'I'm sorry to bother you, but I don't suppose there are any Hungarians at Glyndebourne at the moment, are there?'

A girl clasping a violin case against her knees looks up. 'There's a violinist who's playing as an extra with us,' she tells him. 'Why are you looking for a Hungarian?'

'There's something I need to have translated, some old family letters. Just roughly, to get an idea of what's in them.' He grins. 'My Hungarian's a little rusty.'

'I'm sure she'd do that, she'd probably find it really interesting. She's got a history degree. Let me ring her, I don't think she's left yet . . .' The girl scrolls down her mobile phone contacts and presses a button. 'Éva? It's Mel. Listen, we've just met this bloke who's got some historic letters in Hungarian and is desperate to find a . . . really? Are you sure? Yes, he's here—' She holds out the phone to Julian.

'*Ha*llo,' says Éva's voice. She sounds like a younger version of his mother-in-law. He's startled; he's so used to the accent that he barely notices it, except out of context, as now. He explains the situation and is astonished when she says she'll be on the next minibus and could meet him in a nearby café in twenty minutes. Julian thanks Mel profusely, then leads the excited Jamie into the appointed café to wait.

'It's like a detective story,' Jamie enthuses. 'I'll be Morse, you be Lewis.'

'It's all your idea,' Julian credits him proudly.

'Can I see them?'

Jamie gazes at the letters: heavy, unformed writing with wild, flying accents and a liberal peppering of exclamation marks. Julian watches his puzzled little face and wonders who wrote those words. Jamie's great-grandmother? Or someone further back?

'Do you think it's a child?' Julian asks him.

'It looks more like a grown-up,' Jamie remarks, 'but a grown-up who doesn't really know how to write.'

'Jimbo,' Julian says, for the second time that day, 'you're a genius.'

Éva, carrying her violin case, is wearing a pink coat, false eyelashes and a rough rose quartz pendant on a chain. Her waterfall of blonde hair turns the head of every man in the café. Sitting opposite Julian and Jamie at a table by the window, she pushes back her sunglasses, asks for an espresso and quizzes Julian. He explains his wife – crucial, he senses, for reasons other than nationality; then her parents; finally her grandmother. Éva's eyes turn into vast blue pools when she hears Mimi's name.

'This is *in*credible,' she cries. 'I don't *be*lieve it! And these might be from her?'

'Or to her. I don't know.'

Jamie, as enchanted by Éva as his father is, pipes up with his own theory. Éva listens and nods, serious. She begins to read. 'Eiyiyi,' she laughs, 'what writing! I see your problem . . .'

She bends over the papers and, adjusting to the scrawl, reads more rapidly, chin on one hand. Soon, she falls still; then takes a long breath.

'What is it?' Julian asks, disturbed.

'It is quite painful, if it is what I think. These were in Mimi's things. So, probably it is close relation of Mimi writing to her. She had Gypsy relations?'

'Possibly.'

'Which is why you are right, Jamie, they might not have known how to write; somebody may have learned as an adult, not a child. So, this is 1944, when the Nazis invaded. And I think this is family of Mimi, asking her to send them money or papers, anything to help them get out.'

'Oh my God.' Julian scrabbles back through his earlier thoughts. Stuff. Relics. Crap. Machiavelli. He could kick himself.

'Look,' says Éva. 'Here he or she writes: "*What did we do to deserve this? Why don't you answer me? We are your family, but you forget us! For our sake, for your own sake, help us, please, please, please help us!*" This date is March 1944. That was the month the Germans marched in. That year, a terrible thing happened to the Gypsies who had been captured.'

'What was it?' Julian asks. He is so perturbed by Éva's story that he forgets to worry about any potential upset for Jamie.

'Well,' says Éva, 'for a long time Hungary seemed safe, and even most Jews seemed safe, but then in 1944 there is a terrible escalation. The Germans don't kick out Miklós Horthy's regency at first, but as the summer progresses, Hitler isn't pleased with the way the Hungarians won't deport enough Jews, though I must say there were already plenty being taken – just not enough for him. They were rounding up the Jews and making them do terrible things like walking through landmined fields to clear them, but many were surviving. Eventually the Nazis turn on Horthy and kidnap his son and he is forced to abdicate. So then Hungarians comply and deport thousands of Jews from the Pécs area in southern Hungary.

'Now, there was a Gypsy section at Auschwitz, perhaps already for two years. They took the Gypsies from the occupied countries and imprisoned them there, and because from the early 1940s the Hungarian government is basically aligned with Germany and its policies, as early as 1943 they were also deporting Gypsies there from Hungary. But then at Auschwitz, the Nazis need to make room for the Jews from Pécs. So they kill the Gypsies. Thousands of Gypsies, in one night. That was on the second of August 1944. And you know, people said that the Jews would go quietly, but not the Gypsies. It was said that you could hear the screams for many miles, all night long. Now the Roma call their holocaust *Porrajmos*, which means "the Great Devouring".'

'Jesus Christ almighty . . . And the letters—?'

She points to the date at the top of the last letter. 'March 1944. As I understand it, they did well to be free until then.'

'Do you think that they . . . ?'

'Who knows? If there are no more letters, then yes, I think it is likely that they died that night of the second of August.'

There's a long silence while both of them, shell-shocked, leaf through more papers in the box. Julian isn't used to feeling lost for words. Who wrote these letters – Jamie's great-great-grandfather? Julian tries to get used to the sensation – dizzying, nearly nauseating – that this long-dead individual was not simply an unfortunate statistic, but was the forefather of his own son, who's sitting beside him, slurping up the foam from his second cup of hot chocolate, fascinated but as yet unaware that the story has any bearing on his life.

'At school we learned all about how the British repulsed the Nazis and so on, but I don't remember anybody mentioning the word "Hungary", let alone the Roma,' Julian remarks at last.

'You don't want to know what *we* were taught at school,' Éva tells him. 'Though our schools, generally speaking, were extremely good, compared to – oh, what's this?' She's uncovered a page written in a different hand, on heavy, fine-quality paper. A florid, cultivated script, full of loops. 'French. I don't know much French.'

Julian has never been a good linguist. He can decipher and understand one line:

'Elle est le trésor de ma vie.'

She is the treasure of my life. There is no signature, only a letter: M.

Karina is holding on to Rohan's arm. They're in the basement of the House of Terror Museum, where the ÁVH's prison cells have been reconstructed. Brick walls, whitewashed and grimy, arched and low, close in on her; the building will crush them and release its ghosts. Her hands are cold and sweaty. She and Rohan are silent, reading the information in front of them.

This wasn't only a prison, but a torture chamber. Electric shocks; beatings; starvation. In some cells, the occupant had to sit in water. In others, he would have been chained. Two floors below street level, the place depended on a ventilation system; one torture method was to turn it off. On a section labelled 'Death Row', prisoners waited to be hanged. 'If they made it that far,' Rohan says.

Karina remembers the facile words that habitually escape her lips when people ask her what became of her grandfather: 'He disappeared. Nobody knew what happened to him.' This is it, then; this, here, under the pallid bricks. He was an academic, a bookish intellectual, a philosopher – everything the regime detested. He lived for and in the mind; how could his body, weakened by the war years, have withstood what was done to it here?

A set of cells, each barely two metres by one metre, represent where he would have been imprisoned. Planks pass for beds. On the walls, photographs: victims. Tamás's picture is not among them; there have been more victims here than any display could show.

'I feel a bit faint.' Karina sits down on the plank bed; Rohan crouches beside her, concerned. 'My grandfather was here,' she tells him.

'Are you sure?'

'There must be a reason my father told me to come here. But also – I can feel him. I just know it.'

If she'd said such a thing to Julian, he'd have talked at her for five solid minutes. He'd have said it's because her father sent her; there's no sixth sense but common sense. Rohan says nothing.

Instead, he holds her hand while she doubles forward to let the blood run to her head. She's freezing, sickened. She can't rationalise her guilt. 'Why them and not me? Why did they have to suffer? How can I live now and not then, with them? I can't bear it that they had to go through this hell.'

'Karrie,' Rohan soothes. 'Let's get out of here.'

They make their way through brighter displays tracing the recovery of Hungary after 1956, then out into the spring air – a progress from darkness to light that Tamás Veres might never have experienced.

'I need to get some water,' Karina says.

The cavernous Burger King is nearby. 'Let's stop here,' Rohan suggests. After ushering Karina to a chair at a formica table, he brings her some Coca-Cola. 'Water, sugar and caffeine. This should sort you out.'

'Thanks,' says Karina. She can't find any more words.

He sits opposite her while she sips. 'There's nothing much I can say that's going to make you feel better,' he tells her. 'But you know, my mother and father lost some close friends in Johannesburg. They were helping people that the authorities didn't want them to help. My father's best friend died in custody. The police said that he fell down the stairs. But some of the people he was close to are in the government now. So you see, I do understand. How it's not you, it's not your life, but it's part of you all the same.' He reaches out to her across the table. His palms are warm against her shoulders, so comforting that she pulls her chair closer and feels his cheek leaning on the top of her head.

'Ro, I'm sorry. This is terrible, and we've got a concert tonight. I shouldn't have brought you.'

'I wouldn't have let you go in there alone, not when I realised what it was. Look, Karrie, these were appalling, vile creatures without a shred of humanity. They still exist, because they always have, they always will and we can't prevent that. But here, they've gone. Your grandfather suffered, but you've come back and tonight you're going to be on the stage of the Liszt Academy playing your violin, just like your grandmother. They'd be so proud of you. You're the evidence that they've won.'

Karina doesn't move. He turns, kisses her forehead, her eyelids, then her mouth. Desultory tourists walk by; somewhere in the stone walls, the cries of No. 60's captives seem frozen, their legacy inverting the air. And to Karina and Rohan it seems as if everything in their lives has led them here, towards this understanding that craves expression as simply as a plant craves growth, in the middle of Burger King, Budapest.

Wandering back to the hotel, they blink in the daylight, half incredulous to find that Budapest is the city of today, calm, mercenary and hopeful under the cranes. They hover by the lift, hands linked, glancing around to make sure they're not being observed. It's four o'clock. Their concert begins at seven thirty.

'Karrie,' says Rohan.

'We have to play tonight.'

'Practising. Rest. Yes?'

'Yes.'

'Later . . .'

'Ro—'

'I know. But how not?'

Alone in her room, Karina prostrates herself on the bed for half an hour, trying to calm down. The spinning head, the sensation of turning inside out, a tightening of energy in her heart and her thighs, she recognises these. She passed a signal at danger the moment she sat down opposite Rohan on the train.

She takes out her violin and begins some warm-up exercises. She hasn't slept, the museum upset her and Rohan hangs in her consciousness like an explosion filmed in slow motion; but she has to concentrate on his new bowings, or risk screwing up the Mozart in the concert. She could have stayed at home. Right now, she'd have been at the Pearsons' with Jamie, in the supermarket with Julian, or teaching Grade I pieces to a seven-year-old. She feels split into two halves that don't match.

A tap on her door at five forty-five turns out to be Genya, who, to her surprise, presents her with a plastic bag containing a sandwich, a banana and some chocolate. 'My job on tour,' he explains. 'I make sure everybody eats something before concert. Our quartet tradition, very important. We need energy.' He glances at her reddened eyes. 'Karina, you are OK?'

'The museum was a little unsettling, but I'm fine now,' she assures him. 'Thanks for the food. See you in half an hour.'

Karina zips her concert dress into its carrier. She checks her equipment: violin, music, make-up, brush, tights, beta blockers, phone, purse, water, the chocolate and banana that she hasn't the appetite to eat after the sandwich. She pulls on her coat and goes downstairs.

The others are waiting in the lobby; with them is their agent, Miklós Hauser, whose alert, clever face reminds Karina of the foxes who sometimes sun themselves in her garden. He shakes her hand and she does her best to greet him in Hungarian: '*Jó estét, Miklós!*'

'It's good to meet all of you, finally,' Miklós declares, with a transatlantic twang. He's no more than thirty, Karina notes; he learned his English after the fall of the Iron Curtain, in an age where English in Europe is American. 'This was a great idea, to play the quintets. The hall is sold out. Next time, we put you in bigger hall! A new one is built now, close to river – it is very fine. And a Hungarian name, Veres Karina! You were born here?'

'No, it's my first visit.'

'We must show you this wonderful city. After the concert we go to dinner at fantastic restaurant. Where did you eat yesterday?'

'A big, old place in Buda. It was good. I think it was called Károlyi.'

'Ah, very nice. It used to be nicer, it was famous before the Second World War – and they have Gypsy music. But tonight we hear very, *very* good Gypsy music in this restaurant. The best. I think you will enjoy.'

'Oh, God, Miki, that stuff drives me up the wall,' Malcolm protests.

'You don't like it, don't come,' Harry ripostes. 'The one last night wasn't bad.'

They walk *en masse* up the road to the Academy. A stone Liszt presides over its front entrance; inside, the foyer is rich with art deco pillaring, marble, dark wood and elaborate tiling, the whole place curlicued into a celebration of art far removed from the concrete of Karina's music college. Miklós leads them through the corridors to the dressing-rooms, where he gives each of them a bottle of mineral water and a copy of the programme.

Karina dumps her things in the room she has to herself, as the only woman, then makes for the toilets. Before she left the orchestra, Julian used to joke that performing was a cheap alternative to colonic irrigation. Nerves, heavy food, emotional upset, maybe all of these . . . She should take a beta blocker to make certain her bow doesn't shake. But beta blockers screen out everything. Nothing is too frightening, but nothing excites you too much. Not taking one would be dangerous. It's a long time since she gave a performance chemically unassisted.

Rohan is rubbing rosin onto his bow when she taps on the dressing-room door, beckons him away and explains how she feels. 'Please don't,' he says. 'You need to take risks sometimes, Karrie.'

'It could be a disaster.'

'If you swallow that thing, you'll lose the edge. You mightn't shake, but you'll deaden yourself. Don't you want to feel, tonight?'

Karina puts the silver sheet of tablets back into her purse. She walks towards the platform, invisible to the assembling audience. The hall has been refurbished; from the side she can see shining organ pipes gaping upwards, wooden floors, a high ceiling. Her grandmother was launched on this stage. In 1929, there were no beta blockers.

It's seven thirty. The men pat one another on the back and Rohan squeezes Karina's hand when the others aren't looking. They form a line and walk onto the platform, towards the spot where Mimi must have stood as a young girl, proud, free and unshakeable, liberated by her violin. Karina sees welcoming eyes among the audience. She thinks herself into Mimi's skin. She will not shake tonight.

22

Karina is so tired that for a moment she can scarcely lift her violin. But two phrases into the G minor Quintet, the electricity grabs her. A connecting current snaps through the five of them; no discrepancies can remain while the music flows. Lifted out of herself, her bow in deep contact with the strings, she's exhilarated, floating. Now and then the same energy used to blaze out in concerts with the orchestra: the Royal Festival Hall, the Châtelet in Paris, a standing ovation at the Salzburg Festival where ninety-seven musicians shared in the glory. Why had she forgotten? How could she have let one malicious remark wreck her confidence?

After all their hard work, the concert flies by in what feels like minutes. Off stage, when the final applause has died down, she's so overwhelmed that she tries to hug the entire St Francis Quartet at the same time.

'You see?' Rohan says. 'You were fantastic.'

'So were you. So were all of you.'

'You don't need pills, Karrie, you need *us*. Let's get out of here and go eat.'

Miklós bustles down the corridor by the dressing-rooms, bringing some guests. Hungarian names flip round her ears; she shakes hands, smiles into faces whose impish generosity reminds her of her teacher, József. She remembers more Hungarian than she'd expected to. She says good evening, thank you, how are you, thank you again; the evening lifts her up and carries her.

Two taxis wait by the artists' entrance on Király Street to take them to the restaurant. Climbing into the car, she imagines Mimi here, wearing silk and a fur coat, not Marks & Spencer charcoal linen; admirers clamouring for her attention; prejudice and threat exiled to the shadows. She and Rohan talk to everyone but each other, joking, comparing the phrases of Hungarian they've learned. Andrássy Street spreads wide and inviting ahead of them while the taxi bowls towards Heroes' Square, the zoo and the park.

Outside the restaurant, they find a terrace with an expanse of tables lamplit golden beneath the trees; inside, the art deco mansion swarms with heady aromas and music. A violin cuts through the ambient noise, sweet and swooping. Miki leads them in, steering a path between the tables – the clientele a mix, Karina thinks, of tourists, businessmen and the new Hungarians of the new Europe celebrating enterprise and capitalism. He has reserved the six of them a prime spot in an alcove, with a good view of the band.

'My God.' Rohan stares at the violinist. The ensemble is playing Brahms: one of the Hungarian Dances, but not as any of the St Francis Quartet and their guest artist have heard it before. A cimbalom glitters at the side, a tárogató points, clarinet-like, and the leader with his violin stands in the centre, wearing a blue waistcoat, flinging showers of notes into the air, his face impassive. Karina has never seen a bow move like this: a blur of white horsehair and brown wood, its owner's pudgy hand controlling it with the assurance of a pointillist painter wielding a brush as he conjures up improvised figurations that nobody will ever hear again.

'Fuck.' Even Malcolm is transfixed.

'This violinist, Zoltán Roth, he is one of best Gypsy players in Budapest,' Miki declares.

'No kidding,' Harry says. 'He ought to be in Carnegie Hall.'

'There is competition.' Miki shrugs. 'Lots of Gypsy violinists in Budapest, and lots are good. But this is not real Hungarian folk music, you understand. It is not even real Gypsy music.'

'Of course not. It's Brahms,' Harry points out.

'Gypsy music is completely different from Hungarian folk music,' Miki insists. 'True Hungarian folk music derives from the Far East, China and Central Asia. These restaurant bands are something else. They take Hungarian or quasi-Hungarian tunes that exist, like this Brahms, embellishing, showing off the technique. It doesn't speak with the genuine voice, you see. Always the Gypsies take on the character of the national music in the countries where they live, but they treat it with their own freedom, virtuoso tricks that impress people.'

'But Miki,' Rohan protests, 'I've never seen playing like this in my life. I don't think you should rubbish it. It's dynamite. I don't know why people here don't value Gypsy musicians more. We could learn so much from them, especially their sense of colour and rhythm.'

'Sure – look, Zoltán Roth is a good musician, I like him, I like his music. But he can't touch your playing, Rohan, not with bargepole!' Miki waves to the wine waiter to order some Bikavér.

'Can we talk to him?' Rohan asks. Zoltán Roth, though, has already spotted the musical instruments beside their table; and now, instead of serenading the customers, he's making a beeline for them. He's playing the ubiquitous Monti's *Csárdás*, but treating it as a springboard into a musical fantasy world that would seem impossible if he didn't make it sound so easy. As he approaches, he fixes Karina with the kind of gaze that she's only ever received from her grandmother.

She leans forward, captivated. Although Harry hints that Zoltán Roth is after a large tip from foreign visitors, she doesn't care. What price the intellect of a Beethoven, the soft songs of a Schumann or the cool perambulations of a Ravel if it's without such fire, such communication? This is how music connects person to person, the violin's song a thread that strings their souls together. Zoltán slides up to an astral harmonic with the precision of a neurosurgeon; the sound makes a direct hit on Karina's unconscious. She's on her feet.

'Karina, what are you doing?' Malcolm demands.

Zoltán holds out a hand to her. 'You are professional, I can tell by the way you watch me,' he says. 'Come and play something with us.' Every eye in the restaurant is turned towards them.

Karina opens her violin case.

Malcolm is outraged. 'He probably grabs a different classical musician out of the audience every night. You can't do it, Karina. You'll be out of your depth.'

'Of course she can do it.' Rohan jumps up – and Zoltán summons him into action too, with a sweep of his bow.

'Ro, Karrie, what food shall we order for you?' Genya calls from the end of the table; he's barely looked up from the menu.

'Fish soup!' Karina calls back. Zoltán is ushering them towards the band and she doesn't know what she's doing, but she's going to do it anyway. Today she's taking risks.

Zoltán begins the *Csárdás* again; Karina and Rohan join the accompaniment, slotting into the harmonies, capturing effects from the cues that the other players send them. It's easier than she'd expected, perhaps because she knows the piece so well, or perhaps because of the exultation that's filling her this night outside time. Zoltán plays a brief solo full of intricate figurations, then indicates that it's Rohan's turn. Rohan tries, but ends up concentrating on sweetness of tone and soft, richly-coloured sounds, instead of the virtuoso flourishes that are second nature to Zoltán. Karina tries next, but, self-conscious, she resorts to patterns from long-remembered études. She spots Harry and Malcolm chortling at the table, while Genya munches bread. Normally she'd feel hurt, but tonight she doesn't care.

Then Zoltán accelerates into the coda and it's like pressing down the gas on a Ferrari. The sound swallows her and Rohan, the insane tempo pulls them on despite themselves, careering towards the final cadence as if trying to burst through the crash barrier, take the air and land unscathed. Her arms move of their own accord; sweat plasters her hair to her forehead. The only way is not to think. If you start thinking, you can't do it, but lose yourself and your mind in listening, and you can fly. The restaurant holds its breath; when the last chord arrives amid a flurry of cimbalom, a shout goes up that nearly knocks them over. Karina's as out of breath as if she'd run a marathon, and as transported. Is this what Mimi left behind to enter the Conservatoire and refine away all that joy?

Zoltán gives them both a quick, formal nod of thanks. Karina's linen suit is clammy beneath her arms and Rohan can't stop laughing. 'I'd never keep up with a guy like that. Never!' he says, grabbing a glass of wine.

'But Rohan, you are a much better violinist,' Miki says. 'You give Zoltán the Mendelssohn concerto or ask him to play in a string quartet and there'd be trouble.'

'That doesn't make anyone a better violinist,' Rohan insists. 'Only a different kind of violinist.'

'Where did we lose out?' Harry thinks aloud. 'Where did we lose the spontaneity?'

'Spontaneity is nice, but isn't everything,' Genya suggests. 'We have other things, as good in their own way. Is like Ro says. Not better or worse. Only different.'

Karina swallows half a glass of wine in one gulp. She's just improvised with Gypsy musicians, throwing out every inhibition her training had locked into her, and she feels so alive that she can almost see the nerve endings glowing in her fingers. Glasses clink, food arrives, and the band begins 'Deux Guitarres'. Wine spurts into her brain as if she's injected it and at some point Rohan slings an arm round her shoulders and she doesn't stop him and doesn't care if the others see, which they can hardly help, and she stays quiet and lets them talk because all she wants to do is feel.

'He didn't spot your background,' Rohan remarks, glancing at Zoltán: the band is having a break and a beer.

'No reason he should.'

'But it means more to you than to us. Or am I imagining it? Am I just a silly romantic, Karrie?'

'I love silly romantics.'

'Are you drunk?'

'Yes. Do you mind?'

Miki is telling a story about a group of Nazi officials – 'I think included Dr Mengele' – who came into a Budapest café and demanded that the band play 'real' Gypsy music, by which they meant Brahms and Liszt. 'We're a bit Brahms and Liszt already, mate,' Harry says, then has to explain Cockney rhyming slang to him. Miki recommends *palacsinta* for dessert – pancakes with ground walnuts and chocolate sauce. A carved wooden clock in a corner begins to strike.

Rohan touches Karina's hand. The night is running on. Both of them decline dessert, but order double espressos.

'Ro, you OK?' Harry asks. 'You never have coffee at night.'

'I like Hungarian coffee,' Rohan declares.

Karina glances at the phone in her bag: three missed calls from home. She switches it off.

Malcolm has been pressing Miki on the possibility of a return visit or even a residency at the Spring Festival. Karina remembers her father's words about the difficulty of establishing an international career from Hungary. 'Do you think that's true?' she asks Miki.

'It's a small country,' he replies. 'We were always the outsiders. In the middle of the Slav nations, we have this crazy Finno-Ugric language that's related basically to nothing. And always somebody wanted to move in and take over. We were always the odd ones out, and pathetic, too, sometimes. In the Trianon Treaty in 1920, we lost two thirds of our territory. Two thirds! We allowed this to happen, we were being punished. The flags flew at half-mast, you know how long for? Eighteen years! And all we do is beat ourselves up about it. People were committing suicide because of this. They don't stick up for themselves, the rulers don't stick up for them, so they turn it inwards. Perhaps it's better not to take it out on other people, but it's still pathetic. Hungarian land was given to Austria, Romania, what's now the Czech Republic and Slovakia, and it's a human disaster, a tragedy. Karina, my family came from a little place in Transylvania, where they'd lived for hundreds of years – suddenly after this treaty, that place isn't Hungary any more, it's Romania, and the Romanians hated the Hungarians, so my family were being persecuted. Then there comes the Second World War, you know all about this. And now, after sixty years of communism – you can pull down a wall, but you can't change the people's mindset so fast. There's defeatism here. I feel it, it's hard to get past it. It's up to my generation to break out of this crazy pattern.'

'So, Miki, how you break out?' Genya asks, scraping up the last of his chocolate sauce.

'Ah, I plan to make my agency very successful and myself very rich by the time I'm forty-five. That's Plan A.'

'And Plan B?' Karina prompts.

'Plan B is one day I go and work in New York. Karina, please, here is last glass of wine, it's for you. And maybe it's a wrap, guys – you must be tired.'

The minutes tick by while Miki asks for the bill and phones for two taxis. Malcolm yawns; Genya asks Rohan if he wants the chocolate that arrived with his coffee; Harry works out what time they need to leave in the morning. Karina and Rohan can't look at each other. They share the second taxi with Malcolm and his cello. Karina pretends to fall asleep.

In the lobby, the others are waiting for the lift. Rohan stops in his tracks beside Karina. 'I can't stand it any more,' he mutters. 'Let's take the stairs.'

Mimi, back from a party in a mansion on Fifth Avenue, lay beside Marc in her underwear. Dénes was nearly seven now, and spoke Hungarian with her and Vali, and English at school and with Uncle Marc. Ani was asleep in her cot. Vali would soon leave them to marry her American beau, who was uppity about their lifestyle. Marc had given up his own apartment when Ani arrived. Bartók was dead, of leukaemia – her instinct about him had been right.

'Tell me about when you were little,' Mimi asked, sharing her cigarette with Marc.

He took a puff and lay back. 'You know what I miss? The sunsets.'

Sunsets, he said, were to him what the madeleine had been to Proust. When the sky paled from blue to jade green, he was a child again, watching the twentieth century stretching out before him, newborn. He'd see the sunset from his bedroom window. Aged seven, he still had his wooden rocking-horse – his mother occasionally threatened to give it away to a poor boy who would appreciate it – and the bat and ball set that he and his brother played with in the garden. Sometimes he'd sit on the rocking-horse and pass the ball gently from hand to hand, feeling the two pulses, the rocking and the ball, clash and phase in and out. He couldn't get the interlocking rhythms out of his head.

'I want to be a musician,' he told his parents.

'You'll grow out of it, son,' said his father through his cigar, without looking up from *Le Figaro*.

The law course went unfinished. His grandmother had the vapours; his father lectured him on how deeply he had disappointed his family. He'd never encountered anyone who could match his passion for music until he heard Mimi play. After her recital, he sat up all night, sketching out a plan for some fantasy pieces about a Gypsy childhood, trying to dream himself into her dreams. Air. Movement. Freedom. The rocking wagon. And – how blessed – no school.

Mimi laughed and laughed. 'My dear, it wasn't entirely like this!'

'What was it like, then?'

'Completely different. You don't want to know. Make love to me.' She pulled off the few pieces of silk she was wearing; he squashed out the last of the cigarette and fell onto her. The war was over, the flags were flying, jubilation filled the city. Lost in one another, they refused to think further ahead than tonight.

Mimi sat at the table, hiding her face in her hands. The first pictures of Bergen-Belsen had reached America. Now that the truth was out, rumour was spreading unchecked. Millions of Jews, but not only Jews: homosexuals, the disabled, the mentally ill – and the Roma. Mass murder. A Polish–Jewish legal scholar had invented a new word: 'genocide'. The letters from the Frankls and the wild scribbles from her brother had stopped arriving long ago.

'What could I have done? Could I have saved them if I'd gone back?'

'You'd have been in danger yourself,' Marc told her. 'Tamás wouldn't have been able to protect you. You could have been killed.'

'But I stayed away. I should have gone back. They're dead.'

'Perhaps not. Perhaps the letters can't get through.'

'Don't joke with me, I can feel it. Something has gone. *They* have gone. He wrote to me for help and I didn't help, and now it's too late.'

She would never tell him what was in those letters. 'Why didn't you?' asked Marc.

'Because my father sold me. Because he said he never wanted to see me again. Because my mother died and nobody sent me word of it. There – now you know.'

During all their years in New York, Mimi had never suggested that they go home. Why would she? Anybody would have done the same, given the choice between freedom and danger, celebrity or persecution, playing concerts in America's most glamorous halls or hiding in cellars in fear of her life. Besides, the ships had been requisitioned to carry troops. She'd treasured letters from the Frankls – which came every week, until 1944 – but she had never lamented over her brother's scrawled missives. She hadn't seen him since she was ten, she told Marc. When they were children, he hadn't known how to write. He'd learned so that he could pester her.

'That suite of yours. "The Minstrel".' Mimi looked up, her eyes red and puffy. 'Minstrel indeed. What else could they do? Nothing! "The Forest"? Where else could they go? Nowhere! They were hounded out of every village. Improvising? Of course! They couldn't read music! You can't read and write, you have no homeland, you have no schooling, people spit at you in the street, you don't know when you'll eat again – why is that romantic? When the Frankls took me in, I spent an hour in the bath. My feet were warm. My feet were warm in winter. My God, the winters . . . I can't forget the cold; it got into my bones. I'll pay for that one day, my dear.'

'And the Frankls?' Marc pressed her hand to his cheek, kissed the palm. She pulled it away. He knew the softness inside her – and the effort she made to hide it.

'I can't bear it. Old people, good people, Marc, thousands upon thousands, slaughtered. And the Frankls never said a word. "Life is difficult, but we manage." "We have to move, here is our new address." That was all. I never thought . . .'

'Couldn't Tamás have helped them?'

'They wouldn't have asked him. They were too proud.'

'But he is – was – your husband,' Marc faltered, 'and you were as good as their daughter . . .'

'They were like that, they never wanted to trouble anybody. I don't know, perhaps they felt they were too old either to fight back or to give up their pride, or to hope.'

She wandered to the window and leaned her forehead against the glass. How could this charmed life carry on, now that they knew? Outside, New York was brown, grey and pale blue, bowling forward and forward when she longed only to turn the clock back and rerun the years, undoing all that was done.

She turned. 'Marc?'

'My love?'

'I want to go home. I want to take my children back to Budapest.'

'Mimi! Are you crazy?'

'Perhaps. But I want to go home. I belong there, I should have gone back, for them, even if it killed me too. Will you phone Saul and ask whether he can investigate a ship?'

She knew he wouldn't argue or ask her to consider the matter a little longer; he knew her too well. When she made up her mind, she stuck to it. She watched him dial Saul's office number without complaint. Who'd have thought that their six-week trip would last over six years?

She dug out and reread Tamás's letter, sent when Germany invaded Poland a month after she and Marc arrived in New York. 'Take my word for it: stay there,' Tamás wrote. A wise man, with foresight, her Tamás. And kindness, too, believing – or so he said – that Marc was no more to her than a friend, confidant and colleague. A good man, a fine human being, and she had deceived him. 'Don't even think about coming back until Hitler is dead,' he wrote. 'People say it won't affect Hungary, but you need only look at that monster's face to know that this plague will reach not only Poland, not only Hungary, but the entire civilised world. Don't worry about me. I only want your safety, and Dini's. Promise me you will stay in the States until Hitler has been wiped off this diseased planet forever.'

Fifteen published compositions, four hundred concerts, seventy concert dresses, twenty pupils a year, a thousand parties and one baby daughter later, she could feel New York finishing. It was time she went home to put back together what pieces remained of her old life. Yet Marc's concerto – the pretext for this whole insane adventure – lay in its drawer, unplayed.

Karina dreams. She's flying, music lifts her. She's holding her violin, and with the tip of her bow she's lighting up the empty stars one by one. They blaze around her while she soars ahead, weightless. A sucking sensation, falling, a jolt. She wakes, sheltered in the warmth of Rohan's tree-trunk body; she doesn't know whether she dreamed the sound of Mozart or of Zoltán Roth improvising, summoning her like Duplessis's minstrel.

Seven o'clock. A cool morning, grey outside. They lie close together, feet touching.

'What are we going to do?' Rohan whispers.

'I don't know.'

'How do you feel, Karrie?'

'Good.'

'Is that all?'

'I feel as if I've been asleep for ten years.'

'I feel as if I've been asleep all my life. Karrie, I love you.'

'I love you too.'

'And you have to go back to your family. I'm improvising now, I don't know what to do next.'

'Nor me. Ro, I—'

'Come here, Karrie. Don't you dare get out of this bed . . .' He strokes her eyelid and her nose with a fingertip. 'Did you dream? What were you dreaming about?'

Karina smiles into his eyes. 'I have these dreams about flying. It's almost like – I don't know, astral travel. Sometimes I'm among the stars. Or sometimes it's as if I'm in a wagon. A horse-drawn wagon, the kind that Mimi might have lived in as a child. I can feel the way it moves. Do you think it's possible to inherit someone's dreams?'

'Of course. Why wouldn't it be?' Rohan kisses her collar-bone. 'There's a mole just there, where your violin sits.'

'Julian gets so annoyed if I suggest I'm tapping into a family memory, or anything that could be remotely psychic or paranormal.'

'Perhaps he thinks you really will start telling Andy and Sarah's fortunes. He's scared! It's a threat – it's beyond anything he can relate to.'

'You're not threatened?'

'No way. It's part of you, I love you, and I love everything that makes you you. And if these things exist, I think they're mysterious, wonderful and as real as we are.'

'I love you so much,' says Karina.

'You know something?' Rohan wraps her against him. 'You *are* Hungary. It's just like you, full of warmth and beauty and sorrow. You've been colonised – taken over. You've lost two thirds of your territory. And you're like that Amati in its glass case. A wonder, too perfect to be allowed to sing as it should. I didn't tell you what that violin made me think of. It was you.'

Karina knows that whatever happens when they go home, which she can't bear to think about, she'll never forget his words.

23

On Dénes and Erzsébet's wooden-armed couch there sits what Karina at first takes to be a beige cushion. Closer examination makes it uncurl and let out a miaow.

'Pom-Pom's downshifted,' Erzsébet explains, making tea. 'She's our cat now. Ninety-eight per cent fluff.' The animal jumps down and curls round Erzsébet's ankles. 'Poor puss, hungry again.' She fills a bowl to the brim with cat food. Pom-Pom has gained weight since moving in. Over the road, the Georgian house is dark. An estate agent has nailed a garish sign to its gatepost.

'Where's Martin?' Karina asks, stroking the cat. Her hands long for soft things to caress. Back for four days from Budapest, she's avoided meeting her mother's eye.

'He brought Pom-Pom over in a basket and said he was going to stay in town. I imagine, with a girlfriend. I haven't seen him for two weeks, except on TV.'

'He's leading the victims' association, isn't he?'

'I believe he wants to sue the government. We can't exactly blame him.'

'And Cynthia? Any news?'

'She phoned me from Marion's and said she loves your idea of recording Lindy's play for charity. And she wants to write her memoirs. I think this is good, even if it upsets everybody. Writing is cathartic. Like playing music, perhaps better. Karrie, come, here's your tea. Tell me things. Tell me about Budapest.'

In her parents' front room, Karina imagines herself back into a time when the past year hadn't begun. A world with Jamie at home, Lindy alive and no Rohan.

'It made an impression?' Erzsébet prompts.

'So familiar and so strange. It's full of paradoxes. There's something about it that's warm and sad, proud and disastrous, central but isolated, open but closed. As if its eyes are half shut.' Rohan's touch seems to have soaked into her bones. 'Mum, will you play me something?'

'Why?' Erzsébet is surprised.

'I'm getting live music withdrawal symptoms. Julian was so busy trying out bits of his latest CDs last night that we didn't hear anything properly.'

'Well, if you want.' Erzsébet sits down at the piano and begins a Chopin mazurka. Cuddling Pom-Pom, Karina watches her. At the piano Erzsébet transforms from housewife to the artist she might have become, given different circumstances. Her back straightens, her face focuses, her poise, ingrained since her earliest training, takes over. Art is a serious matter to the Veres family. Art, music, literature, culture: these make you human, they'd told Karina; and she had felt its truth that night in Budapest. Still, she can't help remembering the faces of Harry, Genya and Malcolm when they came down to breakfast and understood, with one glance, exactly what had been happening overnight.

At Heathrow, pulling their suitcases through the EU Arrivals channel, Rohan touched her hand and said, 'We've still got a few more minutes.' But five seconds later the doors opened and Karina saw her husband and son waiting there, and Julian had brought flowers and Jamie shouted and hurtled towards her and she picked him up and hugged him until he was nearly blue, and when she turned, it was just in time to see Rohan with the other three, waving goodbye as if the earth hadn't reversed its direction, as if night wasn't day nor day night, and there was nothing, but nothing, that she could do about it.

Erzsébet finishes her mazurka. 'Karrie, what's wrong? Tell me.'

'There's nothing to tell.'

'Are you sure?'

'Yes, Mum. I promise.'

Karina couldn't begin to describe to her mother what Julian had found while she was away.

'Darling, I'm sorry,' he'd said. 'I wanted to clear some space in the attic, but I didn't want to throw anything out without making sure of what it was.' He explained Glyndebourne, Éva, the letters. The horror was more than Karina, overwrought, could take in.

'I must go and look this up.' She'd used it as an excuse to escape, running upstairs to dig out her book about Duplessis, then locking herself in the bathroom with it.

The letter scripted in French – was it from Duplessis? Was Mimi '*le trésor de ma vie*'? So was he talking to somebody else about Mimi? If so, why would Mimi have had the letter? It was addressed simply to '*Mon amie*.'

Karina has taken to reading in the bath.

Marc Duplessis and Mimi Rácz returned to Europe from New York on the newly refurbished Queen Elizabeth, wrote Pierre Vincente. *Perhaps it was a strange decision of Rácz's to bring her son up not in the USA but the war-torn world of central Europe, yet there was no stopping her, Duplessis said, when her mind was made up. He insisted he would not consider staying in New York without her.*

From Paris, Rácz travelled by train to Budapest, where she rejoined her husband, Tamás Veres, who had not seen his son since he was eight months old. Duplessis related that the small Dénes had come to regard him as his father, although Rácz had always spoken of him as 'Uncle Marc'. He suspected the ensuing separation must have hit the boy somewhat harder than it appeared to have hit his mother.

In New York, Duplessis had noticed that when Dénes was allowed, briefly, to pick up his mother's precious Italian violin, he showed a natural tendency to hold it like a cello. Suspecting that the boy might become a cellist, Duplessis, renting a small apartment in the quietest corner of Neuilly-sur-Seine, composed a short cello piece for beginners and posted it to his 'nephew' in Budapest. Probably this was a wordless way of telling the lad that he was still there, still cared and, indeed, missed him deeply. Whether it ever reached its destination, or survived the later traumas that struck the glorious city astride the Danube, we will never know.

After seeing the foreign powers of fascism and communism engaged in mortal combat in the streets of Budapest, while he survived in hiding in the cellars of the university, Tamás Veres must have felt so fortunate to be alive that his joy at seeing his wife again perhaps outweighed any anxiety about how she had been living during those years of enforced separation.

'Karrie?' says Rohan, in Brighton, to Karina's mobile.

'I can't talk.' Karina is still in the bath.

'Please, Karrie. We can't just leave it. Please meet me this week. I have to go to Germany next Tuesday.'

'I don't know what to say.'

'Nor do I. When can you come?'

'I can't. Jamie's home until the weekend . . .'

'Monday, then? Karrie, please. I need to see you, even if it's only for five minutes. I'm going out of my mind.'

'So am I.'

'I love you.'

'I have to go.'

Budapest feels like a dream from which Karina has woken to find that her vital organs have been stolen. She composes herself, pulls on her dressing-gown and phones her grandmother.

'*Ha*llo, my dear!' Mimi has been having a good day. 'Listen to this.' Down the line comes the sound of a long-ago violin: the Duplessis Suite.

'I've just been playing in Budapest,' Karina says. 'We gave a concert at the Liszt Academy. Where you made your debut.'

There's a delighted chuckle. 'So! We come full circle.'

'Grandma, did you ever go back?'

'To Budapest? Oh, yes. Before – you know. All this stupid illness.'

'What was it like? Going back?'

'Ah, no, Karina. I didn't like it, not at all.'

'It must have changed so much.'

'No, no, no, that was the problem. It was exactly the same.'

'Grandma, we found a letter in one of your boxes – it's in French and it says something like "*Elle est le trésor—*"'

'Karina, darlink, my soup is about to boil. You must excuse me, we talk soon. Goodnight, my dear.' There's a click; silence, then a hum. Mimi has rung off.

'Mummy,' says Jamie in the car, on the way to school with a suitcase full of summer sports gear, 'do I have to go back?'

'Yes, Schnooks, you do.'

'But why?' Jamie begins to whimper. 'I don't *learn* anything there. The food's horrible, the teachers are horrible, everything's horrible, I hate it.'

'Jimbo, that's enough.' Julian, driving, barely glances at his son in the rear-view mirror.

'I know you'd rather be at home,' says Karina, 'but if you don't go back tonight, you're going to be behind on the lessons.'

'I hate exams. It's horrible.'

Jamie is eight years old; he shouldn't have to take exams. Resentment billows through Karina like smoke. Julian, sensing it, prods her kneecap hard with one finger to keep her quiet.

'You have to learn how to do them,' he tells Jamie. 'It's important. You can't go round the problem, you have to go through it. Learn how to solve it.'

Jamie's whine crescendos into a howl.

At school, Karina has to prise his arms from her waist again. It should be getting better. Instead, it's getting worse.

'It's only because he's been on holiday,' Julian says, unruffled, while they walk to the car park.

Karina rounds on him. 'I don't understand you. He's your son, for Christ's sake. How can you stand it?'

'He's got to learn, and so have you. He's got to toughen up. Come on, Vitamin K, let's go home. What shall we listen to? Why don't you choose us a nice CD?'

'Fuck,' says Karina, biting her lip to repress tears. Julian opens the car door, gets in and slams it.

They drive to the sound of a Schumann symphony. Karina weeps silently through the slow movement. Julian doesn't take his eyes off the road.

She'd thought she could meet Rohan for Monday lunch at Lane's, talk things through, resolve them. It has to stop. If her marriage were to fall apart, how would Jamie cope?

They sit over lasagne and salad, fingers interlaced, barely able to speak, let alone eat. The pasta sheets feel like sandpaper in her mouth, the orange juice turns to lemon.

'What have you been doing?' Rohan asks, half-hearted.

'The usual. Teaching. Juggling Julian and Jamie. You?'

'Missing you.'

'Apart from that.'

'What else is there?'

'Aren't you practising?'

'Yes. But I'm not there. I'm with you.'

'Ro, you can't do this. You can't let me take over your life.'

'Can you sit there, after Budapest, and say you feel nothing?'

'How I feel isn't the point.' Karina's voice cracks. Next thing she knows he's leaning over the table to kiss her. She'd planned everything she needed to say, sentence by sentence. None of it has been said; none of it will be. They leave their lunch unfinished.

In his bed, with the sea sparkling in the far distance, Rohan pushes her hair back from her forehead. 'Leave him, Karrie. Move in with me.'

'I can't. What about Jamie?'

'Bring him. Take him out of that stupid school. He'll live with us.'

'Do you really think the Rookfield family's going to let me do that?'

'He's your son too. Anyway, whether they "let" you or not isn't the point. It's your choice. You married Julian on the rebound, way too fast.'

'I didn't!'

'Of course you did. You may as well admit it, it's clear as day to everyone else.'

'Ro, I can't put Jamie through that.'

'Thousands of kids go through far worse than "that" every day,' Rohan reminds her. 'This is 2007.'

'I'd never forgive myself if he was hurt.' Karina throws back the duvet.

'Hey. Come back here. You're not getting out of this bed. Not now.' He wraps the covers round both of them. 'Please, Karrie, don't let all the crap get between us. Just because we met at a lousy time, it doesn't mean we can't be together. Come back . . .'

She'd meant to leave, run away, but she can't, not from him and the deepest, gentlest communion she's ever known. How can bodies speak to one another more strongly than minds? She'd thought their connection could be a meeting of spirits, with the body an unfortunate encumbrance. Now, though, she understands that this is far more erotic than a straightforward physical attraction. He grasps her, enters her while she's softened and drenched with her need of him, and, improvising, she arches back and lets go, pouring her love out to him like molasses until nothing of herself is left.

The rows of tracks extended ahead of Mimi, like a repeated image superimposed again and again in a recurring nightmare. The gateways were murky with soot; layers of it coated the city. She thought of New York's cool, modern colours. Budapest was old, dark, growing darker. Youngsters outside the station, their fingers pallid with chill, were distributing pamphlets plastered with communist slogans. Mimi stared at the rails and listened to the clank, rattle and whistle of trains arriving and leaving.

From this station, her family, along with hundreds of thousands of Gypsies and Jews, must have taken their last view of Budapest. Péter, her brother, should have been thirty-six now. She pictured him as he was the night he accosted her outside the Liszt Academy's stage door, a Gypsy in Gypsy's clothes with a Gypsy's face and the crowd had recoiled and Herbert Wilhelm had ushered her away. She imagined him with a shadowy wife – sympathetic, loving – and two or three children clinging to her long skirts, and their father, looking older than he was, worn down by hardship and hunger, loss and fear.

Perhaps here, too, an elderly Jewish couple took leave of their city, trying to face their predicament with dignity. The Frankls had written not a word of their increasing hardship to Mimi. 'We have to move house. Here is our new address,' was all the letter had said when they were forced into the ghetto. She hadn't opened her eyes, hadn't guessed, hadn't had a clue. A signal changing. Steam oozing, the train crawling north. Now she knew where they might have been taken as a staging post before their last journey into Poland: there was an internment camp in, of all places, Kistarcsa. Denying her family, had she been no better than a Nazi herself?

'Madam, may I help you?' a voice asked by her side. A stationmaster, attentive because of Mimi's fur wrap, had noticed her distress. She hadn't realised that her cheeks were clammy with tears. Maybe I could have helped them. Maybe I could have saved them. Aloud, she said only, 'Thank you, but no.'

She walked out of the station, trying to regain her equilibrium. At home, she needed to feed her two growing children and her husband, who was ill and emaciated. She must think of the future. She must telephone Herbert Wilhelm to tell him that she needed to find some work. Urgently.

'Grandma?' Karina has come to visit her. Mimi opens her eyes. She wishes that the past would stay in the past, not insist on colonising the present.

'Darlink, how you like my city?' she asks.

'It was wonderful.' Karina kisses Mimi and clasps her hand. Mimi beams, basking in her warmth. Such a lovely girl; what a privilege to be grandmother to such a woman. She notices a tremor in Karina's fingers, unusual moisture in the palm. Ill? Worried? In love? All three? She listens to her talk about the beauty of old Buda, how proud she was to play at the Liszt Academy, how welcoming, kind and open the people were; in other words, about nothing.

'Ah, you were a visitor,' Mimi interrupts. 'You didn't see what they don't want you to see. Or you were too busy to look. We often don't see past our instruments. Our worlds are coloured by the sound of weeping violins; that keeps us human. The danger is that we forget others sometimes are not. That some see no further than their instinct for hatred. It is fear of The Other.'

'That's changed, Grandma. Hungary's like anywhere else in the EU now,' Karina reminds her.

'Impossible. Each place is always different, Hungary will always be Hungary. I saw on television the riots in Budapest last autumn, and it was the fiftieth anniversary of the uprising . . . My God, crooked politicians, crooked rioters, far right and far left and all the same in the end, eiyiyiyi. You can change overnight a system, but not its people. And for the Roma, all over Eastern Europe, now it is worse than ever.'

Mimi is being so coherent that Karina wonders whether to take advantage of it and ask questions. If she does, Mimi may retreat into her favourite mental fog. Still, it has occurred to her that an explanation might exist for Mimi's fog that nobody's considered and that isn't medical: it may be deliberate.

'Grandma, my friend Rohan – you met him – lent me a book about Marc Duplessis. You're in it.'

'Quite a lot in it, I imagine.' Mimi's eyebrows curve ceilingwards.

'There's something that confuses me. At one point he says you were descended from what he calls a long line of Gypsy musicians, some way back. Why "some way back"?'

'My dear, you have to be careful what you tell people and when. Do you think anybody would have given me the time of day in Europe then if they thought I was really a Gypsy? Marc Duplessis was loyal to me and he would not have told this man, Pierre Vincente, or anybody else. Anyway, I was adopted. I was taken away, thank you very much.'

Karina gazes at her grandmother, who as usual is half sitting, half lying, in her armchair close to the window overlooking the gardens.

'You never hid it from me.'

'Why should I? You are my granddaughter.'

'But if you wanted to reject everything, leave it all behind . . .'

'You can do that, but only to a point. There came a time when . . . I decided that . . .' She yawns, stretching her thin arms.

'Grandma, please, I'm dying to know about this.'

'My dear, enough of the past. I want to know things too. Your new young man, how is he?'

Karina tries to say that Rohan isn't her new young man, but the words won't come out. She rubs her forehead with both hands.

'It's difficult,' says Mimi, reading her. 'I know, my dear. You love him?'

Karina's mind rings with her father's words about the strength of the Roma family, the importance of fidelity, the deep-seated nature of that inheritance. What would her grandmother think of her now?

'Grandma, I don't know what to do,' she says finally. What's the use in hiding it? 'He wants me to leave Julian and live with him.'

'What do you want to do?'

'I don't know.'

'So find out what you want to do, then do it. Karina, I was the first person in my family ever to become completely myself. My new "parents", the Frankls, taught me the importance of such a thing. The importance of not being bound by traditions, questioning everything, finding the way forward that is true to yourself.'

'So you didn't think that fidelity—?'

'Oh, fidelity is vital. But you have to be careful to whom you are being faithful, and how, and why, and when. Because the first fidelity, that must be to *you*.'

Were her father's words about Marc Duplessis a smokescreen? She daren't ask, not yet. 'And the violin, Grandma? The Amati? Did you lose it during the war?'

'No. It was 1956.'

'But you lost it then?'

Mimi sighs. 'All these questions. Like I said, you must be careful what you tell people, and when. Now, my dear, let me rest . . .'

24

On Friday afternoon, a week before the franchise announcement is due, the phone rings in Julian's office. 'Andrew Williamson for you,' says his PA.

'Andy, hi.' Julian's nerves bound into action.

'Hello, old man,' Andy drawls. 'I'm not calling with news. I'm not calling to tell you that the franchise is going to your German chappie. I'm not calling to tell you anything at all, right? You never hear any news from me, do you?'

'Of course not.' Julian leans back in his leather chair and puts his feet on his desk. He wants to spin round the room in a war dance of triumph.

'So maybe we should organise a little dinner, non-celebratory, naturally, with Karrie and Sarah, say end of next week? I reckon Herr Schmidt might find an excuse to visit London.'

'I'll book something. How about Le Gavroche?'

'Sounds good to me. Talk to you soon. Best to Karrie.'

'And to Sarah. Thanks for calling.' Julian hangs up, then laughs aloud, clapping his hands together, as Karina would. Another client, another jackpot. They should be able to do the loft conversion, have a good, luxurious holiday and even . . .

Julian has a secret goal. He wants to buy Karina a violin. A real violin: Italian, preferably eighteenth-century, with a name. A Stradivarius would be excessive, but there are others: Gagliano, Ruggieri, Maggini and more. Karina's fiddle is a beat-up old object, pretty enough and with a pleasing tone, but glued back together so many times that Julian feels sorry for it. It must have been a tall order for her to hold her own with the St Francis Quartet on that thing. If she's to resume her career, she needs a decent instrument. If only that crazy family hadn't lost the bloody Amati in bloody Budapest.

Dénes had presented the 'Matchbox' to Karina on her eighteenth birthday, when it was clear she'd become a professional violinist; he'd bought it through some kind of wheeling and dealing with a friend at the Academy. All slightly shadowy, but Julian knows better than to poke his nose too closely into the violin business. He's convinced it stinks to high heaven, full of false certificates, false labelling, false identification and downright fakes.

Julian has never mentioned his idea to Karina; he wouldn't want to disappoint her if, for some reason, it didn't work out. She's the least materialistic woman he's ever met; as far as he knows, she only spends money on Jamie. Not for her the rafts of shoes and designer labels that, according to Andy, Sarah keeps in her wall-to-wall wardrobe in Pimlico. Karina's clothes mostly come from Marks & Spencer and she tends to wear the same few pairs of shoes until they fall apart. She's not stingy; she's simply not interested in owning things. It's about time he bought her something serious that would benefit her directly. If he were to ask her, she'd say she has no need for a posh fiddle. That's not the point. She deserves one.

While he's driving home, his phone rings. He answers on his hands-free set. 'Jules, dear,' says his mother, 'could you stop in for a drink on your way back? We'd like to talk to you.'

'Oh, Mother, can't it wait? Karina's been down in the dumps and I'd rather not leave her on her own more than I have to.'

'Dear, I'm afraid this business isn't calculated to cheer her up – and it's quite urgent.'

Julian's mind fills with question marks. He assents, then phones home to tell Karina. No reply. She must still be fetching Jamie. He'd have thought she'd be back by now.

Julian parks in the drive and paces round to the side door that the family always uses. A marquee has been erected on the back lawn for a wedding the next day. Julian winces; its pink frills are a tasteless blot on what should be a perfect vista. From Hilary's apartment, a lamp shines through the blue twilight. Julian can see his brother's hunched figure bending over his desk, apparently working, though on what, Julian can't imagine.

'Mother?' he calls, inside.

'In here, Jules,' comes Anne's sing-song voice. He paces into the drawing room and knows at once that all is not well.

'It's Hilary,' Arthur tells him.

'What's happened?'

'Oh, Jules,' Anne begins, then turns away. 'I'm sorry.'

Julian feels the need for a drink parachuting towards him. He makes for the sideboard and pours a whisky from the decanter.

'I won't give in,' Anne says. 'I'm not going to let this get to me.'

'Father, please will you fill me in?' says Julian.

'As you can see, there's a wedding tomorrow,' Arthur begins. 'Fine. They don't intrude too much, they don't use the house apart from the hall, but it's essential that we keep out of things. To coin a phrase, we take the money and run. But Hils has been making a nuisance of himself. He corners people and starts talking about his car. Some of them have been extremely tolerant, but last weekend, the bride arrived in a vintage Bentley and Hils spotted it pulling up. He went bounding down, and while they were trying to get the bride and her meringue into the hall before it rained, he started chattering to the chauffeur and trying to draw in the father of the bride. Two days later I received a stiff letter from the father, declaring that the wedding had been badly disrupted by "one of our residents", and demanding a refund.'

'He's just trying it on, Father.'

'That's what I thought, but the man means business. And I'm afraid Hils just hasn't been the same since I took him to task over it . . .'

'Oh, Christ.'

'I knew it was a sign,' Anne says, her face turned away. 'It's been building for a while. We were so unsettled when poor Lindy died. He hasn't the resources to deal with these things – he just retreats into his own world . . . He says he's working, but when I went up there, he had these bizarre line-drawings all over his desk. I don't know what he thinks they are.'

'Have you spoken to the consultant?'

'He's adjusted the medication, but I don't think it's made any difference. Jules, if it gets worse I'm wondering whether to call Keswick.'

'Oh, Mother, I'm so sorry.' Julian goes across and pats her shoulder.

'I won't give in,' she says through her teeth. 'I won't let this defeat me.'

'You really think that Lindy—? It's not as if they were particularly close.'

'He's sensitive, you see. He picks up atmospheres and they affect him. Seeing his cousin die, that whole family in shreds . . .'

Julian reflects, quietly, that work is a greater help than is generally recognised. If Hilary had had a job, even a menial one, wouldn't it have helped him to keep his focus? He too was upset about his cousin's death; but as long as he had his work, and his wife, nothing could shake his sanity.

'Jules,' says Arthur, 'because of all this, I've made a decision. I want you to know that we're leaving Fairfallows to you.'

Julian wants to say 'Oh, no.' Instead he says nothing.

'Hilary can't possibly inherit the house,' Arthur continues. 'He can't take on that responsibility. I know it will be hard for him, but I believe this is the only option.'

Julian sips his whisky. How to tell Karina? He knows what she thinks of Fairfallows. And Jamie . . .

'Jamie will like that.'

Anne smiles at him, infinitely sad. He wonders how it must feel to watch your eldest son disintegrating, decade by decade. 'I'll make it up to you, Mother,' he promises. 'I'll try to do it properly, for everyone's sake.'

'Jules,' says Anne, 'you should also know that your father has put a clause in his will stipulating that the house must stay in the family. He feels very strongly about this. In a way, it's all he has left.'

Julian takes this in – no National Trust, no English Heritage, then? He gets to his feet and says, 'I'd like to go up and see Hilary now, if that's OK.'

Fortified by the whisky, Julian heads up the stairs and knocks on his brother's door.

'Come,' calls Hilary's voice. At the desk in the window, he looks no different from usual, though when he turns, his gaze is, perhaps, a little unfocused. It's hard to tell in the lamplight. 'Jules, old boy! How's the Jag?'

'Fine, thanks. What are you up to?'

'Look at this.' Hilary lifts up a sheet of paper. He's covered its expanse with close-set patterns of fine lines, some long, others minute. Staring at it, Julian feels his eyes begin to cross.

'This is just the beginning. Now look.' Hilary unscrews the bulb in the lamp and replaces it with one tinted red. The light turns his white hair salmon pink; on the page, it casts an inexplicable distortion into the lines. '*Voilà!* You can see all kinds of things in it. One picture creates many! It's the future of modern art. Now watch.' Hilary replaces the red bulb with a green one; the light is less sinister but equally uncomfortable. 'It's totally different. I'm going to experiment with canvas and oils next, and then, when the style is really formed, I'll have an exhibition, invite old Saatchi along, see what vital statistics we can coordinate. You could hang one in your office and then your clients will want to buy them, and . . .'

Julian listens, silently upset. How can anyone get to grips with a condition known only by one of those frustrating medical acronyms containing a 'U' for 'Unspecified'? It's too easy to start thinking that his brother can't be so deluded, that it must be his own fault for not understanding . . . 'Hils, I have to get going,' he says. 'Karrie will be wondering where I am, and Jamie's home tonight. I'll see you very soon.'

'Righty-ho, then. Bye-bye, little bro.' Hilary puts back the normal bulb and resumes precisely the pose he was in when Julian arrived.

When he walks into the house, Karina is stirring something on the stove; chicken *paprikás*, Jamie's favourite.

'Dad!' shouts Jamie, torpedoing across from the sofa, where he'd been curled up watching *The Simpsons*.

Julian picks him up. The place isn't the same without him, but one assumes that is par for the course. 'Karrie, darling. How's Vitamin K? It's been a long day . . .'

She glances up, but doesn't stop stirring.

'What is it, love?' He puts Jamie down, then goes over and kisses her. 'I'm sorry I'm so late,' he adds quickly, in case the problem is that simple. 'Mother asked me to go to the house – there's some news – actually several pieces of news . . .'

Karina gazes at him, dusky in a brown cotton jersey. A chocolate bird of paradise. One whose plumage seems severely ruffled. He wants to lift her up and heal her with a hug, like Jamie – though, of course, he doesn't. She's silent for so long that he begins to suspect that whatever's wrong is worse than he thought. He's about to ask her where she was earlier, but she speaks first.

'What's happened? Tell me.'

'*Pas devant l'enfant.*'

'*Papa, je parle très bien le français!*' Jamie butts in, laughing. '*C'est mon sujet préféré à l'école!*'

'I mean it, Jimbo. Back to your telly! Away with you! Karrie, come upstairs?'

Karina turns down the flame and follows him. Passing the bathroom, he notices that the tub is wet and the mirror steamed up. Since when is she so fixated on hot baths?

Karina has been in Brighton. The music on Rohan's stand, including the Duplessis Suite, was covered with pencil marks so intense that they'd indented the next three pages: metronome markings and bowing indications, erased and replaced many times. It's vital, he said. He has to give his first solo recital in New York in three weeks' time.

'I wish I could come with you,' said Karina.

'Can you get away?'

'No. It's impossible.'

'Karrie, you've got to tell him today. Promise?' And soon Karina, throwing down her jersey beside his shirt, couldn't not promise. She knew she had to drive to Chichester, but her body, in contact with Rohan's, rebelled against anything as non-visceral as good sense.

So she'd been late to fetch Jamie. She'd been the last mother to arrive and found him sitting in the entrance hall with his bag, snuffling into three tissues. Then there'd been roadworks on the A27 and Julian had been summoned by the lord of the manor. Nothing has gone right today, but she promised Rohan. Why put it off? It's not going to change, let alone grow easier. She has to tell her husband that she loves another man.

She's thought it through, or tried to; she must explain gently but firmly, deflect his fury, use Jamie's presence as a shield if need be. If she has to leave at once, she'll drive to Forest Road and pray that her parents will be willing to absorb the shock. If he won't let her leave at all, though, she must talk him into a trial separation. What she can't begin to decide is how she'll explain it to Jamie.

'Listen, Karrie, I know this is going to be a bit of a shock,' says Julian, in the study, 'but Hils has had a kind of relapse, and Father told me tonight that they've decided to leave Fairfallows to us.'

'Shit.' Karina's problems tumble under the Rookfield family steamroller.

'Look, it won't happen for years, maybe decades. I don't want to worry about it now, and I don't want you to worry either. It's not going to be a problem.'

'Jules, I can't live there.'

'Come here, darling one.' He pats his knee. 'I can tell you it'll be less of a worry for us to own the place than to let Hils have it. We'll find a way.'

'They should turn it over to the National Trust.' Karina wanders to the window and traces the wooden sash frames with one hand as if they're the bars of a prison. 'Or we should, when the time comes.'

'Karrie – Mother just told me that there's a clause in the will forbidding it.'

'You have to be joking.'

Julian balks at the sight of her expression. 'I wish I were.'

'Oh, Christ.' Karina turns and flies out of the room. A second later Julian hears the front door crash behind her.

For a moment Julian is paralysed with disbelief. A second later, he remembers that he can't leave Jamie on his own, so he grabs the startled child from the sofa, bundles him into the car and drives out after Karina.

She's walking up the hill rather than running; it's steep, and she's out of puff. Above them, Lewes Castle is floodlit, a fairy tale image pasted into the wrong book. Julian hoots. She doesn't stop.

'Sweetheart, please calm down,' he orders through the open window. 'Please don't go all Hungarian and hysterical on me now. That's all we need.'

'Your bloody family,' Karina returns. 'They expect you to do everything their way, and you expect *me* to. Supposing I won't? Who do they think they are, telling me how to live my life?'

'Karina, don't be ridiculous. You sound like a spoilt brat.'

'And you sound like a hectoring snob.'

'Do you know how many people in the world would give their eye-teeth for one room to call home? And you react to the prospect of inheriting a manor house as if you've been sentenced to life imprisonment!'

'Oh, I have been, Jules, I have been. They're so stupid. If they sold the Gainsborough, it would solve everything. But they're too pigheaded to do anything but shunt the problems onto us and at the same time make it impossible for us to solve them. They're going to ruin both our lives, and Jamie's.'

'Karrie, get into the car, *now*.'

'Mum,' wails Jamie from inside, 'why are you cross? I'm hungry!'

Julian, crawling the car along, surveys his wife. His mind is casting a light on this more sinister than Hilary's coloured bulbs. 'Darling one, there's some good news too,' he encourages, trying a new tactic, stalling his own understanding. 'Schmidt's won the franchise. We should celebrate, have a proper holiday. Maybe Barbados . . .'

'You don't listen to me, do you?'

'Listen to what? You've been swearing at me! Fairfallows isn't my fault, but it's happened, and we need to make the best of it. Can't you think of anything but yourself?'

'And can't you, just occasionally, think of me?'

'Daddy, I'm hungry!' Jamie howls.

'Karina, it's nearly nine o'clock and Jimbo needs his dinner. Let's go home, for Christ's sake.'

Karina climbs in and slams the door.

At ten thirty, her mobile rings.

'Well?' says Rohan.

'I can't talk. I'll call you tomorrow.'

'Karrie—'

'Tomorrow.' She hangs up.

By the time Julian, Karina and Jamie arrive at Fairfallows for Sunday lunch, Anne has spoken to the director at Keswick about Hilary.

He's to go there for a week, after which they'll advise on the best course of action. Arthur, in his slippers, shuffles out of his study, where he's been going through the paperwork, his face grey at the sight of the cost.

'I don't want Jamie to have to see him,' Julian grunts. It's not fair on an eight-year-old, especially not one whose unquestioning instinct is to love his only uncle.

'Hilary,' Arthur tells them, pouring sherry, 'had one more surprise up his sleeve. He managed to get an agreement to have the travellers moved on. God alone knows how. Must be the plus side of being obsessive.'

Karina refuses the sherry. 'What's going to happen to them?' she demands.

'My dear, I haven't a clue. Presumably they'll go and bother some other blameless community for a while. That, or possibly prison. I understand the children may be taken into care.

'But they weren't harming anyone.'

'So they'd like people to think. There've been stories all over the county about muggings, robberies . . .'

'But I met them! They were gentle, normal people trying to get on with—'

'Normal?' Arthur interrupts. 'You call that *normal*? Living in a caravan, sponging off the state, never doing an honest day's work in your life?'

'How dare you?' Karina's eyes are blazing. 'How can you stand by and see children removed from their parents just because they live in caravans? Just because they live differently from you?'

'Darling,' says Anne, staying calm, 'it wasn't just because of the caravans. They were trespassing. The men were blind drunk at ten thirty in the morning. The mothers were letting the children run riot. They didn't go to school. They couldn't read and write. They—'

'I don't care! When I think what my grandmother suffered, what my parents went through, how Lindy died, and you sit here blithely ruining the lives of a whole family, just because that field is "yours" . . .'

Julian grips her arm and manoeuvres her out of the room. Jamie is sitting beside his grandmother, motionless.

* * *

'Karrie,' Julian says, in the entrance hall, 'while you're in your Hungarian three-year-old mode, I'm going to ask you whether you're having an affair with Rohan.'

'Not hard to guess, then.'

'Are you in love with him?'

'Of course. Why would I have an affair with him otherwise?'

'How do I deserve this, Karina?'

'You don't.'

'We can't talk about this here. Get Jamie. I'll make our excuses.'

Mimi, blooming with health after her years in America, crouched beside Tamás, stroking his hand. The little girl asleep in the cot had long limbs, big feet and blue eyes.

'You're asking me to bring her up as mine?' said Tamás.

The war years had left him as raddled with ruin as their apartment block, close to the Liszt Academy. His face was skeletal, his skin as wrinkled as that of a man ten years older; Mimi was convinced, too, that his persistent cough was more than the lingering irritation he claimed.

'It's asking a lot,' she said. 'But I am asking anyway, because I have no choice.'

'Why didn't you go to France and live with him?'

'Because I belong here, with you.'

'Why wasn't that so before?'

'It always was. But you told me not to come back. Do you remember?'

'Mimi, how could you do this to me?'

'Life has done this to us. We must get through.'

'If you love me, how could you have a child with him?'

'I love you,' said Mimi, 'but for a while I loved him too. Not instead of you, but as well. I genuinely loved both of you. Do you understand? I don't. I've tried to understand, so many times, but I still can't.'

'Why did you insist that he went with you to America?'

'It was for a concert tour and a chance to make contacts. It was supposed to be a few weeks. We didn't think there would be a war. And you, Tamás? In six years, did you never love anybody else?'

Tamás was silent. His shoulders radiated defiance. Mimi kissed his cheeks, his eyelids and his mouth. He pulled away, coughing, hiding his face in his arm. 'Love? In this hell-hole?' he said. 'What the Russians did, Mimi . . . I can't tell you what they did to the women – nobody can speak of it, there aren't the words . . . I thanked God every hour for keeping you away.'

'If you can't accept me with Ani,' said Mimi, 'if it is too much, if you can never love her . . . I'd understand. It's my fault. I'll take the consequences.'

He raised his head and she realised, incredulous, that his smile was soft with heartbreak. 'Mimi, she's the daughter I wish we had. She's a sweet, lovely child, and she's yours; I can't help but love her. This innocent creature – it's not her fault. That's why it's so hard . . . Mimi, stay with me. I still love you. We'll get through.'

Mimi lowered her head into his lap and kissed his hand. 'We'll get through,' she echoed.

Walking through Budapest, taking in the devastation, Mimi shook with tears, those unwept the more painful. The Jewish ghetto had centred on a claustrophobic complex of interlocking courtyards in the Seventh District. Empty; haunted. She couldn't look at it without imagining the Frankls believing, even as they went to their deaths, in a world where this could never happen again. The ghetto was a vacuum, swallowing the voices of its own ghost children.

Another day, she found her way to the distant Gypsy suburb beyond the city boundary where she had last seen her father. She stared into archways and courtyards where children used to play, drains that used to be clogged with rotting cabbage leaves, discarded bottles and other smelly, healthy signs of vitality, run-down bars where István might have lingered with his friends, drinking coffee or spritzers. It might have been poor, chaotic and miserable, but it had been alive. War had gouged out Budapest's soul, while she was living in luxury in New York. On a corner, she saw a solitary Gypsy fiddler playing for stray forints; passers-by bent their heads in their hats, moving on. Guilt drove through her like a pickaxe. At least Dénes and Ani had not had to hide in cellars. At least they were safe and well.

Marc had written her a strange, formal letter, stating that if she chose to send Ani to him in Paris, he would bring her up. Paris was damaged, but still Paris; and she knew what devotion Marc would lavish on Ani. Yet how could she send her little girl away? Ani was tiny; Dini adored her; they loved and depended on each other. Here in Budapest, they were a family – not a peculiar, dispossessed composer living alone from hand to mouth while nobody was particularly interested in his music. Life would be harder in Budapest, no doubt – but nobody ever said it should be easy. Besides, if Ani went to Paris, people would soon know where she had gone, and why; that would do none of them any good. If Tamás had answered her differently, she might have answered Marc differently as well. Now Ani would stay.

It was early in 1950 that Dénes came home from school carrying a pamphlet that made Mimi put down her violin. On it was a picture of Stalin.

'What's going on?' she asked her son.

'Mr Nemeth, our maths teacher, says I'm the best in the class,' Dénes declared. 'He says we should be proud of being Gypsies because we are the people close to the earth and the soil and the work of—'

'Dini,' said Tamás, 'please don't get too excited about this.'

Tamás's family owned land in the country, near Szeged. There'd been a seat – Mimi had never seen it – where the Vereses had lived for centuries. Now the new communist government, which had taken over the previous year from the postwar coalition, was gradually tugging Hungary closer to the Moscow regime. Tamás told Mimi that they had reduced the amount of land that people were permitted to own – a reduction, as it happened, on an earlier reduction. Tamás wasn't interested in land for its own sake; he only cared about his books.

He was the only one left of the Veres siblings. His brother had been killed in action; his sister died of a perforated stomach ulcer after the war ended. Mimi had hated her. She'd hated all of them, since they'd ostracised Tamás for marrying a Gypsy, no matter that she was a famous classical violinist. So much for Dr Frankl's meritocracy. Tamás stood his ground, but the memories lived on long after the people who had caused them. The fuss they'd made! And for what? Now they were dead.

As for Stalin, she didn't know what to think. The idea was – as far as she could tell – that Gypsies should no longer be treated as second-class citizens, that communism was going to equalise everyone. Her son was the best in his class, though a couple of decades ago he'd have had no education at all. It sounded good to her.

But Tamás wasn't as happy as she was with the outlook. 'I don't care about giving up the land myself, but it's the principle I don't like,' he said to Mimi late one night, back from the café on Andrássy where he and his colleagues met to talk books, university politics and philosophy. 'If it was an isolated matter . . . but what will they do next? There's talk of moving elderly people out to collectives in the country – can you believe that? Forcing them to leave their homes and families so that the younger workers can have their apartments? It's monstrous. Inhuman.'

Mimi had stayed home to look after the children, practise and write some desperate letters about finding concerts. She listened to him, assailed by doubts. 'They can't force people to do that, can they?'

'They can, and they will. I'm not sure there's any division now between communism and fascism, Mimi. We've been talking about this all evening, but you know, after we had this discussion, which became quite heated, I came away feeling that perhaps we shouldn't have spoken about such things in public. You start to wonder who was in there. Who might have heard you. When you know what people are capable of when they have a little power . . .'

'It won't happen,' said Mimi.

When the floor falls in, you can see it. You can walk round the hole, call a builder, or buy some wood and repair it yourself. The problem in Karina and Julian's home is that everything that can be seen, touched or physically avoided is intact.

They lie in bed, backs turned, the silence smothering them.

'Why?' Julian asks. 'What's he got that I haven't?'

'If you don't know, I can't explain.'

'Try being rational.'

'Supposing I am?'

'You think it's rational to leave your child's father for some footloose musician who scrapes his way from A to B and can't bear commitment?'

'He wants me to live with him.'

'What do you have in common? You play the violin. His father knew your grandmother's French friend. So what?'

'Do you think you and I have anything in common?'

'You don't count our son, then?'

'Rohan and I both come from immigrant families, we're both musicians and we understand each other.'

'Oh, for God's sake, you mean you like shagging him. That's all it is, Karrie. A bloody good shag.'

'*Baszd meg!*'

'If you want to say fuck off, then say it in plain English.'

'Fuck off, then. What am I? Someone to look after your kid when you can be bothered to have him at home? Someone to cook and clean and look good on your arm at fancy dinners? An exotic-looking woman with thin legs and big tits and an arty pastime that you would never stoop to call a profession, enhancing the fabulous success of your fabulous firm and family?'

'Karrie, shut up.'

Karina hides her face in the pillow. Perhaps she deserves this. Perhaps it's all her own fault. Karina Veres, professional pushover. The outsider, compromising too far in her eagerness to please. Whatever her difficulties in the orchestra, she'd earned her place in that great musical mechanism and its standing ovation at the Salzburg Festival; but when Julian snapped his fingers, she'd let everything go. Moving to Lewes? She'd let him choose. As for Jamie's boarding-school . . . Is all this Julian's fault for pushing her around? Or hers, for letting him?

'Jules, I can't live by going through the motions. All I've done since Jamie was born is go through the motions.'

'What? All that don't-take-my-child-away-from-me stuff was a front?'

'No! I'd give my life for Jamie. But I miss the person I used to be. Anyway, I didn't want to be in love with anyone else. Sometimes people just fall in love. It happens so fast, there's nothing you can do about it.'

'I'll tell you exactly what you do. You don't see him, you don't contact him, and sooner or later it fades. It has to.'

'Have you tried?'

'Of course not.'

'Then don't lecture me. When we first met, you liked it that I seemed odd and exotic and artistic, but all you've tried to do since then is force me to fit your family. I feel as if you want to squash out everything that makes me who I am. I can't keep going through the motions of being the Rookfield family's perfect son's perfect wife.'

'There are plenty worse things you could be.' Julian, out of bed, scrabbles for his slippers. 'You could be starving in Africa or dying of AIDS. You could be trying to escape Hungary in 1956. You could have been on that train with Lindy. Why don't you try counting your blessings for a change?'

'I need to grow, Jules. And if you won't let me, if you won't grow with me, I'll have to do it without you.'

'There's one more thing you could be.' He rounds on her. 'You could be the wife of a string quartet leader, encumbered by your son. Your fiddler will be ambitious, and, Karina, if you let me walk on you, what do you think you'll let *him* do? He'll trample all over you, with your full permission. He'll go on tour while you scratch around for pupils to pay the bills, and he'll just be waiting for that violin of your grandmother's to reappear so that he can sell it for megabucks or use it to boost his own career. And he'll be so busy with his violin that he'll never let you impinge on him for a moment once the novelty wears off. You'll never know what he's up to. He'll be off to a different country every week, sampling the local produce before you can say Amo, Amas, Amati.'

'Shut up, Jules. You should hear yourself.'

'Bloody hell.' Julian stamps out; she hears him thumping up the back stairs to the spare room. She's grateful that he cracked first.

Somehow, she sleeps. When she wakes, before six, it's to the sound, rising from the living room, of Richard Strauss's *Der Rosenkavalier*: the final trio, three angelic, radiant voices. The opera's heroine, Karina vaguely remembers, is giving up the younger man she loves to a younger girl.

She goes downstairs, rubbing sleep from her eyes. Julian is sitting in her armchair near the fireplace. The sky is lavender above the spring garden, which is full of tulips that she planted years ago, the bulbs more resilient than she is to the passage of time. Julian is quiet, his eyes damp. He wipes them periodically with his sleeve. In ten years, Karina has never seen him cry.

She sits on the floor and leans her head against his knee. They listen together until the music is over.

'So,' he says finally, when silence falls. 'Try it. Go with him. See if you're as happy as you expect. See if you find what you're looking for. When you realise it's a terrible mistake, come back to me.'

'I'll make some coffee,' says Karina.

25

Erzsébet and Dénes listen to Karina with sober expressions and few words. Karina has enough words of her own. She's brought her suitcase; Rohan is away teaching at the Menuhin School, and she can't go straight to him.

'But what will you do?' Erzsébet prods.

'Find more teaching. Start playing again.'

'That's the smallest problem,' Dénes insists. 'What you will tell Jamie?'

'The truth. His father and I are having a trial separation.'

'Eiyiyi.' Erzsébet shakes her head.

'Mum, I need to take this risk. We never took risks when I was a child, did we? You never even took a risk buying new furniture.'

'We took a big risk each, escaping here from Hungary,' Dénes points out. 'Then we took another big risk, marrying each other. That's enough risk for one lifetime.'

Karina picks up Pom-Pom, who's purring by her ankles. The Rookfields' house has been sold. The cat's snubby face seems to bear a permanently outraged expression, as if she can't believe that humans could let themselves fall so far from the feline's natural state of grace.

Karina has reclaimed her old bedroom for the time being. She still feels shaky and can't face food. She gazes out towards the dark window that was once Lindy's. What would Lindy have said about all this? Karina suspects she'd have understood.

Her phone beeps: a text from Rohan. 'Back 5 p.m. tmrw, c u at flat, love u x'.

She texts back: 'Have to teach, c u after. xxx'. She needs somewhere other than the house to give her lessons. She phones the headmistress of Jamie's old primary school and begs for the special dispensation of a room to use after hours; all the children there who learn the violin are with her, so it makes sense. The logistics of leaving a marriage, she's discovering, are almost as bad as the emotions; but at least she can deal with practicalities one at a time.

Later, after her mother has forced her to eat some soup, Karina takes her mobile phone upstairs and calls Rohan. They talk for twenty minutes, but mainly about flights to New York. Rohan surfs the Internet on his laptop while they talk, looking for the best prices. Logistics. When she hangs up, her phone beeps again: Jamie's text. 'Nite nite, Mum'. She texts back: 'Nite nite, Schnooky'. Though she doesn't believe in lying to children, she hasn't yet told him the truth.

Three a.m. Lights in the street, a black car, heavy boots on wooden stairs, a knock. A few questions, they said. They let Tamás dress. Mimi wanted to fly at them, to scream and strike and resist, but he pushed her back into the bedroom and whispered, 'Lock the door, my love.'

Footsteps. Silence. Outside, the roar of that revolting car fading into the distance, towards Stalin Avenue, which used to be Andrássy. She felt numb. It was only when she saw her son in the doorway, rubbing his eyes, that the anguish overwhelmed her.

'Where's Papa?' he asked.

'Hush, darling. Go back to sleep.'

'What's happening?'

'Don't wake Ani.'

'Nothing *ever* wakes Ani. Mama, you have to tell me what's going on. I'm not a child.' Dénes was thirteen; not the easiest age for a boy. She beckoned him over and gave him a long, long hug.

'You have to be brave,' she whispered. 'Are you?'

He nodded, waiting.

She told him. 'We don't know where they've taken him or for how long. But your father is a strong man and I know, and you know too, that he'll come back to us. Now, will you be strong like him and help me look after your sister while he's away?'

'Of course I will.' Dénes raised his chin. Scared, but braver than she is. 'I'll always look after Ani, I promise.' She detected a splinter in his tone. Perhaps it was emotion, or perhaps the first bend of his voice before it broke.

She coaxed him back to bed and put out the light. In her bedroom, she rolled onto the patch of mattress that was still warm from Tamás's body and breathed the scent of his sweat before she gave way to tears.

After several weeks, the children stopped asking where he was. Mimi had work to do – the state agency was assigning her plenty of concerts in the Eastern bloc, poorly paid and lavishly taxed, but keeping her busy – and she took the children with her whenever she could. Traces of her two loves: Tamás's in Dénes, Marc's in gawky little Ani, whose attempts at starting the violin weren't going well. She seemed unable to coordinate her hands; but her giggles when it all went wrong meant that that never quite mattered.

Marc hadn't contacted her since she'd refused to send Ani to Paris. Sometimes, when she felt the darkness descending, the greying of the air, the downcast gazes of people in the streets, she'd wonder whether she'd chosen well for her daughter.

She wrote to him, asking how he was. The letter came back, unopened: no forwarding address. She sat on her bed holding the envelope, sensing the closing of gates. If only they'd known, they'd never have left New York. Or would they? She'd have stayed there, free but trapped inside her guilt, for the rest of her life.

She took out the Amati; the strings emitted faint murmurs under her fingers. It was a smallish violin, dark brown rather than red or golden, and in need of a good overhaul, if only there were anyone in Budapest she'd trust with it. Nobody would guess its worth by its appearance – but set it free in a player's hands and its song could break every heart in heaven.

'This is yours,' Marc had said, putting the case into her arms.

Mimi hadn't known how to respond. A girl of twenty-one, fresh out of Hungary, overwhelmed by Notre Dame Cathedral, Parisian fashion and French cuisine. 'I can't possibly accept this.'

'It's yours. It has to be yours.'

Marc had steered her to the auction house's pre-sale viewing as if by accident and suggested that they 'pop in' to try some instruments. She'd picked up the Amati and begun to play Ravel's *Tzigane*, and the roomful of visitors and potential buyers had fallen silent on the spot.

'It could have been made for you. You can't not have it,' said Marc.

'Don't be silly,' said Mimi.

Yet he'd bought it; and the premiere, only weeks away, needed a violin that could project through the sizeable Châtelet better than her cheap Hungarian fiddle. She took Marc's gift; and once she realised its full capabilities, the horizons of her musical world began to crack apart. She understood then that Marc Duplessis knew her better than she knew herself.

Night is falling; the windows are lamplit. Cars chunter by as if this day is like any other. In the distance Karina can hear a whisper of sea; overhead, the whining of seagulls. She stands on Rohan's doorstep, suitcase in hand, and presses the bell by the label MASTERSON. The door buzzes and admits her. She goes up the curving stairs towards the top floor, where Rohan's door is open, waiting for her.

'You have to be kidding,' says Andy, over pasta. Julian, uncharacteristically, had rung at the last minute to see whether he was free for lunch. 'What's she *doing*? Finding herself, or shit like that?'

'Who knows?' Julian decides not to mention Rohan. After Karina's name-day dinner, Andy had remarked, 'Good-looking chap, the South African fiddler, but a bit out of it.'

'What are you going to do?'

'Keep going. What else can I do? And you know what the fucking stupid thing is? She's mad at me for sending Jamie to St Matthew's because she thinks boarding-school is bad for him. This is a hundred times worse, but I haven't noticed that stopping her.'

Andy nods, without meeting Julian's eye. Julian wonders whether there are problems between him and Sarah, a girl whose looks seem chiselled to a template of perfection, but might conceal the kind of neuroses that you don't need after a long day at the Department for Transport.

'You've got to try not to let it get to you,' Andy says. 'Not at work. You've still got that; it's yours and she can't take it away. It's the best remedy.'

'I'm doing my best.' Julian's said nothing about Hilary, whom he has to drive to Keswick the day after tomorrow. Andy looks tired, as exhausted as Julian feels. Ambition can wear you out, especially when you're the DfT's resident Sisyphus.

'It's good to be involved in stuff that's bigger than you are,' Andy remarks. 'Keeps you on the rails, if you'll excuse the analogy. Another beer?'

The franchise announcement has been and gone. Flayed by the empty house, Karina's decimated wardrobe, the absent violin case, Julian barely noticed. Carsten Schmidt, negotiating for a franchise in Krakow, had taken the news without a hint of surprise or gratitude, let alone pleasure; he certainly can't find time to fly in for a celebratory dinner, thank heavens.

Home mercifully late, Julian takes refuge in his CD collection. He pulls out some rival recordings of Beethoven string quartets to compare – then chooses piano music instead. The sound of violins would be more than he could stand.

Rohan goes into the bedroom to practise. He's working on the Duplessis Suite for New York. Karina has crammed her clothes beside his in the cupboard; now, while he works, she hovers in his kitchen, absorbing impressions. The TV chatters in the flat downstairs; motorbikes buzz by; spring breezes catch in the trees. Flowers, freshly planted, adorn the window-boxes. On the desk in the living room lies a pile of manuscript paper, covered with notes in Rohan's small, intense, precise script; he's pushed some books over it, evidently in a hurry to hide his composerly efforts from her. Her nose tells her that something's off in the fridge. She finds a cucumber decomposing into greenish-grey liquid, a pat of butter marked USE BY: 31 JAN 07, and two onions evincing ambitions to become plants. She clears the lot into the bin and sponges down the shelves. When the fridge is spotless, she starts on the oven.

Rohan peers round the bedroom door. 'Just another half an hour, love,' he says. The bedclothes are still in chaos after the welcome he gave her there.

Karina curls up on the sofa and opens her laptop computer. The machine seems confused when she tries to connect to the Internet; it's accustomed to logging on to Julian's wireless home network. She must prioritise setting one up here, not that she has any idea how to do so. She uses Rohan's PC instead and looks up some news sites to make sure she is still in the world she seems to have left.

A flourish from the violin, a twang, then quiet, and Rohan is with her. 'Tea?' he offers. 'What are you reading?'

She shows him; he glances at the screen with a nod. She thinks he'll ask again how she's left things with Julian or what she's said to Jamie, but his mind is somewhere else.

'Karrie, you know the Forest Scene in the Duplessis? Did Mimi tell you anything much about it?'

'Oh . . .' She tries to pull her mind into music. 'Once she mentioned that for Duplessis the forest was symbolic. It represented the subconscious, the source of everything forbidden and tempting. The sort of dark that you're scared of, but can't do without. That's how she put it.'

'I was thinking more about the bowing. You know the bit where . . .'

'Ro,' Karina says, 'I just need to call Jamie. Then we can talk Duplessis.'

Rohan nods and tactfully removes himself to the bedroom, while Karina, forcing herself to sound normal, rings her son to say goodnight, and to tell him that she's coming to visit him tomorrow.

'Cool,' says Jamie's small, distant voice. 'Can I say goodnight to Daddy?'

Karina flinches. 'He's not here, sweetheart,' she tells him. 'See you tomorrow.'

An ÁVH man was standing by Mimi's door, puffing on a cigarette and looking intensely bored. Transfixed by the gun at his hip, she stared up at him and waited.

'Mrs Veres? Come with me. You're going to see your husband.' He looked her up and down, impassive. 'Bring him some food if you want to.'

Her body turned to water. She threw into her shopping basket everything she had in the kitchen – some bread, a piece of smoked sausage, two apples and some strudel she'd been keeping for the children. She tied a scarf over her hair and grabbed her coat – from New York, its elbows nearly worn through. 'I'm ready,' she managed to say. Next thing she knew, she was climbing, voluntarily, into the black car waiting in the street, while several passing neighbours pretended that they didn't know her.

* * *

She walked up the flight of carpeted stairs beyond the central courtyard, under the biggest chandelier she had seen since leaving America. It was light and quiet; this place's daily business occurred well out of view. Upstairs, a door opened; her guide pointed. She stepped forward. Heavy curtains concealed seven eighths of the window; a fat, moustachioed man in shirt sleeves lurked at a leather-topped desk behind a lamp; nearby, on a wooden chair, there hunched another figure, a bony hand shielding his eyes from the scant sunlight.

'Tamás!' cried Mimi. She ran to him; nobody stopped her.

'This is your wife?' The officer at the desk addressed Tamás.

Tamás reached out to Mimi and they held each other for five long seconds. She could feel nothing but bones. 'I brought you food,' she said in a rush. 'The children are well. They'll be so happy. Darling, there's so much to tell you.'

'This is your wife?' repeated the officer: it was a demand. Tamás and Mimi, interlocked, turned and froze.

'She is,' Tamás said.

'You will now sign this statement, otherwise we'll rape her. She's a Gypsy whore.'

Why were the curtains drawn? Because Tamás had not seen daylight for eighteen months? Because they didn't want her to see the scars on his legs and wrists? Or so that nobody should witness what went on in this room? She tried to open her mouth to tell him not to do it, not to sign, but one glance from his eyes – their wonderful green vigour long beaten out of them – told her everything she needed to know.

'You've demeaned yourself already, Professor, marrying a Gypsy whore.' The officer yawned. 'Signing is fun, don't you think? Intellectuals have always enjoyed signing autographs.' The statement seemed as natural to him as a remark about the unavailability of certain kinds of ham.

'I will not sign it, and you will not touch my wife,' said Tamás.

'Take her.'

Four hands, stronger than she was, seized her from behind – she had no idea where they'd come from, all these people, she'd seen nothing but Tamás. Stinking male breath on her face; alcoholic fumes, acrid sweat. Tamás tried to struggle to his feet; she heard a crack as someone lunged out. She unfroze. She was a child in the forest again and she knew how to scream. The sound leapt back from the walls and ceiling. The official made some notes, a hand over one ear. And Mimi remembered how to spit into eyes and how to utter curses, and when that didn't work she found a way to bite, curse and scream at the same time. They could silence her with a bullet – though that might be too kind. Her teeth made contact with a wrist and she felt its flesh give way like bread.

'Fucking demon!' came its owner's shriek. 'Creature from hell!'

'You don't want her? Let her go, then. Go on, stupid woman.' The officer had the air of a bored puppeteer. 'Just think, Gypsy Mimi, you could have stayed in America. You came back.' The hands dropped away from her. In the half-light, she could barely see Tamás on the floor, a figure standing over him, stabbing at his body with fists and feet. Something shattered.

'Get out of here, filthy Gypsy whore,' the others jeered. She didn't want to move. Her whole body needed, as an absolute imperative, to kill every ÁVH man in the room, tear out their throats and carry Tamás home to nurse him better. One step towards him, though, and they'd both be dead.

Behind the desk, another yawn. 'Go away. Go play your fucking fiddle.'

She walked through the open door, knowing the guns were trained on her back. They'd had their fun; if Tamás were unconscious he wouldn't have seen them rape her, which was the whole point. Walking, head up, maintaining concert-platform dignity no matter how her feet shook in her old shoes, she waited for another ÁVH minion to appear, drag her to a cell and finish her off, but the carpet stretched ahead and she could see the door. Don't run, her instinct told her. If you run, they'll shoot. Why hadn't they shot her when she screamed? They should have. Her only hope was that Tamás would stay unconscious long enough not to know what was happening to him.

She never had any idea how she reached home that day, but when she arrived, the staircase felt different. She blinked; it seemed someone had tipped it over by forty-five degrees. She clung to the banisters, walking step by step by step, remembering to breathe.

The children mustn't know. She found herself at her door; she went in and her legs gave way under her.

Later Dénes and Ani came home from school; Ani, laughing with wide blue eyes like Marc's, was singing a song in Russian. Mimi grabbed them both, held them to her so that they couldn't see her face, and said, 'Darlings, I'm sorry. There's no strudel today.'

She'd blamed her mother for rejecting her, and her father for selling her. Now she understood. Given the chance to send her children away from this cage of a city, she'd do the same. She'd rejected her family and her heritage; she'd failed them when they needed her. Mimi Rácz, under the tutelage of Dr Frankl, had grown up believing in self-determination and meritocracy: not fate, not heaven or hell, and certainly not divine retribution. Dear God, was this her punishment?

'Mama,' Dénes said, 'what is it?' He had his father's intelligence and his grandfather's bullishness: a dangerous combination, but galvanising.

'Nothing, Dini. Get your cello and let's do some work,' said Mimi.

'You look so strange. You're pale. You look – as if you've given away all your strength.'

Mimi settled Ani in the bedroom with some books, then closed the door. 'Dini, come here. Listen.' He sat opposite her at the kitchen table and leaned his chin on his hands, gaze fixed on her face. Mimi took a breath. 'Your father is alive,' she said. 'I don't know when he'll come home, but this morning, he was alive.'

Dénes's face did not change outwardly, but behind his eyes a light glowed. Mimi no longer minded if he sensed how shattered and weak she felt. He wanted to know, because now he was the strongest of them. 'Come, my dear,' she said. 'Let's do some work.'

26

Jamie and Karina wander round the school grounds, skirting the football pitch. Karina is more tearful than her child as she tries to explain that she and his father aren't going to live in the same house any more. 'It doesn't make any difference,' she insists. 'We'll still be seeing you every weekend.'

'Did I do something bad?' Jamie looks away towards the grass.

'Goodness, no, Schnooks. You mustn't think that for a second. We're the problem. Not you.'

'Is that why you wanted me to go to boarding-school? So's you could go away and I wouldn't be there? You wanted to get rid of me, didn't you?'

'Darling, *no*.' Karina clasps his hand. He pulls it away and folds his arms behind his back as he walks, as Arthur often does.

'Where did you go?' he demands.

'Brighton.'

'Why?'

'I'm staying with a friend. Rohan. Do you remember him? He came to dinner.'

'Oh, him.'

'You liked him, didn't you?'

'I want my daddy.'

'Jamie, love.' She tries to put an arm around him.

'Geroff,' Jamie mutters.

'Come on, Schnooky. Don't be that way, it's not going to help.'

'And don't call me Schnooky. It's stupid.'

'My mum and dad still call me Schnooky.'

'I don't care, I hate it. I hate you. I hate everything.'

Karina tries to hold on to him, but he's off, a small figure in grey uniform hurtling across the muddy sports field towards the cloakroom door.

'It's too fast,' Erzsébet warns her by phone. Karina is talking as quietly as she can in the front room in Brighton so as not to disturb Rohan, practising at the back. 'You move in straight away?'

'Why leave it, Mum? Why wait? I had to be honest with them all.'

'And are you happy?'

'No, but I need to be with Rohan.'

'I don't want to watch you spoil your life. You only have one life.'

'That's why I've left.'

'Karina, listen. You think your father and I have had an easy marriage? We've been through some bad times. Your father can be a difficult man, and your grandmother hasn't always made things pleasant for me. I didn't want you to see, and if you didn't, I'm glad. But if you don't work at your relationships, nothing will ever be right, not with either of these men.'

Soon there's quiet, but for Rohan's playing. Karina listens. Everything she'd taken for granted seems to have collapsed in the wake of Lindy's death. One constant remains: the sound of the violin.

'Jeez,' says Rohan, emerging and giving her a grin. 'Duplessis must have been a sadist. The more I play this piece, the more I realise how bloody difficult it is. Who was on the phone?'

'My mother. She thinks I've moved too fast.'

'And have you, love?' Rohan hugs her.

'No,' says Karina. 'But I have to move faster now, because I'm due at school.'

'Karrie, just one thing I want to show you, very quickly . . .' Rohan dives over to the computer and moves the mouse.

A violin appears on the screen. A Nicolò Amati, 1671, for sale in an auction house in New York. From the instrument's history, outlined briefly below the photo, the word 'Budapest' leaps out like a flashing light.

Karina stares. 'Surely not?'

'Even if it's not the one, they might have information or leads or contacts. Karrie, the viewing is while we're there for the recital. We have to go and see it.'

'Ro, supposing the violin literally doesn't exist? Supposing it was destroyed?'

'They'd tell us, wouldn't they?'

'You don't know my father. He can be – well, a little perverse, though he's got a heart of gold. I have to run. I'm going to be late.' Karina kisses the end of Rohan's long nose, grabs her violin case and makes for the door. Part of her wonders why Rohan should be so fixated on Mimi's Amati, when there are plenty of other good violins in the world.

When she comes back, six pupils later, tired and slightly dispirited, Rohan is still practising. He has put a pan of soup on the stove to heat for supper; it's boiled over. Immersed in Duplessis's song of the minstrel and the forest shadows, he's forgotten all about it.

Marc Duplessis, wrote Pierre Vincente, *sensed that the war-shattered world was beginning to regroup. The Parisian sunlight held new hopes, the trees outside his apartment block in Neuilly-sur-Seine were turning to jade. Everywhere there thundered building works, road repairs, a rhetoric calling for change.*

After six and a half years in New York, he and Mimi Rácz had parted company once and for all; and his concerto had never been played. Now the critics habitually panned his works for being old-fashioned; he feared he might never hear them performed again. His parents were dead; his brother had taken umbrage at the way Duplessis had followed a married woman to America. The new world, Duplessis remarked later, seemed as blank as manuscript paper, and he must put notes on its stave. He had to make a fresh start. Why in France? Why not somewhere else? Somewhere new, hopeful, untouched by the twin demons of fascism and communism.

Six months later Marc Duplessis stood on the deck of a Union-Castle Line steamer, leaning on the rail with the ocean pulsing beneath his feet, drinking in the fierce white sun of Africa and an extraordinary image: a mountain rising out of the sea, its flat-topped silhouette scalpel-sharp against the sky. In his cabin, at the bottom of a trunk, lay the pages of his Gypsy Violin Concerto, wrapped in a pair of pyjamas. He wouldn't know, until he had tried, whether anyone in South Africa would be more receptive to his music than the concert promoters in Europe and America. He chose the Cape of Good Hope for its name.

A report the size of Big Ben concerning the Wood Green disaster has landed on Andy Williamson's desk. The victims' association, led by Martin Rookfield, wants to sue the train company for corporate manslaughter and criminal negligence. Andy knows, not least via Julian, that if this produces no results, Rookfield has set his sights on suing the government. Andy has been muttering to his PA, Pippa, between cups of strong coffee, that accidents no longer exist. Whenever anything goes wrong, it's deemed someone's fault and someone else will demand money. As if that would bring back Rookfield's daughter and the other poor blighters who'd died that day. Even he, a trained lawyer, feels a certain disgust at the burgeoning litigation culture, which he reckons is demeaning to everyone concerned and to the law itself. Yet now – for his sins – he must do all he can to grasp how and why the crash happened, and who was passing the buck to whom.

'Don't overdo it, Mr Williamson,' Pippa remarks. She's a temp, standing in for Andy's secretary who's away on jury service, and she likes to put in extra time to show willing.

'Don't mind me, Pippa, I'll be here for a while yet,' Andy says. 'Going out tonight, are you?'

'Yeah, that's the plan. If it's all the same to you, Mr W, I should really be off. Hate to leave you here still up to your eyeballs.' She shrugs on a denim jacket.

'Going somewhere nice?' Andy turns a page.

'Meeting the girls for a drink, and we might go clubbing later.'

'Friday night in London, and you're young and free.' Andy sits back and watches her with a flood of feeling, which, he realises with distress, could be described as wistfulness. He doesn't think of himself as a wistful kind of man.

'Are you busy with the kids this weekend?' Pippa asks kindly.

'The usual. Ballet class for Marsha, football coaching for Cos. Homework, parties, Marsha's going to a sleep-over in Notting Hill and Sarah's going to cook me dinner without wheat.

Apparently wheat is bad for you – did you know that? I only live on the ruddy stuff.'

'Oh, Mr W. Why don't you come out for a drink with us?' Pippa says. He deduces, from the surprise on her face, that she didn't mean to say this, but feels so sorry for him, twenty years older and sadder than she is, that the words more or less slipped out of their own accord.

'You don't want boring old blokes hanging around on your girls' night out.'

'You're not boring, you're not hanging around and you're not exactly old. Just older than us.' Pippa grins. 'Come on, Mr W. Let your hair down for once.'

Ten minutes later, Andy, to his own amazement, finds he's walking beside Pippa out of the building, past Victoria Station and towards the River Thames and the freedom beckoning on its other side.

Andy doesn't know how or why young women in Britain can drink so much alcohol. When they find Pippa's friends Kirsty and Lavenda in a noisy bar close to County Hall, the girls are already well tanked up – on vodka, which they say contains fewer calories than other drinks. They order two bottles of wine, with a bowl of vegetable crisps and a few olives. 'Waste of calories, food,' Lavenda declares. She and Kirsty, one Caribbean, the other Scottish, are surprised that Pippa's brought her boss, but they're agreeable, if drunk, and the booze on emptyish stomachs sends them all spinning into a parallel universe so fast that nobody even asks Andy what he does at the DfT.

The evening flies by with another bottle or two, and when Big Ben strikes eleven, Lavenda's warm rump is on Andy's lap and Kirsty, in a top with a neckline that has nothing to do with her neck, is draping herself forward so that he can't help but gaze down her cleavage. He averts his eyes. Pippa suggests they go to a cellar club near Trafalgar Square. Andy's too sozzled, and too besotted with life outside office and home, to resist. He texts Sarah: 'Working late, don't wait up.'

Around one a.m., his head under assault from mixed drinks, the infernal din and a faint despair at being the oldest man in the club, Andy navigates an unsteady path out into the fresh air. The girls are still down there, coiling their slender bodies around strange boys, and Andy's had one beer too many and feels nauseous. The bouncers, two enormous fellows in leather, stare down at him from a great height. One fixes him with a gaze too perceptive for comfort. Andy wonders whether he's been recognised. He casts around for a cab. Otherwise it's the night bus, or Shanks's pony home to Pimlico.

'Listen, mate,' says the bouncer, 'I know a club'd suit you better than this one.'

'What?' Andy mumbles.

The bouncer tells him where to turn off the main road. 'Corner place. You can't miss it, know what I mean? Anyone asks you, yeah, tell them Wayne sent you.'

'Um. Yeah. Right,' Andy stammers. And maybe because Wayne is watching him, he walks obediently in the direction he's been pointed. Towards Soho, the streets look different at this time of night, sepia-patched under the tall lamps and populated by nocturnal types who don't conform to any social standard that Andy's familiar with. Creatures from another world, he thinks, fed on white dust and dangerous liquors, and the other club, which he can glimpse on the next corner, will be full of them. Taxis drive past; they're all taken. He hesitates, noticing a bus stop nearby.

'Going where I'm going?'

He turns. Beside him there stands a youth half his age, with a black T-shirt, spiked hair and the biggest, bluest eyes in London, perhaps widened by drugs. Andy registers that he's wearing mascara. 'You're not from round here?' the boy persists. 'C'mon. I'll show you the ropes.'

And why Andy should turn away from the bus stop and go with him past the carmine glass and more bouncers into that throbbing interior is something that he can't understand even as he does it.

Mimi bowed her head, worked hard and gave concerts in schools and factories in the countryside whenever the state concert agency demanded it. She had no choice but to be managed by them; with Tamás a dissident in prison, she was lucky to work at all. In transit, on trains and buses in the furthest corners of the country, she wrapped herself against the cold in a headscarf; immediately, to other travellers, she was just a Gypsy with a violin, though an odd one, being a woman. She wondered why, under a system that was supposed to equalise the populace, she still received the same filthy looks and muttered insults that had always followed her father's family when they weren't playing their instruments.

A cellist from London, Ursula Pollens, whom she'd met on tour ten years earlier, wrote to Mimi while the early summer sun streamed into the kitchen in 1956. She was coming to Budapest to play a concerto with a British chamber orchestra; a small and extremely rare reciprocal gesture – at least, she thought so – after the Hungarian state folk dance assembly had performed in London. What could she bring for Mimi? 'Medicines,' Mimi wrote back. 'Tampons. Toilet paper.'

When Ursula arrived, tall, fair and flustered, on a clandestine visit, she presented them with an outsize tin of leaf tea and a big jar of marmalade. 'Nectar and ambrosia!' Dénes cried. He clicked his heels together and kissed her hand to make her laugh. Ursula did laugh, beaming an enchanted English smile into the young man's face. Mimi didn't know that one day Dénes would regard those three words as the most important he had ever spoken.

Looking at the tea, she could have cried. She was grateful, of course, and Dénes and Ani fell on the marmalade in ecstasy; but when she'd said medicine, tampons and toilet paper, she'd meant it, and Ursula hadn't believed her.

Dénes, replete with marmalade-drenched bread, shyly asked Ursula if he could play to her. While the cellist listened to his Beethoven sonata, Mimi noticed her eyes stray now and then to the giggly, ill-proportioned girl who looked so very unlike her brother.

'You should come to England and study with me,' Ursula told Dénes. His face filled with longing, but he uttered a polite thank-you in which hope didn't feature. When time ran out and Ursula picked up her cello case, Mimi hugged her for so long that she looked slightly embarrassed.

'It can't go on,' she encouraged Mimi in a whisper. 'Something has to happen. Now that Khrushchev's been so critical of Stalin, everyone's saying things have to change. Then Tamás will come back.'

'How can it ever change?' Mimi asked. 'It would be like trying to turn round a dinosaur. One of the biggest and most stupid ones.' She'd only heard about the Russian premier's speech, which he'd given back in February, when the Hungarian Communist Party had got round to responding to it two weeks ago. Optimism no longer came as naturally to her as it used to.

'Don't stop hoping, Mimi,' Ursula insisted. 'Don't give up. Promise?'

Mimi promised.

Rohan arrives at Harry's at eleven a.m. on the dot for a quartet rehearsal and is surprised to find his colleagues ensconced at the kitchen table, the remains of a box of Lyuba biscuits and three virtually drained coffee cups in front of them. They've evidently been there for a while.

'Rohan,' Harry says, his face impassive, letting him dump his coat on the sofa, 'how's Karina settling in?'

'Oh, she's fine, thanks. She's coming with me to New York, and – what is it, chaps? What's going on?'

'We have to have a little chat,' Malcolm declares from the table. 'Come and sit down.'

Two days later, Karina and Rohan, pulling their suitcases on wheels, set off from the flat for New York. Walking up to Brighton station, Karina tells Rohan about Jamie's defiant mood, and his set, angry face when she explained she'd be away in America for five days; she's convinced Julian must be poisoning his view of her. Rohan tells Karina about his plans to hold a chamber music master-class at the Southbank Centre. He looks worried, but she attributes this to nerves over the New York recital, combined with some quartet rehearsals in which the usual sparks had flown.

At Gatwick, once they've checked in and steered Rohan's violin through security, he suggests a coffee.

'Ro,' Karina says, looking at his stance and expression, 'what's the matter?'

Sipping latte in the airport Starbucks underneath the departure screens, Rohan lets out a long breath. 'It's not about us,' he assures her. 'I don't want you to worry. Hopefully it'll blow over. The thing is, the chaps are angry with me. It should be funny, but as you know, Malcolm hasn't much sense of humour and Harry and Genya worry about money. So . . .'

'I don't get it.'

Rohan holds her hand and looks at the floor. 'Budapest.'

'Budapest? But – because of me? But they agreed!'

'Yes, they did, but the other day they had a go at me. Don't worry, it's nothing to do with you or your playing. The thing is, it meant a reduction in everyone's fee – the same money, which wasn't much, shared between five instead of four. Yes, they thought it was a good idea at the time. But now they've decided that it was my way of getting you away from your husband, and since you've moved in . . . well, I don't need to tell you what they think.'

'Why didn't you say so before?' Karina protests.

'I didn't want to worry you, you've got enough on your plate. It was just bad timing. I reckon Malcolm's been stirring, pressing all Harry and Genya's usual buttons. He's been telling them they lost some of their rightful fee just because I wanted to get off with you.'

'But you and I are none of their business!'

'Of course not, but Malcolm has an agenda and he'll twist whatever he likes to fit it. It's nothing new. We grumble about him, but he runs the quartet and when it comes to the crunch, he gets his way. Harry and Genya are good blokes, but they'll always capitulate and toe the line when he tells them to. He's a shit, and there's fuck all I can do about it.'

'I'll pay them back the amount they lost, then. I didn't do that concert for the money.'

'Don't even think about it. You worked harder than those three put together. Anyway, it wouldn't make any difference.'

'Ro, what's going to happen?'

'I don't know. They need me, we've got concerts. But the atmosphere's – well, you can imagine. Basically, they want me out, and I'd like to go. I'd like never to see any of them again. But it's not so easy.'

'You can't let them force you out over this! It's crazy.'

'Karrie, it's not just because of this. This is the last straw. They think I'm overambitious, arrogant, selfish, you name it. It's jealousy, of course, because I've got a New York recital. They'd have liked me to say "Oh no, I don't want a solo recital, I want to bring my string quartet." Imagine any of *them* doing that, given the same chance.'

'Ro, you mustn't worry. If you leave, it's their loss.'

'Yes, but we have to eat.'

'We'll manage. You've got to tell me if things like that happen – don't go being noble to spare my feelings. I need to know. Promise?'

An announcement rings out: the New York flight is boarding. Karina gets up. 'That's us,' she says. 'I'll just run to the newsagent and grab something to read.'

Coming back, newspaper in hand, she glances at the front page and pulls up short.

'ABERRATION' IN DEN OF INIQUITY

Transport minister 'won't resign' after cameras catch father-of-two revelling in notorious gay nightclub in London's West End . . .

Below is pictured a throng of clamouring reporters; and, trapped among them, Andy Williamson, one arm raised to conceal his face.

27

Cars, horns and mayhem greet Karina and Rohan, travelling by yellow taxi towards the Upper West Side. It's nearly midnight, but there doesn't seem to be a difference here between rush hour and any other time of day. On a clearer stretch of road, a beat-up Ford overtakes them, tyres screeching, missing the wing mirror by two millimetres. Their cab-driver erupts with fury. The car lurches as he accelerates, leaning out of the window, gesticulating and shouting, 'Fucking Taliban!' Karina and Rohan shrink back in the seat. Above them the blocks soar towards the night sky, the darkness drained by the city lights. Sounds bounce up the skyscrapers, the walls acting as natural amplification. Karina feels lost in a tunnel of noise.

The taxi-driver swerves and careers past the Ford. The Ford honks. Yells emerge from its depths. Karina hears: 'Do that again and we'll blow out your fucking brains!' In the deluge of lights and metal and distorted reflections, she thinks she sees the dull gleam of a gun.

'It's OK, mate,' Rohan says to the driver. 'Relax. Take it easy, we don't want you to have a problem.'

'Hey, *you* relax. I'm drivin' the friggin' car.'

'At least if we die, we die together,' Rohan mumbles to Karina.

It feels like a year, though in reality it's only minutes, until the taxi loses the Ford, rounds several corners, then slows down on Riverside Drive. 'Here,' says Rohan at a side-street. A friend of his has agreed to lend them her studio apartment while she's away. The taxi comes to a halt outside a brownstone; Karina climbs out, her knees weak.

'We made it.' Rohan smiles, grabbing the cases. 'All right, love?'

It's a long time since Karina was last in New York. They'd gone for a weekend to celebrate Julian's fortieth birthday and stayed at the Park Plaza, leaving the small Jamie at Forest Road with his grandparents. Karina, trying desperately to enjoy the Metropolitan Museum and Bloomingdale's, had instead spent the whole time worrying about him, phoning home almost every hour until her mother gave her an earful and insisted she stop.

She follows Rohan up the front stairs, carrying his violin. She's startled at the images that had flown through her imagination when she saw the gun: the news reaching home, Julian telling Jamie, Jamie, grown up, trying to remember her. The idea of dying doesn't bother her unduly, she realises – with luck, once it's happened we'll know nothing about it. It's the thought of those left behind. What it does to them. Especially a child.

A loquacious next-door neighbour lets them in. The studio, on the top floor, is hot and airless, but Rohan – who seems to know where things are – dashes about turning on air-conditioning and boiling water for tea in a pot on the stove (New Yorkers, he remarks, don't seem keen on kettles). Karina finds somewhere to hang their clothes and gazes through the window at the lightscape outside. The street is quiet, but she can still hear the whirr of New York traffic, as ambient as the sea in Brighton, but rather more intrusive.

'I've lived in Lewes so long that I'd forgotten what it's like to be in the middle of a big city,' she tells Rohan.

'New York's a one-off. I feel the same every time I come here. Thrilled and bloody terrified. Though it's supposed to be safer than it used to be.'

The studio belongs to a freelance violinist named Sophia who, Rohan explains, is constantly on the move, playing in sessions, period-instrument ensembles and occasionally symphony orchestras. When she comes to Britain, she stays at Rohan's flat; when he goes to New York, she returns the favour. Karina divines her personality. African wall-hangings. A patchwork bedspread. A shelf piled with boxes of organic herbal teas; an amply filled bookcase; a wardrobe containing long skirts, jeans and loose, batik-print shirts. 'She's great,' Rohan assures Karina. 'A good spirit. You'd like her.'

'Old girlfriend?'

'Kind of.' He rubs her back. 'Ancient history. In case you're wondering, yes, the wall hangings are South African; we did go there together once. Years ago. Come on, Karrie, let's get something to eat. There's a good shop round the corner.'

Karina remembers Rohan remarking that he had had 'lots of affairs'; the music world, as she discovered in her orchestral days, is replete with temporary, fluid relationships that wax and wane at different rates while their protagonists circle the globe. She's been so busy dealing with her own past that she hasn't had much time, yet, to think about his.

On Broadway, they find an all-night grocery where they buy bagels, hummus, salad, fruit, milk, cereal and coffee (Sophia's cupboard contains only decaffeinated). Outside, the streets are dotted with late-evening dog walkers. Karina looks left and right at the long perspective of traffic lights at each corner, changing in unison from red to amber to green. Broadway is hard, bright and dark, a beehive overwhelming its own bees. At home, it's four a.m. She imagines Jamie asleep in his cubicle room at school, and her innards, still shaken by the taxi ride, ache for him.

Rohan, too keyed up to worry about jet lag, bounds out the next morning to rehearse with his pianist, who lives fifteen blocks away, down West End Avenue. 'You can't get lost in New York,' he assures her. Karina isn't convinced. She takes herself for a walk in the sunshine, uncertain and disoriented.

She passes great gothic apartment buildings on Riverside Drive and goes into the park under the trees. Rollerbladers career past her, dogs on leashes snuff at one another and at the bottom of a bank of grass some huge rodents are rootling about. Rats. Karina discovers that her feet won't move closer to them. She decides to walk round the park instead of through it.

She drifts, unanchored. New York is hers for the day. She can go to the shops and make the most of the favourable exchange rate of pound to dollar; she can visit a gallery, or wander the streets, recharging herself with the city's relentless energy. Boggled by so many choices, she goes into a café and orders coffee and a muffin that turns out to be twice the size of the ones she's used to at home. Somehow the morning passes.

At two, in another café after some fruitless window-shopping, she phones her mother to let her know that they've arrived safely. In the background, three thousand miles away, she can hear two cellos: her father is teaching.

'Wait,' Erzsébet says, 'he wants to talk to you.'

'Don't interrupt him.' Dénes hates being disturbed in the studio.

'No, this is important. Just a second, Schnooky.'

The cellos break off; Karina hears her father's footsteps. 'Karina, how you get to Carnegie Hall? Practise, practise, practise! Listen, my child, you're in New York, you've got some time?'

'Yes. Rohan's working.'

'Rohan. What a crazy name. Now, Karina, will you do something for me, and, I think, for you? Can you look somebody up?'

'Of course. Tell me?'

'Her name is Vali Shapiro. She'll be getting on in years now. Older than me, younger than your grandmother.'

'A friend from Hungary?'

'Once upon a time, Vali was my nurse. Nanny, you'd say. She married a New Yorker and stayed there when we went back to Budapest. She writes to me every Christmas and sometimes I write back. Listen, take this down.' He rattles off a Brooklyn address. 'Now, don't forget while you're busy looking after your friend.'

Karina had wanted to tell her parents about the terrifying taxi ride, her anxiety over knowing so little of Rohan's past, the way she misses Jamie so much that she could scream. She says nothing. She writes down Vali Shapiro's address, promises her father she'll investigate, then rings off. Britney Spears blares out of loudspeakers above her. Two enormous women at the next table shovel cake into their mouths. Karina gathers her things and prepares to leave. At least now she has a task to accomplish.

Back at the flat, she searches Pierre Vincente's biography of Duplessis, which she takes everywhere, for any mention of Vali Shapiro. One anecdote describes Mimi arriving in Paris with an 'entourage' including a nurse for the baby. There's nothing more.

She picks up Sophia's phone book. She feels some distaste at staying in the flat with Rohan when he'd evidently spent time there in the same capacity with its owner. She imagines Sophia

– blonde, polished, but Bohemian enough to be charming – rifling through this book. Shapiro . . . there must be a million Shapiros in New York.

Finding Vali is easier than she expected, though; the address that her father gave her is still current. Plucking up the courage to phone is another matter. Karina takes a deep breath and forces herself.

There's a response after a ring and a half. 'Yes?'

'Is that Mrs Shapiro?'

'Yes? Can I help you?' According to Dénes, Vali must have been in New York for something like sixty years – presumably she's around eighty-five – but her accent is almost as powerful as Mimi's.

'My name is Karina Veres. I'm Dénes Veres's daughter.'

A silence – shock? Disbelief? 'Are you?' says Vali Shapiro. 'Are you, indeed? And you're in New York?'

'Yes, just for a few days. My father asked me to look you up and send you his love.'

There's a cackle as Vali laughs, her voice deep and suddenly warm. 'Little Dini! How good to hear news of him. It's a long time since we spoke. And you, I have never spoken to you. How old are you?'

'Thirty-six.'

'Thirty-six! My goodness, so young, yet so much time goes by. I was always so sad, you know, about Ani.'

Karina stalls. Annie? The only Annie she can think of is Marc Duplessis's daughter, Annette.

'I've never met her, but I think she's in South Africa,' she ventures.

'No, no,' says Vali, 'I'm talking about *Ani*.'

Is there someone she should know or remember, but doesn't? Surely her own mind must be at fault? She wonders what to say; her imagination remains blank. 'Mrs Shapiro, if you have time in the next few days, could I possibly come and see you?' she suggests. 'We're here until Monday.'

'It would be a pleasure. Come to my place. Why not tomorrow, about half past three? Is that good?'

'That's great. Thank you.' Karina scribbles down the directions that Vali gives her. Who is Annie?

Rohan whirls in at five thirty, plonks down his violin case and envelops Karina. 'I've missed you all day,' he says. 'Darling, I still can't believe it, I come back and you're here! Get this thing off.' He begins to unfasten Karina's belt.

'Ro, the weirdest—'

'My love, my darling, I want you right now. Take off those silly clothes! Nobody should make you wear clothes, you're so beautiful without them I can't bear it . . . come here . . .'

They stay in Sophia's bed until nearly seven, when Rohan goes as far as the kitchenette to open the bottle of wine he brought back with him. They settle against the pillows and sip. An image returns to Karina: Richard; wine in bed; singing. She begins to hum softly, Simon and Garfunkel.

'The Franck was a disaster,' Rohan says, ignoring the humming. 'How do you make the world's most insensitive pianist play a little more quietly? He hits all the right notes, but he bashes, and if I ask him to change anything he throws hissy fits.'

'Why are you playing with him, anyway?'

Rohan explains that they have the same agent, who's trying to do some musical matchmaking. But Karina's preoccupied. She can't understand why the mysterious Annie should cause her so much unease. Perhaps it isn't her; perhaps Vali Shapiro's marbles are as loose as Mimi's?

'Do you know anything about Vali Shapiro?' she asks. 'She was my father's nanny. I'm going to meet her tomorrow.'

'No, I've never heard the name. When are you going to see her? Because, you know, tomorrow we could go and look at that violin. It's the last day of the viewings before the sale. Fuck, my wrist hurts.'

'Try and rest it,' Karina urges, rubbing his arm. 'You've got to be on form.'

'Nice idea. I'll rest when I'm dead. Hungry, love?'

'Kind of.'

'There's just a little work I need to do. I have to go through some fingering, make sure I'm happy with what we did today, and we didn't get to the Duplessis . . . We could go out later?'

Rohan, tall and spindly, casts around the room for his underpants. How long did he spend here with Sophia? Probably not long, but long enough to know where to find the corkscrew. Karina pulls the duvet over her and picks up Pierre Vincente's book.

Two and a half hours later, Rohan puts down his violin and says, 'Cripes, is that the time? I'm sorry, I meant to stop ages ago. Darling, you must be starved. There's a good Chinese place round the corner. Shall we go there?'

Karina, though her stomach is rumbling, has been absorbed. Reading the book for the fourth time, she's looking not for what it includes, but for what's missing. Notably, a mention of anyone called Annie. Annette, yes: Duplessis's daughter. But by the time she was born, in Cape Town in 1948, Vali would have been in America for nine years. How could she have been close to Annette Duplessis?

Duplessis settled into his new life in Cape Town with ease. The city's small yet dedicated artistic community quickly took him to its heart. A real French composer, direct from Paris, he was soon snapped up by the music faculty of Cape Town University, where for the rest of his life he not only taught aspiring young composers, but became their mentor, role model and surrogate father. The climate he found congenial and the food superb for its freshness. Although he complained by letter from time to time about the cuisine's lack of sophistication, he was fascinated to discover many varieties of fish that, he remarked, had never been served at La Coupole. Kingklip was a favourite, and the local crayfish was a perpetual joy.

After only one term in his new job, Duplessis met a young music student named Shirley Cohn. One morning, he told me, he heard the sound of a piano drifting from a practice room in the music faculty and recognised, to his astonishment, one of his own piano études. He discovered that the pianist was an attractive young woman with nut-brown hair, dark eyes and the sweetest smile he had ever seen.

After a whirlwind romance, Shirley Cohn and Marc Duplessis were married, despite the scathing disapproval of her family, who disliked the idea of her marrying a man more than twenty years her senior and, moreover, a musician. Within the year Duplessis had become a father. His daughter Annette was his pride and joy, and the happy family's delight grew further when a son, Michael, was born two years later.

The casualty of so much happiness was, unfortunately, Duplessis's music. It has been said that a man must perfect either his life or his work, but both will be impossible; and with his life perfected almost by accident, the creative fire behind Duplessis's compositions began to go out. He struggled to fulfil a commission for a cello concerto for the university orchestra; the work was completed only three days before the premiere, the orchestra did not have enough time to rehearse the difficult score sufficiently, and the unlucky soloist virtually had to sight-read. The performance, predictably, was a disaster. Duplessis was not commissioned again in the city, although his professor continued to give him every support and his students never ceased to adore him.

The Duplessis family settled in Stellenbosch, in a villa overlooking a landscape of rolling hills covered in vineyards – many times Duplessis declared it the best of Burgundy and Provence rolled into one. There, he took up a new hobby of gardening, his compositions slowly forgotten.

'How peculiar,' Karina reflects in the Chinese restaurant, 'that he seems to have been too happy with life to compose, after all that.'

'If he was,' remarks Rohan. 'That book doesn't say what happened to him later.'

Vincente's book finishes with a last glimpse of Duplessis tending the proteas in his garden, Shirley serving fresh lemonade on the veranda, the children playing in the swimming pool. The back cover gives the date of Duplessis's death – 1961 – but not the cause. Karina is about to ask Rohan what more he knows, but before she can, he says, 'Oh, Karrie, you know that bit in the Forest Scene when . . .'

Julian is alone in the house in Lewes. How easy it would be to run back to Fairfallows, to the comfort of his mother's cooking and his father's grumbling. If they lectured him about Karina, at least that, too, would be comforting by dint of familiarity. What his father would say about Andy is another matter. Julian's worried: work is bound to leach away from the company after Andy's resignation. Whenever a politician says he won't resign, it means that pretty soon he will. Why the fuck does this have to happen *now*?

He sips a whisky in his armchair, listening to a Mozart piano concerto. Beautiful, but essentially unemotive stuff, he reckons. It's interesting to compare an historically-informed version on fortepiano and period-instrument orchestra against Daniel Barenboim's classic recording from the 1960s. He tries hard to like the fortepiano, but doesn't. Is that because he knows Karina would hate it? He stops the CD and, on impulse, takes off the shelf a disc of Schubert played by the St Francis Quartet. A disc that he certainly didn't buy.

So this fine fiddler is Karina's lover. He uses a powerful vibrato. He swoops up and down the strings as if he were in the nineteenth century. He sounds like Fritz bloody Kreisler. Julian finds the sexual impression evoked by the combination of intense vibration and slippery ease deeply disturbing. He switches off the CD. Perhaps he should go to the pub, if only to get away from the emptiness of the house.

The nearest pub, with low, beamed ceilings and a log fire in winter, is a five-minute stroll away up the hill. He's been going there for years. In the long vac from Cambridge, it had been a favourite hang-out for him with Hilary, Andy and their friends. It's a welcome refuge and tonight, as he approaches, he senses liveliness buzzing inside.

A collection of musical instrument cases alerts him to a bunch of extremely merry musicians from Glyndebourne's touring orchestra. Among them, his eye is caught by some bright hair and a pink crystal pendant glinting on a chain. Julian wanders over and says, '*Jó estét*, Éva!'

Ten minutes later, when he's bought a round of drinks for her and her three friends, Julian begins to wonder whether he could face comforting himself with another Hungarian violinist. Éva is more Hungarian than Karina ever was. She comes from Budapest, has read every biography of Kodály in English and Hungarian, and is a fount of information about the country and its history. She makes Karina seem like – well, a plain English girl from Twickenham.

'Are you at Glyndebourne much longer?' he asks her as the bell sounds for last orders. 'Fancy meeting up one evening? There's a lovely restaurant down in Polegate. I could take you there if you like. Saturday's good, if you're free.'

'That is so kind of you!' Éva twinkles at him. 'I like very much! And Julian, maybe you would like to come to something with me? There's this interesting guy speaking at the Meeting House on Saturday. It is at four, it should be over by half past five, and afterwards we could go to your restaurant?'

Julian looks down at the leaflet she's pressed into his hand. The crystal should have been a giveaway: Éva is a New Age acolyte. What is it, then? A spiritual guru? An astrology course? An environmental forum? It's none of these; but it is a familiar face. 'Bloody hell,' Julian says, staring at the name CHRISTOPHER FANNING. 'I was at school with this bloke. He was friendly with my brother, and my cousin had the most humungous crush on him. We used to come to this pub together twenty-five years ago. What's he doing?'

'Don't let her push you around, mate,' says one of the boys. 'Evie's hooked on this self-help crap.'

Chris's talk is entitled GET IT TOGETHER: HOW TO HEAL YOUR LIFE.

'He is extremely inspirational,' Éva enthuses, ignoring her friend. 'He speaks so well. It's practical advice, very sensible.'

'*You* need to heal your life?' Julian surveys Éva's svelte figure in her skinny jeans. 'Surely not?'

'Oh, but I do! Julian, my life is such a mess, you would not believe.'

'So's mine,' he tells her. 'You would not believe either. But, you know, it's not my scene, New Age lectures, and I wouldn't want to spoil it for you. Why don't I just pick you up afterwards?'

'Oh, but *Julian*!' Éva cries, 'Don't you see? It is such incredible coincidence that it must be more than this! You come to pub tonight; we are here; you once came here with Chris; and Chris speaks on Saturday, and this Saturday night the performance is opera that I don't play, so I'm free! You see, it is all *meant* that you find us today and you come to hear him. This is part of the great plan.'

'What great plan?'

'Everything in our life is preordained, even if we fight against it,' Éva insists. 'These coincidences are signposts on our path.'

'Oh, for heaven's sake,' Julian begins. Then he hesitates. He doesn't want to put Éva off the idea of having dinner with him.

'All right, then,' he says instead, smiling down at her. 'You've convinced me. I'll book the restaurant.'

'I will look forward,' Éva declares. Julian stops himself from saying that maybe he could help heal her life unaided. He'd love to go to bed with her; what man wouldn't? If only she was anything but a Hungarian violinist.

28

Karina takes the subway to Brooklyn. She follows Vali Shapiro's directions, past a park where beds of tulips and wallflowers are in full bloom, then uphill towards the street of brownstones where Vali lives. When she presses the bell, Vali's voice on the entry-phone says at once, '*Ha*llo, Karina Veres! Please come in.'

Across the hall, a tiny, white-haired woman is waiting to greet her. Karina walks over and shakes her hand, but Vali reaches out to kiss her on both cheeks.

'*So!*' She surveys Karina. 'Dini's daughter! I am so glad to see you here. You're very like your grandmother. Come in, please, come in.'

Vali's flat is full of Hungarian souvenirs. Painted vases top a wooden dresser in the kitchen, a folksy embroidered cloth is spread on the kitchen table and old family photographs on the wall show a country village, a flat, dusty landscape, children by a lake, women in headscarves.

'This was my husband,' Vali says, pointing at a photo in a silver frame. 'We had five happy decades together. Fifty years, Karina! I have been very lucky in my life, I have known real happiness. He is dead now, but not an hour goes by when I do not think of him.'

'He's handsome,' Karina remarks.

'He was indeed. He didn't approve of your grandmother, you know! We had to agree to differ. Come, my dear, I'll make you a *nice cup of tea*, isn't that what the British like?'

'Thank you.' Karina sits down at the table and watches Vali bustling by the stove, taking willow-patterned china cups down from a tidy shelf. She tries to imagine her as a young girl, pushing the infant Dénes in his pram through Central Park.

'This is so odd,' she confesses. She feels comfortable with Vali despite the weirdness of the occasion. 'He's never told me anything about you.'

'Aha,' Vali chuckles, 'but he's told me all about you! How talented you are. How like his mother.'

'I'm nothing like her, though, not really.'

'Oh, but you are, I can see. Your father was very upset about what became of your violin playing, my dear. He said you could have been a fine artist if you hadn't let the wrong people sway you.'

'The orchestra? He called them "Rottweilers".'

Vali laughs. 'Yes, but he thinks you should maybe not have tried to be in an orchestra, you weren't this kind of musician. You were too strong, too individual. It's unusual, he said, for such a young musician to get into such a good orchestra, straight out of college, so either you must have played too well, or someone fancied you, no?'

'You're fond of music?' Karina asks her.

'Yes, yes, I love music, though I don't know much about it. But what I know, my dear, I learned from your grandmother. Did she tell you about the time Professor Bartók came to dinner?'

'*Bartók?*'

'Ah, they knew everybody in New York then. I tell you, Karina, I answer the door and there is Professor Bartók, come to see his compatriot Mimi Rácz. Mr Duplessis turned so pale I thought he would faint!'

'He was there too?'

'Of course.' Vali's sparkly gaze bores into Karina's forehead. 'He had his own apartment uptown, but he didn't use it much. You did know that they really lived together, didn't you?'

'Not exactly.' Karina's heartbeat is speeding up. 'I knew he was in love with her, but . . .'

'I can see why you are like your grandmother. You live for love, no?'

Karina is so confused that she can scarcely get her words out. 'I live for . . . well, my son. My family.'

'But why were you looking for a job in an orchestra? Your father said it was so you could support some man you were in love with. A composer, he said, who wrote very bad music! Just like Mr Duplessis. Only people said his music was good, just a little out of date.'

'But . . .'

'And now you're here with a new boyfriend? I can see you glowing. Don't fool yourself, Karina. If you live for love, then do so. Be honest with yourself. Be strong. Most of us need to be reminded, sometimes, of how strong we are.'

'That's true. But please, tell me more about my grandmother and Duplessis.'

Vali sips her tea. 'With Mimi,' she begins, 'we lived in an incredible apartment in the Dakota building, beside Central Park. Everybody has lived in that building. More recently Leonard Bernstein and of course John Lennon. We had one of the smaller units, but it was more magnificent than anything I'd ever seen before. The living room was the size of this whole apartment. And outside, there were tennis-courts. I didn't care that I had to use the staff entrance, I just loved to be there. A long way from Szeged, my dear. Anyhow, Mr Duplessis basically lived there with us – he would stay more nights than not. And my fiancé told me I had to get away from your grandmother and Mr Duplessis, because he thought they were immoral and a bad influence. That was difficult, because I loved them both very dearly.

'In Hungary this would have been unthinkable: a married woman with her lover, no divorce, the children, one from each. It would have been a scandal; they'd have been ostracised, like devil-worshippers. Budapest, my dear, was not an advanced society that way. In New York, people gossiped, I don't know who believed what, because of course nobody told the truth, but the gossip was part of the glamour. Something to be expected from "Bohemians" and "artists" . . .'

'What did you say?' Karina interrupts. 'About children? Did you say one from each?'

'Indeed,' says Vali. 'Dénes, your father, was Tamás Veres's son. Then along came Ani.'

'What?'

'The sweetest baby, my dear. What an angel. Blue, blue eyes, always laughing.'

'Vali, are you saying that my grandmother *had another child*?'

'You didn't know?'

Karina's mouth opens but no sound comes out.

Vali gets up quickly from the table and turns to a cupboard, where she opens a door and rummages about. Karina can't see her face. 'I'm sorry,' Vali says. 'I thought you would know. It was a great tragedy. Of all the silly things that a talented, headstrong young woman could do in the 1940s, my dear, going back to Hungary was probably the silliest.'

Karina sits with her head in her hands, silent, while Vali tumbles some biscuits onto a plate. When Karina looks up, she sees tears gleaming in the cataract-pearled eyes.

'Are you sure,' Karina ventures, 'that – I mean – I don't know how to say this, but—'

'Was she real?' Vali smiles. 'Am I going senile? No, dear, let me show you something.' She glides out of the kitchen and returns a minute later with a dog-eared photograph. Karina takes it and gazes. Mimi; Marc Duplessis; her father, aged about six, holding the hand of a toddler. A little girl with enormous eyes the image of Duplessis's. She feels winded. Vali's hand presses hers, the liver-spotted skin as delicate as organza, but the fingers remarkably strong and warm.

'So they didn't tell you,' she remarks. 'Well, I'm not so surprised. Ani is not alive, you wouldn't have known her, and for your father it must be difficult.'

Karina blows her nose. 'But I've always been so close to my parents. I tell them everything. I don't understand why they've never told me about this.'

'The past can be hard to talk about, especially a trauma like your father's. Don't blame your grandmother for her fickleness, my dear. Mr Duplessis was a very good man. She was a young, vulnerable, passionate girl – she put her art first, it was the only way she could live. And he was so in love with her. When they first knew each other, Mr Duplessis bought her that violin. It was a real love-gift. He used all his savings on it; after she'd tried it out, he sent a friend to buy it in his place so that nobody official would know it was him. Of course she took it back to Hungary with her. I imagine the ÁVH would have grabbed it and had it sent to Moscow.'

'My partner, Rohan, is a violinist, and later this afternoon we're going to look at an Amati that's going to be auctioned, just in case it's Mimi's,' Karina tells her.

'It won't be, dear. You're wasting your time.'

'Rohan's desperate for a good instrument.'

'You see what I tell you? You're like your grandmother, you will do anything for someone you love. Of course, it wasn't just her. Mr Duplessis worshipped her. He followed her about like a big, gentle dog. When she was having the baby, he decided we should go to California and hide for half a year; he told everybody she had gone back to Budapest to see her husband, though why they believed him – if they did – God alone knows. She would have had to cross the ocean at the height of the war. But it was a more innocent time, you see, information was not so available as it is now, and America felt a safe distance from the horrors. He took good care of her, that I can promise. I am sure she loved him, but in the end one feels she used him terribly as well. Beautiful women have always trodden on men who are too devoted – and vice versa, if I may say so.

'Anyhow, when the war was over, Mimi decided overnight to go home to Hungary, and when they arrived in Paris, she took the children and left Mr Duplessis behind. He wanted to keep Ani, to bring her up in France, but Mimi would have none of it. She went to her husband, with this child from another man, and begged him to take them all back. I don't know what he had thought in the years between – probably he thought nothing, he just tried to stay alive – but he agreed. And Mr Duplessis missed that little girl so badly, I don't know how he could bear it. He used to write to me about her. My dear, I have three children and I couldn't bear to live without any of them, not for a moment! Now I have ten grandchildren and four great-grandchildren. I spend my life buying presents and sending cards. It's a wonderful thing, a large family.'

'But Vali, is that why Duplessis emigrated? To leave his history with Mimi behind?'

'I think that when he knew Mimi had taken Ani away for good, he felt there was nothing more for him in Europe. It is so sad, his story.'

'He did well in South Africa, though. He got married, he had a family, but he stopped composing, more or less. He was too happy.'

'Oh, that's what that silly biography says. What nonsense. Look how he died.'

'What?'

'So nobody tells you this either. Eiyiyi. Not the books, and the programme notes just spew up the books. Nobody likes the truth. Nobody likes to hold up a mirror, look into it and say: this is you and me, this is our world, a world we have created together. It's easier to deny everything than face the truth.'

'Did you see him again?'

'Never, my dear, but we kept writing. Perhaps he thought of me as a last link with Mimi. I've still got his letters. He describes his children so tenderly – they named their daughter Annette, almost after Ani, who was really Anna. Shirley was a sweet, sweet girl – I met her once when she came to America and we corresponded from time to time. He was very fortunate in her. But he was so damaged. Just imagine. First, there was the guilt, loving another man's wife in the lap of luxury in New York while Europe was in tatters. Then Mimi and the children leaving him. His music not being played – it wasn't avant-garde, it wasn't *cool*. And he'd seen what had become of Europe – the prejudice, the genocide. He dreamed of a better world where everyone would be equal and nobody would be judged by anything but their own natures and abilities. Then he ended up in South Africa. Living under another Nazi regime. Can you imagine? He thought he'd seen it all, Auschwitz, Belsen, Hiroshima. Then there's apartheid; and the massacre at Sharpeville. And he realised, I think, that this world can only grow worse. Losing Mimi, he lost his impetus to write music. Something pushed him into a real depression, beyond where Shirley could reach him. Somehow, he lost the will to live. Karina, you may read that he died of a rare blood cancer, but Marc Duplessis died, I think, of grief.'

'Oh my God.'

'Not that Shirley would ever accept that. We're the sum total, Karina, of our own stories. She wasn't going to let this notion become part of his, or her own. She made sure it was never written about. And by the time she died, nobody was interested in Marc Duplessis any more. No one plays his music now, except for the Suite.'

'Rohan's playing it in his recital.'

'Mr Duplessis used to grumble that it was played to death although it wasn't his best work. Eventually he didn't want to hear it any more, I think because it was so tied up with Mimi. He wrote it before he met her, when she was nothing but a golden girl on a stage, a Gypsy gone classical, playing like an angel, or maybe a devil. An ideal, unattainable, essentially his muse. At the end of his life, he couldn't cope with the piece any more, because it kept that first image of Mimi alive for him – as fresh and vivid as the day he dreamed it up. Wait, my dear, I have some letters from Duplessis. Perhaps you would like to see them. I go and get them . . .'

Karina breathes and tries to steady herself. 'Vali,' she asks, 'what became of the . . . their daughter?'

'Ah.' Vali pauses in the doorway, her expression clouded. 'My dear, this I think you must ask your father.'

Karina is late to meet Rohan. She texts him to say so, because when she leaves Vali's apartment her voice has dried up. Either she's talked too much, or she's getting sick, or she's in shock; possibly all three.

'Good Lord, what happened?' Rohan, pacing up and down on the pavement near the Lincoln Center, assesses her with one glance.

'It's a very, very long story,' she tells him, coughing.

'Darling, you'll have to tell me later because the viewing closes at six. Is that OK?'

Karina tries to catch up as he makes for the auction house entrance. She has no choice. This story will take all evening; it can wait. With the alacrity of a pointer at a kill, Rohan is striding through some sleek revolving doors and towards a receptionist, apologising for lateness and asking for the Fine Stringed Instruments viewing.

'Vali says we're wasting our time,' Karina tells him while they wait in the lobby.

'She would, wouldn't she?' says Rohan. 'None of them want to believe that that fiddle survived. Because if it did, it proves that they were responsible for losing it.'

'They lost much more, as it turns out.'

'Karrie?' Rohan looks at her, concerned, and takes her hand. She imagines Marc with Mimi. They were lovers; they had a child. What does that mean for her and Rohan? She has no more time to think: the auction house's stringed instrument expert, a Mr Stranin, is approaching to welcome them.

The viewing is in a reception room lined with photos of valuable Italian instruments and famous musicians playing them. The violins and violas waiting for auction are arrayed together on an antique wooden table, each bearing a label displaying its lot number. To one side, two Japanese businessmen are examining a viola with a magnifying glass.

'You're lucky, you've missed the hordes,' Mr Stranin tells them. 'So it's the Amati you're interested in? Here it is. Lot number 211. Nicolò Amati, 1671.'

Rohan bends over the table of violins as if it's a cradle, then lifts up the Amati as tenderly as he would a baby. Mr Stranin brings him a bow, the frog of which is still warm from the last violinist who's been in to try the instruments.

The Amati looks little different from the violins beside it – a Guarneri del Gesù, a Storioni and a Gagliano. The wood is exquisite, tawny in the evening sun, and Rohan, trying out Duplessis, closes his eyes and experiments with weight, power and softness. The sound blooms in their ears.

'It's in exceptionally fine condition and the reserve price is $400,000,' says Mr Stranin. Rohan stops playing, his face contorted with longing. Amati: loved ones, thinks Karina. Distant beloved, Beethoven's '*ferne Geliebte*'. A muse. An unattainable violin. It may be cheaper than a Stradivarius by at least two million dollars, but even so, the only way Rohan will be able to have it, or one like it, is if someone lends it to him, sponsors its purchase, arranges a crippling loan for him, or steals it.

'It's amazing. It's so easy to play. It has this marvellous resonance, and it's so even-toned. It's fantastic in every register.' Rohan gives a deep sigh. 'It reminds me of something I've played before, but I can't think what. Do you know much about its history?'

Mr Stranin hands him an auction catalogue printed with details of the instruments' provenances. Unless it's a fake – and judging from its sound, it probably isn't – this Amati's history has been meticulously documented. The list of owners' names doesn't include Francesco Avignola or Mimi Rácz. The owner from Budapest had been the leader of an orchestra before Mimi was born.

'It's not the one we hoped it might be,' Rohan admits. 'But, my God, it's wonderful.'

He walks to the far end of the room with the instrument and begins to play Bach, more to himself than to Karina. He stoops slightly as he plays; his eyes close and he's gone, deep in communion with the violin that rests on his shoulder, near his heart. Mr Stranin's eyebrows twitch upwards as he listens; he whispers to Karina to please remind him when Rohan's recital is.

On the way out, Karina takes Rohan's arm to comfort him.

'It's too bloody marvellous,' he mutters. 'I can't bear it.'

'There has to be a way for you to get a good instrument,' she says. 'Aren't there funding schemes, or special loans, or . . . ?'

'Darling, it's all I can do to manage my mortgage,' Rohan admits. 'I'd need to find a sponsor to buy the violin and lend it to me. And I doubt whether anybody would.'

'Why not? Someone who loves your playing. Someone who has the money, or access to it, and really believes in you . . .'

'The thing is, I'm not sixteen, I'm not a pretty girl, I'm not an Adonis, I've never won a competition, I'm too old to be young and too young to be distinguished, I lead a quartet that can't afford to commission World Music Fusion, and when I do play concertos nobody bothers to review them. How I play seems to be the last thing that concerns anyone.'

'Why don't we stop for a drink,' Karina suggests, 'and I'll tell you what happened today?'

'Let's go home and I'll cook you dinner while you tell me, how about that?'

On the subway travelling uptown, Karina stares at their feet side by side: hers a smallish 36 in trainers, Rohan's a hefty 44 in moccasins, like different species. '*Elle est le trésor de ma vie.*' She remembers the line, etched on the letter from the loft. The handwriting matches the Duplessis letters that Vali showed her. Now she understands: that letter was Marc writing to Mimi, asking her to send Ani to him. And the treasure of his life was not his lover, but his daughter.

Should she phone her father now? He's told her nothing before, and probably he'd make excuses, as usual. The cost of the call from New York, the time difference, a student arriving. No, the only way to make him tell her the truth is to be there and trap him. She'll wait until she next goes to Forest Road, when he won't be able to run away.

They climb the stairs to the flat. 'I know pasta with pesto is a cop-out,' Rohan remarks, 'but could you fancy it?'

Karina pours two glasses of wine; Rohan fills a pot with water, puts it on to boil, then looks hopefully towards the bed.

'Ro,' says Karina, 'come and sit down.' She takes both his hands and begins to explain her afternoon.

By the time the story is over, they're lying side by side on the bed, motionless. Rohan says nothing for several minutes, moved beyond words. Eventually he reaches out and embraces her.

'I never knew him,' he remarks. 'But I know so well what he must have felt for Mimi. I know exactly.'

'But they never told me. I can't believe it.'

'People are complicated. This is really complicated.'

'It sounds as if Shirley knew everything.'

'She'd have wanted to hush it up. In her family, it would have been a massive scandal if her husband had had an illegitimate child with another woman. She'd have had to keep shtumm. Karrie, what became of Ani?'

'I don't know,' Karina admits. 'She isn't alive, that's all Vali said . . . She told me I must ask my father. I didn't press her – it might sound strange, but I want *him* to tell me the truth.'

'That's not strange at all.' Rohan kisses her.

They're quiet for a long time. Outside the building, New York's roar swishes upwards through the blue-gold evening. 'We can make up for their mistakes and enjoy the love that they couldn't,' Rohan ventures. 'That's what it means for me. And you?'

'I'm frightened, Ro. There's so much I don't know, and it's so close to me. But when Mimi split herself in half, it doesn't seem to have bothered her as much as it bothers me.'

'Are you still split in half, Karrie? Hasn't the balance changed?'

'It doesn't change Jamie,' says Karina.

On the stove, there's a hiss and a splash as the pasta pot bubbles over. 'Let's eat,' says Rohan, turning away.

Life must go on; Rohan's concert is tomorrow, so he still has to practise tonight. Karina tries to pull herself back into the present. While he works through the centrifugal vortex that is the final episode of Ravel's *Tzigane*, she looks up news from home on Sophia's computer.

Andy Williamson, the headlines declare, is expected to resign soon. He's offered no excuses for his exploit. His wife has announced that she will stand by him. This junior transport minister, whom few people would have recognised before, is suddenly a household name. Columnists in every paper spit accusations: sleaze, corruption, the degeneracy of a government that's been too long in power. Could this, they cry, be the last straw for New Labour?

Julian rings; Karina takes her phone to the bathroom so that he can't hear Rohan practising. They have a stilted, artificial conversation about Jamie, who, it turns out, has stayed at school for the weekend.

'Why?' she asks.

Julian's tone sounds oddly keyed up. 'Because you're in New York and I've been busy today.' In Lewes, it's past one a.m. He doesn't elaborate.

'Have you spoken to Andy?'

'Yes, the idiot. If you have to have a mid-life crisis, you don't do it where the newspapers can see you.'

'So was he gay all along?'

'Possibly. I wouldn't know.'

'But why, Jules? Why did he do it, why now?'

'Why, indeed? Since you ask, it's because *you* left *me*. When you watch your oldest friend's nice, stable marriage suddenly disintegrate, it can make you question things you might never have questioned before. There aren't any certainties. We have to find a way to live with that.'

'Jules, you don't sound yourself. You sound – kind of high.'

'I went to a talk this afternoon, by a bloke who was pally with Hils at Elthingbourne. Chris Fanning, the one Lindy used to fancy. I'm not high, but I did realise there's no point being *low*. Don't forget to ring Jamie tomorrow, will you? Dear.'

'Goodnight,' says the puzzled Karina.

She lies awake while Rohan sleeps. Jet lag. Ani. Lies, cover-ups, books that omit facts instead of revealing them; traumas hidden for their pain; loves buried for their disgrace. She lets her head rest against Rohan's shoulder-blade. Maybe Vali's right. Maybe she does live for love.

In the morning they take the subway towards Fifth Avenue, then walk several blocks to the Frick Collection. Henry Clay Frick's mansion is an imitation of a French château, incongruous amid the hubbub, the skyscrapers and the skateboarders in Central Park across the road. Inside, it's busy yet tranquil; Karina is tempted to linger with the tourists around its treasure trove of Constable, Rembrandt, Ingres, Vermeer and rather a lot of Gainsborough portraits which, she thinks, show up the one at Fairfallows as rather less than the artist's finest work. She wonders whether it really is a Gainsborough. Perhaps that's why they guard it so closely; after all, if they were to have it valued for potential sale, they might discover that it isn't.

In the heart of the museum, a well-equipped lecture room hosts talks and concerts; recitals take place most Sunday afternoons. Nearby, a roofed-in courtyard encloses a fountain amid beds of azaleas, aquilegias and orchids in riotous bloom. If I were a New Yorker, Karina thinks, following Rohan through it towards the recital room, I'd come here, to the Garden Court, to escape.

'Patrick, this is my girlfriend, Karina,' Rohan says to the pianist who's showing off at the resident grand.

'Hey, Karina. Good to meet you.' He stands up and shakes her hand. Karina makes small-talk. Rohan warms up on his fiddle, his back turned. This performance could make or break his career in the US, depending on who turns up.

'Do you want to stay and listen?' Rohan encourages her. He's nervous, but trying not to show it. She sits halfway down the rows of seats. The programme is ambitious: Mozart, Franck and Debussy sonatas, the Duplessis suite, Ravel's *Tzigane* to end. The promoter had balked at the idea of including Rohan's own pieces. His violin sounds warm and sweet, as always, although its projection isn't up to that of the Amati he tried yesterday. When there's no sign of him stopping around one o'clock, Karina signals to him that she's going to go out. She wants to buy him a sandwich to make sure he remembers to eat.

Fifth Avenue is clogged with traffic, a few daring bicycles slaloming in between the cars and buses. A pedestrian light orders 'DON'T WALK'. Karina doesn't. Where to go? The Metropolitan Museum is a matter of blocks away; cafés galore dot the perpendicular streets; over the road, if she can ever get there, Central Park beckons with bright May blossoms, through which hundreds of New Yorkers are taking a Sunday stroll. She might find a take-out sandwich stall in the park. She fishes out her phone to check for texts or messages from Jamie while she waits for an opportunity to cross.

Then she looks up and sees a face.

That face.

No.

She's walking towards Fifth Avenue out of the park. She's wearing a pale blue skinny top and a denim skirt. Her hair is dyed brown, not black, and her blue eyes are frosted with silvery shadow. The cheekbones, high, balanced, Pre-Raphaelite. The lock of hair escaping from the pony-tail. The atmosphere about her skin, her irises and her clothes, silvery blue, grey and white. This is madness. Lindy is dead.

'Lindy?' Karina says aloud. The woman walks at the same brisk speed as Lindy, wears similar clothes, has an identical expression. She doesn't turn at Karina's call; maybe she can't hear her. Perhaps Karina has imagined it – the syndrome by which we see everywhere people who resemble too closely the person we miss.

'Lindy!' shouts Karina, stepping out into Fifth Avenue.

There's an impact, the street jumping up sideways, brakes slamming, a crunch of metal. She's on the ground, winded, a blunt pain pressing into her head. Feet surround her, and some knees. A hand takes her wrist, pressing her pulse. In front of her, she can see two slender wheels, one of them buckled. She squints down at her dark cotton jumper and trousers. Splinters of glass are spattered over her hand – her watch has smashed on the road. Her mobile phone lies beside her in several pieces. There's a long mark down her left side and, on her hip, the dusty imprint of a thin tyre. She can't work out how she got there.

'Can you hear me?' a voice demands. 'What's your name? Can you hear me?'

'I'm Karina,' she manages to say. 'Yes, I can hear you.'

'Are you hurt, Karina? Show me where you're hurt.'

Karina touches her head and her hip. To one side, the unfortunate cyclist, distressed, is being accosted by a policeman. He's not only knocked Karina down, he's also caused a pile-up of cars; hence the metallic scrunch. 'But she just walked right out in front of me,' he's protesting.

'Can you stand up?' asks Karina's rescuer, whom she registers is another policeman.

'Yes, I think so. I'm just a bit shocked, I guess . . .'

'Ma'am, the ambulance will be here momentarily to get you to hospital. Do you have insurance?'

'I'm British. But please, no, I don't need to go to hospital.' Things are rushing back to her. Rohan. If she's in hospital, she won't be at his concert. How can she tell him on such a vital day that she's been knocked down by a bicycle on Fifth Avenue just because she imagined she'd seen somebody who's been dead for nearly a year?

'I think you ought to, ma'am,' the policeman warns her. 'That's a nasty bump on your head. Can you walk?'

Karina swims to her feet. There's a pounding sensation right through her, as if she's lying under a kettledrum. Her legs are quivering and the bicycle bruise throbs. 'I'm fine,' she says.

'You feel sick or giddy or you start thinking you're going to pass out, you go straight to hospital,' the policeman warns. 'I don't like this, ma'am, I don't like to see you risk your health this way.'

Karina can't believe she's hearing the voice she hears next.

'Officer, I've got first-aid training, and we know each other. I'll look after her.' Lindy: cool and unperturbed, as natural as the grass beyond the gate. 'Hi, Karrie.'

'May I take your name, lady?' the officer says.

'Caroline Birch,' says Lindy. 'I'm a playwright. I live in the East Village.'

The touch of Lindy's hand on her elbow. Blue eyes, flecked with slate grey. 'What—?' says Karina.

'Come on, Karrie. Taxi!'

A second later Lindy has bundled her into a cab and they're heading downtown.

29

'Keep still.' Lindy dabs Karina's grazes with pink antiseptic wash.

'What's going on?' Karina asks again. She's said nothing else since leaving Fifth Avenue. Lindy hasn't replied, although she pointed out the sights of the city as they drove past. Without talking, she's led Karina up into a compact, book-lined apartment overlooking a courtyard.

Once she's cleaned Karina's cuts, she makes her a cup of tea. 'Two sugars, for the shock,' she says. Taking the mug, Karina begins to cry.

'Lindy? Are you real?'

'I could ask you the same thing. What are you doing in New York, throwing yourself under bicycles?'

'Lin—'

'My name's Caroline,' Lindy interrupts. 'My boyfriend calls me Caro.'

'Your name's Lindy, it always was and it always will be.'

'No. I'll show you.' Lindy dashes to the desk and, from a drawer, retrieves an American passport. Karina opens it. Inside, there's a photo of Lindy that Karina remembers being taken in a booth at Camden Town station. The name reads CAROLINE ELIZABETH BIRCH.

'How did you get that?'

'Friends. Contacts. It was easy. It cost a fortune, but it wasn't hard, once I'd made up my mind. The difficult bit was deciding.'

'But that's a false passport!'

'No, it's *my* passport. Issued legally by the USA. I have my social security card, my birth certificate, my green card, my driving licence, a credit card or two, and I pay American taxes in my name, which is Caroline Birch.'

'I don't understand.'

'OK.' Lindy sits down beside her. 'Let's get this straight. In case you hadn't noticed, I'm not dead. I decided to make myself a new life. Thanks to the train crash, I did it a little more dramatically than I intended.'

The fences around Karina's mind are in flames.

'Shh.' Lindy holds out her arms. Karina falls onto her shoulder, shaking. 'There, there. It's OK.'

Glancing up through what feels like a lake of salt water, Karina feels half her usual weight. She could rise up to the ceiling and hover there. 'But we cremated you almost a year ago.'

'Sorry,' says Lindy. 'Don't tell me what's happening in London, I don't want to know.'

'God, Lin, don't be heartless! There's nobody who loved you who hasn't been to hell and back. Do you have *no notion* of what you've done?'

'Like I said, I don't want to know.'

'Your parents have broken up and sold the house. Your father's obsessed with getting compensation for the crash victims. Charles is taking early retirement, Hilary's in hospital again. And Jamie keeps saying you're going to come back.'

'Clever boy.' Lindy shrugs. 'I miss Jamie a lot. I miss my mother a little and my father not at all. They should have broken up years ago. Charles is a wanker and Hilary should have been strangled at birth. Here, Karrie, let's see that leg.'

She winces when Lindy tries to rub in some arnica ointment. 'It hurts too much.'

'Try some tablets instead. They're homeopathic and they really work. Here. Now, since you insist on telling me what's happened, tell me more?'

'Lindy, you've nearly brought down the government.'

Lindy stares in astonishment into Karina's face, then begins to laugh. Soon Karina too is collapsing with laughter, and together they're the same as they ever were, and Karina's tears and helium lightness mingle into a flying sensation that might be incipient concussion but might also be mad, pure joy.

'I can't believe it! Oh, Lin, how? Why? I can't believe it . . .'

'Just tell me why I nearly brought down the government!'

'Look – oh heck, I should explain, Jules and I are in trouble – it's my fault, I fell in love with someone else and that's why I'm in New York, I'm with him – and I think if you hadn't died – if I hadn't thought you were dead – I'd never have done what I did, because I wouldn't have taken the risk . . . anyway, Jules told Andy Williamson, and Andy had a kind of mid-life crisis and went to a gay nightclub. Now it's in all the papers, and everyone's saying it's going to spell electoral disaster!'

'Oh, yeah, right, all my fault. Poor bugger, though, I feel sorry for him. These things come out of the blue. One minute you're fine being the you that everyone thinks you are, and the next – you just can't hack it any more.'

'That's what happened to you?'

'You bet.'

'I could hit you, you know.'

'Go on then,' says Lindy. 'Hit me. It won't change anything.'

'I can't. I'm too glad to see you.'

Karina glances around the room. The largest bookcase holds a complete set of Shakespeare and studies of Arthur Miller, Tennesee Williams and John Osborne. On the walls hang posters from Broadway productions. Through the kitchen doorway, she spots a coffee machine rather more sophisticated than the one Lindy had in London. This looks like an apartment where someone has lived for a good while – not a runaway with false papers, and not necessarily Lindy.

'It's my boyfriend's place,' Lindy says. 'I moved in a month ago. His name's David and he's a theatre director. Those are his shows.' She waves a hand at the posters. 'Are you OK? Do you want a blanket?'

Karina, still shivering with shock, lets Lindy wrap her in a blue mohair rug. She gazes at Lindy's silhouette. 'Tell me everything,' she demands. 'From the beginning.'

Lindy settles in the armchair opposite, gives Karina a shrewd gaze and takes a breath. 'OK,' she says. 'Here goes.

'I had to decide very fast. It was in my mind already, because when bloody Charles came to *Distant Beloved* with his wifey and kiddies I felt as if I might as well not exist. I began to imagine disappearing in earnest. I know being hopping mad isn't a reason to make people think you're dead. But it planted a seed. Disappearing. Airlifting yourself out of all your problems. The night before the train crash, I went out with Alban and got very upset and very drunk, so he took me back to his place and I slept in the spare room. In the morning I tried to go to work by train, and if I'd got there ten minutes earlier I really would have been in the crash. So, the line was down, there was smoke everywhere and while I was wondering what to do, I remembered hearing about people staging their own deaths in accidents or terrorist attacks, letting people think they'd been killed, grabbing the chance to start over.

'I was about to take a bus to Camden instead, but there were such crowds – and I remembered how you couldn't get on the bus that day. Then neither could I. I found I was walking back to Alban's place and I knew I wasn't going to go to work, not that day and not ever. We'd been talking, as it happened, about how people disappear. Do you remember, after the *Distant Beloved* premiere, you found me on the phone upstairs? I was talking to Alban then. Christ, Karrie, I was bloody miserable. We discussed it later that same night. He made some calls, then told me what they could do and what it would cost. I'd thought about just vanishing, picking up and going, though not about making out I was dead. Alban told me I had to be sure I could be consistent in a whole new identity.'

'So Alban deals with false passports, identity fraud and suchlike?'

'Sometimes.'

'How could you be friends with someone like that?'

'He's not a bad guy. He helped me.'

'I don't call that "helping".'

'Do you want to know what happened or don't you? What really did it was when my mother decided that that body was me.'

'You mean you were sitting in Alban's flat *the whole time*?'

'More or less. There were pictures in the paper, so I kept a low profile. I went out a few times in a burka so that nobody would spot me. That was an experience – someone called me a terrorist, and I couldn't work out how to drink my tea. Well, Mummy thought the body was mine, and she got a death certificate and planned that silly service.'

'You knew about that?'

'Of course. Eventually the papers arrived and all I had to do was head for the airport and pray. Smooth as silk. It was easy, Karrie.'

'But that's impossible! This is America!'

'Exactly. They've got all these systems, biometric this and that, but here's what I think: first they're looking for shifty Arabic students with beards, carrying the Koran and a Kalashnikov; next, they're looking for people who have nothing and speak only Spanish; after that, people who have too much and speak only Russian. What they're *not* looking for is a nice white girl called Caroline Birch who was born in the States, grew up in Britain and turns up to go home with a posh accent and all her papers in order.'

Lindy dives over to a cupboard and brings out a birth certificate. Caroline Elizabeth Birch, born in West Hollywood 1970, parents Harrison P. Birch, civil engineer, and Mary S. Birch née Wilde, housewife. 'Not that I've ever had to show this, but I quite enjoyed being the daughter of Mary Silvia Birch, born Wilde. It's such a totally made-up name and nobody batted an eyelid.'

'But—?'

'What next? I checked into the YMCA, then I found a place in Harlem with some girls who were advertising for a room-mate. They were great. I was just Caro, fresh out of London, looking for a job. We had a lot of fun – they loved Ubiquitous Bean Stew. I took my green card to a few bookshops. I worked in one for six months and then my favourite second-hand shop in Greenwich Village had a vacancy, and I applied, so now I work there four days a week and write on the other three. It's great. I've got a new life.'

'You've lied your way into it.'

'Nonsense. I might have a fake reference, but I've plenty of genuine experience. Problem there was none.'

'But how can you stand it?'

'Stand it? I love it! I'm free. What did I have to lose? I was fed up. My love-life was going nowhere, my job was going nowhere, my plays were going nowhere *fast*, my father was a sleazy bastard, my mother was a silly flapper putting up with him, and all I wanted was not to be like her or, worse, like both of them, especially when I know I'm bloody not. The only thing I didn't want to leave was Jamie.'

'What about me?' Karina says. 'What was I? Collateral damage? Best friend badly wounded, oops, sorry, couldn't help it? Why couldn't you have made yourself a new life without deciding everyone should think you'd been killed?'

'Once my mother identified that body, there was no going back.'

'Of course there was. You could have told her she'd got it wrong. Someone might be looking for that body. Someone will never know it was their daughter.'

'It wasn't my fault if my mother decided someone else was me. Shows how well she knew me. Anyhow, if you disappear without people thinking you're dead, they think you're alive, so they look for you. I don't have to hide. I can walk around New York and work in a bookshop, because nobody thinks I'm here. I've never met anyone who knew me from before. Yes, I could have come back, but I don't want to. My life is my own and I take responsibility for it. I'm sorry if people are upset. But maybe it's made my mother get her act together. And I've met this lovely man, who's not only a knockout in the sack, but he's going to stage my first real play. He's an experienced director and he genuinely likes it. He wouldn't do it otherwise. I don't count *Distant* fucking *Beloved*. It was complete crap.'

'We're recording it,' Karina tells her. 'Charles organised it. It's a memorial to you.'

'Christ, get it stopped. I don't want it. I disown the whole thing.'

'You can't. You're dead,' Karina points out. 'What's the new one about?'

'Funnily enough, it's about a young woman's efforts to come to terms with parents she can't stand. It's called *Life Without Mother*.'

Karina notices a clock on the desk: it's four thirty.

'Lin, I'm late for something. Can I use your phone? Mine's bust.'

Lindy passes it to her. Karina quickly punches in Rohan's number, but his voicemail is on. It's only half an hour until he's on stage; he should be warming up by now. Supposing he's gone out to look for her? Supposing someone saw the accident and told him and he's scouring the hospitals? 'Ro,' she says to the voicemail, 'it's me. It's a long story and my phone's broken, but I'm fine and I'll see you later. Don't worry. Go and play your concert. I'll get there as soon as I can.' She looks down at Lindy's phone: its number is emblazoned in a frame in the middle of the receiver. She commits it quickly to memory.

'So, tell me more,' says Lindy, when Karina rings off. 'This guy sounds interesting.'

Karina explains Rohan.

'And it's a big love-thang? Are you happy?'

'Not exactly,' Karina admits, 'but I feel alive. I'm learning who I am at last – he's made me want to discover all kinds of things that I never knew about my background, and about myself. He's wonderful. He's helped me so much. I hope I can help him too.'

'Good. He's making you do something for yourself, not just for other people.'

'There's such a thing as being too selfish,' Karina points out, acid.

'There's also such a thing as being too unselfish. Letting people use you, because everyone knows you'll do anything to prove how unselfish you are. That's the most profound form of selfishness.'

'What's that supposed to mean?'

'Don't accuse me of being selfish when everybody's in a mess that would never have happened if you'd been a little more selfish sooner.'

'I don't know what you're talking about.' Karina's head is hurting in earnest. Julian, abandoned in Lewes. Jamie, abandoned in school. Rohan. 'I have to get back to the Frick,' she adds. 'Rohan's on in fifteen minutes.'

'You won't make it in fifteen. You might make the second half. Are you well enough?'

'Yes. Listen, can we meet tomorrow? Our plane doesn't go till the evening.'

Lindy drinks tea, silent. Karina's gaze travels over the Broadway posters.

'No,' says Lindy.

'What?'

'No means no. I don't want my old life. I want this one.'

Now Karina understands, and it's worse than she thought. 'Lin, surely you don't expect me not to tell your mother that you're alive?'

'You breathe one word of my existence, Karrie, and there'll be trouble.'

Karina is briefly speechless. Concussion, fright, shock, she doesn't know why, but she's never felt so angry in her life. 'And what would you do? Set Alban's mates on me? You'd have to call him to do that, and he's your old life too. You can't get away from it – you're still you, whether you like it or not. You can't expect me not to tell your parents and you can't expect me not to tell you to come home!'

'This *is* home. I'm not goin' nowhere.'

'But how can you live with yourself?'

'Very easily. God, I need a drink. Do you want one?' Lindy dumps her cup in the sink and takes an open bottle of white wine out of the fridge.

'I have to go,' says Karina. A trapdoor within her has slammed shut.

'Karrie, listen.' Lindy puts the wine aside, sits down and takes her hand. 'Do you remember telling me about the dreams you had when we were kids? About flying through the stars, feeling you were plummeting back to earth before you woke up?'

'What about it?'

'The night I knew my mother had decided I was dead, Alban and I went for a drive into the countryside. There was a freak meteor shower, the weather was clear and we wanted to watch it from somewhere dark. We lay in a field. And when I saw all those shooting stars, flaming across the sky and burning themselves out, I felt that way too, as if I was up among them, flying. It's natural to move, Karrie. It's natural to go from one part of the sky to another. What's unnatural is to stay still. There's only one thing worse than the prospect of total change, and that's the prospect of no change.'

'I understand perfectly,' says Karina. 'Now I have to go.'

'Let me come with you,' Lindy protests. 'You're not well.'

'Lindy, you may be able to cope with this, but I can't.'

'Karrie, wait.' Lindy grasps both her hands. 'Don't you see?

You're trying to find out who you are, but you're looking in the wrong place. You're not your family! You have to break away from the past because it only stifles you with limits that aren't yours. You have to look forward, not back. I hated my family for long enough. Now I can say: this is *me*. And if you have a problem with that, Karrie, that's tough, because I'm happy, I'm building a life and my play is going to be on bloody Broadway.'

'I have to go,' says Karina, disengaged, casting around for her things.

Lindy gazes at her, shrewd. 'Do you suppose,' she says, 'that maybe it would be better if I really were dead?'

Karina jumps up, grabs her bag and makes for the door without looking back.

Outside, before Lindy can come after her, she spots a bus pulling in at a nearby stop and hurries aboard.

'Fifth Avenue?' she asks. 'The Frick Collection?'

'You OK, lady?' the driver asks her, staring at her bruised forehead. She explains; he shakes his head and makes derogatory remarks about cyclists. 'I'll tell you which stop,' he promises. She slumps into the nearest seat.

One half of New York has been to lunch with the other half and is now driving home. The bus crawls; time ticks by; Rohan's recital will be well underway. She's in a shipwreck, hanging on to driftwood while the vessel breaks apart. Is Lindy right? Would it have been better if she had been dead? Although she's alive, she's not the Lindy that Karina knew. This Lindy has betrayed everybody, without remorse. Yet the Frick, bizarrely, is exactly where it stood that morning, on a Fifth Avenue that has knocked over far more than merely Karina's body. 'Here we go,' calls the driver. 'Frick Collection.'

'Thanks.' Karina's head hammers. She gives the driver a bright smile and takes the steps carefully.

The violin and piano echo through the gallery, the last movement of the Duplessis Suite; she's missed almost everything. But, thank God, he's playing. She slides in during the applause after the Duplessis. Most seats are taken, but she spots an empty chair at the side. Rohan's eyes meet hers from the stage; a quick warmth flashes through them. She thinks of Duplessis's music, the minstrel.

Who are you? he whispers. What do you expect of me, of everyone else, and of yourself?

Rohan's bow circles towards the strings and out fly the first declamatory notes of Ravel's *Tzigane*. He closes his eyes, losing himself as Ravel's fantasy Gypsy casts a hypnotic spell, then summons the piano to attention and begins to build that mesmeric vortex, whirling faster and faster towards cataclysm. Karina is transfixed: she's never seen Rohan play like this, with the white-hot compulsion of a possessed shamanic medium. And she recognises something she has never let herself admit: if Rohan belongs to anyone or anything, it's the violin. This passion is all-encompassing; if there's nothing of him left for her, why should that be so strange?

She watches him, her mind splintering. Rohan on the train, begging for her number; in her kitchen, hands bloodied with cherry juice; kissing her for the first time in the Budapest burger bar. But this extreme, all-giving Rohan is his essence; everything else, the easy-going smile, the sweet, dopey enthusiasm, is just a veneer. Not only can she not tame this; she shouldn't even try. Her head throbs and her grazes sting as if he's poured salt over them. With the violin in his hand, Rohan is the wanderer who longs to strike out for the ends of the musical earth, and whose relationships with Sophia, the dog-owning flautist and goodness knows how many other women must trail behind the demon that tells him to keep playing or die. No wonder he wants the Amati. And he does. He really does.

She's going through the motions again. Gauging the applause, hearing the encore as if from a great distance, then, when the throngs get up to leave, making her way backstage, finding him drenched in sweat, exhausted and relieved to see her. 'Darling! My God, what happened to you?' In his generous, trusting embrace, she almost forgets her decision.

He's soon introducing her to people: an agent, a critic, the gallery's concert manager. The sea rolls over her driftwood.

'Ro,' she says, 'I'm not feeling fantastic. I fell over on Fifth Avenue, it's all my own fault. I'll tell you later. I need to go and lie down – do you mind?'

Rohan kisses the bump on her head. 'I'll be back soon,' he whispers. 'Love you.'

'Love you too,' says Karina, without looking at him. A few moments later she's out in the bright spring evening with the streets and skyscrapers of New York thrumming around her.

She has just enough cash for the two journeys she needs to make. First, back to the flat to make some calls, pack her case and swallow some pills. Then to the airport.

30

The overnight flight lands at Heathrow at dawn. An ill-advised combination of a stiff drink and more painkillers had knocked Karina into merciful semi-consciousness an hour after take-off and she'd slept, or at least dozed, all the way to London. She imagines Rohan in Sophia's flat, violin case over his shoulder, reading her note; Lindy, asleep in the East Village, her body entwined with that of the lover who calls her Caro; Vali in Brooklyn, talking to her dead husband's photograph; Marc Duplessis's letters lying, dust-coated, in their boxes.

Her head thudding, Karina somnambulates through passport control, the baggage hall and customs. It's only when she sees her mother waiting for her that she notices the lights above them spinning in ellipses and realises just how ill she feels.

'You silly girl.' Dénes sits on the edge of Karina's childhood bed. 'You get knocked down, you don't go to hospital, you leave your lovely boyfriend high and dry, you fly three thousand miles and then you wonder why you collapse! I tell you, Karina, you are neck in pain.'

'Dad, I'm ill.'

'Concussion! You come home to us with concussion!'

'I need to call Jamie. He's been at school all weekend. He's not used to it.'

'That boy is staying where he is until you're well enough to take care of him. You wait here until you knock some sense into that knocked head.'

'I have to call him. He'll be trying to call my mobile and it's bust.'

'Don't worry about silly things. I have spare phone. All my old phones are here, they all work. I give you phone.'

Karina smiles – her father, who claims to hate 'stuff', hoards ancient mobiles and SIM cards to give his students. 'I bring you,' he says, pacing out. He returns with a battered handset, pressing buttons to set it up. 'Here. Is your phone now. I will organise for you.'

'Thanks, Dad. I don't think I could have worked it out myself today.'

'Nor you should. You sleep now, Karrie, I must go and teach.'

'Dad, wait. I have to tell you, I saw Vali.'

Dénes freezes. 'Yes?'

'I need to ask you things.'

'What you need to ask me, Karina? What goes on?'

'Everything. I want to know how you got out of Hungary.'

'You never wanted to know before.'

'You never told me.'

'So, OK, I tell you. But first you must rest. You've been very sick, you've had a silly journey and my pupil arrives any moment now. Karina, listen, this is a long and serious story. I'm not willing to do it in three stupid minutes.'

'Dad, I want to know what happened to Ani.'

Dénes pauses; then reaches out a fine-fingered hand and strokes her hair. 'When you're feeling better, I tell you about my sister,' he says simply.

Karina, lying back and trying to control her nausea, knows he's stalling as she'd anticipated – but a ring on the doorbell proves he's telling the truth, which is more than she's told them. She hasn't breathed a word about Lindy or why she really ran away from New York.

Lindy, alive? Not death, but betrayal? Karina's spinning head swirls images together: Cynthia, ravaged by grief, Martin speaking like an automaton on the TV about the daughter he hadn't appreciated, Jamie by the window chanting, the empty Rookery, the silver watch on the desk. All that; yet Lindy's been in New York the whole time, living with a director and staging her play under an assumed name? Karina moans aloud. How could Lindy do such a thing to both their families and, ultimately, to her? This was her best friend?

Karina takes Dénes's old mobile phone and calls Lindy's number, which she's branded into her brain. An answering machine kicks in, giving 'Caro's' mobile number. She scribbles it down, programmes it into the phone and texts: 'LINDY, COME HOME. K.' She lies down and waits. There's silence, but for Dénes's student playing Elgar downstairs.

Erzsébet appears in the doorway, with a cup of peppermint tea. 'It is good for settling the stomach,' she says.

How would she have managed without her mother? Calm, dignified, loving; if only she could have been like her, instead of the volatile Mimi. If only she could tell her the truth. If she were to tell everyone that Lindy is alive, the girl would have no choice but to come back. But would it do even more damage to break the news like that? To shatter illusions built out of other illusions that were already shattered? She sips her tea and fights herself. 'I feel like I'm ten years old again,' she says.

Erzsébet sits on the bed and smiles down at her, just as she used to when Karina was small. 'When I was your age, it was more than two decades since I last saw my parents,' she says. 'We had to grow up very, very fast. You know, I talk to my pupils' parents and they tell me young people maybe have things too easy now. Maybe you did, Schnooky, but we wanted that for you. We didn't want you ever to have experiences like ours. I don't believe we were wrong.'

'I can't imagine what it must have been like,' Karina says, 'and I know I can't compare anything in my life to what you went through. But . . .'

'What happened in New York, Schnooky? There's something, isn't there? Something that shocked you.'

'Maybe it was all a bad dream.' Karina shuts her eyes. She can't take bright light.

'Those bruises are real. What happened over there?'

'Mum, it's a very long story. I need to feel up to it before I explain.'

'I understand. In your good time, no? Now, drink your tea and try to rest.' Erzsébet slips out and closes the door.

Karina turns off the lamp and burrows under the duvet. Her head feels like fresh-cut raw meat and the lack of Rohan is a tearing, physical ache in her chest. What if she's wrong? 'Darling,

I understand. I'm going home,' she'd written. But where is home? She's left Julian, she's left Rohan, and regressing to childhood in Forest Road isn't going to solve anything. And now, the grief over Lindy. So many lives turned upside down – for what? Her death may have been devastating; her resurrection feels infinitely worse.

Early in the morning, the house phone gives a shrill ring. Karina listens to her mother answering: 'Yes, she is here; yes, she's kind of OK; I will call her.' A moment later Erzsébet looks round the door and hands her a receiver.

'Ro?' says Karina into the phone.

'Karrie, what's going on? I'm at Gatwick, I want to come and get you.' He sounds exhausted and lonely. 'It took me an hour to track down someone who knew your father and had his number.'

'Ro,' says Karina, 'it's over.'

'No, Karrie, you can't do that. You can't just walk out on me and say "it's over".'

'You don't want me, you want Mimi's Amati and I'm only a way to get to it, assuming it even exists. That's not enough.'

'Karrie, that's insane. I love you. I thought you loved me.'

'I do. But . . .'

'Was it the old Hungarian lady? What other stories did she tell you?'

'Ro, I'm ill. I've got a touch of concussion. I'll be down in a day or two to get my things.'

'And then what? Home to Julian?'

'I don't know. I don't know anything any more.'

'Darling, please let me come and get you. I can't bear the idea that you're sitting there suffering and I can't reach you.'

Karina, struggling, can't speak for a minute. The words 'Lindy's alive' hover, unspoken, on her tongue. 'I just need,' she says eventually, 'a little time.'

The sound of the cello downstairs breaks off and Karina hears her father's steps coming towards her room. He's carrying a CD and the kitchen ghetto blaster.

'Karrie, I want you to hear something,' he says softly. 'It's boring for you listening to me teach, so here, you play this.'

'What is it?'

'Bartók, the *Cantata Profana*. It's based on a Romanian folktale. I tell you story. It is of nine enchanted stags. The nine sons of a hunter are raised to roam free, becoming great hunters themselves in the dark forests. Gradually they are transformed into stags, the very creature they have been hunting. Their father tries to shoot them until they tell him who they are. Then he says that their mother mourns them and they must please come home. But now they reply: they can't get in through the door because their antlers are too wide. They can't go home, because they have become something new. It is how people hunt their true selves, find them and grow into them, and then they can't go back. Bartók had a special place in his heart for this piece, Karrie. It's about exile, but also about transformation in the soul. Now, you listen.'

He leaves Karina alone with the disc. Downstairs, the cello begins again. Karina pictures her father as a child in New York: a wide-eyed boy rather like Jamie, looking round a door, watching his mother and Bartók play music together. She plugs in the machine, puts on the CD and lets Bartók's clashing harmonies and intertwining Hungarian voices carry her into the shadows of Mimi's forests, stalking the stags.

Dénes's teaching runs into the evening. Each lesson is supposed to be an hour long, but that hour usually becomes two, sometimes three, powered by caffeine, Erzsébet's baking and off-cello discussions ranging from the price of rehairing bows to the misleading lines drawn in society between the immoral and the illegal. 'Where else kids are going to learn to think?' Dénes demands when Erzsébet protests at the time he spends on such matters. 'Music is not only sound, music is spirit and philosophy and humanity. If I don't teach them, they learn nothing from anyone else. They just watch stupid TV and deafen themselves with headbang pop noise on their iPods. That's what freedom's for? I tell you, Erzsi, it's crap!'

Finally, the front door closes at eight o'clock. Karina has scarcely ventured out of bed all day. Through her window, she glimpses the student ambling away, cello case on his back. She pulls on a dressing-gown that belongs to her mother and pads downstairs, where she finds Erzsébet cooking dinner.

'Karrie, you listen to disc?' Dénes demands.

'Yes. It's incredible.'

'Good. So you understand. And now I am going to tell you another story. It's time the cat stopped tiptoeing around the hot porridge. Come and sit down, Schnooky.'

He pours a glass of wine for each of them, then pats the sofa next to him. He's tired and sweaty – he puts as much energy into teaching as he would into a recital. 'Achhh, that's good!' He takes a long draught. 'What a glorious invention is wine! So now, my child. You want to know? I tell you. Where you want me to start?'

'At the beginning. With Ani.'

'But Ani was not the beginning.'

She was his sister – nothing more, nothing less. She was born in America; she'd be American, which troubled him at the time because he couldn't imagine how it would feel to be anything but Hungarian. New York was a giant playground, especially Central Park; every day was an adventure. School, when it began, was glorious and all in English. Still, he would declare, 'I am Hungarian boy from Budapest,' and swell with pride at the thought of a city he couldn't remember. His mother and Vali spoke Hungarian at home, so he and Ani did too; sometimes his schoolmates teased him about his accent. He vaguely knew that Uncle Marc was French. He didn't know why other kids lived with mothers and fathers, but he lived with a mother and occasionally an uncle. He didn't tell anybody about that.

Staring into the pram at the tiny pink creature with blue eyes and open, squalling mouth, trying to get used to having a sister – that took some doing and he'd needed to pull himself together. He hadn't known what was going on beforehand, just that they'd been in California for six months and he'd played on the beach while his mother got fatter and fatter and wore voluminous dresses to hide the bulge. Uncle Marc helped him through, holding his hand almost all the way back to New York on the train. He hadn't known that they lived through those months partly on the money his mother had been saving and partly on what Marc could make by giving piano lessons instead of composing.

Had he missed him? Would he have missed his right arm? He

might have been Uncle Marc, not Papa, but he taught Dénes to play ball, to read music, to get a grip on his emotions, to share, to let his little sister join his games and eat his ice-creams. Dénes remembered running the length of the thirty-foot living room to leap into his arms, seeing how much momentum he could build up over that distance, because Uncle Marc was as big as a tree and it would surely be impossible to knock him over.

He hadn't understood why they were leaving New York – he wasn't sure that his mother or Marc understood either – but the boat had been tremendous fun. He and Ani played on the deck all day long, enjoying the dipping and plunging of the water. One afternoon there'd been a fancy-dress party for all the children on board and Mimi and Marc had improvised costumes for them. He'd been a pirate with an eye-patch, shouting 'Shiver me timbers!' Ani wanted to go as a fairy, but she was so unfairylike that Mimi suggested a milkmaid instead. Not knowing that a milkmaid wasn't a magical creature, little Ani was happy. She was always laughing and smiling, because everyone loved her so much.

What do you do, though, when the man you treat like your father kisses you and your mother and sister, then turns away and lets you take a different train without him? And then the three of you ride for what feels like days and days towards the rising sun, and suddenly you're in a new city, charcoal black, unfamiliar, frightening and full of massive craters where something has knocked down the buildings, nobody speaks English, and now your mother tells you you're home? You can only hold your little sister's hand and your mother's and look after them both, because now you're the man, until you find your real father, and your mother introduces you to him: 'Isn't he handsome?'

He wasn't. He was terribly pale and looked as if he lay awake all night watching the ghosts dance. And he turned that haunted expression towards Ani, who stood clutching Dénes's hand and sucking her thumb, and his eyes became moist, which Dénes didn't think was very manly. A minute later he'd lifted Ani and embraced her and Ani was too bewildered even to cry. 'I want to go back to America,' said Dénes.

Tamás had seen the Nazis take over in 1944; the Jews forced to stitch yellow stars to their clothes, then hounded into a ghetto;

next the round-ups, lorries slamming through the streets with their human cargo, columns of poor, sick people, old and newborn alike herded away for deportation. While the city's huge Jewish population was evaporating in front of his eyes, Tamás seriously thought about suicide. Taking one's own life, he wrote in one of his philosophical papers, was part of the national consciousness. Hungarians, time and again, couldn't determine the fate of their country while other nations tore it to pieces. This would not change in his lifetime. Yet people could still be the arbiters of their own death.

He decided, instead, to fight back in his own way. He was an academic, a specialist in language, literature and philosophy; those would be his weapons. He wouldn't write at his office, but at home. Minding the children while Mimi gave concerts, he wrote tracts on war, peace and love; about literature, music, art; about the strength of the human spirit, the capacity for endurance, the galvanising life-force that keeps us going when everything around us has disintegrated. The will to live, breathe, move and love, despite ourselves, sometimes against our better judgment.

Some drafts he destroyed when the danger became clear. A few were published in subversive magazines and academic journals – only in Hungarian, of course. That, Dénes smouldered, was the tragedy: nobody who couldn't understand Hungarian would ever read his father's words. Nobody would translate the philosophical ramblings of an obscure academic, and Tamás could have done it himself, but wouldn't. In spare moments, between cello practice and lessons, Dénes would spirit the published papers to his bed; later he'd read them under the covers, by torchlight. He hadn't understood much at the time. Looking back, later, he could see that it was all theory, not practice; it was free thought, no following of Marx or Engels or, heaven help us, Nietzsche. What makes us human, Tamás asked? What sets us apart from pigs and dogs, scavenging for food and sex? Not superman; just mankind at its most transcendent? No wonder the ÁVH arrested him; no wonder they restricted Mimi's travelling when other musicians were often allowed in and out with relative ease.

They muddled through the first three, greying, postwar years when the Arrow Cross thugs had been booted out and the government was a coalition; for the first year and a half, or thereabouts, they still believed that what they'd taken for a democracy would hold. Day by day, with Tamás's few relatives who were still alive, they became a family; an odd family, but a family nonetheless. Dénes struck up a friendship with two brothers who lived three blocks away: József, who was his own age, played the violin and gazed with awe at Mimi, and Iván, three years his senior, who wanted to be a writer. Dénes made good progress with his cello. Ani made everyone smile.

Mimi gave concerts, travelling when she could, where she could. After Tamás disappeared, in 1951, they could have wrecked her career wholesale; instead, they just stopped her from going to the West. It was a matter of PR, Dénes reckoned: Mimi was so well known in America and Western Europe that the regime needed her for propaganda. If she played in the Eastern bloc but nowhere else, they could put it about that that had been her own decision.

Trains through Eastern Europe. The children went along: Sofia, Bucharest or Krakow, on a good day. Minsk, Gdansk, Katowice on a bad one. She didn't like to leave Ani, who sometimes wet her bed, and did so more often after Tamás was arrested.

Dénes could scarcely guess at how Mimi had reached her state of collapse on returning from the ÁVH headquarters – she only told him what had happened long after they settled in Britain – but he held on to her words, 'Your father is alive,' even after three years, when it seemed ridiculous to imagine that it was true. And he and Ani grew despite everything – if not up, Mimi joked, then at least a little bigger – and somehow the family held together from day to day, studying, finding friends, living from one small triumph to another: a successful concert, a cello prize, a party on someone's name day, with toast after toast offered to good company, the greatest joy and one that couldn't be taken away from them.

Dénes was just eighteen when his friend József, who was starting his violin studies at the Ferenc Liszt Conservatory while Dénes was admitted as a cellist, set off one autumn morning for Szeged to visit an uncle who taught Physics at the university there. He came back two days later. Around ten at night, the doorbell rang and Dénes answered.

'Józsi! What is it?'

'I've just been watching Uncle András's students pulling down a statue of Stalin.'

'*What?*'

A revolt; a will for change. It all stemmed, József told him, from Stalin's death three years earlier and the speech Khrushchev had made in February criticising Stalin's policies. There'd already been unrest in Poland and now the students were leading the way. József had watched in wonder as a huge group, working as one, brought the loathed effigy down in a nosedive. A stone monolith, vile, horrible, not even well carved, and they smashed it – and oh, the joy, the glee on their faces! The future was open, hope flew free, and it all began in Szeged, that day. It was October 1956.

'I'm going to the demonstration this afternoon,' József told him on 23 October. He'd bounded all the way up their stairs and his face was red with effort and excitement. The sun poured in through their kitchen window. 'There's a whole bunch of us going. My brother's helping organise it.' József's brother Iván was at the Loránd Eötvös University and was a member of the Petöfi Circle of intellectuals, many of them freethinking communists and would-be writers, like Iván. 'Why don't you come, Dini? We're meeting at the statue of Petöfi and marching to the statue of Bem in Buda, and then to Parliament.'

'I want to come too!' Ani shouted.

'We'll all go,' Mimi announced. 'We'll go later, once we've done a good day's work.'

As the day wore on and Dénes tried to concentrate on his cello lesson, he sensed even from the college that something was different. From the window, he saw people running, flags waving, heard singing and shouting nearby. His professor, a harried-looking fellow with a big moustache and hangdog rings under his eyes, was as excited as anybody, unusually for him.

'You're young,' he grunted, catching Dénes fingering a study automatically, his gaze drifting to the window. 'You should be out there.'

'I'm sorry, Professor. I'll go later this afternoon.'

'Go on. Go out there. Today isn't like other days. Come along, I give you permission to leave a little early.'

Dénes didn't wait for him to change his mind. He made a dash for the nearest main thoroughfare, but the streets were so jammed with people that the trams weren't running and Dénes found that he couldn't either. He swerved through the backstreets instead, jogging with his cello case on his back, to fetch Mimi and Ani.

Two student rallies were marching towards Bem Square, converging from their individual routes, one from Pest, one from Buda. By the time Mimi, Dénes and Ani bounded out of their door, the day's action was well advanced. They shouldered their way along as the crowds built around them. Dénes would never forget the thrill of those moments: so many bodies marching and surging together, and the flags soaring over them, and the commotion, the roaring, the excitement. To experience this, Dénes thought, is to know what hope means.

In the crowds a new energy had begun to breed. Perhaps it was osmosis, for as far as Dénes knew there had been no plans beyond marching in solidarity with the Poles in Poznań, where the students were leading an uprising. He sensed the air changing: as if someone had turned on the mains and suddenly the electric light was pure and potent, illuminating every spirit in the street.

They were making progress through Pest, close to the Danube. Mimi spotted a neighbour whose son was at university with Iván and asked if she knew where their group might be. The neighbour cupped a hand behind her ear to hear Mimi better amid the racket. 'They were going towards Parliament,' she said. 'Kossuth Square. They're probably there now. I just heard that they're calling for Imre Nagy to be reinstated!'

'The radio station,' someone else shouted. 'They're heading for the radio station. Somebody said the Sixteen Points may be broadcast.'

'What are those?' Ani asked.

'The main demands that the leaders of today have made,' Dénes explained. 'Here, they're on these leaflets.' He picked one up off the ground to show her.

They had paused in their tracks, unsure of their direction. Parliament or radio station? Mimi stared at the ground, feeling something. 'I think we should go home,' she said. 'I don't like this.

It's all rumour, speculation. They'll never let the Sixteen Points be heard on the radio.'

'No!' Dénes had never wanted to be anywhere as much as he wanted to be on the streets of Budapest tonight. 'We can't go home. Let's just go to the Parliament.'

'No,' Mimi said. 'Something's not right.'

The carved stone turrets and the huge dome rose black against the evening sky while the Danube slid by in its wide bed just as it would if young people carrying flags from which the central hammer and sickle had been ripped out weren't flocking across the bridges, shouting '*Russkik haza!*' – Russians, go home! – and calling for Imre Nagy to speak.

'This is unbelievable,' Dénes mumbled.

'Who are they?' Ani asked him, pointing; some truckloads of youngsters, not much older than herself, went careening by.

'They're from the Csepel armaments factories,' Dénes said. 'Believe me, I should know.' An extremely sexy girl who worked in the café nearest to the Academy, and who flirted with him something rotten, had a brother who worked there. But that was when the first question mark crossed his mind.

Jostled from every side, they ploughed forward through the encroaching night towards the Parliament; row after row of dark coats and hats made it impossible to get much closer. Kossuth Square held thousands, shouting, chanting, and Dénes, looking at his mother's face, saw tears in her eyes as she felt the sudden release of the years that had destroyed her husband. Just when Dénes thought no more magic could happen, the lights went off inside Parliament. A collective gasp swept the square, and a moment later Dénes realised that flaming lanterns were shining in the night all around. He had a copy of *A Free People*, the communist newspaper, and without even stopping to think about it, within a second he had rolled it up and set it alight. Ani gasped with joy as flame illuminated the upturned, wondering faces around them.

Around nine o'clock, a figure appeared at last, a figure with a sizeable moustache and round-rimmed glasses, on a balcony high on the Parliament building: Imre Nagy. He began to speak; they could just make out his words.

'Dear comrades,' said Imre Nagy.

Dénes clapped a hand to his forehead. 'Dear comrades'? Anyone could see that this demonstration was about nobody wanting to be a 'comrade' for a moment longer.

'We're not comrades!' he yelled. Even as his voice rose from the crowd, so, he thought, did everyone else's. Boos, whistles. He'd never known such spontaneity in his life, not here, where applause usually had to be reserved for matters one detested. And this was the man they *wanted* to reinstate to lead them?

Nagy was imploring the crowd to be sensible, be good and go home. No chance, thought Dénes. Not tonight, on this wave of energy. He glanced around. At the back of the crowd lurked some ÁVH men with guns. A minibus screeched by, then another.

'Quick!' shouted someone from one of them, Dénes couldn't see who. 'To the radio station! The ÁVH is firing on the crowd, stop them!'

Later Dénes, and many of his fellow refugees, wondered whether the minibus crews were planted. Had the firing in truth begun later, when more of the demonstrators had swallowed this bait? Or was it true that the first shot was simply fired in panic, without orders from above, after the outrage of hearing the detested First Minister, Ernő Gerő, insulting the crowd, when they had hoped to hear the Sixteen Points instead, grew too much for the demonstrators? Dénes, Mimi and Ani found themselves swept forward in the general stampede; it was only when they smelled gas, felt it pricking their eyes like barbed wire, and heard gunfire ricochet through the narrow cobbled street that led to the radio station, that they seemed to regain control of their own feet. Mimi began to run. Dénes did not; Ani hovered, scared, close beside him. Their mother stopped and screamed.

'We're going home, *now*, to take your sister to safety! Otherwise I won't answer for the consequences!'

'Mama, this is the greatest day of my life and I'm not leaving it.'

'So then, if something happens to her, Dini, you will remember *it is your fault*.' Dénes was no match for Mimi at her fiercest. Their wills locked over Ani's head; he lost. Ani glanced from mother to brother and back again, powerless.

'All right.' He took Ani's reluctant arm, and Mimi's. They headed for home. From the kitchen they could hear, in the distance, the sounds of battle as Budapest made its bid for freedom. Dénes stood at the window, listening to the symphony of guns, longing to be part of it.

The Russian military stationed nearby came to the Hungarian government's aid to re-establish order in Budapest. In other words, Dénes grouched, they tried to murder the demonstrators, shooting at them in Kossuth Square, on the spot where Dénes, Mimi and Ani had stood forty-eight hours earlier. Then, to Dénes's astonishment, the Russians withdrew. David was beating Goliath. He didn't know how it had happened; it was too good to be true. The waitress from the café asked him to go with her to the hospital and give blood. There, he passed patients with gunshot wounds who smiled through their pain.

Mimi and Ani went out together to buy food. For once, it was plentiful, instead of rationed. In solidarity with the capital, peasants had been flocking in from the collective farms, bringing whatever food they could to help the fighters. The joyful Ani carried a whole bag of apples and another of carrots and potatoes; and someone, recognising Mimi from a concert, tossed a plucked chicken towards her and refused to take payment. But even as she caught it, Mimi thought she could glimpse, two blocks ahead, a long grey sack with a skewed purple ball on top, dangling from a tree. She grabbed Ani and turned her face the other way. The crowd had lynched an ÁVH man. On Váci Street, smoke caught in their nostrils. Flakes of singed paper fluttered down and settled on their coats. A bonfire of books was aflame outside the Soviet bookshop. Communist tracts?

'Not only those,' József told him when Dénes met him for an update. 'Iván says it won't just be Marx and Lenin. No, a lot of them *like* Marx and Lenin. Nobody's trying to get rid of communism, just the fucking corrupt Gang of Four-style communism – Gerő, Rákosi, the bloody thugs. This'll also be books burned for the sake of it. Intellect incarnate. They'll burn your father's thesis too, and my Uncle András's physics textbook, given half a chance.'

'If that's so, then we must get out, right now.' Dénes imagined he could feel the flames licking at his own skin. At home, he told

Mimi what else he'd learned: 'The borders are open – thousands of people are heading for Austria. We should go.'

'I can't,' Mimi announced. 'I've got a concert on the third of November.'

Stripped of international celebrity in the West, Mimi could pride herself on one more thing: her professionalism. She would never let anybody down – with the exception of that unplanned six-month period in California when she'd refrained from appearing, claiming an 'injury'. She had given concerts with a high fever; once, after eating bad oysters, she'd glided gracefully into the wings and thrown up; and now, even when she was too worried to sleep or eat, she would set aside all other concerns when it was time to perform. Her husband having been arrested, tortured and probably murdered, she counted herself lucky to play her violin at all. Her conscience hewed away at her mind.

She truly believed that everything they suffered was divine payback for all that had happened before: the way she had turned her back on her parents, her heritage and the Frankls. Retribution, too, for her escape to the States, the life she'd led there, her relationship with Marc. She'd been so confident, so arrogant. That was the sin: arrogance. Her encounter with the ÁVH headquarters was enough to destroy the last of it. It was in vain that Dénes tried to tell her that the government of Hungary had nothing whatsoever to do with her personal morality.

On the evening of 3 November, Mimi sailed onto the stage of the Ferenc Liszt Academy and changed her programme. Instead of the advertised pieces – Mozart, Beethoven and Prokofiev – she substituted music by Brahms dedicated to his Hungarian violinist friend József Joachim, plus some of his Hungarian Dances; then music by Bartók; the Duplessis Suite; and Ravel's *Tzigane*, written for Jelly d'Arányi. The queue at the box office spilled out along the street, although winter had set in and the air was bitter. 'Let them in,' Mimi pleaded when all the tickets had gone but the queue hadn't. Finally the doors simply opened and the waiting crowd surged forward into the foyer. They stood there throughout, spellbound; for once, everybody in Budapest seemed willing to forget that she was a Gypsy.

Dénes's eyes filled with tears of pride. As his mother took her sixth curtain call, golden autumn flowers pelting her from the balcony, a cloth bundle flew towards her: someone had tossed on stage a Hungarian flag from which the hated circular centre had been torn. Mimi picked it up, unfurled it and with a flourish, draped it round her shoulders. Her pianist came back carrying a pile of music and they played encore after encore. Dénes had seen nothing like it, before or since.

The concert finally drew to a close around eleven fifteen. Back at the apartment, Mimi, Dénes, Ani and their friends celebrated with tea, cake and Pálinka. After everybody had left, Dénes fell asleep to the sound of his mother's voice singing quietly to herself in the next room – a Gypsy lullaby, or perhaps a love song, the words of which he'd never know.

Before dawn, another sound woke him. A metallic clanking, whirring its inexorable way along the street. As it passed, the walls shook. Budapest was trembling. Fifty years later, Dénes could still feel that vibration through the thin mattress. He got up and went to the kitchen window. Ani joined him. Overhead in the dark sky flew small, strange green lights.

'What's that?' Ani whispered.

'Russian projectiles for reconnaissance,' said Dénes, who understood at once what was going on. 'And the rumbling comes from tanks.' Ani huddled up to him and they held each other. 'Don't be afraid,' he whispered. The next sound he remembered was the whine and thunder as the Russian attack began.

Any other time, Dénes liked to think, they'd never have got away with what they did to Budapest that day and during those that followed. The West was looking at the Suez Crisis, not Hungary. Any other time, they'd have come to help. Surely they would?

It was several hours before the magnitude of the attack sunk in. Finally, around midday, Mimi and Ani scurried down the stairs, making for the cellar, where many of the neighbours had already taken refuge. 'Doesn't seem long since last time,' remarked a jovial fellow who'd lived in the apartment below theirs for fifteen years. Nobody laughed.

Dénes hesitated. He wanted to see what was happening. While he hovered, ushering his mother and sister down to safety, he saw József in the doorway, his eyes frantic.

'Iván's out there.' József needed to say no more; Dénes dashed out to join him.

The boys ploughed through the streets, ducking from glowering doorway to stone arch, their clothes dusty with falling plaster. Dénes couldn't absorb anything: the noise, the shooting and shelling, layered perspective on perspective near and further and far, people dashing for cover, dark coats pulled round them, faces shielded by their arms. Machine gun fire, from which side he couldn't tell. A city of faceless, scampering coats, desperate for safety.

'Józsi, stop,' Dénes urged. 'This is crazy.'

On Rákóczi Street, a lorry bearing a black flag drove past them, laden with Hungarian corpses. Through the November air, his nostrils and throat thick with dust, he could smell smoke, blood and gunpowder. Around them unfolded the nightmare of tumbling stone and brick, ground down under their feet as they crossed Stalin Avenue – not even when he'd first seen it, when they'd arrived from America after the war, had the destruction been so extreme. The last chance had gone. The city was being shelled half to pieces.

Dénes saw a heap of wreckage, which was all that remained of a great block with carved lintels and iron balconies; amid the rubble, he glimpsed what looked like a child's hobby-horse, and a flicker of blue material that might once have been a woman's scarf. Opposite, outside what was once his father's favourite café, lay a hundred plates each smashed into a hundred pieces. They walked on, passing boy soldiers in trench coats clutching machine-guns. People around them simply stepped over the corpses of Russian soldiers who'd been shot; nobody would collect them. 'It's hopeless,' József said, his cheeks wet with tears. 'He's dead. How could we ever find him?'

Like everything in these mad thirteen days, Dénes thought, it happened by accident. They stumbled across Iván on the pavement of the Museum Boulevard. The lorries hadn't reached his body yet. He'd fallen sideways, a bullet in his head. His fingertips skimmed the grille of a drain. From his coat pocket protruded the programme from Mimi's recital. József knelt and reached out to close his brother's sightless eyes.

'Help me lift him?' he asked, taking Iván's shoulders in his arms. And as Dénes raised the heavy, bloodstained legs, he made a silent vow never to give in: not to the Russians, not to the ÁVH thugs, not to anyone.

There'd be camps over the border in Austria to receive those who'd made it out of Hungary; at least that's what he'd heard. It was a risk, but other people had done it and so could they. 'We have to go,' said Dénes. 'We've lost. They've got rid of Nagy, and János Kádár's a Russian puppet. Bloody Rottweilers!'

'I'm an artist,' Mimi protested. 'People know me. There must be a better way. Let me write to Saul in New York.' She wrote, praying. If Saul helped them, they could wait for matters to calm down, then leave legitimately. And so they waited. Silence. Much later they learned that Saul never received the letter.

'Ani could go,' said Dénes. 'She's still American, isn't she?'

Mimi wouldn't hear of it. 'No. She's too young to travel through a place like this alone. We must stay together.'

József's grandmother, who was over eighty, had been relocated to the countryside and József's mother had insisted on going with her. Now, after Iván's death, she was desperate for her remaining son to join them. József, who hadn't slept since he'd found his brother's body, asked Dénes whether he could go with him. After college, Dénes dashed to the station to meet him for an early evening train.

'Identity cards,' a leather-jacketed official snapped at them half an hour out of the city. The boys produced their papers. He seized them and stomped out of the carriage. They never saw their identity cards again.

Without those cards, they'd be lost. You couldn't move without your identity card. Dénes felt his last shred of acceptance slide away; he wondered how he could have let it last so long. 'Józsi,' he said, 'we can't live like this.'

'What about college?' protested József, who'd brought his violin.

What was more important: studying or freedom? What was the point of perfecting your musical ability if you were to be a prisoner for the rest of your life? 'I don't care,' Dénes said. 'The college will find other students.'

József hesitated. 'But look, Dini, we tried. Hungary got its pride back, because we tried, even if we lost. Wasn't it worth it?'

'Of course it was worth it. But it's not enough, not for me. And after what happened to Iván, I don't know how you can even think it's enough for you.'

Home again, after a return journey in which he'd scarcely breathed for fear of what would happen should anyone demand his identity card this time, Dénes gazed at his mother, who was forty-one but looked fifty-five, and his little sister, thirteen, skinny and pale with stress and fright. Was it worth it? Was it enough? Ani's face clinched his decision.

'I'm going to get out,' he said. 'I'll go with Józsi.' József had come back from the country after two weeks and at the Academy Dénes was doing his best to talk him round.

'I want to go,' Ani declared.

'Ani, you're not even fourteen,' Mimi protested. 'We have to stay together.'

'I want to! If Dini's going, I'm going. Dini, please, please, take me with you?'

Dénes leaned forward and held both his mother's frozen hands in his. Outside, snow was falling. 'Mama, come with us,' Dénes coaxed. 'Let's stay together – but not here. It's a risk, but I'd rather save my spirit than my life. Papa is dead, there's no way we can keep hoping now. What's left? Let's go. Let's make a try for it. If we can get to England, perhaps Ursula will help us. She said that she'd teach me.'

Mimi picked up her violin case and cradled it, as if for comfort. 'I don't know how to do it,' she said, more to the Amati than to her children. 'It's so silly. I can play the hardest violin music ever written, I lived six years in New York, but now I don't know how to leave this country.'

'I'll do everything, Mama. Leave it to me,' said Dénes, who didn't know how either but wasn't going to let that be a problem. It was a matter of improvising. He met József outside the Academy to make a plan.

'It's too late,' said József. 'We could have gone at the beginning, but not now. It's been three weeks. They'll have cracked down on the borders.'

'We're going anyway,' Dénes insisted. 'If we don't make it, then so be it, but I won't give up without trying. Come with us.'

'My mother won't leave my grandmother. And I can't leave her.'

Dénes stamped his foot with frustration, but there was no budging the reluctant violinist. Ironically enough, József won an international competition a few years later, sailed out of Hungary to give a concert in France, and never returned. It was a considerably simpler exit than that of Dénes, Ani and Mimi.

When desperate people want to flee a country, there is always someone – an Alban, perhaps – who is willing to help them, for the right price. It took Dénes only a few hours of watching, listening and questioning in the city centre to learn that a bus would leave early the next morning, travelling towards the Austrian border.

Mimi wanted to bring as many mementos as she could stuff into a suitcase, and Ani wanted to bring a much-chewed American teddy bear from her infancy that she didn't know was a gift from her real father. 'Leave the papers,' Dénes bargained, seeing his mother despairing over boxes of old programmes and letters. 'I'll give them to Jószi, he'll look after them and send them to us later.' József obliged; the boys spent several frantic hours on that last evening shifting Mimi's archive, while she looked on in tears. She refused to leave behind the silver spoons that the Frankls had given her and Tamás on their wedding day.

'What about all our things?' Ani asked. 'Papa's books, and Mama's dresses, and—'

'Forget about them. They're only things.' For himself, Dénes packed only some clean underwear, two shirts and a photograph of his father.

Before dawn, he woke his mother and sister and led them out into the winter morning. Ani glanced over her shoulder one last time at their apartment block. She carried Mimi's violin in its case – it was her job, her little ritual when they toured with their mother. Dénes left his cello behind with József. If he made it, there'd be cellos in England. If he didn't, he wouldn't need it again.

The drive lasted all day, trundling up endless, potholed roads. The bus stopped several times, but nobody got off; every passenger was trying to leave the country. As twilight set in, the driver pulled up at the second-last stop and switched off the engine. 'If anybody "isn't going anywhere",' he announced, 'it's a good idea to get off here. The Russians are patrolling close to our last stop.'

Dénes, holding their bags, let everyone else climb out first. Mimi followed him; last off was Ani, the Amati in its case clasped to her chest.

'Come here, Ani,' Mimi said. 'There's a smudge on your cheek.' She wiped soot from Ani's face with the attention of one preparing a daughter for a debutantes' ball.

Not knowing what to do next, they began to walk along the road in the same direction the bus had been travelling. Perhaps they'd find a house or a village where there'd be help, or at least directions. The sound of an engine made Dénes glance round. A truck was coming towards them. He flagged it down and talked to the driver, who had swarthy skin, perhaps Roma. The man stared at him, as the Roma sometimes did: was he one of them? Dénes's careful choice of words didn't last long – this character knew at once that they were aiming for the border. 'All right,' he said. 'I can help you.'

'How much?' Dénes asked.

'How much have you got?'

Dénes told him.

'That's what it costs.' The driver's eyes lighted on Ani's fair hair. 'Come on, get in.'

He opened the tail doors and Dénes nearly laughed aloud: the truck was already full of refugees, maybe twenty-eight of them, children, young parents and old people, huddled together, keeping quiet. Two men who looked like the driver's brothers were in the back with them, on guard; their gazes too strayed towards Ani. Dénes tried to make his mother comfortable, then held Ani close to him while the truck lurched on through the night. A squash of bodies, everyone with the same idea and the same lack of idea. The odours of damp cloth and sweat mingled with earth and incipient mould – the van had probably been used for carrying potatoes up until a few weeks ago. Nobody spoke.

Stopping. Climbing out, cold, stiff-limbed. Frozen earth underfoot. Black sky. A peasant, middle-aged, bearded, suspicious, surveying the runaways with contempt rather than pity, the way an abattoir worker might watch a herd of befuddled sows. No light except, in the far distance, a blue beam from a watch-tower. That way, the border. No moon, so no moonlight: Dénes had accidentally chosen the right day for their escape.

The peasant and the lorry crew gathered the refugees into a circle. The purses and banknotes came out. Everything. The men even made Ani turn out her pockets. They must have been amassing the fortune of their dreams, but nobody cared how much it cost them, as long as they got out.

'This will take around six hours,' declared the bearded peasant. 'I will walk at the front, my friend in the middle and the last one at the back. Don't talk, just keep going. You will see some lights. The Russians are patrolling the border and we will go between the lights. If you see a flare, lie down and keep bloody still. There will be three large ponds, which are frozen. There's a river and a bridge. Cross it and you're in Austria. There's a reception camp in the next village.'

Dénes held Ani's hand. He carried two cases in his other hand and let his mother take the last. Ani carried the violin, the routine serving as an odd comfort. Frozen puddles punctuated the earth; snow lay thin and brittle, its slush frozen and refrozen, the surface treacherous. 'Walk where you see grass; it's less slippery,' Dénes whispered to Ani. He thanked heaven for his strong shoes. Ani, though, was wearing her holiday boots, the one reasonably pretty pair she possessed; she'd refused to leave them behind and Dénes, in the rush to get them all to the bus on time, had forgotten to tell her to be sensible. Now her feet hurt, and her heels left pockmarks in the frozen earth.

The rest of the group wasn't quiet enough. Behind them, an elderly woman was wheezing and coughing. A baby squawked; there came a frantic shushing from its parents, almost as loud as the cry. 'Papa, are we nearly there?' pleaded a small boy at the top of his voice, which made everybody laugh. The lights were growing nearer; the lad wasn't wrong.

What happened next was so quick that Dénes didn't have time to think. A shout: 'Hands up! Guns!' The line scattered. He took three jumps and threw himself face down. Eyes screwed shut, chill seeping across his belly, he heard whispers, prayers, somebody whimpering, 'Dear Lord, let us go in peace . . .' Then silence. He waited. He counted to ten, then lifted his head and opened an eye. He was sweating profusely, despite the cold. It was too dark to see anything or anyone. 'Ani?' he whispered. 'Mama?'

He slunk forward on his knees, feeling around him with one hand. After several appalling moments grasping in the void, he touched something firm, mud-caked – a girl's shoe, with an inappropriate heel. 'Dini?' came Ani's small voice. He gasped with relief. When he'd taken his leaps, Mimi and Ani had followed; they were on the ground together, waiting for him. Ani was quaking with fear and cold. He couldn't see anyone else from their party.

'Remember what he said about going between the lights,' he whispered.

They began to move forwards. In between the silver-blue rays stretched a corridor of darkness. They bent low, half walking, half crawling. Whenever a beam swerved through the blackness, they threw themselves flat. Time liquified. Dénes had no idea how long they'd been there. To his astonishment, he wasn't afraid. He just wanted to cross the border without dying. If he felt fear, it was for his sister and mother, who were less strong than he was, female, and the wrong ages. As a boy of eighteen, he had nothing to lose.

They were past the lights. The night deepened; the corridor of darkness merged with the flat land ahead. Dénes thought he could glimpse several dull expanses in the distance. Three stretches of water, like ponds – frozen. Find the bridge, cross it and you're in Austria. His mouth dry, he mumbled encouragement to Mimi and Ani. They fixed their gazes on the ice and moved forward.

The flare shot into the sky behind them. A flash, a shout; a shot. Dénes felt the ground slap his face and body. He could hear his mother's rapid breaths a foot away. A rattle of gunfire. Keep down, keep still. Another flare, fireworks, new year, ha ha, the beautiful blue Danube. And a sudden flurry; someone leaping up in panic, tripping, stumbling. Ani? Surely not Ani? The light caught her; the shots and the shriek he would hear in his sleep every night for the rest of his life. He grabbed his mother, shoved a hand over her mouth. Strait-jacketed in his arms, Mimi keened silently back and forth.

The pursuing patrol was off after the rest of their party. Around them, everything went silent. Dénes cautiously loosened his grip on Mimi.

'I have to go to her,' gasped Mimi. 'I can't leave her.'

'We have to, or we'll be shot too. There's nothing we can do,' Dénes urged. 'She's dead.'

'The violin,' said Mimi.

'Leave the fucking violin!'

'Supposing she's not dead? How can we be sure?'

'Stay here. I'll go.'

Dénes crawled, his breath rasping in his throat, in the direction of Ani's scream. He'd experienced enough in Budapest these last weeks to know a mortal cry when he heard one.

She was lying on her front, hat askew above her fair pigtails, gawky limbs splayed at impossible angles. Dark patches of blood seeped from her back where the bullets had sprayed her. Death would have been instant. Dénes wept. A little girl in her holiday boots, threatening nobody, looking for nothing but the chance to live a full life. Slaughtered, like those lynched ÁVH pigs. Dénes remembered Marc Duplessis teaching him to get a grip: control yourself; raging changes nothing; be a man, be strong.

Gently, he rolled his sister's body over. Her left arm still clasped her mother's violin case. Had they shot her from the front, instead of from behind like the cowardly criminals they were, the violin might have saved her life. Instead, she had saved it. He lifted the case. A bullet had bored straight through it from one side to the other.

He didn't see the soldier approaching. A Russian soldier – standing beside him, staring down at the rag-doll body of the dead girl with a horror that Dénes abruptly understood matched his own. The soldier's eyes met his – and he was only a boy himself, no more than seventeen, with the wide cheekbones, slanting eyes and dark hair that betrayed the far reaches of the USSR, the eastern lands that had been sucked into the monster regime like milk up Stalin's straw. Most likely he thought he was at Suez, not in Hungary. He'd believe that Hungarian was Arabic; he probably couldn't understand why it was snowing, or why there was no canal.

'My sister,' said Dénes without moving. If the soldier were to shoot him now, he wouldn't give a fuck. 'Come on, then. Kill me too. Why should I live when my sister is dead?'

Yet this boy soldier, for reasons best known to himself, wasn't going to hurt him. Could be, Dénes thought, he'd never shot anybody before in his life. The boy looked at the violin, then lowered his gun and reached out a hand to the grieving Dénes. His finger touched Dénes's elbow. For a second, contact. Enemies connecting: each as terrified as the other. The lad mumbled something: a condolence, maybe a prayer. Then he jerked his head and said in Russian, 'Go. Quick.'

'*Köszönöm, barátom,*' said Dénes. Thank you, my friend. His mother's violin in his arms, he turned and walked away towards Austria.

Karina's face is wet with tears. Dénes gives her a kiss, then swallows a long swig of wine. He's been holding her hand through the latter part of his story, his grip growing tighter. 'Now you see why we didn't tell you?' he says.

'You've been living with this, all these years.'

'What else to do? Maybe I'm responsible for my sister's death. Your grandmother blamed me then, and continued to blame me. When we crossed the Channel to Britain, some days after we reached Austria, do you know, she would barely speak to me. But we were survivors. We had only each other, a little hope and two or three phone numbers. How do we live with it? God alone knows that. She had it worse. I lost a father and a sister. She lost a husband and a child. And, in Duplessis, her lover. And, of course, she had lost her real parents, her brother and her adopted parents long before. But on those days we call her bad days, I know that it's Ani she's crying for. The dreams stay with you, Karina, they never stop. She's ninety-one and every night, she sees it all again.'

'And when you got to Britain—?'

'Yes, after a few weeks locked inside a camp for refugee immigrants we swallowed our pride and called Ursula. She told us to come to her, which we did, because we didn't feel safe where we were, not one bit. I'll never forget the first morning in the camp, Karrie. We ate cornflakes. I'd never seen a cornflake in my life. I couldn't imagine who invented such a thing. And there were plenty of decent people there, like us. But there were a few real desperados, too, and we were scared, we had to get away. Ursula vouched for us; she found us somewhere to stay, she found someone who could lend me a cello, she gave me lessons and instead of paying her I cleaned her house twice a week. I tell you, Karina, if it wasn't for her, if I hadn't charmed her by saying "nectar and ambrosia" . . . Well, a year or two later I won a special scholarship for Hungarian refugees and went to college at last. Your grandmother was in great demand, of course, as soon as people knew she was in Britain.'

Dénes smiled. 'One month after we arrived, we were invited to tea with Yehudi Menuhin. And because so many people knew my mother, we landed plumb in the middle of this wonderful world that was London's musical scene. It took time to build things up, to get the concerts, but we couldn't imagine what great things were coming. The sixties, Karina! Everything bloomed. It was like a rebirth. She played with everybody – Daniel Barenboim, Jacqueline du Pré, Leonard Bernstein, Stephen Kovacevich, Georg Solti, the best musicians in the world.'

'I don't know how I can worry about my stupid life when I think of what you went through,' Karina says into her father's shoulder. 'I can't get my head around it – that one world can hold so many different experiences all at the same time. My life seemed so bleak yesterday. Now I don't know how I can even hold my head up in front of you and Grandma. Everything must seem banal to you, compared to that.'

'Silly girl.' Dénes strokes her hair. 'We did it all for you. If you suffer like we suffered, that means we didn't do enough. And personally, I think we did! We exist together in this huge soup, we're all different and yet we're all the same. That's what this life is, a silly great collage pasted of cunts and Rottweilers and, just now and then, an angel or two. You have to do what you can with the little bit that's yours. And if nobody is dying, then life is good.'

'Compared to all that, the fate of a violin doesn't count for much,' Karina says. 'But you did take it with you?'

Dénes reaches for the bottle of wine and refills their glasses. 'The violin didn't escape altogether. That bullet went straight through the top part of the case and out the other side. The scroll was blown clean off the body.'

'The *scroll*?'

'Yes. So we took it to Jonny Goldsmith senior, your Jonny Goldsmith's father, who ran the business then. He mended the scroll, built it up and glued it back on. A patch-up job because a bullet is a bullet, you know what I'm saying? The sound was as fine as ever, but when my mother tried to play it, she broke down: the wound in that fiddle reminded her every time of Ani's death. Then a sponsor bought her a beautiful Guadagnini which carried no memories, and she played that for the rest of her career. But there's still a battered old Amati with a damaged and repaired scroll, and it has been very well concealed.'

'But Dad . . . ?'

'Like I tell you, Karina, today everybody wants that fucking fiddle! "Oh, Mr Veres, what happened to your mother's Amati? Can I have it, please?" Karina, tell me, if you want to hide, where do you hide?'

Karina thinks of Jamie under the bed at Fairfallows, covered in dust, easy to find with one giveaway cough; and Lindy in New York, unnoticed in the sheer normality of daily life as Caroline Birch.

'We made up this cock-and-bull story when you turned eighteen,' her father declares, 'and we gave you the bloody Amati saying it's a Polish matchbox. It's a convincing matchbox, I tell you. Life didn't treat it well. And if it looks old, that's because it is. Very old.'

Karina didn't take her violin to New York. It's in Brighton, under Rohan's bed. Her father's eyes are twinkling at her. She wants to shake him, hard. 'But how could you have let me carry it around, insured for all of fifteen thousand pounds?'

'So, you lose the fiddle, you think it's worth fifteen grand, you buy another for fifteen grand and you'd never know the difference.' Dénes sighs. 'Value is in the head. It's all about what people make you believe.'

'Didn't Jonny Goldsmith know what it was?'

'Yes, of course he did. But my mother was so upset over the entire bloody saga that she insisted he didn't tell nobody nothing. She paid him not to put it in his records. Yes, Karina, it was a bribe. He wasn't happy, but that didn't stop him taking the money and doing as she asked. And by the time your Jonny Goldsmith inherited the business this was all long in the past. You have taken it to him?'

'No, never. I just go to a local repairer. And he always said he thought it was a better instrument than I'd told him – but I didn't believe him.'

'You thought maybe he just wants to keep your business!' Dénes says with a laugh.

'But Dad – it's crazy. I still don't understand why you'd give me the Amati and not tell me what it was.' Karina is tussling with a new image of her father's mind: warped, damaged, a tad paranoiac? And no wonder.

'Crazy? Of course it's crazy,' Dénes says. 'Ask anyone, Karina, any of my students, they'll all say, ah, Veres, that mad Hungarian, we love him, but you know, he's nuts.'

Karina stares down at the carpet's ancient stains. Mimi lost her parents, her adoptive parents, her brother, her husband, her lover, her daughter. She weeps, fifty years later, for her daughter more than all the rest. 'I should call Jamie before school bedtime,' she says.

'OK, Schnooky. I'll tell your mother I've told you. She needs to know.'

Karina picks up the phone. 'Jamie, love, it's Mum.'

Dénes, unburdened at last, switches on the TV where the seven o'clock news is beginning, then falls asleep in his chair. 'Crisis on the Underground,' blares the headline. 'Derailment traps passengers in "cattle truck" conditions . . .'

31

Julian is wedged into a corner of the trapped train, trying to breathe. The tube was built for Victorians; today, taller individuals like him have to stoop and pray for safety. He's been there for an hour and people have begun to crumple around him – though the carriage is so crowded that many can scarcely move.

His mind hums: why here, why now? Why the very day that the Jag went in for servicing? There'd been a bump, a lurch, moments of turbulence, some smoke, screams, darkness. The driver had announced that the front few carriages had derailed – Julian is near the back. What if it's a bomb attack and they can't be told lest people panic? It's remarkably quiet now; they are waiting for rescue. A few passengers chat softly; some try to make light of their predicament; others are in tears. Despite the oppressive heat and the decreasing supply of oxygen, Julian takes the opportunity to think.

Take control, said Chris in Lewes, while Éva and the riveted audience hung on his every word. You are the author of your own history. Take control. Pain may not be necessary for gain, but hard work is. Don't make excuses, don't bend reality to suit yourself. Look sharp, see clearly. Tell it like it is; then you can pinpoint the areas where change is needed. Identify the elements holding you back, the ingrowing, inherited patterns blocking you from fulfilling your potential. If something hobbles you, even if you love it, make a decision to let it go.

He's been turning this over, astonished at how difficult it is to do.

'Jules, what a surprise!' Chris had pumped his hand after the talk. 'How completely excellent to see you again, mate! It's been a long time.'

'My friend brought me,' said Julian, introducing Éva. 'She's a big fan of yours.' He noticed at once that Chris, who was the same age as Hilary, looked ten years younger. The old charisma was stronger than ever. His face was friendly and confident, his skin remarkably unlined. He'd lost very little of his curly hair. He's a good advert, Julian thought, for his own philosophies.

'Here's my card,' said Chris. 'Any time you want to talk, just give me a buzz, yeah?'

'Thank you. I may take you up on that.'

Why does it take a New Age life-coach to make him realise that he must let Karina go? How hard must his face be rubbed in her betrayal? Why should her family's problems – the temperamental old grandma, the difficult father, the refugee history – drag him down with her? He can't heal them, any more than Karina can heal his family's problems. Growth and change, said Chris, are organic to every cell in our body, therefore organic to life and its progress. Recognise them, accept them, embrace them. Once Julian would have scoffed, but now the words thump him in the goolies.

While the train waits for help, it occurs to Julian that if nothing happens soon, this rush-hour carriage may suffocate all its passengers. Segments of window are open at either end, but is this enough? All that's coming in seems to be smoke and dust. Why doesn't the system get its act together and walk them out through the tunnel? Something must be stopping them, something bad – a fire? Toxic fumes?

Fires are sucked through sloping tunnels, and hence become extra fierce; think of Lindy. Could two members of the same family be killed the same way within a year? Wouldn't the laws of probability go against that? And Jamie . . . Julian puts his hand over his face. Jamie is eight years old, he hasn't seen him for two weeks, and he can't blame Karina for this. Every day the boy is at school is one day less spent in his company.

'You have to let go of the thought patterns that hold you back,' Chris lectured. 'Recognition and release. Let them go. The chances are that they're not yours anyway, but your parents'.'

Halfway up the carriage, a small child has wet himself and is howling with misery. The smell is pungent, exaggerated. Tired, frightened passengers shuffle away from the puddle as best they can, trying not to make the toddler's upset mother feel any worse. The whiff plunges Julian back into his school dorm. Five years old. Abandonment. Has it stayed with him? Has Karina abandoned him because he expects abandonment, because it's all he really knows? Is that the pattern that holds him back?

The transport system is little better, despite the hours he spends on its legalities. Without him, everything would carry on much the same. Tell it like it is, said Chris. Look at the reality, not at what you want reality to be. The more the passengers sit helpless, the more Julian realises that none of his work has improved ordinary people's daily experiences. He's put all his brainpower into the legal management of what should have been the rejuvenation of the railways. But Andy – in his last phone call before his resignation – had reported the latest advice from the government's advisor: Britain's transport problems should be solved by scrapping plans for high-speed rail links, charging tolls on the roads and expanding the airports. All Julian has done, in the end, is make money for his company, which he's using to send his son to an expensive school, by which he has alienated Karina, who should have been the most precious element of his life.

He shuts his eyes, asks himself for the unblinkered truth. The truth is that he loves his wife – more than ever. The thought of life without her hangs over him like a guillotine. Yet now it's too late, with her damaged family, her overreactions to Fairfallows, her overidentification with Jamie and finally her affair; however much he loves her, he has to recognise that she's become part of the trouble, not its solution.

Identify the problem, said Chris, then let it go. Julian identifies it. It's not only Karina. It's the rat-trap of the life they live. If he were to choose a different way of life, maybe even in another country, nobody could stop him. Settle matters with Karina – then go. What's so hard about that? He's highly qualified, he has an MBA as well as a law degree, he knows transport issues inside out. He reckons he could set up a consultancy anywhere he likes. Yet he may never have a chance to do it, because he may not emerge from this train alive. Is his life over? Has he missed the point of the whole damn thing?

Two hours have passed. A young woman collapses in a faint. If I ever get out of here, Julian resolves, trying to help her, life will be different. I'll make certain of that.

By the next afternoon, Karina's head has cleared of the effects of concussion, if nothing else. Her father has to teach, her mother is anxious; she must get out of their way. Her car, her violin, her computer, most of her clothes and all her pupils are in Sussex. Erzsébet drives her to the station and she heads for Brighton.

Lindy hasn't answered her text. Rattling from Clapham towards Haywards Heath, she takes out her phone and tries again: 'LINDY/CARO, PLEASE COME HOME.'

This time a message beeps back after five minutes.

'OPENING NITE "LIFE W/OUT MOTHER" 21 OCT PLSE COME.'

'NOT THE POINT', texts Karina.

'YES', texts Lindy.

'YES, YOU WILL COME HOME?'

The phone rings and Karina nearly jumps out of her seat. Her opposite neighbour, who's holding a floppy-haired Yorkshire terrier on her lap, pretends to look the other way.

'Lindy,' Karina says into the phone.

'Caroline,' says Lindy. 'Karrie, this is crazy. You can't bully me by mobile.'

'I can and I will, until you agree first to let me tell your mother and secondly to come back and make peace.'

'Come see the play. The actors are great and David's doing a brilliant job.'

'What if it's a smash hit?'

'There goes another of those flying pigs,' Lindy remarks. 'They're quite common over the East Village.'

'But it could be,' Karina presses. 'It might be a huge success. If that happens, it'll be all over the Internet in no time, and of course someone will find you. You might have been able to vanish forever if you worked in a supermarket or on a farm, but . . .'

The eyebrows of the woman with the dog rise despite themselves. Karina wonders what on earth she can be making of this. The hopeful dog wriggles.

'I'll cut my hair,' says Lindy, after a moment's reflection. 'Or wear a wig.'

'You've already changed your hair so much that it won't make any difference.'

'I'll wear dark glasses.'

'Don't be silly, Lin. It won't work, and deep down, you know it.'

'Well, then, I won't come back and you can't tell Mum,' Lindy says flatly. Karina notices, though, that Lindy has just referred to Cynthia as 'Mum', not 'my mother', for the first time since Lindy's reappearance.

'If I don't tell her, sooner or later someone else will,' she says. 'It would be so much better if you'd do it yourself.'

Lindy breathes long and deep. 'Karrie,' she remarks, three thousand miles away, 'how would you do it, if you were me?'

'I don't know, but I'd find a way.'

'I have to go. I'm late for work.'

'Go on, then. Have a bagel for me. But I'll call you again, and I'll keep on calling you until you see sense.'

'Fuck.' Lindy rings off.

The train passes Haywards Heath. Karina thinks of Rohan, leaving the train in the autumn night only eight months ago. Her mind is full of people going away. Moving on, starting again, leaving her behind. She rubs her eyes and her bruised forehead. Then she smiles at the woman opposite and says, 'Could I hold your dog for a bit, please?'

Rohan isn't there when she arrives at the flat, still brushing dog hair from her cotton jersey. This bright, amiable space was about to become her home, until now. She gazes about at the indications of Rohan's presence: his brown jacket on the peg, a carton of lentil soup in the fridge, the intensely annotated music on its stand. She goes to the bedroom, pulls her violin case from under the bed and opens it.

The Amati gleams in her hands. Matchbox indeed. She lifts it and kisses the mended scroll. Well, she'd always known the tone was good. Too good. No wonder its strength and sweetness had stuck out in the orchestra. How can a wooden box made more than three centuries ago carry the soul of everything it's seen? Oh, what nonsense. She has to get out before Rohan returns. She wraps the fiddle in its silk scarf, then begins to pack her clothes.

There's a click downstairs, footsteps mounting towards the first floor. The door opens and shuts. 'Karrie?' calls Rohan's voice. She's taken too long. She goes to meet him. He's been rehearsing with the quartet. He puts down his violin case and gazes, crestfallen, at her and the suitcase open on the floor. 'You're packing?'

'I can't stay here, Ro. I have to try and mend things at home, because all I really have is Jamie. You see, you don't need me and he does.'

'Karrie, I need you like I've never needed anyone in my life. And who says you can't have Jamie if you're with me? Bring him, for goodness' sake . . .'

'I have to pack.' She turns back towards the bedroom. He follows without a word. 'How's the quartet?' she asks, to dispel the silence.

'I'll leave if I can work out how to live. I need to write some applications for teaching posts, maybe think about starting a new group. Though I have to say some good things happened in New York, which you don't know about yet.'

'Tell me.'

'You want to know?' The sugar in Rohan's eyes has turned to vinegar.

'Of course,' she says, pain jolting her.

'Well, a conductor offered me some concertos. It's an orchestra from upstate New York. There's a chance of a little tour, including Carnegie Hall, playing Bartók, the Second Concerto.'

'But that's fantastic!'

'I don't care, I don't want to do it. It doesn't mean anything if you're not there.' He looks at the open violin case. 'Were you practising?'

'Not really. I had a talk with my father yesterday about how the scroll came off. I'll tell you sometime.' She folds her bronze cashmere jersey and places it in her suitcase.

'What happened?' Rohan sits down beside the violin he doesn't know he's been hunting for.

'It's a very long story,' Karina says.

He picks up her violin and bow, picks out some figurations and a wisp of Duplessis melody. 'Nice,' he remarks. 'Funny fiddle, your matchbox. It's rather good. It's so even, across all the strings, much more than mine, and it has this lovely resonance . . .'

'Yes.' Karina fetches her toiletries from the bathroom. She's doing the right thing: Rohan, watching her pack, is still most interested in talking about her violin.

'Please don't go. Please, Karrie. Don't just give up.'

'I'd rather go now than in a year's time, or two, or ten.'

'Why do you suddenly not love me? Because I had to work in New York when you fell over and I should have been there to catch you? Karrie, I didn't have a clue where you were! I was worried sick and you know it.'

'Please, stop asking *why*.' Karina zips up her case. 'It's not that I don't love you. But I need to do the right thing.'

'Karrie, please, just come here.' Rohan stands up and reaches out to her. They hold each other for a long minute.

'I must go.'

'Wait, Karrie. I won't ask again that you stay, but will you do one thing for and with me?'

'What is it?'

'Will you come to Kingsbury and meet my mother?'

Karina bites her lip.

'I've always wanted you to meet her,' says Rohan, 'but she's been away, teaching in Soweto, and since she got back she's been having some work done in the house. But she's very keen for me to bring you, and I'd rather you met her now than not at all.'

Karina hesitates. 'Why?'

'I'm not telling why until you say you will.'

'But, Ro—'

'Next Sunday?' Rohan presses. 'Please, Karrie. You'll be glad. I promise.' He takes her hand and squeezes.

'We'll talk.' Karina squeezes back; she can't not. They look at each other, fingers entwined.

'We'll talk,' says Rohan.

Karina unlocks the front door of her Lewes home. The house feels strangely normal. Jamie's photo stands on the mantelpiece, the tiered garden is running a May riot of roses and wallflowers, and a pile of CDs indicates that Julian has been home, listening and comparing. A programme from a lecture is on the coffee table beside his chair. *Chris Fanning: Get It Together*.

She wanders up to Jamie's room and lies on his bed, staring at the pictures – a pop group, a Simpsons' poster, a panoramic view of Fairfallows. How strange that she'll never know how it feels to *be* Jamie. He will always be separate from her, and only more so with the years. How many poets and philosophers, over millennia, have written that each of us is ultimately alone? Just because everyone's said it, that doesn't make it less true.

She rings Julian on his mobile. His voice sounds absent, distracted.

'Jules,' she says, 'can you talk?'

'What is it?'

'It's over. Me and Rohan.'

'No, really? What a surprise. Where are you?'

'At home.'

'Lewes?'

'Yes, of course.'

'Karina,' Julian says, 'I want you to leave, please.'

Karina sits down in shock. She can't speak.

'Too much baggage. Both of us. We've tried for ten years, but if you're going to bugger off having affairs the minute the least little thing disrupts your life, then I think we're not exactly made for one another. It's better if we separate and have done with it.'

'Jules—'

'I've done some thinking and I've decided several things, which you need to know. First, I'm considering leaving the company. Secondly, if I do, I may move to Europe, I'm not sure where yet, but possibly Sweden. I can set up a transport consultancy anywhere and Martin has good contacts there. And last but not least, I'd want to take Jamie with me.'

'*What?*'

'I have to hand it to you, Karrie: you were right about boarding-school. It's not good for Jimbo. Anyway, the rat race is no way for a kid to live. I want him to grow up somewhere where daily life feels simple and straightforward.'

'Jules, have you gone mad?' Karina manages to say.

'Quite the opposite. Karina, yesterday I was in that Underground train that derailed. We were stuck for nearly three hours and I thought I was going to die. It gave me a chance to chew things over. I want a divorce.'

'Jules, we can't sort this out on the phone.'

'Very well, we'll talk once I'm home. But I'm warning you, Karrie, I don't intend to waste time. Stay tonight if you must, but you're sleeping in the spare room.'

In what was once her home, Karina sits motionless for five minutes with her hands over her face. Then she pours herself a large dose of Julian's whisky and switches on the television so that she doesn't need to feel so alone.

The local news is showing, of all things, Fairfallows. In the meadow, the travellers are being evicted. Karina spots Caitlin with her children, the environmental health staff standing by, bailiffs' heavies, policemen with semi-concealed truncheons. The caravans are being moved to a travellers' site a few villages away. Dave, who's narrowly escaped arrest, is on camera railing against the government edict that removed the obligation for councils to provide land for travellers, and the council guidance which spells out that they should be treated in the same way as everybody else, proving that officials need to be reminded of this. Human excrement, the journalist reports, was recently found smeared on the door of Fairfallows Place. Arthur blusters about landowners' rights and the damage inflicted upon Fairfallows's reputation; why, he grumbles, has it taken nearly a year for anything to be done?

Karina finds she's shivering with cold although it's a warm day. She tells herself to focus on practical things. It's all that will help. She glances at her violin and her suitcase, then picks up the phone to call Jamie.

'Listen, love,' she says, 'as a special treat, how do you fancy spending next weekend in Twickenham with me and your grandparents? I'll rearrange my teaching. We can visit your great-grandmother and we can go into London and do fun things. We could go on the London Eye.'

'Yeah. Whatever,' says Jamie's small voice, resigned. Trying to make the best of it. It's the defeated, dispirited tone in his voice that she loathes – it wasn't there before boarding-school. Tiredness . . .

'You haven't been having any more midnight feasts, have you?' she demands.

'We got caught and Mr Whitehouse gave us detentions for days and days. And now they're going to put up CCTV cameras in the corridor.'

CCTV to stop small boys eating chocolate muffins? Karina feels an all-too-familiar lurch of disgust. 'I'll see you very soon, love,' she says, and rings off.

There is only one thing that can keep her company now. She takes out the Amati and begins to play some studies, squinting down the body of the violin past the bullet-seared scroll towards the fireplace, the rose-patterned tiles, the garden in high spring.

What will she do? Where can she go? The Roma, she thinks, have been wandering minstrels forever. Mimi's family belonged with their instruments and with each other. Perhaps that's where she belongs: with her son and her violin. She can face losing Julian, her home, and Lindy again, if her efforts should fail; she can even face losing Rohan; but she can't lose Jamie. If she's to keep him with her, she needs more work. Teaching is good, but now that she's found her way back to her violin, and it has found its true Amati self, it's time to knuckle down. She should ask advice from the person who knows life and the violin better than anyone else: Mimi.

Jamie, sitting on the sofa in Mimi's flat, tries not to wriggle. Visiting his very old and excessively scary great-grandmother isn't how he'd have liked to spend his first weekend home in what feels like ages, but since his parents aren't talking to each other, it's not a bad option. They do talk, of course. They talk politely, calmly and reasonably. That means they're not talking.

For some reason Dad, who's gone a bit crazy, has been saying that he's thinking of taking him to live abroad. Mum says Dad wouldn't have a legal leg to stand on if he tried to move a child overseas without his mother's agreement, and the pastoral tutor at school says so too, which is a relief, though funny when you remember that Dad's a lawyer. Jamie doesn't want to go abroad, but he does want to live at home, not at school.

He watches his mother tightening the bow and tuning the violin; then Grandma Mimi's eyes when Mum brings her the instrument and lets her hold it. Jamie has never seen eyes as astonishing as Grandma Mimi's; when she takes the fiddle, they melt with more emotions, and stranger ones, than he'd thought the world contained.

'So you know?' she says to Mum, who nods, silent, smiling yet with tears in her eyes. Mum's also gone a bit crazy recently. Jamie sighs. God, grown-ups are stupid. If they'd ever had to deal with Mr Whitehouse's detentions, not to mention cross-country running, school dinners and, to cap it all, SATS, they'd know how lucky they were.

'I know everything, Grandma,' Mum says. 'The violin. Marc. Ani.'

'Good, my dear. It was time. Now, play to me and we'll work.'

'I don't want to overload you.'

'I'm well and happy today, my dear, thanks to you. I don't have so many bad days now. Somewhere, something is set free. Come along, play me Marc's piece.'

She plays the suite about the Gypsy childhood, and Grandma Mimi talks her through it. Jamie can't help being interested, despite himself. He didn't know his great-grandmother gave lessons. Isn't she supposed to be gaga? She doesn't sound it. She isn't a hundred yet, but it can't be long until she is. He hopes she'll get her telegram from the Queen, and he wants to be there when she opens it.

He knows the music well because Mum practises it so often, but Grandma Mimi advises, singing in her unsteady voice, telling Mum to play softer instead of louder, or to move the bow in another way, or change the fingering, and suddenly it sounds different and rather better.

'You should play a concert at our school, Mum,' he says. 'Or maybe you could come and teach. The violin teacher's leaving.'

'Schnooky, that's a very good idea.' Mum looks genuinely pleased and Jamie feels his stomach glow. There's something about making Mum smile that he enjoys: when she smiles, so does everyone else. He's proud to have the fittest mum of anyone in his class.

Grandma Mimi gives a big yawn and says they've worked enough. 'But my dear, if it's advice you want, I can tell you for certain you play very beautifully,' she says to Mum. 'You need to work hard, but you managed your Budapest trip, you played Mozart string quintets after playing so little for a while, so you will be fine. Work hard, and this time, *don't stop.*' The words sound fierce, but Mum looks so happy that Jamie finds he's beaming too, even though he doesn't see what the fuss is about. Of course Mum plays beautifully. She always has.

'I'd like to go on a course,' she says, 'and learn how to play in the Gypsy style. There are plenty around – I've been hunting on the Internet.'

'Internet,' Mimi sniffs. 'I've lived quite happily for ninety-two years without it, my dear. Go to Hungary, Karina. Get away from computer screens and posh English schools. Go and play to the Roma children, and with them. There, or Romania, or Slovakia. Learn the language, talk to them; they need you. You will be shocked by the discrimination and the prejudice, but now you could help, and you'll learn from them.'

'Maybe I will,' Mum replies. 'One step at a time, but if they'll have me, maybe I will. Grandma, could you tell me something? Did Duplessis ever finish that concerto?'

'The Gypsy Violin Concerto? Oh yes. He finished it.'

'Did you ever play it?'

'We played it at the piano, at home. Together. It was good, my dear. It wasn't a masterpiece, not like Bartók's concertos, but it was good music, appealing, with character, and some real beauty. He put such love into it. If there's real love, you can hear it and even if the structure is a little weak, or it was the wrong time for it – imagine a "Gypsy concerto" in the 1930s, eiyiyi! – the love was there just the same.'

'But where is it now?'

'He took it with him to Paris, I went to Budapest. I never saw him or the concerto again. Maybe that writer talks about it in his silly book that's full of lies, or rather that's not full of truth. Either way, it's gone, with him and our love and our daughter.'

'Didn't you try to find him? After Tamás died and you came to Britain?'

'I heard he was in South Africa and happily married. It was best to leave things alone. I hurt him, as I hurt everyone. Always hurting, though I never meant to. I didn't want to make it worse. I loved each of them, you know. It wasn't either-or. I didn't love one more than the other. It was real, the love, always real . . .'

'Hush, Grandma. I'm sorry. I shouldn't have asked.' Mum soothes her. Silly women, thinks Jamie, always crying. He's glad there are no girls at his school.

'No, my dear, it is good that you ask,' says Grandma Mimi, calming down. 'You know, I can remember one melody, the best one. It was the slow movement. A wonderful love-song – the way he imagined a Gypsy love-song, the silly man.'

She begins to hum. Karina sits very still, head on one side, trying to catch the tune.

'No,' says Mimi. 'My dear, give me please my violin?'

Mimi's hands, as knarled as wooden carvings, close around the fingerboard and the bow. Jamie notices that her fingers are shaking. 'My' violin? He thought she hadn't played a violin for ages. As he watches, Mimi closes her eyes, leans her cheek against the chin-rest and feels her way across the strings. The sound begins to speak; hesitant, tremulous, as if from another world. He can see that his mother is concentrating, trying to remember every note of the strange theme that sings out of the fiddle.

'May I try it?' she asks, when Mimi has finished.

'Yes, Karina. Take the melody. Play it, or it is lost forever. It's yours now.'

Jamie watches his mother obey. She plays; Mimi corrects her; they carry on, going over and over, again and again, until the tune is perfect and Mum can play it without faltering.

'What came next?' she asks, when they've reached the last phrase. 'How did it continue?'

'No, I can't,' says Mimi. 'I haven't seen this piece in more than fifty years. I'm sure he burned it. Try to remember it as far as this, no? But also remember, the only important thing: you are here, Jamie is here, we have each other. The family continues. Love continues, the sweetest of melodies.'

Mum bends and kisses her. Jamie can sense something shifting in the air, though he doesn't know what. Life has begun to feel like an adventure. He senses a window springing open, the air dancing in. You're not supposed to feel good when your parents separate. He keeps quiet about it.

Mum has brought shopping to make lunch for the three of them. She cooks chicken *paprikás* with noodles in Grandma Mimi's kitchenette. Mimi eats little, but seems to enjoy the food. Mum reaches over to Jamie's plate to cut up his chicken for him.

'Geroff, Mum,' says Jamie. 'I can do it myself.'

32

On Sunday morning, Karina leaves Jamie with his grandparents in Forest Road and picks up Rohan at Twickenham station. She's uncomfortable. Who in their right mind agrees to go to Sunday lunch to meet the mother of a partner they're trying to leave? Karina Veres, professional pushover, hunting for her identity in other people's pasts. Perhaps she should drop Rohan at a tube station and bottle out.

He's waiting on the pavement, pacing up and down, carrying his violin case. She still feels the pull, the intuitive kinship telling her she's known him for longer than they've both lived. That won't change; but it doesn't mean that they would be happy together. He climbs into the car, kisses her cheek, slips an arm round her.

'I'm not coming to lunch,' she tells him. 'I'll drop you somewhere to get the tube, maybe Richmond, and—'

'Christ. I knew you'd say that. Karina, you're coming to Kingsbury and you won't be sorry, I promise.'

'You said "I promise" about my phone number once. You promised that you knew I was married and you wouldn't pester me.'

'And I didn't. I fell in love with you.'

'I'm dropping you off. Then I'm going back to Mimi's and I'm going to play to her again if she's up to it.' Her violin in its case is on the back seat.

'Rubbish,' says Rohan. 'Let's get going, we'll be late.'

'*You'll* be late.'

'Karina, what will it take to make you come to Kingsbury? For heaven's sake! Don't you know I would never have invited you with all this shit going on between us if it wasn't bloody important?'

'How do you mean?'

'Let's go, then you'll see. Now, we need the North Circular.'

* * *

Streets of small houses like the Vereses'; a stretch of green belt across a hillside; a school, a public swimming pool, Indian restaurants galore. In the sky, the giant, tipped-over arch of the new Wembley Stadium. So this is where Rohan grew up. Of course, he'd gone away to school. His schooling had been geared to the violin, like everything else in his life. Rohan points. 'Here we are, Karrie, it's the next on the right.'

Karina parks a little way down the road and lifts her violin out of the car. Diana Masterson's small front garden is richly stocked and well kept. Through the window Karina spots rush mats on the floor and carved wooden animals beside a fireplace. Rohan presses out a rhythm on the bell. Footsteps inside and the door swings open. Rohan's mother: tall, with huge brown eyes like Rohan's. A forest of curls, which must once have been brown but are now grey. Long limbs, large but graceful hands and Rohan's cheekbones.

'Karina,' she says, clasping her hand. 'I can't tell you how happy I am to meet you. I'm Diana Masterson.' An arrow slices through Karina: this warm, welcoming, artistic woman could have been her mother-in-law.

The house has an almost identical layout to her parents'. She gazes around, imagining Rohan here as a child. The carved African animals are made of dark wood: a crouching lion, an antelope, a giraffe three feet high. On the lounge wall hang heavy-hewn wooden masks, a shield covered in striped hide and a painting of Table Mountain signed 'D. Masterson'.

'I always wanted to paint,' Diana tells Karina. 'I miss Ian so much, but I've finally had the guts to take his study to pieces, knock in a skylight and make myself a work-space at the back here. I've been trying to paint a little each day.' Through the doorway off the lounge, Karina glimpses an easel bearing a canvas.

'Your house is just like ours,' she says. 'I feel as if I've walked into my childhood home, but redesigned.'

'Sweetie, half the houses in Britain look like this.' Diana laughs. 'Come, what can I get you to drink? As Ro will have told you, I've just been to South Africa and I've brought back some fantastic rooibos tea. Can I tempt you?'

'Yes, please,' says Karina. Diana has the same soft magnetism as Rohan; her smile is wide, soft and dazzling, like his. Photographs on the mantelpiece show her with Rohan's father, Ian; the pair with a twelve-year-old Rohan and his small, camera-worshipping sister; and there, in black and white, are the much younger Ian and Diana with their South African neighbours: Marc Duplessis, older yet happier, and a tiny, dark-eyed woman who must be Shirley.

'The studio looks great, Mum,' Rohan says.

'You hadn't seen it before?' Karina asks him.

'It's brand new.'

'In eighteen years, I've never been able to bear to redo this room,' Diana admits. Karina detects tears threatening; this woman had known what love was. 'But now I'm glad I've taken that step. I had to clear a lot of papers and I can tell you, finding the guts to throw them out was one of the worst things I've ever had to do.'

'You said you wanted us to look at something?' Rohan prompts.

'Yes. I found something that I think Karina ought to see.'

She carries an old envelope, dog-eared and faded, over to the table and places it in front of them. Karina holds her breath. Rohan did have a reason to bring her here, as he promised.

Rohan extracts the letter. 'Oh my God, that's my grandmother's writing,' says Karina.

London, 2 September 1958

Marc, my dear,

I hope you are well. I understand that you are married and that you have two children. I am so happy for you. My best wishes to you, your wife and the little ones. How I wish I could see them.

Dénes and I now live in London. You will find our address at the foot of this letter. Dénes's studies are progressing well. He will be a fine cellist, though his character is somewhat difficult and has become more so recently. It is no wonder. We have both suffered, my dear, and at twenty my son has suffered more than most men twice his age.

I have some bad news. There is no gentle or easy way to tell you. We had a difficult time in the winter of 1956 leaving Hungary and during our escape, Ani died. In the days that followed, I remembered, in my grief, your offer to take her to Paris and my pigheaded refusal. I blame myself for this tragedy that will stain my heart for the rest of my life. No moment goes by when I do not miss her.

I want you to know that your daughter was a beautiful, sweet girl who lit up the world even in our darkest days. She was the treasure of your life, and of mine. It has taken nearly two years for me to find the words to tell you this, my dear, and to beg your forgiveness.

I ask your forgiveness for everything that happened between us. Please believe me when I tell you that my other great sorrow is the knowledge that I have caused pain to those I love, though I wanted only to love them. When we cannot reach one another in this mad world, when idiot things in our surroundings, in society's conventions or even in ourselves prevent us being together, the casualty is the natural progress of honest love. Yet love is all that can save us.

I love you now, as I did then, and I always will.

Yours ever,
Mimi

'Why did your husband have this?' Karina asks Diana, barely looking up from the letter.

Diana begins cautiously. 'It's likely that Shirley gave it to him for safekeeping, perhaps to stop Marc from burning it, or perhaps to make sure that nobody else would find it among his things – I had no idea that he'd had a daughter with Mimi Rácz until I saw this for the first time two weeks ago. I do know that in the last few years of his life, Marc became extremely depressed. He made bonfires out of his old manuscripts and letters. But I think in the case of this one, something happened . . . Ian used to tell me that people don't die of a broken heart, but of heart disease, or in Marc's case, cancer, but that that can sometimes be the physical manifestation of a spiritual crisis.'

Karina stares at the page, her vision blurring a little. 'I think that when my grandmother wrote this letter to him, telling him about Ani's death, perhaps that's what pushed him into that depression.'

'Who knows? But it seems possible,' Diana agrees. 'It's good to have the full story. Knowing such truths doesn't always change our lives, but it joins up the dots, it helps make the picture clear. And the clearer the picture is behind us, the clearer the picture can become ahead. Do you feel that too?'

Rohan isn't listening. 'Mum,' he says, 'you didn't find any sign of the concerto, did you?'

'I know you were desperate, Ro – but I promise, I went through everything with a tooth-comb. There was no music. I'm certain Marc burned it. We'd know by now, if he hadn't.'

'That's a tragedy, then.' Rohan shakes his head. 'All that work, all that feeling, going up in smoke. What a waste.'

The melody that Mimi had taught her, handed down in the way István Rácz would have handed on music to his children, lingers in Karina's mind, urging her on: speak now, or never. She could let it rest, with its creator. Or . . .

'Ro,' she says, 'I had an interesting session with my grandmother yesterday. I want to play you something.'

Rohan glances up.

'I don't know why she decided to teach it to me now, and not sooner. But maybe I wasn't ready to hear it before.' Karina takes out her violin. She hopes the theme has stayed with her. 'There isn't much of it, but it's all she can remember. And this violin could probably play it on its own.'

Rohan mouths 'Why?' but no sound comes out.

'I've been talking to my father. There was a good reason we couldn't find the Amati. The scroll was blown off by a bullet when he and my grandmother escaped from Hungary.'

Karina will never forget the look on Rohan's face as the understanding strikes home.

A Gypsy love-song, or Duplessis's fantasy of one: a fragment of memory, an essence distilled into a few perfect phrases that are all that remains of his dream. She lifts the violin and the notes find their way out of Mimi's memory and hers, out of her violin, and into the living air.

'Holy cow,' Rohan breathes. 'It's beautiful. Play it again?'

Karina plays, the melody basking under her fingers. If this isn't a love-song, then whatever could be? If Brahms had written it, or

Bartók or Kodály, by now it would have been recorded a hundred times by the finest violinists on earth. When she finishes, there's a very long silence.

'Karrie,' says Rohan, gently grasping her wrist, 'come upstairs with me a minute? And bring the violin?'

In Rohan's childhood room, Karina wanders to the window and gazes down at Diana's garden. She imagines Rohan coming home for the holidays to this little room. There'd have been a music stand, books on the shelves, LPs stacked near the old gramophone. Outside she notices a shrub in the full sun, covered in small flowers of three different hues: dark purple, lilac and pale cream.

'What a lovely plant. What is it?' she asks Rohan. 'The one by the fence? I don't recognise it.'

'It's South African,' he tells her. 'One of Mum's favourites. It's called Yesterday, Today and Tomorrow.' He goes to his old desk that stands in the window, just as Karina's had in Forest Road, and pulls out the bottom drawer. Inside lies a book of blank manuscript paper. 'Yes!' He brandishes it, triumphant. 'I thought it was still here. This was for my Music A-level harmony exercises. Now, Karrie, play it to me, slowly. I'm going to write it down.'

'Seriously?'

'Of course. We can't lose it again. Off you go.'

Rohan takes a pen from his pocket and settles at the desk with the manuscript paper. Karina begins the first phrase.

'Stop. Again,' says Rohan after a few bars. Karina waits, plays, watches him checking what he's written. Slowly, as she repeats it, the melody takes shape on the page. Rohan writes, pressing hard, focusing. 'Is that dotted, or triplets?' he asks from time to time, or, 'Do you think there should be a pause there?' or 'Up-bow to start that bar?'

Eventually Karina remarks, 'Ro, don't worry so much about the details. It's a wonderful memory, but it's yours now and you can add your own ideas.'

He turns round, pen in hand, and Karina sees his eyes shining in a way that they haven't for some time. 'I want to write a new piece for you, based on it,' he says. 'If you like it, will you play it?'

'You should play it yourself. Write a new Gypsy Concerto. It's all you need – your scoop, your big break. You'd have the original violin, the original theme and a world premiere. It could be everything you've been waiting for.'

'No. I only want to write for you.'

Karina squeezes his shoulder; his hand comes up and swamps hers. He pulls her down to sit on his lap; she hides her face in his neck. Her ribs crumble.

'The violin is yours to use whenever you like,' she says.

'No, it's yours. It always was.'

'But you could use it. It's the one you've dreamed about.'

'This is going to be your day, Karrie. I want you to have the fiddle and the piece – if it turns out any damn good, which I can't promise.'

'You'd give up that chance for me?'

'It's all for you.'

'But the violin—'

'Couldn't it be *ours*?'

'I don't know yet, Ro.'

'Why not, Karrie? What's confused you?' He sits back, looking at her, head on one side. 'Listen, I know you love me. It's written all over you. Something's got in the way. Tell me what. Please? Otherwise we're wrecked and I can't bear that. If something's happened, please tell me, right now.'

Worn away, needing the Rohan who can read her mind, Karina lets go. She says, 'Ro, Lindy's alive.'

'No,' says Lindy. 'My play's in rehearsal.'

Karina is in the primary school's little music room, waiting for her next pupil, who's late. She's commuting to Lewes from Twickenham, living out of a suitcase. 'I can't go on like this,' she says into her mobile. 'I've found you and sooner or later, someone else will too. You can't keep hiding and the longer you leave it, the worse it will be. You've got to come back.'

'Karrie, it's *my life*.'

'And it's screwing up mine. You're asking too much.'

'I don't give a damn. I left for a reason and it's the best thing I ever did.'

'But don't you see?' Karina, her fingers curled into a fist, notices red indents in her palms. 'You've gained your strength now and if you come back you'll still have it. It won't change.'

'You find this hard? Just try being me.'

'Lin, deep down, you know it's the right thing. Even if you've grown too much to get your antlers through the door, you have to make your peace, otherwise it'll hang over you forever. No?'

There's a hesitation in New York. 'What do you mean, my antlers?' Lindy asks. Karina detects a tiny break in her voice.

'You've grown, so you can't go back to your old life and I'm not saying you should. But you can't let your mother keep suffering.'

'Oh, bloody hell.' Karina can hear the clack of Lindy's shoes as she paces about on a wooden floor. 'It's out of the question.'

'Why?'

'Well, could *you*? What would I say?'

'You don't have to say anything. You just have to be there.'

Lindy is silent.

'Please, Lindy. One day you'll thank me. Just come back. I'll hold your hand if you need me to. We'll improvise.'

'Do you know how I paid Alban?'

'I dread to think.'

'I couldn't get at my savings, because I was supposed to be dead. So Alban said I should pay him back afterwards. Now I pay him every month, with interest, and I'll be paying him half my monthly bookshop salary for something like ten years.'

'Serves you right,' Karina tells her. 'I knew he was a crook. But that doesn't mean you can't come back. I need a very good reason and I haven't heard one yet. And by the way, I *have* told someone.'

'Fuck you, Karrie! Who the hell—?'

'Rohan. And don't swear at me.'

'And what does precious lover boy think I ought to do?'

'Don't talk about him like that.'

'"Infidelity is always wrong, no matter how strong the love is." Don't you remember that?'

'If you must know,' Karina says, keeping control, 'he thought I should go straight to your mother and tell her. She's suffered far too much.'

'And meek, obedient little Karina did as he said?'

'No, I didn't. I want you to tell her yourself.'

'Karina, shut it!' Lindy snaps. 'I can't, I won't and I'm not going to, so just bloody leave me alone. Christ, you're a fine one to lecture me. Look at you! What a mess. Back in Forest Road with Mummy and Daddy, your kid doesn't know what's happening, you and your husband and your lover are all kicking each other out of different housies – I'm *so* going to listen to your advice. Go fix your own life instead of sticking your nose in mine! And don't you dare call me again, now or ever.'

The line goes dead. Karina presses her hands to her eyelids. It's over. She's blown it.

Footsteps patter in the corridor, and her pupil, who happens to be Olly Pearson, taps on the door, eighteen minutes late. She opens the door and tries to scold the small, guilty face before her.

There's one person she can bring back, even if not Lindy.

Jamie, puffing and sweating in the sunshine during the cross-country run, is dreading maths prep and wondering who, this time, will have made him an apple-pie bed or sent rude text messages calling him a Gypsy joker. The run is nearly over. The crowd of small boys in tracksuits jogs down the lane and turns in to the front entrance of St Matthew's, heading up the drive past the car park. Jamie narrows his eyes. Is he seeing things, or is that a red Golf? The car flashes its lights and hoots. Jamie stops.

'Rookfield! Get a move on!'

'Sorry, sir. That's my mum.' On a Tuesday afternoon? Charging towards the car while she climbs out, Jamie finds the energy to run faster than he's run for the last half hour or, probably, ever before.

She hugs him as hard as he wants to hug her. He buries his face in her cotton blouse, feeling the flat pearly buttons against his cheek and breathing in her scent, something out of a gold-topped bottle that to him means – he doesn't know what. Just her. Just his mother.

'Get your stuff, Jimbo,' she says. 'We're going home.'

33

Christmas in Mimi's sheltered housing has the advantage of an official tree which the residents can enjoy without the strain of having to source, transport and decorate it themselves. Mimi usually spurns coffee mornings in the communal lounge, not to mention Sunday afternoon sing-songs round the piano, but the Christmas Eve treat that Karina has arranged is to be altogether exceptional.

Mimi atypically takes the trouble to visit her neighbours in the preceding days. History will be made, she tells them, in this modest corner of Middlesex. Their enthusiasm thrills her; everyone's bringing family or friends. 'There are people of ninety in here,' she tells Dénes, 'with more spirit than most youngsters of twenty. My dear, I've made fifteen new friends in three hours!'

The Rookfields arrive first. Julian is smiling and relaxed, tanned from reconnoitring in Spain; he's considering relocation to Barcelona instead of Sweden, which is too cold. Martin sits with him, keen to discuss the possibility of setting up in business together. Arthur fidgets with his Orthodox cross and Anne embraces Cynthia, who has had her memoirs printed privately and is glowing with the catharsis of imminent revenge. Dénes strides in with a brisk, generalised greeting. Andy and Sarah Williamson sit together, talking neither to each other nor to anyone else except Julian. Jamie reserves himself a seat beside Olly Pearson, who's tentatively agreed to be his best friend again; then he charges across the room and throws his arms around his frail great-grandmother, whom he's decided is his favourite relation of them all.

Cynthia ignores Martin. She goes to Mimi, gives her a kiss and places a CD in her hands: the newly issued *Distant Beloved* recording. Then she taps on the door of Mimi's flat to give Karina a note from Charles; he's written from France to apologise for his absence, enclosing a photograph of himself with Nicki, for whom he's left his family.

Jamie and Olly have prepared a programme sheet according to Karina's instructions; they stand at the lounge entrance to hand it out.

ROHAN MASTERSON, after a theme by MARC DUPLESSIS:
Andante amoroso alla zingaresca, world premiere
Karina Veres (violin), Erzsébet Veres (piano)
In memoriam

Rohan slides through the door. Jamie looks up at him and waves. He waves back. Julian glares across the room. Rohan meets his eye, acknowledging him with a nod, then takes a seat beside the radiant Diana, at whom Martin can't stop gazing. Sarah, beside Andy, catches Rohan's eye and flushes scarlet. A distant thread of violin reaches their ears: Karina, in Mimi's flat, is warming up.

She stands in the doorway of Mimi's kitchenette, denim-clad, blonde once more, her eyes shadowy with jet lag and less afraid than Karina thinks they ought to be. Her suitcase, unopened, lurks near the door, a sticky airport tag looped round the handle. 'So, Ms Last-minute,' Karina says, 'how do you feel?'

'Do you remember *The Winter's Tale*?' says Lindy. 'When Queen Hermione comes back?'

'It's hardly comparable.' Karina picks out a pattern on the violin, a figuration from the rhapsodic cadenza that Rohan has composed for her. 'Christ, Lin. You could have warned me.'

'Sorry. I was afraid I'd lose my nerve. I think I can face them now. I couldn't before.'

'Why?'

'Maybe because I've got it out of my system writing the play. I had to think myself into my mum's mind to do that. I'll never understand my father, I'll never really love him, but – I miss her. I can't help it. She's still my mum, and she's still there in my head, no matter where I am.'

Karina focuses on her violin. She refuses to cry.

'It's so good that you're playing, Karrie,' Lindy remarks. 'It's been years since I saw you working like this.'

'You've helped me find a way forward, even if you didn't mean to,' Karina admits. 'I never realised how much of myself the violin was, how much I loved it and missed it. It's my life and I want it back before it's too late. I don't know what I'm going to do, but I'm ready to see where it takes me.'

'Good girl.' Lindy nods approval. 'You were right, you know: I'm stronger, and I'm not going to lose that.' She grins. 'No doubt Mum'll write a sequel. Oops. Great timing. I hope the print run didn't cost her too much.'

'What about your CD?'

'I don't give a damn about it. Too many bad memories. You didn't invite Alban today, did you?'

'I don't know where he is. Do you?'

'I know his bank details. Yes, he's a crook. On the other hand, he's also been my fairy godfather.'

Karina twangs a string. 'Time to turn back into a pumpkin, then.'

Lindy watches her, as if assessing a new incarnation of her old friend. 'What about you and Julian?'

'It's funny, but something in Jules is different. He's finally got some perspective. Maybe it was meeting Chris again, or the day he was trapped in the tube.'

'Tripe. It was you leaving him. I bet that was the real wake-up call.'

'I'm still married to him, he's Jamie's dad and I actually like him a lot more, now that he's decided to change his life. He's more relaxed, he's more sensible and open, and he's fine about Jamie's school.'

'What about Fairfallows and Arthur's blasted will?'

'Progress, of sorts. Jules has been having long conversations with Arthur and I think he'll make him see sense sooner or later.'

'But you're going to divorce, so it doesn't matter.'

'I don't know, Lin. He's stopped saying he wants a divorce on the spot and I'm starting to think there really is potential to mend things, if he'll agree. The trouble is, I'm still in love with Rohan.'

'Oh, fuck. What are you going to do?'

'Mimi says she loved Tamás and Marc Duplessis equally, in different ways, and perhaps what's happened to me is the same thing. There isn't an easy answer. I'm living in Lewes to look after Jamie, but I speak to Rohan every day. I see him in Brighton, sometimes I tell him I can't see him any more, but next thing I know, we're in bed. One minute I think we could never be happy together, the next I think I can never be happy without him.' She plays a phrase of the new piece. 'Now we're together in art, if nothing else. Maybe I'll end up on my own with Jamie, but if I do, that's all right. I can cope. A year or two ago, I couldn't have. And Jamie's a tougher little cookie than I thought.'

'Oh, Karrie, I can't wait to see him. I missed him so much. I missed *you* so much.'

The girls embrace. Their tears meet and immerse in each other. Not many people are lucky enough to find that their loved ones who have died are returned to life. 'You've done us all some good,' Karina says. 'Even if you didn't mean to.'

Lindy blows her nose. 'I'll wait here. I'm sorry not to hear you play Rohan's piece.'

'Come back in April, then. I'm going to play the orchestral version in a new music showcase at St Luke's in London. It's meant to be broadcast on the radio, so it could be Rohan's breakthrough, at least as a composer. I wanted him to play it and have the scoop as a violinist, but he insists I have to do it.'

'It could be your breakthrough too,' Lindy points out.

Karina shrugs off the idea. 'Let's get through today first. Once the fuss has died down, Lin, look up the Bartók *Cantata Profana*, the one about the hunters who turn into the creature they hunt. If I've turned into the stag, or rather the violinist that I was hunting, and now I can't go home because my antlers are too wide, perhaps it's not so different from what you've done.'

'What I did was unforgivable. But will you forgive me?'

Karina smiles. 'I might.'

Mimi's next-door neighbour has made mulled wine for the party after the performance. Karina slips out into the corridor, where Erzsébet is waiting for her, and breathes in the clove-scented air of the present, the chill of the past, the fragile molecules of the future. Cradling the violin that was once her grandmother's voice and is now hers, she kisses her mother on both cheeks. 'Ready, Mum?'

'So, now.' Erzsébet takes her hand. 'It all depends on you. You are the artist, the architect and the director of your life. And today, don't forget: you are the violin.'

They go together into the lounge; there's a welcoming sparkle of applause from fifty people, most of whom have no idea how significant this afternoon is, but are ready to enjoy it. Rohan switches on a minidisc recorder. Jamie beams, proud; Dénes, his face in that unfathomable half smile, half scowl, sits beside the piano to turn Rohan's handwritten pages for Erzsébet. He hasn't heard this melody since the night of 3 November 1956, when Mimi sang herself to sleep with it after her concert.

In the ensuing silence, Karina raises the Amati and feels her way into the first haunting, declamatory phrase of Duplessis's Gypsy love-song. Erzsébet, at the piano, lets the cimbalom-like tremolando that Rohan has penned shiver under her fingertips. Karina turns the Hungarian phrase endings and soars up into the arabesques, closing her eyes, freeing herself and losing herself as if she were Rohan. Within moments, her listeners are rapt.

Mimi sits motionless while the new piece fashioned out of the old melody unfurls before her. She thinks of Jamie embracing her earlier: a young child, vivid with energy, renewing her, just as Rohan's music embraces and renews what's left of Marc's.

'*Mimi?*'

'*Marc, my dear.*'

'*Come with me. There's enough love, here, for everyone.*'

Silver stars, rocking wagon, everything is preserved in his notes, resurrected through Rohan's work in Karina's hands. Perhaps, at last, they are all one. Mimi leans back in her chair with a silent sigh. Nobody is watching Mimi, though, as the last note dies away. Karina fixes her gaze on the door and gives a nod. Lindy's shape shines against the darkened windows as she walks forward into the light.